Sleepless Nights and Hockey Fights

HOT FLASH HOOKUPS
BOOK FOUR

MARIKA RAY

SYLVIE STEWART

Description

I'm a hot-headed pro hockey player with a reputation for two things: reckless fights on the ice and a taste for older women off of it. But this time I might just be in over my head with an older single mom.

With the team's new head coach on my case, I can't afford any more screw-ups. He thinks I need to grow up, and I'm out to prove I can get my act together once and for all. In fact, I just hired a realtor to help me buy a house. How's that for grown up?

Except the realtor turns out to be the quiet, captivating single mom of a boy I mentor on a youth hockey league. I should keep things strictly business, but she knocks me off my skates with those pencil skirts and mom voice.

Molly insists she's too old for me, and I say opposites attract. As I fight for my spot on the ice and battle some personal demons, she's juggling an unpredictable pre-teen, an ex who belongs in the penalty box, and a case of insomnia that has me calling new plays between the sheets.

If I push too hard, I know she'll run. But there's no way I'm throwing in the towel–not when I've realized her heart is the only thing worth fighting for.

Trigger Warning

This story touches on physical violence, references to abuse, and situations involving homophobia.

Chapter One

Bobby

I slam my hand against the steering wheel of my Cybertruck and instantly regret it when my left turn signal, high beams, and thumping rap music all turn on at the same time. That's what I get for hitting my baby in anger.

"Sorry, Wolverine," I whisper to it, stroking the wheel.

Another car honks at me before I get the high beams off, which is par for the course in Tampa, Florida. Someone's always honking or flipping you off, even if you're just minding your own business and driving like a normal person. I've had more than my fair share of middle fingers just for driving this outlandish beast, but I don't care. This thing is a monster of a truck and I fucking love it.

I am pissed though, and it has nothing to do with the guy who cuts me off right before I turn into the parking garage below my apartment building. After parking in my reserved space, I lean my head back against the headrest and let the bass reverberate through my chest. Visions of our new head coach,

Andre Marsh, yelling at me to get my shit together flash through my brain. He really handed me my ass the other day in his office. Coach Bowman would never have talked to me like that. Then again, I didn't fuck up as much under his watch. He kept my brain busy with calculating stats and watching game film to figure out what was going wrong with our first-line offense. Coach Marsh just doesn't understand me yet and doesn't seem like he wants to.

A groan leaves my mouth but gets swallowed by the loud music. Chloe Cooper, my friend and the fiancée to one of my teammates, overheard the ass whooping in vivid detail. And she didn't exactly take my side. She told me to straighten my shit up. Settle into this new contract of mine with the Storm Chasers and pull up my big boy pants.

I hit the button to turn off the truck, leaving me in deafening silence. Grabbing my bag, I exit the truck and glance down at myself. Whereas the other guys left practice in sweats and whatever questionable T-shirts they happened to have in their lockers, I changed into my favorite pair of jeans and this polo shirt the sales gal talked me into last time I visited Neiman Marcus. But no matter how impressive my outfit, I always make sure to pair it with a fun pair of boxers. Today's have skeletons riding flamingos, a nod to both the state I now live in and the fact that pumpkin spice is back on the menu. My life philosophy is that undressing should be like opening a gift. The right pair of boxers either make a woman's face light up or an eyebrow lift. And I prefer she do both, right before she rips the boxers off me. So, yeah, sorry Coach Marsh and Chloe and everyone else in my life who's told me to grow up. I don't have big boy underpants. I have *fun* underpants. Might even start calling them funderpants.

I slam the door and head for the elevators. Despite my dark mood, I force myself to whistle a tune. A quick Google search last year told me to interrupt the angry thoughts in my head by singing. I can't carry a tune to save my life, so I've taken to whistling, much to the annoyance of my entire team. Doctor Google also told me to express my anger constructively. I'm not really sure what that means. Am I supposed to build a birdhouse or some shit? Punch a bad guy in the face instead of one of my teammates? Pretty sure Coach would bench me for hanging out in dark alleys at night and I have zero use for an apartment full of birdhouses.

The elevator opens and I hustle to my door. My oversized muscles are screaming for food after a tough practice. The television is on in the living room, which is weird. I drop my bag silently by the door and lick my lips, thinking I might have a chance to punch a bad guy after all. Except it's my fucking brother. On my couch, hand down his pants, rubbing one out to the weather chick on channel nine.

"What the fuck, Dick?"

Richie tucks and rolls, landing on the ground on all fours. I know where that hand's been and I don't appreciate it on my fucking rug. His hair—the same dirty-blond shade as mine but longer—is a mess, like he's just woken up for the day. "Why aren't you at the bar?"

"I should ask you the same question!" I gesture to the end table strewn with three cups and a half-eaten donut. Powdered sugar fills in the empty space. "What the fuck are you doing here?"

Richie pushes to his feet and adjusts himself, making me grimace. "I ran out of milk."

As if that explains why he made himself at home in my apartment without asking. "So you thought you'd sip my milk and choke the chicken on my couch?" I glance at the television. She is kind of pretty with that knee length dress and helmet hair. Dammit, that's beside the point. "Come on, man. Just a simple text to ask permission would be nice. And Jesus, keep your hands out of your pants."

"Sorry, sorry." Richie collects the glasses and heads for the kitchen as I follow. "I'm off tonight and I figured you'd be at the bar after practice like usual. Didn't think you'd mind if I stopped by. I planned to be gone before you got home with some bunny."

I roll my eyes and open the fridge to see what I have on hand to make for dinner. "I'm cleaning up my act, Richie boy. No more bars. Definitely no bunnies."

He snorts and then wrinkles his nose at my shoes. "What's with the loafers and no socks? You look like the director of a porno."

My Gucci slides are first class. They just happen to be bright red. "Don't worry about my shoes. Worry about how you're gonna clean my couch, bro."

He gives me a look I know all too well. Richie doesn't know how to clean shit except for the pint glasses at the bar where he works, the Irish Rogue. One of the bars I should be at right now.

I sigh and pull out a box of spinach. "You have dinner?" He opens his mouth and I cut him off. "Donuts aren't dinner, dumbass."

Before I can place the spinach on the counter, the dude wrangles his lanky arm around my neck and yanks me down in a headlock. His knuckles try to drill a hole in my skull while I flail to save our dinner. I see red when he doesn't let up, so I jab a quick fist into his kidneys. He lets me go, but not before sweeping a foot behind my knees, making them buckle. I grab his shorts on the way down and he shouts an obscenity as he finds himself pantsed. We're both red-faced and pissed off as we call a truce. I make him wash his hands before we throw dinner together. He snacks on potato chips while I grill up some chicken and pair it with a salad. The dude would subsist on junk food if I didn't feed him at least twice a week when I'm in town.

He's got a mouthful of chicken at the small kitchenette table when he returns to the subject of my being home instead of at the bar. "Seriously, why are you here?"

"I live here," I answer blandly. He kicks my shin under the table. "Fuck! You don't have to resort to violence." I reach down and rub the spot.

"We all resort to violence. That's what we do, little bro."

He's not wrong. There are five of us Rhodes brothers. I'm the youngest, which means I took the brunt of everyone's teasing and physical assaults. I learned to give as good as I got. Survival, baby. Richie lives here in Tampa near me, while the other three live back in Georgia where we grew up. I tease Richie he's like the little fish that swims around with the shark, feeding off the leftovers. Honestly, I don't mind him being here with me–except when he's waxing the carrot on my couch. Richie puts his chin in his hand and stares at me. I know he won't leave until I spill the details.

"Fine. Coach wasn't pleased at me for getting in a scuffle with Mac the other day in the locker room. Said I'll be benched if I don't get my act together."

Richie blinks repeatedly. His brain takes a little longer to process things. "So, you can't go to bars now?"

I shove my plate away from me. I've lost my appetite. "I can go to bars, but not every day. And I can't start any fights. Chloe suggested I buy a house with a fuckin' white picket fence. Marry a girl. Wear an ugly sweater and get a dog. Or maybe it was the dog who should wear the sweater, I can't remember."

Richie sits straight up and slaps his thigh, guffawing like a donkey. "That's the funniest shit I've heard all day."

I see red, but instead of punching him in the arm to shut him up, I start whistling. It's effective, but not in the way I intended. Richie quits laughing and stares at me like I've lost my mind.

"It's not funny, douchebag. If I get benched, I get traded. Which means you have to move too. Which also means I'm seen as a liability player who can't stick with a team, which means after this contract is up, my career might be done too. Which means you might have to start supporting us for once."

Richie's ruddy cheeks pale.

"Yeah. Not laughing now, are you?"

He helps me clean up our dinner plates, which might be a first. I guess I scared him with that talk of being traded. We watch some television–I sit in the recliner, not the defiled couch–but I change it from the news so he doesn't get any ideas. I get bored within minutes and pick up my phone to do the word of the day puzzle, solving it after three tries. Then I navigate to my favorite dating app, Chloe's words in the back of my mind.

Thing is, I quit bringing home puck bunnies a couple years ago. They just weren't doing it for me anymore. I blame that trip three Christmases ago when Richie and I flew home for the holidays. We found ourselves falling off our barstools at the local bar with all my brothers. I was heading for the bathroom when I ran smack into a busty redhead in a black tank top and a skintight jeans skirt. She looked familiar but I couldn't quite place her. Hell, I couldn't even see straight after all those shots, but when she pushed me up against the wall just outside the men's restroom and ran her finger down my chest, everything below the belt worked just fine.

I ended up taking her into a stall for some privacy. She was a decade or two older than me, based on the lines that fanned out from the corners of her eyes and the gray hair that threaded through the red, but I liked how she took control. She turned around, put her hands on the door, and told me to flip her skirt up and show her a good time. She even barked at me to get her off twice before I was allowed to come. Something about being told what to do was kind of hot. Turns out she looked familiar because she's my old high school chemistry teacher. Believe me, my brothers never let me forget it when we walked back out of the bathroom together, hair disheveled and Ms. Moore walking bowlegged.

I've had a thing ever since for older women. If I have to find a girl and settle down like Chloe suggested, it's going to be with a woman who's capable and pats me on the head like a good boy. I flip through the over-forty selection on the app, swiping right and hoping for a match.

Operation Save My Hockey Career has begun.

Chapter Two

Molly

"Well, that went well."

I turn in my chair to see my ex-husband emerge from the hall, both hands scrubbing his face. I know just how he feels.

"Do I detect a note of sarcasm?" I ask, despite the fact that even a toddler could have spotted the jest in Blake's tone.

"How about an entire symphony?" He drops into the painted chair next to mine at the kitchenette table nestled in the corner of my small kitchen. His elbows land on the table as he eyes me. "He nixed the therapy idea, like you said. First, he pretended not to know what I was talking about, and when I informed him I knew about the detention, he claimed it was all a misunderstanding."

I sigh and clutch my coffee cup with both hands. "I thought boys were supposed to be easier as they got older," I lament.

Blake throws his head of shoulder-length brown hair back and cackles. "Who the hell told you that?"

I frown at him before taking a sip of the hot elixir of life. "Everybody." This latest parenting crisis is doing nothing to help my insomnia, thus the gallon of coffee in front of me.

Still grinning, Blake reaches over to pat my arm. "Oh, honey, you've obviously been talking to the wrong *everybody*. I can tell you from personal experience that boys only get more complicated the older they get. *Believe me.*" This is followed by a beleaguered sigh that I know is intended to have me asking about his love life, but now is not the time. This is about our kid—our kid who is clearly struggling if his detention record at school this year is any indication.

I slide the other steaming coffee mug toward Blake, who snatches it up like its contents were drawn straight from the Fountain of Youth. "I just don't know how to relate to him with all this anger and aggression. Where is this coming from?"

"Your guess is as good as mine. Apart from the shoving match, though, you've got to admit the insult was pretty creative. I've never been called a finger sniffer, have you?" When I narrow my eyes, Blake throws both hands up. "Right. Sorry."

"If it was from the divorce, we would have seen it two years ago, Right?" I ask.

"Definitely."

Nodding absently, I run my finger along the rim of my coffee mug and stare blankly out the kitchen window. Matty was always such a calm kid, going with the flow no matter what. He weathered the divorce better than anyone could have predicted. But ever since he turned twelve this summer, it's like a switch has been flipped. He flies off the handle at the smallest things, behaving so unpredictably that I'm at my wit's end. I thought maybe his dad might have some magical Y-chromosome insight, but it seems not.

I turn my attention back to Blake and lower my voice.

"You know he broke his skateboard last week? He said he crashed and it just snapped, but I saw him bash it against the fence after he fell off a few times trying a new trick."

"Shit." Blake's brow creases before his voice tightens. "I hope he knows we're not buying him a new one."

"It hasn't come up." I wave it off and worry my lip, reopening the small crack from a week's worth of biting it. The coppery tang of blood hits my tongue, and I push my chair back from the table to get a tissue. "It's not the skateboard I'm worried about. We need to figure out what's behind all of this, and a counselor is the only idea I've got."

Blake rises from his seat and steps close, pulling a tissue from the box on the counter and pressing it gently to my lip. "Hey," he whispers. His tone is too soft and the gesture too intimate, which he appears to realize when I take a small step back. "Sorry." He relinquishes the red-stained tissue and backs up to give me more space, shoving his hands in his jeans pockets.

I detest these awkward moments.

"No." I force a smile. "It's fine." Because it is. My brain knows Blake's actions come purely from a place of concern and friendship, but my body sometimes takes a minute to catch up.

It's been over two years since my husband of a decade and a half broke the news that he's gay. And even then, it was almost a relief. Things hadn't been right for a while, and finally understanding the reason made it easier to come to terms with. In fact, in some ways, our friendship is even stronger now than it was before. But we're still in transition mode in a certain sense.

Blake's phone rings, and he pulls it from his back pocket. "Shit. I gotta go." He looks up at me again, driving his fingers through his long hair to slick it back. "The band is hitting the road in two hours, and I still need to pick up Jess and Gordie."

I force another smile, knowing that hardly anything comes between my ex-husband and his band. When we were married, it was more of a side gig, but they're playing full time now.

"Where to this time?" The band has a decent following and they make enough money to live on, unlike a lot of musicians. But Blake isn't rolling in it, by any means. We always kept our heads above water when we were together, but things have been tighter since our split. Yet another thing that keeps me up at night.

"We've got a couple of gigs in Tallahassee, then we're off to South Carolina." He can't help his grin at first but soon manages to bring himself back to earth. "Hey, Dollface." Blake's voice softens as he steps close again, addressing me with the nickname he's used since the day we met. "Don't worry. The therapist will know what to do for Matty. I'm sure half the boys in Matty's class are raging with hormones and behaving like jackasses."

Blake isn't crossing into my personal space this time, instead allowing me to choose. I close the distance and he wraps me up in a hug.

"I hope you're right," I say into the shoulder of his thin T-shirt. What I don't say is that it will be hard for a therapist to do much of anything if Matty refuses to enter their office in the first place.

As if to punctuate my thought, the front door closes with a bang, Matty's voice delivering a barely audible, "I'll be back later."

Blake and I both pull back to look at each other. "By the way," he says, "He's got two boxes of crackers under his bed."

My nose wrinkles. "Seriously?"

One corner of Blake's mouth lifts. "Hey, at least it's not stiff tube socks he's collecting under there."

My dumbstruck expression has him laughing all the way to the door.

"Sorry to bug you," I say as I knock on my boss's open office door. "But I wanted to touch base before I leave to take Matty to hockey practice."

"Come in," she beckons from behind her marble-topped desk with a wave of one graceful hand. "Sit." When my only response is to stay put and look at my watch, Coco delivers one of her well-practiced side-eyes. I swear the woman could talk the Pope himself out of Sunday Mass. "Sit," she repeats in a firmer tone.

I don't try very hard to hide my sigh, but it only makes her grin.

"You still have another twenty minutes before you need to leave, and you've been running around all day like a chicken with its head cut off. Take a minute to breathe, will you?" she admonishes.

She's not wrong. Today has been nuts, and I'm operating on only four hours of sleep. Who knew one of the signs of impending menopause was sleepless nights that turn you into a zombie? First, my car wouldn't start, so I had to dig around under the hood and tighten the terminal nut that keeps coming loose. Of course, that resulted in a grease stain on my most versatile ivory blouse, which necessitated me changing outfits faster than a Vegas showgirl between acts and breaking the speed limit to make it to the morning meeting at Farnsworth Realty.

Friday being the biggest day of the week for new listings meant endless trips to the printer and back while juggling client emails and phone calls. As the newest—and thus lowest-ranking—agent in the office, I pretty much get the scraps when it comes to property leads while the more lucrative prospects are handed off to Maude and Jason, two other agents with more seniority and not a small degree of entitlement to match.

Honestly, it's for the best, though. I'm not ready for a big listing.

Coco studies me for a few silent beats while I force my feet not to tap on her wood floor. I finally can't take it anymore. "What?"

"How's your sex life these days?"

I choke on my own saliva and proceed to cough into the inside of my elbow for a good thirty seconds. "Coco!" I manage to scold once I'm partway recovered. "I thought bosses weren't allowed to ask stuff like that!"

Even her laugh is classy as hell, a light tinkling sound that's purely feminine. "Darling, we're off the clock. This is girl time." She pats her silver-blond updo and stares me down more effectively than even Dame Maggie Smith could have.

I purse my lips. "In that case, I might ask the same of you," I volley back. This turns out to be a poor decision.

"Fabulous, as always. I may even stop my Botox, these men are keeping me so young."

"Oh, god," I mumble under my breath.

She lowers both palms to her desktop. "Look at you. You're a hot commodity just waiting to be snatched off the market by some hunky stud."

"I'm not a house for sale, for god's sake. And I'm fine with just me and Matty." This isn't strictly true. Some days I'd give my right arm to have a partner to share my troubles and triumphs—other days, I remind myself I need that arm to give myself the only orgasms available to me.

"Liar, liar, panties on fire," Coco croons as she swipes her phone up with one hand, the perfectly manicured index finger of the other tapping at the screen.

"You're calling *me* a liar?" I cock my head in disbelief. "Just yesterday I heard you telling that guy from that fancy investment firm that you're forty-six."

She doesn't even look up from her phone. "How many times do I have to tell you? Age is a mindset, darling. I *feel* forty-six, so it's not a lie at all."

I suppose she has a point. Coco Farnsworth, owner and realtor extraordinaire here at Farnsworth Luxury Realty, looks and acts much younger than her sixty-two years. And, while some of the credit must go to her plastic surgeon, the rest is undeniably Coco.

"Ah!" she exclaims. "Here it is!" Her blue eyes positively twinkle as they meet mine across the desk. "We're signing you up for a dating app."

We've all heard the expression, *the blood drained from her face*, but I can't remember another instance where I could literally feel the blood inside my skull ducking for cover and hauling ass out of Dodge. "I might faint," I mumble before dropping my head down between my knees. *Deep breaths, Molly.*

"Oh, don't be such a drama queen. That's my job," Coco says, amusement suffusing her words.

I give myself a good twenty seconds before slowly lifting my head again. No white spots in my vision, so that's a good sign, right? "I'm not taking out a billboard offering free booty calls to strange men." Just the thought of a handsome man flirting with me is enough to make me blush after all this time.

"Oh, it's easy to weed the weirdos out, I promise." Coco is now typing with both thumbs clacking away on her phone screen.

"You've officially lost the plot, boss." I shake my head and stand, both hands gripping the chair arms in case my head decides to get light again. "I've got to go."

I only get two steps.

"There. You're all signed up. I'm texting you the app's link plus your username and password."

"I'm deleting it," I reply, quickening my pace. "I'm too old for dating apps." Hell, I feel too old for dating in general. It's a young person's game. I wouldn't know what to do.

"Bite your tongue, Molly Sparks. Besides, have I ever steered you wrong?"

I groan this time since she knows the answer to that question as well as I do.

Coco took me under her wing from the moment I walked through her agency's door two years ago to inquire about a receptionist job. I wouldn't have ever thought to pursue my real estate license if it hadn't been for her encouragement and support. Her belief in me is unwavering, and I have the deepest respect for her business sense and savvy. Coco's entire attitude and outlook on life are something to aspire to.

So, yeah, her advice is never a thing to be tossed casually aside. Still, there's an exception to every rule.

I reach the doorway and open my mouth to throw a teasing "No comment" her way before I stop short, only now remembering why I knocked on her door in the first place. "Oh. I forgot to tell you. I was driving by that gorgeous Victorian on Newland Boulevard and saw a man hammering a "For Sale by Owner" sign into the yard.

Coco's eyes widen, her lips stretching into a blindingly white smile. "That's my girl."

I can't help grinning to myself all the way to my car. My phone pings from inside my giant handbag just as I shut the driver's side door, and I rifle through various bits and bobs until I locate the device.

My grin dies on my face when I see the new text from Coco, accompanied by a link.

> Coco: Your username is @SparkleIsMy-StripperName and your password is MamaNeeds2GetSome. You're welcome.

Chapter Three

Bobby

"How's that new asshole working out for you?" Benny–otherwise known as our first-line center Banks Bennet–asks, flopping down on the bench next to me with his skates in hand. He's one of the senior players on our team, a fact I bring up as much as humanly possible.

I give him my best scathing look, when what I want to do is punch something. Coach has been riding me hard since our chat about straightening up my shit, though I didn't think anyone else noticed.

"The ladies seem to like it," I quip. Benny doesn't smile.

"Kaitlyn says she has a plan for you." He looks out at the ice where Chloe is setting up brightly colored cones before her rec league practice starts. He's engaged to my agent, Kaitlyn, which probably means she's filled him in on the gory details of my ass chewing from Coach. "She's tough as nails, but I can speak from experience: her plans work. If you give her shit and make her go into labor, I swear your new asshole will be the least of your problems."

I put my hand up in the scout's honor salute, but we all know I've never been a Boy Scout. I'm just not promising anything until I hear this plan of hers. I want to clean up my act and keep my spot on the team, but I also know my limitations. Benny laces up his skates and heads off to the ice without another word.

Chloe didn't ask for my help with her practice today, but I have a meeting scheduled with Kaitlyn at six. Practice got out at three and since I can't go to a bar to pass the time like I normally would, I might as well help out the youth of America. Hopefully Coach looks out his window and sees me doing a good deed. Kids start streaming in and the volume inside the rink goes way up. Benny's Little from the Big Brothers program, Eli, comes swaggering in with another boy hot on his heels. I perk up, realizing the other boy is the kid spawned from that hot mom I always notice.

At that exact moment, Chloe skates by and snaps at me. "You gonna help, or sit and pout all day?"

Since children are present, I have to clench my hands into fists to keep from flipping her off. Did I say we're friends? I lied. She's dead to me. Which isn't true, because I get my ass off the bench and skate out onto the ice to help her, telling myself it's for the kids and bolstering my reputation. Eli and the other kid come whizzing past me, warming up on the side of the rink I'm on, which is where the older kids practice.

I holler at a tall redhead to get off the ice and tie her skates properly before she maims herself. I know Chloe covered proper lacing on day one. There's no excuse for sloppy equipment in a game where razor blades are strapped to the bottoms of your feet. Eli whizzes by me again, sticking his tongue out the side of his mouth like he's the Michael Jordan of hockey.

The kid behind him tries to keep up, but hits a rough patch of ice left over from our practice. His arms pinwheel and his eyes go wide in panic. I push off my right foot and get to his side just as he regains his balance.

Unfortunately, his pants don't escape mishap. They drop, showing a pair of bright blue underwear that I could swear have Spongebob printed on the front. I don't waste time gawking. I just reach over, yank the pants back up, and pat him on the shoulder like we're having a chat.

"Easy there, killer. Gotta watch out for those divots. They'll take you out every time." I give him a stern nod, hoping I didn't give him a wedgie in my hurry to save him from social ruin.

Eyes still wide, he turns the color of a tomato as he stares at me in horror.

I lean in. "Hey, nobody saw anything, man. You're good. Right? You're good?"

His barely-there Adam's apple bobs in his skinny throat, but he seems to collect himself. "Yeah." His voice cracks so he clears it and tries again. "Thanks."

I pat him on the shoulder some more. "Any time. Did you ever hear about the time some ass–butthole–from the Gliders pulled my pants down during warmups? He claims it was an accident, but the fu–fudger knew what he was doing. I hadn't laced up tight yet because we were just stretching." I shake my head when his freckled nose wrinkles and he laughs. "I got him back, though, by taking his mom to dinner that weekend and making sure the paparazzi took pictures."

The kid's jaw drops. "Dude. That's epic."

I shrug. "I probably should have let it go, but sometimes you have to pay people back when they're rude."

He nods sagely. "I get that."

Chloe's whistle breaks up our conversation and the kids

skate off to form a circle for warm-ups. I stay to help out, actually enjoying myself with the kids and forgetting to even check if Coach sees me out here. Parents arrive before I realize that much time has passed, signaling the end of practice.

One particular mom with auburn hair in a slicked back ponytail and the hottest pencil skirt I've ever seen catches my attention like she always does. I pretend to concern myself with collecting cones over where the mom is waiting for her son. She's biting her bottom lip and scrolling on her phone when I get close. I can't see her screen, but that doesn't stop me from using it as an opening.

"No need to scroll. Just swipe right on me."

Her head whips up and her teeth let go of her lip. I shoot her a wink, then notice how beautiful her wide eyes are. Stunning, actually. They're hazel, with a green ring close to her pupil and an unusual golden brown everywhere else. We stand there for a few moments, both of us mute and staring. Then her cheeks stain as red as her son's and she snaps her mouth shut.

"I . . . I wasn't–you know." She shakes her head. "Okay, bye." She turns, her ponytail swinging around and almost hitting me in the face. I watch her go, too preoccupied with watching those full hips swing as she marches off to notice that Chloe is also watching this interaction. She sprays ice up on my pants as she abruptly stops in front of me.

"Not one of my moms, Bobby," she warns, finger in my face.

I throw my hands in the air in a gesture of peace. "I was just being friendly."

Chloe narrows her eyes. "Uh huh. Your definition of friendly varies widely from mine."

I give her my best innocent aw shucks grin, the one that worked on my mother every single time us boys got in trouble. Apparently, I've still got it because Chloe relents and doesn't say another word as we exit the rink and take our skates off.

I don't bother changing to meet up with Kaitlyn at a casual restaurant just off the beaten path in downtown Tampa. She's due any day now with her and Benny's first child and she said she wanted spicy Thai food to hurry things along. I don't know what that means and I don't want to find out. The way a woman's body can make a baby is nothing short of a miracle, but I don't want to see the inner workings up close and personal as she brings that life into this world.

Kaitlyn's already seated at a table when I get there. She's sitting sideways, her swollen feet in flip flops and propped up on another chair. One hand rubs her massive belly, and the other hand is shoveling a spring roll in her mouth. She chews and gestures for me to come over. I do, giving her a friendly pat on the shoulder and pulling out a chair opposite her.

"Am I late? I could have sworn you said six." I place a napkin on my lap.

She swallows and then takes a big gulp of water before speaking. "Nope! Right on time. I just got hungry. I swear, this baby better come soon, or I won't have enough room for food."

She shoves another spring roll in her mouth, taking an obnoxiously large bite and chewing like it's the last meal she'll ever have. I grimace. It's like being live at the filming of a mukbang video with the sounds that are coming out of her mouth. Are all pregnant women like this? Or is this just Kaitlyn?

"Benny says you have a plan for me?" I try to get her on task before I lose my appetite completely.

She nods and holds up a finger while still managing to maintain a grasp on what's left of the poor spring roll. Her other hand points to her oversized bag sitting on the floor next to her. At first, I thought she was using this pregnancy to command men to do her bidding. Now that she's further along, I see that she really can't bend over to reach things. I rummage around and pull out a stack of papers.

"Just the top one," she says around the food. I put the rest back and hold the top sheet between us. It's a list in Kaitlyn's handwriting. "Listen, you've screwed up one too many times with the new coach. Everyone is well aware you're the enforcer–for now–but save the fighting for the opponents who deserve it. You can't get in scuffles with your own teammates or pick fights with rookies like last season. I got a text today that Marsh has been entertaining the possibility of trading you."

My heart dips down into my stomach. Fuck. I can't change teams again. I finally have a team that wants me long term. Or at least I thought they did. I like the guys I play with. Hell, despite the crazy drivers, I like Tampa. I know new coaches like to make a huge splash as the new boss, flexing their muscles and laying down the law, but this is ridiculous.

"Relax, we're not going to let that happen. Hence my list." She motions for me to read it aloud while she eats the other half of the roll.

"Buy a home. Steady girlfriend/no bunnies. No alcohol binges/no bars. Get involved in a charity in Tampa. Stop dressing like a YouTube influencer trying to get girls. Take anger management classes. Eat vegetables daily."

I throw the paper back down on the table, managing humor like usual even though I feel like my world is imploding. "Daily vegetables? That's where I draw the line, woman."

It's actually the least offensive thing on the list. Despite my constant teasing and acting up, I eat plenty of healthy food. It's just everything else that sounds like a boring midlife for other people, not me. Might as well start driving a minivan and wearing sandals with socks. And not even fun socks. Stupid big boy socks to go with my big boy underwear.

Kaitlyn must hear the defiance in my tone because she finally wipes off her fingers on the cloth napkin and ignores the food. "Listen, I know it sounds crazy, but it worked for Banks. It'll work for you too. I promise." She motions to her bag again, and following directions, I snag a business card out of the outside pocket. "Start by calling my friend Coco. She helped Banks and me buy our house. She's an older woman, you'll love her."

I give her a flat look, not appreciating my agent giving me shit for my proclivity for older women.

The server interrupts with two steaming bowls of veggies in a broth of some sort before Kaitlyn can keep going on everything I have to do on top of playing incredible hockey. "Jungle curry, extra spicy." The woman grimaces and then bows her head before leaving, like she just said a prayer we'll survive the meal.

Kaitlyn wears a maniacal look as she dips a spoon in her bowl. "Eat up, Bobby. Hope you don't mind spicy."

She slurps up the veggies and immediately pants like a dog. I tentatively let a trickle of the broth enter my mouth and instantly regret it. Fire so hot it feels cold floods my mouth. I grab for my water and drain it in one gulp, looking around wildly for a refill. I wag my tongue outside my mouth, hoping to catch a cool draft of air somewhere. Kaitlyn's full-on sweating. Or maybe she's crying, I can't really tell. What the fuck is this jungle curry? I push my bowl away, scared straight. My sinuses are so clear I can smell Richie's stinky socks he left at my apartment the other night all the way from here. I'll do whatever's on that list, but I'm not eating any more of that shit.

"Oh god," Kaitlyn moans.

I have to wipe a bead of sweat off my brow before it drips into my eyes. "Yeah, no shit. That's ridiculously hot."

"No, I mean, oh god, I think my water just broke."

I shove away from the table and leap to my feet. She's not wrong. It looks like she just peed herself.

"Oh, fuck me. Benny's gonna kill me."

Kaitlyn looks up at me with wide eyes. "Forget Banks! I'm gonna kill you if you don't get me to the hospital!"

Chapter Four

Molly

"There's a panic room. I feel like I'm in a Jodi Foster movie."

Not looking the least bit surprised by my news, Coco turns to face me from across the massive coastal-inspired kitchen. She's wearing a blue Chanel suit and matching Louboutins with a heel that could easily puncture some cheating boyfriend's tire.

"Everybody has a panic room these days, darling," she dismisses my comment. "It's the new home gym."

Maybe Coco's listings do, but mine? Yeah...no. Although one of them does have a tiny pool, so that's something at least. Of course, I don't mention the lack of panic rooms in my listings. I wouldn't want her to think me ungrateful.

"So, what else do we need to do before the official start time?" I ask instead.

I'm helping Coco with an open house at one of her properties today—her idea. She thought I might be able to schmooze a little and maybe pick up a new client. The house we're showing is a gorgeous Key West style home in Sunset Park with a list price that has more zeros than I care to think about.

My boss consults her phone. "Just the flowers."

"Already done," I say. "One small arrangement in each bedroom and a large one in the entry. The place smells like hydrangeas and money."

"Perfect." Coco does a quick check of her lipstick in a compact mirror before snapping it shut. I don't know why she bothers. Her makeup is always impeccable. With no compact of my own, I quickly check my reflection in the glass of the oven door, immediately noticing the bags under my eyes. Do cucumber slices actually shrink those suckers? I should probably try that sometime.

I glance around the sprawling kitchen and dining area for something to straighten, but the place is immaculate from the Spanish tile floor to the crown moldings bordering the twelve-foot ceilings.

"I guess I should go over the listing sheet in case there's a hidden passageway or something I should know about." I take one from the stack on the kitchen island and begin leafing through it.

Coco rounds the island to sidle up next to me. "Since you're clearly not going to bring it up yourself, I have to ask. Have you gotten any matches on the app?"

"What app?" I ask distractedly, following it immediately with, "Is the pool saltwater or chlorine?"

"Saltwater." Coco snatches the listing from my hand. "What do you mean *what app*?"

I look at my boss and blink a couple times before it all comes back to me. I'd forgotten all about the ridiculous dating app the minute I picked Matty up for hockey practice the other day. After his detention, he was grounded from video games and electronics, but I came home to find he had snuck his Nintendo Switch from its hiding place in my bedroom. Looks like I need to be a little craftier in the future. We argued, of course, and he gave me the silent treatment all the way to practice.

I ended up dropping him off and running errands until pickup time. *Oh god.* And I embarrassed the hell out of myself with that young guy—that *hot* young guy. I think he's on the Storm Chasers' team, but they all look the same in their uniforms as far as I'm concerned. In street clothes, however, this guy stands out like a triple fudge brownie sundae in a sea of plain vanilla cones.

The memory has my cheeks heating. He was helping Coach Chloe and was obviously just making a light comment in passing. But there I was staring at him like some horny zombie and making a fool of myself. I don't even remember what I said before turning tail and fleeing.

"I already told you I'm not joining a dating app, Coco."

She scowls at me. "Darling, you need more fun in your life. What does it hurt to scroll a little? You're not agreeing to have a man's baby by taking a peek at his profile." She flicks nonexistent dust off her suit jacket before plucking my phone from the counter where I left it. Knowing it will be easier to just go along and delete it later, I let her have her way.

"Face." She turns the phone to me to unlock it before scrolling directly to the app store and starting a search. "Face again." The app begins installing and I catch the name for the first time.

"*Catnip?* What the hell kind of dating app is called Catnip?"

I get Coco's side-eye in response. "What did I say about trusting me? It's the best dating app out there, bar none."

She continues scrolling and tapping as something horrifying occurs to me. "You didn't post my picture on there, did you?" I can just imagine my creepy dry cleaner cruising dating sites and finding my photo next to "Sparkle Is My Stripper Name." I suppress a shudder.

"Don't be silly, darling. No name and no pictures. If you find someone interesting, you can exchange that later. It's all perfectly safe," she assures. "Ha!" Her sudden shout startles me, making me gape at her. She only grins in return. "You already have six matches!"

A familiar heat begins creeping up my neck. "Let me see that." I take the phone from Coco and see that she's right. There are six "Cat Chat" requests from my "Meow Matches." Are these people serious with this shit? I mean, I guess it's just for fun like Coco said, but it's also, well, a little absurd.

I shove down my panic and hand the phone back to my boss, momentarily forgetting it's my damn phone. "What do dates from this app consist of? A shared can of tuna over candlelight in the alley behind Long John Silver?"

Before Coco can answer, voices sound from the entryway, and we quickly stash our personal things under the counter before straightening and heading for the hall.

"Welcome!" she declares in what I like to call her queen voice. Thus begins our busy first hour of the open house.

Coco is showing a young tech executive and her husband the upstairs while I walk another couple around the enclosed yard and wraparound veranda. I can tell they're not really in the market and are just what we refer to as lookie-loos, but you never know. Everyone can be a potential client down the road.

They take my card before returning to their car parked at the curb. As soon as they pull out, one of those insane Cybertrucks swerves into the spot, coming to an abrupt stop, inches from the car in front of it. I turn to go back into the house when a voice catches my attention.

"Hey, I know you."

The comment—and the deep baritone of the commenter's voice—have me turning back. The hot young guy from hockey practice stands in the open door of the Cybertruck, looking up at me with a million-dollar smile and —holy crap—are those dimples in his unfairly handsome face?

"Oh. Um, hello," I manage as he swaggers toward me with an ease I instinctively know he was born with. *Please don't blush. Please don't blush. Please don't . . .* too late. Damn my fair complexion! "Welcome!" I try channeling my best queen Coco vibe, but it comes out way too loud for our proximity.

"Thanks." His smile remains as he comes to a stop on the porch. His dirty-blond hair is damp at the ends, telling me he just showered—something I already could have guessed from the intoxicating scent wafting my way. He smells like citrus and sandalwood with maybe a hint of pepper, and it takes zero time for me to be mesmerized by his melty chocolate eyes. Again!

I need to snap out of it, so I thrust a hand toward him and force my voice to adopt a professional tone. "I'm Molly Sparks with Farnsworth Luxury Realty."

His eyes widen at the mention of my last name. Yeah, it can be an attention-getter, but it's leagues better than my maiden name, Hooker. Try escaping high school unscathed with that name.

"Bobby Rhodes," he replies, taking my offered hand. My blush kicks up a notch when he brings his other hand up to join the first, essentially cradling my hand in both of his large ones. "Your kid plays hockey."

"So do you," I reply. He still hasn't let go of my hand.

"I do."

We're both silent for a beat, and I finally rip my hand from his grasp and hook my thumb to the open doorway behind me. "You want to see the house?"

"Absolutely." Bobby nods before shrugging a shoulder. "I'm actually here to meet somebody named Coco to help me find a house, but I'd love it if you showed me around this one."

"Oh. She's inside with a potential buyer." I step through the doorway, gesturing for him to follow. What are the chances of this guy showing up here? There are over three million people living in the greater Tampa area. Although, I've heard it said that rich people all run in the same circles. And he's got to be rich, right? With a professional sports career and that crazy Tesla?

"I've got time," Bobby says in a tone that tells me he's well practiced at this easygoing vibe he's got going on. "Especially for you," he adds.

Unsure what to do with my hands or my heated cheeks, I default into realtor mode. "The house is just over six thousand square feet if you count the walk-out basement and home theater. It's owned by the original builder, who's maintained it in pristine condition, as you can see." I continue to list the property's qualities and features while we tour the first floor. Bobby nods at each of my comments as he follows me around, hands clasped behind his back as if he's afraid to touch anything. My nervousness dissipates the longer I talk until I realize fifteen minutes have gone by and he hasn't said a word. Crap.

"Do you have any questions before we go downstairs?" I fold my hands in front of me and offer him a polite smile.

He shakes his head slowly, one corner of his lips tipping up. "No. I'll take it."

I open my mouth and close it again. I must have heard him wrong. I try again. "I . . . I'm sorry, did you just say you want to *buy* this house?"

He's nodding before I even finish my question. Both dimples are on show this time, and I swear his eyes twinkle.

I step closer and throw both my hands forward in a halting gesture as I look up at him. "You can't!" I insist.

The amusement remains. "Why not? Has somebody already bought it?"

"No," I reply. "You haven't even seen the whole property yet! Or asked about the price! People don't just walk into houses and decide to buy them without even seeing the bedrooms or peeking in the medicine cabinet," I continue in dismay, my voice rising with each word. "You might hate the configuration of the basement or get freaked out by the panic room." I tilt my head and give it another thought. "Although your Cybertruck indicates you may already be preparing for the apocalypse, so what do I know?" His smile grows at that, and I shake my head, determined to talk sense into him. "This is the first house you've toured, isn't it?"

He shrugs, completely unbothered. "Yeah. But I need a house and this one is nice." His eyes scan the great room and its numerous seating areas.

I take a breath and study him for a few seconds. "Listen, Mr. Rhodes."

"Bobby," he corrects me.

"Fine. Bobby. I'm sure Coco will be thrilled to help you find a house. But it's important to take time to prioritize and consider what you're looking for in a home before making any decisions. Do you want a big yard or do you prefer something small and lower maintenance? How many bedrooms do you need? Do you prefer an open concept design or something more traditional and intimate? There are lots of factors to consider."

"Okay." He nods, taking it all in stride. He pauses for another second before declaring, "I want you to be my agent. We can figure it out together."

My jaw goes slack. "No! I can't. I . . . I mean, that's a very flattering proposal, but I'm just a junior agent. Coco can really set you up. She's been doing this for decades, and she's a master at it. She knows everyone."

"But I want you," Bobby responds, and something in his tone—and those long-lashed baby browns—makes it sound like he's not just talking about houses. Oh. My. God. What is happening here?

I force myself to take a reality check. He's obviously just a natural-born flirter, that's all it is. He's got to be fifteen years younger than me and he's a professional hockey player, for goodness' sake. He's not hitting on me.

I clear my throat and return to professional mode. "Excuse me for a moment." I walk calmly toward the staircase, intent on fetching Coco to right this ship. But I swear I can feel Bobby's stare searing through my knockoff Dior suit. Good lord. I'm so distracted that I almost plow right into Coco when I round the corner.

She reaches out to steady me from her spot in front of an alcove, and I start to apologize. But suspicion gives me pause. "Were you . . ." I take in her expression and finish my question in an accusing whisper-hiss, ". . . *eavesdropping?*"

Instead of answering, she hooks her arm through mine and forces me back to the hallway where Bobby Rhodes and his dimples wait.

"You must be Bobby Rhodes," Coco declares, her voice and manner as queenly as ever. "How *wonderful* to meet you. You're going to *love* working with Molly."

Chapter Five

Bobby

I can't wipe the grin off my face. Molly looks like a fish, opening and closing her pretty mouth like she has something to say but won't say it now that her boss is here. Coco, the older woman of the two, has diamonds flashing from every surface. She's beautiful and she knows it. She also has a co-conspirator glint in her eye that spells good things for my future working with Molly.

"Excellent." I clap my hands. "Shall I sign something now, making you my personal agent?"

Molly's cheeks flush a deeper red, but Coco doesn't miss a beat. "I have the paperwork in the kitchen. My girl isn't cheap, but I think you'll find she's worth the extra."

I really thought finding a home was going to be a pain in the ass, along with everything else on Kaitlyn's list. But watching Molly blush while spelling out all the qualities of this house in a nervous rant, followed by not allowing me to make an offer, has me intrigued. I also like the way she fills out that pencil skirt. What is it about a pencil skirt that drives me crazy? The flare of hips? The highlighted round ass? Pretty sure the matching sky-high heels have something to do with it too.

Coco lets go of Molly and grabs my arm, tugging me into the kitchen with a force I wouldn't have guessed for a woman her age. Her cloud of Chanel perfume is like an extra person between us. "Don't stare, darling. She's skittish as a newborn colt," she whispers in my ear. "You have to ease this one into the bedroom. Then release the stallion."

My eyes widen at the mixed metaphor. Coco utters a twinkling laugh. She stops us at the oversized kitchen island.

"Sign here." She taps her fingernail on a form. She's back to all business in the blink of an eye.

I briefly look over the clauses of the contract, mostly just assuring I'll pay Molly for her services, and sign my name at the bottom. Molly trails behind us, wringing her hands and looking even cuter than when I flirted with her at the rink, before she walked away without a word. Coco swipes up the signed paper and shakes my hand before gliding out of the room. Molly nervously licks her lips and something tightens in my gut.

"Looks like you're stuck with me."

She doesn't return my flirtatious grin. She stiffens her spine, drops her hands, and gives me a queenly nod. And then she twirls around and stalks out of the kitchen. My bark of laughter echoes off the tile and granite.

This is game three of a road trip through Canada. I got

one on the scoreboard tonight, helping the Storm Chasers continue our winning streak. Coach even gave me a pat on the back when the final buzzer sounded and we headed for the locker room. He's currently huddled in the back corner with Hugh "Cappy" Picard, our backup goalie. Based on the muscle twitching in Cappy's jaw, I don't think Coach is too happy he let one in the net tonight. Druggy, our veteran goalie, has been stepping back to let Cappy play more this season, saving his hips and knees for our most important matches. I'm just happy Coach's perennial bad mood is focused elsewhere today.

It's been a week away from home, and I've missed seeing Molly's backside. Honestly, I'm starting to think I see more of her backside as she walks away from me than I see of those bewitching eyes. There's just something about her that pulls me in. Maybe it's her complete lack of ability to flirt. Or her wit when she does let herself speak what's on her mind. And let's not forget those sexy pencil skirts.

My phone dings in my locker. I shove my gloves in there and open my phone to see a picture from Benny. He's got a bundle of newborn baby in his arms, a goofy grin on both their faces. I went to see Benny and Kaitlyn before we left on this trip. Thankfully, Benny didn't kick my ass for Kaitlyn's water breaking on my watch, but he did make me hold Mei, their newborn daughter. She's pretty damn cute for something that belches and poops all day long.

"Golden Girls sent you a naked selfie, Roadie?" Dan-O elbows me from his locker next to me. "You got that glazed look again."

I frown at the captain of our team. The boys always give me shit for going for the older women. They nicknamed them collectively Golden Girls, a joke I find obnoxious. Okay, fine. It's kind of funny. It'd be the type of shit I'd say if it was someone else dating the over-forty set.

"It's a naked selfie all right." I waggle my eyebrows and that fucker Dan-O leans over to catch a glimpse. "Hey!" I hold the phone to my chest. "Sara would not approve."

Dan-O flips me off at the mention of his wife and removes his shirt. Dude needs to start manscaping again. He's hairier than a wildebeest. "That looks like Mei."

I shrug and get undressed, needing food after all the play time I'm getting with Benny being on paternity leave. "It is. I told Benny to send me daily pictures. These kiddos grow up so fast." I say that last part with a falsetto voice. It's true though. She already looks different from the day I saw her.

Dan-O slaps me on the back on his way to the showers. "Ah, Roadie's getting soft in his old age."

My gaze flicks to the corner where Coach is still letting Cappy have it. My voice increases in volume. "I guess so. I even went house shopping the other day."

"Now you just need a wife and a baby in a baby carriage," Forns sing-songs as he throws a towel at me.

I flip him off, then look over at Coach to make sure he didn't see that. I've successfully gone two weeks without instigating even a verbal argument with anyone outside my purview as enforcer. Thankfully Cappy's got his full attention.

I join the boys over in the shower area and scrub away the game. I redress in slacks, brown loafers, a button-down blue shirt, sport coat, and my favorite Panama hat. This one has a peacock feather tucked into the ribbon that matches my shirt. The feather is technically removable but who would want to take the feather off? It's a goddamn work of art.

Half of the post-game press conference is focused on Benny being out, Cappy taking over as goalie, and my outfit. I don't mind fielding questions about my attire, unlike some of the other guys who think the questions should be focused on our game play.

On the bus back to our hotel, Dan-O leans across the aisle. "What's up with the hat? Planning on going on a safari?"

I shake my head at his lack of fashion knowledge. "This is a Panama hat. Natural fibers sourced from Ecuador and woven by hand. Every gentleman should own at least one Panama hat."

Dan-O busts up laughing. "Okay, Roadie. I'll add that to my Christmas list this year."

"You do that. Sara would appreciate a gentleman."

He smirks. "Nah. She likes me *un*gentlemanly, if you know what I mean."

Druggy turns around in his seat in front of me. I brace for a scathing remark. "Chloe tells me it is called 'a gentleman in the streets and a freak in the sheets.'"

The bus erupts with everyone congratulating Druggy on finally getting an American phrase correct and giving their opinion on what the ladies actually want from their men. As for me, I tune them all out and text Molly with yet another listing I want to go see with her. I've pretty much sent her five houses a day since I've been gone. She told me to be selective, so that's what I'm doing. And if it means I get to spend hours with her, touring all the houses, so be it. She texts back right away, asking if we can start our tours two days from now.

Me: I'll be flying home tomorrow morning so if we can do a few tomorrow night, that would be great too.

Molly: Let me see if that'll work.

Me: Do you have another client tomorrow night?

Molly: No.

> Me: Then . . . why won't that work?

I'm not trying to be a dick, but I've been wanting to see Molly all week and I don't want to wait.

> Molly: If you must know, I have to see if I can use Coco's car.

I frown, wondering why we can't use Molly's car. Then again, maybe she doesn't have a car. Even though my brain hasn't left her side all week, I don't actually know much about her.

> Me: Problem solved. We'll use mine. Send me your address and I'll pick you up at six.

> Molly: In the Cybertruck?

> Me: The one and only! You'll love Wolverine.

Think it would be tacky to ask her to wear another one of her pencil skirts?

The bus comes to a stop outside our hotel and all the guys start getting up, saving me from texting back. Asking about her clothing might be a little skeevy, even for me. I get off the bus and head up to my room, ignoring the younger guys talking about which bar they intend to hit up tonight. No game tomorrow, so in the past, I'd be one of them, staying out all night and experiencing the nightlife in whatever town we were in.

Big Boy Bobby goes to his hotel room and orders room service. I also ignore Mac, my roommate on this trip, as he calls his girlfriend back home. He starts talking in low tones and suddenly gets off his bed to head for the bathroom. I shove earbuds in my ears and play some music, not wanting to know what he's doing in there. I'm already annoyed Coach set me up with a roommate. It's a not-so-subtle slap on the wrist.

I pull up my favorite dating app to pass the time until my food arrives, scrolling through the women I've connected with in the past. I have a new notification, so I go to my inbox to see I've been matched with someone. Unfortunately, her username is *@SparkleIsMyStripperName*. Not that my username is much better, being a stupid phrase from my favorite show.

Kaitlyn told me to get a steady girlfriend to help clean up my image, but I'm pretty sure she didn't mean someone like that. Personally, I have nothing against strippers. I think they're amazing people and I'd be proud to date one. Hell, I've dated several in the past, but Kaitlyn drummed on about cleaning up my image right before she peed herself in public. I snicker, thinking about her expression when her water broke. Wish I could have taken a picture.

I message Sparkle back, letting her down easy.

> @PitterPatterLetsGetAtHer: Hey, sorry for the confusion. I'm actually looking for a serious girlfriend these days.

A knock sounds on the door. I let the room service attendant in to set up our dinner on the table, tipping him extra when he doesn't ask for an autograph and leaves quickly. I dig into my burger, not waiting for Mac. I'm not interrupting whatever's going on in that bathroom. I'm working on the fries when my phone dings that Sparkle has written me back.

> @SparkleIsMyStripperName: Oh, um, sure. I'm not even sure how this thing connected with you. Sorry.

> @PitterPatterLetsGetAtHer: No worries. New to Catnip?

@SparkleIsMyStripperName: That obvious? Don't answer that. Hey, do you know how to change a username?

That has me grinning and abandoning the rest of my fries.

@PitterPatterLetsGetAtHer: Are stripper names supposed to be top secret?

@SparkleIsMyStripperName: I have no idea. I'll have to ask a stripper.

@PitterPatterLetsGetAtHer: You're not one?

@SparkleIsMyStripperName: Gosh no! My boss signed me up for this app. She thinks I need to get laid.

@PitterPatterLetsGetAtHer: Do you?

@SparkleIsMyStripperName: Honestly? Probably.

I head back to my bed, flopping back on the mattress and settling into this conversation with a stripper/not a stripper.

@PitterPatterLetsGetAtHer: Head to the three lines at the top right. Usernames are under Activity instead of Settings for some reason. Not gonna lie though, I kind of like the name. It's straightforward. No surprises.

@Singlemomcatlady: So's this one.

I laugh out loud, right as Mac exits the bathroom, face lighting up when he sees the food.

"Wash those hands first!" I holler.

Chapter Six

Molly

Holding my hair up with one hand and knocking on Matty's door with the other, I announce, "Dinner's ready." When there's no answer, I grab the knob, but it doesn't turn. "Matty?"

"What?" comes his raised voice from the other side.

I'm torn between insisting he unlock the door so I can warn him about his tone and just letting it go. Twelve is an age where privacy is becoming a big thing, right? Hell, I don't know.

"Dinner," I repeat, adding, "I made hurricane tacos," to tempt him. It works. The door swings open a second later to reveal my kid, brown and copper hair a tousled mess and bringing with him an odor I like to call *eau de boy.*

"Why didn't you say so in the first place?" He shoots me a devilish grin that makes me wonder if I imagined his earlier tone. But before he can race off to devour the tacos, his eyes drop to the hand not holding my ponytail in place. "What is *that*?!"

I hold up the auburn hairpiece for his inspection. It's the longer one I integrate into my own thinning hair to make my ponytail full and bouncy. Another gift of middle age. "It's just hair. Not a tarantula." He doesn't appear the least bit comforted, so I show him the little clips that secure it to my head. "Women have lots of secrets, kid. It's probably best you learn these things early on."

His lip curls. "It's still creepy."

I give him a friendly shove toward the kitchen and follow him there. "'Tis the season, I suppose. Speaking of which, we're seriously running short on time for your Halloween costume."

We never do store-bought costumes at the Sparks house. Blake used to be the one to dream up ideas with Matty, and then we'd work on the costumes together, sometimes all of us dressing up in a theme. Last year was the first time Matty wanted to go it alone, even insisting on trick-or-treating with a friend instead of allowing me or his dad to tag along.

"Halloween costumes are for losers." He drops a knee to a chair and reaches over to grab a taco from the plate in the center of the table, and I halt, frowning at him.

"Since when?" I try keeping any emotion out of my voice. I knew this day would come, of course, but I didn't expect it to be so sudden or feel so jarring.

Matty just rolls his eyes, his mouth occupied now with the taco. Dinner needed a short prep time tonight since I'm meeting up with my new client in less than thirty minutes. Hurricane tacos provided the perfect solution, named as such when I invented them while we hunkered down with no power during Hurricane Irma several years back. Just some canned chicken, diced tomatoes, cheese, and a dash of taco seasoning, all wrapped up in a tortilla. They're one of Matty's favorites.

I duck into the half-bathroom just off the kitchen to finish my hair. "So, I guess candy is for losers too, then?" I ask, raising my voice to be heard.

"Yeah, right," Matty scoffs. "We're still trick-or-treating; we're just not wearing costumes," he clarifies. I don't bother asking if the *we* includes me since I know it doesn't. Sigh. Oh well. I'll just hang back and enjoy the cute little kids in their adorable costumes while I hand out candy here.

Securing the last clip in place and smoothing down any flyaways, I bustle back to the kitchen and grab my bag. "I've got some showings to do. Don't forget to finish your home-work before any video games, okay?" I eye him meaningfully. He hasn't tripped up since his detention over a week ago, and I'd like to keep it that way. "I'll be back by eight-thirty. Ramona's home next door. Call if you need anything."

Then I bend to drop a quick kiss on his head before he can duck away. Ha! Too slow for this mom.

Twenty minutes later, I pace in the lobby of the realty office, chewing my lip to shreds while I wait for Bobby Rhodes and his spaceship truck. I was able to push my nervousness off while he was out of town, but as his arrival looms, my sweat glands lose their grip and go into turbo mode. No amount of fanning or flapping my arms can help the wetness from seeping into the armpits of my blouse. Dammit!

Of course, Bobby is right on time, loping up the walkway and smiling broadly when he spies me through the glass doors.

"Nice digs," he says as soon as he enters. I follow his gaze around the lobby, taking in the familiar furnishings and art. Of course, it was all selected by Coco and, therefore, is exquisite.

"That settee belonged to Gianni Versace himself," I say,

hoping Bobby will keep his eyes on the furniture and not my growing sweat stains. Unlike me, he appears cool as a wedge salad, all loose-limbed and dressed to kill in designer jeans and a shirt with a loud retro pattern I'm guessing only about five guys in the world could pull off—Bobby Rhodes being one of them.

"If you'll excuse me for just one moment," I say with a polite smile before hauling ass to the restroom where I instruct my reflection to hold her shit together while I dab at my armpits with paper towels.

"Ready?" I ask when I return, my tone striking the perfect balance between cheerful and professional.

Bobby's eyes briefly scan me from top to toe before he cocks his head and holds the door open for me. "Ladies first." He's equally polite when opening the car door, and I half expect a cloud of vapor to billow out of the Cybertruck. It doesn't, of course, so I'm soon settled in the passenger seat after a hand up from Bobby.

I read him the first address, and he enters it into the vehicle's navigation system before smoothly pulling out of the small parking lot.

"How's your son liking hockey?" he asks. "His name is Matt, right?"

I glance over from the printed listings in my lap and nod. "Matthew. He seems to love it, although I think he's frustrated he hasn't mastered all the skills yet."

Bobby flashes me a dimple and I ignore the flipping of my belly. "I've been playing for twenty years and I still haven't mastered them all."

I smile and shrug one shoulder. "The impatience of youth." It's not lost on me that Bobby could be closer to Matty's age than my own—just one more reason not to let my hormones get feisty. To that point, I turn back to professional mode. "This first house is still occupied. That's why we're viewing it before the other two, which are vacant. We've got more wiggle room with timing on those."

"Isn't it going to be weird if we're walking around in these people's houses while they're eating dinner or whatever?"

I blink a couple times before looking over at Bobby with a knit brow. "They're not going to be home, Bobby. That's why I made an appointment."

One of his hands goes to the back of his neck, his expression turning chagrined. "Oh. I guess that makes more sense."

Without thinking, I reach over to pat his denim-covered knee. "It's okay. This is your first rodeo house hunting." His eyes drop to my hand, and I quickly snatch it away, but not before taking note of the hard muscles under my palm. What was I thinking? God, he's either assuming I think he's a child or I'm trying to cop a feel. Good Christ. I start talking to cover my embarrassment. "You're actually way ahead of the game in a lot of ways. Not many other people your age are taking on mortgages and picking out backsplashes."

His lips curve as he turns left at an intersection, as instructed by his navigation system—which has a sultry Australian accent, of course. "First, what the hell is a backsplash? And second, how young do you think I am?"

"Oh." I pause. It was probably a faux pas to bring up his age, but it's too late now. "Um, twenty-five?" I guess. "And a backsplash is the tile behind the kitchen sink."

"Noted." He shoots me a glare, but it's playful. "And I'll have you know I'm twenty-eight, almost twenty-nine," he boasts in a manner that reminds me of every young kid I know who can't wait to get another year older. I don't point that out. Bobby may be a little older than I thought, but he's still way too young for me to consider developing a silly crush on. After all, I'm forty, the age where a lot of people start counting backward instead of being eager to jump ahead like a kid.

Still, I can't keep myself from commenting, "Practically ancient," in a light tone.

We drive the rest of the short journey to the Mediterranean-style home in Hyde Park. It sits in a trendy neighborhood with newer construction and tight lots. When Bobby filled out a questionnaire the day after I became his agent, it was clear he didn't know enough about home styles to narrow in on what he wanted. So, we're checking out a variety of neighborhoods and architecture styles to see what feels right.

"This one has three bedrooms, three and a half baths, and an impressive outdoor entertainment space," I remind him as we mount the front steps and I punch the code into the key box to retrieve the key.

He watches, not commenting until I've turned the key in the lock and opened the door. "Clever. I was wondering how we were going to get in if nobody was home." This boy is easily impressed.

Our footsteps on the tile floor echo off the walls in the entry as we begin our tour. Bobby looks to me for permission before opening the coat closet to investigate. "Feel free to open any doors or cabinets you like," I tell him. "Storage is important."

He shrugs and shuts the door again. "I don't really have all that much stuff, to be honest."

"You'd be surprised how quickly you start accumulating things when you own a home," I warn. He told me he's been renting in a high-rise right near the hockey facility. "Pretty soon you'll have a lawnmower, three ladders, and a carpet cleaner with twelve attachments. And if you're planning on starting a family anytime soon, you'll need room for a whole lot more. Babies have more accessories and belongings than supermodels."

He chuckles and raises his palms in defense. "Slow down,

Molly. My brain is still stuck on backsplashes. I don't have the capacity to consider marriage and tiny humans too."

"Noted," I repeat his earlier response and grin back at him before gesturing for him to precede me to the kitchen. But he stops abruptly, causing me to crash into his back. I throw my hands out to steady myself, encountering hard muscle hiding behind his crazy shirt. Hard and incredibly warm. He turns, grabbing my elbow to help keep me standing while his movement causes my outstretched hands to glide from his muscled back to his tight abs. My eyes widen and I quickly step back on a heel to create some distance.

Heat crawls up my neck as Bobby drops my elbow and his eyes drop to my chest where I can feel my nipples have hardened into tight peaks under my blouse. Great! Nothing says professional like pit stains *and* blinking headlights.

He quickly averts his gaze, aiming it at the phone he's pulled from his pocket. "Sorry. I just . . . that talk of babies made me think of my teammate, Benny, and his girlfriend. They just had a cute little rugrat." He extends the phone, the screen pointed my way showing the most precious newborn baby with a tiny Florida Storm Chasers jersey draped over its chest. "The jersey was from me. Figured the kid better start representing as soon as possible." Bobby turns the screen to look down at it again, and I glance up to see his enamored expression. My gasping ovaries high five each other. *Not now, bitches!*

"Adorable," I murmur, not sure if I'm talking about the baby or the hunky hockey player. Then, I sidestep Bobby as I will away my blush, determined to press on with the tour. Yes, he's handsome. And kind of sweet. And charming, of course, with those ridiculous dimples. And he's *almost* thirty, right? I consult the printed listing once again and firm my spine. "The kitchen features a Wolf induction stovetop and a—" but I'm cut off by Bobby's sharp gasp behind me.

I spin on my heel to see his attention is no longer on the phone or on the kitchen ahead but has instead wandered to a room off the entry. "Sick!" he exclaims before bounding out of sight. "An air hockey table *and* a pinball machine!" His head appears once more around the corner, his entire expression infused with youthful delight. "You think they come with the house?!"

My ovaries slowly lower their hands back to their sides in defeat.

Chapter Seven

Bobby

Who knew shopping for a house could be so much fun? It helps that I have the hottest realtor in all of Tampa and following her around house after house is no hardship. When I drop Molly off at the realtor's office and she safely goes inside, I do start to wonder if a pencil skirt fetish is a thing. Like, is there a support group? Or maybe just a Reddit thread where we can discuss why a simple business skirt can lead a man to lose his goddamn mind? Kaitlyn's voice floats through my brain, reprimanding me for being an asshole for having dirty thoughts about my realtor.

"I could really use a beer right now," I say out loud as I zoom down the road toward my high-rise. My truck responds in a custom aftermarket Aussie accent, asking if I need directions. Wolverine really is the greatest vehicle ever made. I'll fight you if you disagree.

"Fuck." Now it's Coach's voice in my brain, the tone

sarcastic and lacking even a hint of respect as he tells me to clean up my act. "No thanks, Wolverine."

I look out the passenger window as I pass The Irish Rogue, the bar Richie works at, and make longing, kissy faces at it. My hands grip the wheel, wanting to turn in and have a quick beer before I head home, but my gaze snags on something on the floor. The light turns red and I stop, reaching down to grab a small glass bottle. I hold it up to see what it is, but the scent of berries, jasmine, and what can only be sandalwood hits my nose. Fuck. This is Molly's perfume. Even if she hadn't been sitting in my car earlier, I would have known this was hers from the scent alone.

When the light turns green, I cross a few lanes when it's safe and flip a U-turn, heading back to the realtor's office. I could wait and hand it back to her next time I see her, but why can't the next time be right fucking now? Seeing Molly is pretty much the only thing better than stopping for a beer and since I can't do that, Molly it is.

The realtor's office is dark now, which I should have anticipated. I blow out a disappointed breath and start to turn the wheel in yet another U-turn, thinking Molly has already left for home. But then I see her standing next to the most hideous car ever made, a yellow Kia Soul. The hood is up, and Molly has her hands on her hips like the power of her frown alone will fix all the many things wrong with that car. I pull into the parking lot and slide out before I have a plan in mind.

"Everything okay?" I ask stupidly.

Molly's head whips up and her ponytail goes flying. One hand grabs her chest, and I hold my hands up in peace. Her hand leaves her chest to rub her forehead when she sees it's me. I walk over to her side to assess the engine that looks almost as bad as the outside of this thing.

"Yeah, I don't know," Molly answers, voice sounding

stressed. "It won't turn over, and the normal trick isn't work-ing. I was about to call my neighbor for a jump."

I puff out my chest. I grew up with four brothers and a dad who tackled any and all problems, even if we should have called a professional. I feel compelled to fix this if for no other reason than male pride. "I have jumper cables in the truck. Let's see if we can get you on your way."

Molly looks over at me with so much relief and hope in those gorgeous hazel eyes, I feel a little like Superman when he arrives on the scene in his superhero outfit. Except without the chafing. Those skintight briefs always looked a little uncom-fortable. I much prefer my hundred percent organic bamboo funderpants. I give Molly a confident smile and turn for my truck. It takes a bit of maneuvering, but I find the portable jump starter the dealership gave me when I bought the truck. I wrap the cables around my fist and look for a power button on the main unit.

"So, I haven't actually used this thing before," I admit as I turn the damn thing around for a third time and still don't see a power button.

Molly laughs softly and takes the cables from my hands. "Well, the first problem is that one of the clamps is broken." I look up and see the red clamp dangling uselessly from her hands.

"Well, damn." There goes my superhero confidence.

Molly holds up a single finger and her eyes light up. "Hold, please." She hustles to the passenger side of her car and rummages around. I would have asked a follow-up question, but she's bent over, that heart shaped ass in the tight pencil skirt that teased me all evening aimed in my direction. My brain pretty much goes completely offline.

She straightens with the most adorable "aha!" I have to rip my gaze away so as not to be caught ogling my realtor in the dark behind the realty office. She comes back over and holds up a paperclip.

"Are we going to collate something?" My mom used to do all the flyers that would go into our backpacks at my elementary school. I can't tell you how many papercuts I sustained from helping her get the flyers organized. Paperclips almost set off a PTSD situation for me.

Molly's teeth bite into her bottom lip as she unbends the paperclip and starts to wrap it around the broken clamp. My gaze decides watching her lips is totally acceptable behavior. There are the barest remnants of red lipstick on her mouth. Something about it makes me want to pull her lip away from her teeth and smear the last of the lipstick across her chin with my thumb. Or maybe my tongue.

"Aha!" Molly exclaims again, holding up the clamp.

I startle, realizing I've been lost in a fantasy about kissing my realtor and taking her up against that blocky little car of hers. Molly's face holds pure delight. I take the red clamp from her outstretched hand and examine it, seeing that she's somehow MacGyver'd the damn thing into something that might actually work.

"Well, damn, Molly," I mutter. "If the zombie apocalypse happens, you're on my team."

Molly's laugh makes the edges of my mouth turn up automatically. I get the cables hooked up to the right terminals on her battery, which looks like it's seen better days. Molly holds the portable starter, so I back away and give her a head nod. She must have found the power button because she hits it and the panel lights up with a bazillion green lights. I take it from her and nod to the car.

"Start her up and let her run for fifteen minutes or so."

Molly rounds the hood and starts the car, which thank god, turns over. She climbs back out, a sheepish smile on her face. Her cheeks are bright red, the state they've been in all evening. I place the pack on the edge of her hood and wave her over to Wolverine.

"Might as well sit in the air conditioning while we let it charge."

She takes my hand and lets me help her into my truck. I get in behind the wheel and message Richie for the number for a good mechanic. He hits me back almost immediately. The guy knows everyone, a perk of the job as a bartender. I place the call to the mechanic shop while Molly looks at me in confusion.

"Hey, can you get a tune-up, oil change, and a battery replacement done tomorrow on a Kia Soul?"

Molly grabs my arm, mimicking slicing something across her throat. I mimic back that I can't understand her. She tugs more forcefully, but I ignore her antics. The person on the other end of the phone clacks away on a computer and says they can get it done around eleven in the morning. I make the appointment and hang up.

"What the hell, Robert Rhodes?" Molly barks, hands flying in the air. Her swinging ponytail seems as angry as her hands.

My jaw drops, right before I burst out laughing. No one calls me Robert except for my mother on occasion when she wants to piss me off. I sober when Molly doesn't join in. Her arms are folded across her chest, her knee bouncing up and down rapidly. She's staring at me like she's imagining popping me in the nose. She's got that mom look down pat.

"Molly. That car is barely drivable." I can't imagine letting her drive that thing around Tampa at all hours. She's lucky she didn't break down on the freeway in the middle of rush hour.

One eyebrow lifts and I'm too slow to realize I've stepped into something I shouldn't have. "That's my business. You had no right to call a mechanic and schedule an appointment that I will not be able to make."

"Sure you will. I'll pick you up tomorrow, take you anywhere you need to go. And I'll have a tow truck pick up the Kia." I hold my hands out, palms up. "Problem solved."

Her mouth gapes open. If it's possible, she's even angrier. "A tow truck? Do you have any idea how much that costs?"

"No." It's true. I don't, but I'm sure she has insurance for that kind of thing, right?

Her hands go flying again and I back away, not wanting to get caught in the windstorm they're creating. "You can't just go around making people appointments for costly things, mister bigshot hockey man!"

I swallow down a laugh, instinctively knowing it won't go over well right now. "Mister bigshot hockey man?"

Her eyes are positively terrifying.

I hold up my hands again, trying to see things from her point of view. All I really know about her personally is that she's a single mom. "Okay, I'm sorry. Truly. I'm sorry for not consulting you, but I don't think driving that thing out there is advisable. I need a realtor who's ready to show me a house before someone else snatches it up. I'll gladly cover the cost of the repairs so you can be ready at a moment's notice. Consider it part of the fee I'll pay for the house I'll eventually buy with your assistance."

"Bobby . . ." she grumbles, head dropping.

Well, at least we're back to Bobby and not Robert.

I dare to put my hand on her arm, careful to avoid even the slightest brush of my fingers against her breast, even if my pinkie finger thinks he can get away with it. "Please, Molly? Let me help you. No strings attached. Just a bigshot hockey man doing a good deed, okay?"

She's back to biting her lip and my fingers twitch, desperate to pull that lip away before she does damage. "Fine, but I'll pay you back from the commissions on the house."

I nod. "If you feel you must."

And then she slips out the door and unhooks the jumper cables herself, handing the unit back to me without meeting my gaze. I'm sure she doesn't love it, but I follow her all the way into a cute but older neighborhood east of Tampa, making sure she gets home safely. I turn around in her neighbor's driveway and head back to my place, beer long forgotten.

After all that, I forgot to give Molly her perfume, and it might be wrong to put it on the nightstand next to my bed so I go to sleep with her scent clinging to me, but I do feel a little like Superman, knowing I've done a good deed in the world. Maybe I should look into a designer cape . . .

Chapter Eight

Molly

"Hey, kiddo," I greet Matty as I close the door. He doesn't look up. I drop my bag on the table and kick off my heels. Why did I wear those things tonight anyway? It's not like I'm trying to impress anybody. *Oh, shut up.*

"Hi!" I try again, this time padding onto the living room carpet and approaching the sofa where Matty has sprawled himself. When he still doesn't respond, I realize he's wearing the earbuds Blake got him for his birthday. I reach out and tug one from his left ear, startling him and bringing him to his feet in a snap.

"Hey! What was that for?" He scowls at me.

"No headphones when there are other people in the room. You know the rules," I remind him.

"I was here by myself. Jeez."

He holds his hand out, and I drop the earbud into his palm, but not before delivering a one-word warning. "Tone."

He has a point, but not if he's going to cop an attitude about it.

He mumbles an apology and turns toward the hall. His slumped shoulders have my brow knitting and that sinking feeling returning to my gut. "Hey, you want to watch an episode of *The Office* before you go to bed?" Introducing my son to one of my favorite shows has been an unexpected bonding opportunity since the divorce.

"Nah. I'm good," is the only response I get before his bedroom door closes behind him.

God, I feel like a failure as a mom. I shouldn't have gone house hunting with Bobby tonight. I should have stayed home and had dinner with my son instead. But working is how I put a roof over his head, I remind myself.

My phone chimes from my bag in the kitchen and when I pull it out, there's a notification from that app Coco signed me up for. I meant to delete the damn thing but completely forgot. It's time to remedy that oversight.

When I click it open, there's a new message from *@Pitter-PatterLetsGetAtHer*. I have no idea what that name is supposed to refer to, and I'm not sure I want to.

> @PitterPatterLetsGetAtHer: So, any luck on your quest?

> @singlemomcatlady: What quest? The getting laid one? Nope. How about you?

It's weird talking to a stranger about my non-existent sex life, but it's not like I'm ever going to meet this person.

> @PitterPatterLetsGetAtHer: The girlfriend one? Not really. Although someone has definitely caught my eye.

@singlemomcatlady: That sounds promising.

I drop into a kitchen chair and start removing the hairpiece from my head.

@PitterPatterLetsGetAtHer: Not sure she's into me.

@singlemomcatlady: Did you ask her out?

@PitterPatterLetsGetAtHer: Well, no. I'm afraid it will make things awkward because we're kind of working together.

@singlemomcatlady: Ah. A workplace romance. That can definitely be tricky.

@PitterPatterLetsGetAtHer: Tell me about it. How about you? You getting the hang of the app yet?

@singlemomcatlady: God no.

I press send before thinking.

@singlemomcatlady: Sorry, that sounded bad. I'm just not sure dating apps are for me.

@PitterPatterLetsGetAtHer: Sometimes it's easier to talk to somebody online instead of face-to-face. Just saying. The anonymity can be kind of freeing.

@singlemomcatlady: I guess I can see that. I mean, it's probably good that the guys on here don't know I'm a two-time Olympic gold-winning sumo wrestler. Wouldn't want them to be too starstruck.

@PitterPatterLetsGetAtHer: Seriously? Me too! What are the chances?

I laugh and check the time, seeing it's after nine.

@singlemomcatlady: Ha! Well, nice chatting. I've got to get my kid to bed. Good luck with the coworker.

@PitterPatterLetsGetAtHer: Thanks. And, sumo wrestling fame aside, I hope you find what you're looking for. Goodnight, cat lady.

I grin down at the phone as I close the app, but when my finger hovers over the Catnip logo to delete it, I can't quite bring myself to do it.

"Matty! The bus is pulling up!" I shout from the front porch early the next morning where I'm standing watch.

I hear his shoes clomping on the entry floor before I see him. He whizzes past me as the bus brakes squeal and hiss to a stop.

"Matty! Your lunch!" I thrust the insulated lunch bag at his retreating back and he turns to grab it.

"It's *Matthew*, Mom. How many times do I have to tell you?"

"Right. Sorry! Go!" I shoo him toward the waiting yellow bus, and he barely makes it on before the doors close. I've been doing my best to use his preferred name, but it's hard to break a twelve-year habit. To me, he'll always be Matty.

"Another close one," comes a voice from behind me. I turn to see my neighbor and best friend, Ramona, approaching with two steaming mugs of what I know to be the nectar of the gods. Coffee. I accept one with greedy hands as she stops at my side.

"I seriously don't know how I've kept the gray hair away."

Romona dips her chin and eyes me over her glasses. "I just assumed you've been dying it like I do."

"You think I'd pick this color if I were dying my hair?" I ask her. I've always hated my hair, wishing I had been born a blond bombshell or a raven-haired temptress instead. Red. That's what my mom gave me. Or auburn, as it has luckily darkened into over the years.

"How are things with *Matthew* this week?" Ramona asks before bringing her mug to her lips.

I groan. "Well, let's see. He's still avoiding sharing breathing space with me, and his response to pretty much everything I say is, "I *know*, Mom. *Jeez*." I do my best adolescent boy voice, one that sits somewhere between boy and man but can't commit to either. "But I did get one smile out of him yesterday, and he hasn't gotten in trouble at school in almost two weeks, so that's something, right?"

Romona reaches over to rub my bicep with a pitying smile. She may not be a mom with all the magical answers, but she's a damn good friend. "How did the talk with Blake go? I forgot to ask."

I shrug and try to muster a smile. "Meh. He said it's probably just hormones. Matty still refused the counselor idea when I brought it up again." I drop my eyes to my mug, mentally adding calling the counseling center again to my list for the day.

"You know I'd ask Amir for his advice, but the man was born forty years old. I'm pretty sure he popped out with chest hair and that deep bass of his."

I cough out a laugh, but she's probably not wrong. Ramona's husband is not only incredibly analytical and even-tempered, he's the epitome of stoic masculinity. It's a good thing, too, because Ramona can be a handful and a half.

"And probably his giant dick too, though I'd never ask his mama that."

This time I choke on my coffee, which makes Ramona outright snort-laugh. I guess I can always count on her to lighten the mood.

"Jesus, Ramona," I finally manage, but she only pats her head wrap with a smug grin.

"Speaking of big dick energy," she continues, "Anything new happening with that hockey player you're working for?"

I shake my head, turning to let us both in the front door. I can't possibly talk about Bobby on my front stoop. "No. I told you it's just business." The conviction I meant to instill in those words falls a little short.

"Are you asking me or telling me?"

I spin around once we reach the kitchen. "Don't you have to get to work? I know *I* do." Which is a lie. Bobby won't be picking me up for almost an hour. Plenty of time to drink my coffee and chat before getting ready. I have no idea how he got me to agree to his plan to chauffeur me around, much less pay for my car repairs—no matter how overdue they are.

Ramona purses her lips at me and invites herself to sit in one of my kitchen chairs. "The man is a professional athlete. A tiny crush is inevitable. Amir knows Tommy Fury and Jalen Hurts are both my hall passes."

"Both?"

"You say that like it's a bad thing. Do you know how many erogenous zones women have?"

"No, but I'm sure you'll tell me."

"This is worse than I thought." She straightens her glasses. "Woman, you need to know your body. You're forty years old, for god's sake!"

I sink into the chair next to her before dropping my head into my hands. "I know, okay. But can you cut me some slack? I was married to a gay man for fifteen years. Neither one of us was very good at knowing how to please a woman."

"Shit. I'm sorry, Molls."

"It's fine." I let my hands fall back to the table and straighten in my seat as I inhale the lovely coffee aroma. "Actually, I've been thinking about getting back out there."

Ramona beams at me. "That's great!"

"Coco signed me up for a dating app."

"Shut up! I love that old broad!" My bestie gives me a hand-it-over gesture. "Let's see it."

"No way! Coco already gave me a username suggesting that I'm a stripper. I'm not letting you get your hands on my profile too."

She rolls her lips between her teeth to keep from laughing.

"I did start talking to one guy, though."

"I'm so proud of you. Go get it." She covers one of my hands with hers.

"He's more of a practice test though. He's interested in somebody at his work, so we're just . . . buddies."

"Hey, it's a start. And who's to say he can't change his mind? Work relationships are the worst. Best to avoid them."

I cock my head and stare. "You and Amir met at work."

"Yeah, and he almost got fired for spending too much time banging me in the supply closet!"

"Whatever. This guy is just a harmless acquaintance. A

guinea pig, if you will. It's been a *long* time since I've been out there."

"Well, I think it's great. Keep talking to dating-app guy and add the hockey player to your hall-pass list. You wouldn't want to date a professional athlete anyway. They get so much tail, you'd get eaten alive." She points at me. "And not in the good way."

I fling my hands out in mild panic. "I refuse to even *think* about developing a crush on Bobby Rhodes. He's over a decade younger than me! Can you imagine? So embarrassing." I can feel my skin heat, giving me away.

Ramona doesn't directly call me out, instead replying, "Oh, my imagination is conjuring up something, all right. I'm gonna have to look this guy up."

"You won't have to. He's picking me up in . . ." I glance at my watch and spring to my feet, mild panic switching to hysteria. "Thirty minutes! Shit!"

Ramona jumps in her chair. "I thought we weren't crushing on him?!"

"I'm not!" I slam back the remainder of my coffee, not caring that I may have just scorched my larynx. "I still need to be presentable, don't I?"

I ignore Ramona's skeptical look as I rush from the room to get to my shower.

Thirty minutes later, as Bobby opens the passenger door of "Wolverine" for me, I can't keep my eyes from darting to Ramona and Amir's house. Which I immediately regret when I spot Ramona through her big picture window, mouth gaping. As soon as we lock eyes, she lifts one hand in the air and rolls her hips like she's riding a fricking bronco. I groan.

"Did you say something?" Bobby asks, beginning to turn his attention to follow my gaze.

I quickly haul my ass up into the passenger seat and paste on a bright smile. "Nothing!"

Chapter Nine

Bobby

Kaitlyn texted me the name of an anger management counselor last night with strict instructions not to be late for my first video appointment later today. I told her to go feed her newborn. To which she sent back the middle finger emoji.

I'm grateful for her help, I really am, but I'm also not looking forward to airing my childhood crap and innermost feelings to a total stranger who will psychoanalyze me and find me sorely lacking. I already know I have a problem—Coach has made that abundantly clear—but to talk to a counselor about all of it? That shit is fundamentally opposite of the Rhodes family way. We stuff down those pesky things called emotions and chug a beer to wash it down.

Picking up Molly this morning is just about the only bright spot in what's sure to be a long day. The woman is wearing a dress today as she steps out of her light yellow house with a purse bigger than my hockey bag slung over her shoulder. The deep blue dress with a cinched in waist looks exactly like what that weather chick was wearing the other night. The one Richie was whacking off to. I can see the appeal, now that I've seen Molly in that type of dress, though I do still miss the pencil skirt. I wave and get a hesitant lift of her hand in return.

I hop out and take the purse from her, storing it in the back of the truck. She can't get into the thing without my assistance, not without flashing her entire neighborhood. I mean, I wouldn't mind as long as I'm part of the neighborhood who gets the show, but I'm sure Molly would prefer not to flash anyone. I give her my hand and she takes it, flicking a glance behind me.

"Good morning, sunshine." She doesn't answer me, just lets out a groan that has the hair on the back of my neck standing on end, thinking about other ways in which I could get her to groan like that. I lean in. "Did you say something?"

Molly's eyes widen and she squeezes my hand. "Nothing!"

Disappointed, I help her into the truck and wait until she gets those tantalizing high heels in before closing the door. They're not as high as yesterday's but they still make her legs look fantastic. I shake my head and round the hood. I catch a flicker of movement at the window of her next-door neighbor's house. No one's there though, so I hurry into the vehicle, not wanting to be late to practice today. Nothing pisses Coach off more than any of us being late.

"You look lovely today," I say as I back out and head out of her neighborhood.

Molly's cheeks flush, making her look even lovelier. "Thanks. I have a few meetings today. You?"

I gape, clutching my chest for extra dramatics. "You're cheating on me? Seeing other clients?"

Molly flicks a glance my way, like she's double checking I'm teasing her. She rolls her eyes, and I feel like maybe, just maybe, we've reached a point in our friendship—clientship?? —where she's starting to feel comfortable around me. "Yes, I do have multiple clients. The world does not revolve around you, Robert."

Well, fuck. Just like that, I'm inappropriately turned on. Why do I like her calling me that all of a sudden? Kaitlyn might be right. I really am a sick puppy in need of a counselor. "Well, I'm shocked and horrified. You're my only realtor. Seems only fair we make this monogamous."

Molly's laugh makes my morning. "What are you doing today?"

I get off the freeway at the exit for her office and come to a stop at a red light. "I have practice. We have a home game tomorrow night against Minnesota. They've beat us the last couple times we've played them, so I'm sure Coach will be riding our asses to win this time."

Molly's giving me a smile I could stare at all day. "You'll get 'em this time, tiger!"

I bark out a laugh and take off as the light turns green. "I'm not sure which I like best: you calling me Robert or tiger."

Her intensifying blush is the cherry on top. I pull up to the curb outside her office and turn to face her. "I'll follow up with the mechanic. If you need a ride home before they're done, just text me. Otherwise, I'll have them drop the car off here."

She shakes her head. "What I wouldn't give to be able to pay an unexpected car repair bill without having to worry about how I'm going to put food on the table."

"Hey, I wasn't always rich. I grew up middle class and picked on by four older brothers. Not saying I don't enjoy the finer things in life now, though." I smooth my hand over Wolverine's pristine steering wheel before hopping out and coming around to help Molly down. I get a whiff of her perfume and feel a little guilty for keeping the bottle the other day. She probably had to buy a new one.

I hand her the purse and watch her walk into the office, hips a mesmerizing sway. Coco waves from the door, shooting me a wink like she knows exactly what I'm staring at. I zoom away from the curb and break all the speed limit laws to get to practice on time.

Coach is already in quite a mood, barking at Mac for goofing off even before we've taken the ice. Not even assistant coach Wainwright can run enough interference to keep us from feeling like we're getting singed by Coach's wrath. He puts us through a grueling set of drills, not even letting us take a water break until we're two hours in. After another hour of scrimmage, he calls the practice and yells at us to get to the weight room for training.

"Who shat in Coach's Cheerios?" Druggy mumbles, accent thick as ever. He sucks in a deep breath and pushes through a set of leg presses while Banks and I take our rest. I volunteered to train with the old guys today, following Kaitlyn's advice about appearing wise and mature. Not that these fuckers have cornered the market on either of those things.

"Is past tense shit really shat?" Benny asks, wiping his face with a towel.

I manage a laugh despite my burning lungs and legs. "Say that five times fast."

Druggy slams the pins into place and stands up. Benny and I have to take off two plates on either side before we can complete our sets. Druggy is a beast. We move on to step-ups on a thirty-six inch plyometric box. Benny is dripping sweat during his set, probably due to his glutes being weak. I told him his ass was going flat last week with all the sitting after Mei was born. He just flipped me off, unperturbed by developing a flat ass. That's what becoming a parent does to you, I guess. Count me out of that shit. I'll have a poppin' ass for the ladies well into my eighties, kids or not.

"Either of you know a charity I can start working with?" I

ask out of the blue, remembering that particular item on the list Kaitlyn gave me. "Kaitlyn told me beating a few old ladies' butts at tile games isn't enough good will and all that." Referring, of course, to the volunteer work we already do as a group at a retirement center.

Druggy sucks down water while Benny drops the dumbbells on the floor and looks like he might puke. He puts his hands on his knees and looks up at me. "I'm too old for this shit."

"That's what I've been telling you," I mutter under my breath. Contrary to when I first joined the team, I actually like Benny now, so I try to keep the teasing to a minimum. Kaitlyn's a miracle worker, hence why I trust her with my career now too.

He narrows his eyes, having clearly heard me. "Would you consider yourself a boob guy?"

That gets a smile out of me, even in the midst of torture. Boobs are always smile worthy. "Fuck, yeah."

Benny nods. "I'll forward the contact of someone who runs a charity centered around boobs."

Well, shit. Maybe this maturing stuff isn't so bad.

We finish up our workout and are finally allowed to leave after taking a dip in the ice baths. Every muscle aches, but I know a good night's sleep is all I need to kick ass on the ice tomorrow. Benny and Druggy might need more recovery, but I'm still a spring chicken. I stop at my favorite salad place and grab a Mediterranean bowl with extra steak before heading home.

Richie occupies my couch in a pair of sweatpants and no shirt. An empty bag of chips lays forgotten on my end table and one of my video game controllers is clutched in his hand. I'll take that over his dick.

"Dude. Did you bring me something too?" he asks, pointing at my to-go bag.

"No, dipshit. Make your own lunch."

"That's why I'm here. I ran out of food."

I have a seat on the couch and open the lid to my salad, inhaling the scent of meat and immediately salivating. "That's what the grocery store is for. You know, the place with the carts and the food on every shelf?"

Richie pouts, somehow always forgetting that he's the older brother. He should be taking care of *me*. That fact always got lost somewhere along the way. My older brothers never went easy on me, that's for sure. Probably why I got so good at hockey. I wasn't afraid of hard work. I just had to have an equal amount of time for play.

I eat my salad like a hungry pack of wolves would devour their prey, then reach for the other video controller.

The alarm on my phone goes off and I groan. "Shit."

"What? Got a bunny mad at you?" Richie doesn't even look away from the television. Something blows up on the screen.

"No, I have my anger management session," I grumble, standing to take my trash to the kitchen before I hop on my laptop.

Richie lets out a strangled yelp and literally falls off the couch laughing his ass off. I toss him a dirty look, but he's too busy wiping his eyes to see it.

"Fuck off," I snap.

"Careful. That sounds very *angery*." Richie bursts into another round of laughter I can hear from the kitchen as I stuff the to-go container in the trash.

"*Angery* is not a word, Dick!" I yell back. I roll my eyes when he just keeps laughing. I grab my laptop off the kitchen counter and head for my bedroom where I can get some peace and quiet to bare my soul.

"Wait 'til I tell the boys!" he hollers at my back, referring to my other jackass brothers.

I shake my head but keep walking. Great. Each of my brothers will be blowing up my phone with commentary about my anger management sessions. Just what I need. I stop at my door and yell back. "Tell those fuckers and I'll tell Mom you're the one who put the scratch in her bumper when you took her new car out for a joy ride at twelve!"

I can hear his gasp. "You're the devil, Bobby Rhodes!" he shouts back in an accent to match the characters in the movie *Water Boy.*

My laptop takes forever to boot up as I sit on my bed, and I'm two minutes late when I finally connect to the Zoom call. I'm sure Kaitlyn will rip me a new one for each second I'm late, but she doesn't understand the pressure of having a sibling always in your home. Richie's worse than a newborn, I'm sure of it.

A woman appears on the screen, big black glasses covering her baby face. Jesus, are the social workers from high school these days? Surely, I need someone a little older to understand my troubled past?

"Hello!" she says, bubbly as shit. "I'm Ashley! You must be Bobby?!"

Everything she says comes with an exclamation mark at the end. "Yes! Nice to meet you!" I answer, matching her energy. Her smile only amps up so I must not have offended her with my imitation. After a few minutes of further introduction and small talk regarding why I'm even seeing her, Ashley gets down to business

"Great! Let's start talking about what you feel when you start to get angry. Can you close your eyes and think of a time you got really mad?" I'm one thousand percent certain this won't help me, but I close my eyes anyway and envision Coach telling me I'm a screw up. I wonder if I can ask Ashley to call me a good boy. I think I might like that.

"Good. Just visualize the scene," she instructs. "Tell me what's happening and what you feel in your body."

"My coach is yelling at me. I think he's being unfair. I guess my hands go tingly first. Then my chest puffs up and my eyes feel like they're full of pressure. Like my whole body is going to explode if I don't yell or tackle someone."

"Great job, Bobby!"

I open my eyes and see Ashley beaming at me. Fuck, I wonder if she gives out gold stars. Then I notice movement over the laptop screen and see Richie standing in my doorway, one hand on the doorknob and the other motioning by his crotch. His tongue's hanging out of his mouth and his hips are downright lewd in their gyrations. I flip him off outside the camera angle so Ashley won't see. Richie falls to the floor in a heap of silent laughter.

"You know what, Ashley?" I say out loud. "I think all my anger stems from one of my brothers. He's here with me now actually. Do you think he can join the session? I really think it'll help me work some things out."

Richie's head pops up from the floor with a look of dread.

"Oh my god, yes!" Ashley claps her hands.

And that's how Richie ends up joining me for my first session of anger management classes. Sadly, we're both screwed up enough Ashley suggests quite firmly that we should meet daily for at least the next few weeks.

Chapter Ten

Molly

"Have I told you lately what a star you are?" Coco stops in front of my desk, perching half of her designer-suited butt on the corner.

Jason's responding scoff is muted enough that I know Coco didn't hear it. Jason and Maude have both made it clear that my getting Bobby's contract is total bullshit in their eyes, and the contentious atmosphere this past week has been brutal. Coco may think she's helping with this display of loyalty, but I fear it will only make things worse.

I send her a meaningful look that she pretends not to notice.

"We just officially acquired the contract for the Victorian on Newland."

My responding smile is instantaneous. "That's amazing!"

"And it's all thanks to you. Niedermeyer and Associates tried swooping in, of course, but the owner and I had already established a rapport by then." She returns to her feet and brushes the invisible wrinkles from her skirt. "Well, I have a lunch date, so I'll be unavailable for the next two hours." She winks at me. I swallow my laugh, and she sashays to the lobby where she stops to chat with P.J., our receptionist.

"Molly, I've been meaning to ask all morning. Did I see you arrive at work in a *Cybertruck*?" Jason asks with a little too much interest for my comfort.

Shit. I square my shoulders and turn to face him. "Yes. I had an early appointment with a client." It's kind of true, isn't it?

Maude's responding laugh is unfriendly, at best. "Is that what we're calling it now? At least it finally makes sense how you got his contract."

I swivel the other way, intent on giving Maude a piece of my mind, but I force myself to stop. She wants me to react, and I refuse to give it to her. "I'm going to lunch," I announce instead, opening the large bottom drawer of my desk to retrieve my bag. Neither Jason nor Maude comments. Good. They need to mind their own business.

It's not until I'm out the door that I remember I have no car, so I'm forced to sneak back in and grab my packed lunch from the break room. I decide to make the three-block trek to the nearby park and eat there.

When I'm settled at a picnic table, I unpack my carrot sticks and hummus and pull out my phone. My first instinct is to call Ramona, but she's at work at the hospital. I briefly consider calling Blake, but I don't want him worrying about me. We've finally reached the point in our divorce where he's gotten over his crushing guilt, and I don't want him to think I'm struggling any more than he already suspects.

Not letting myself think too hard about it, I open Catnip, scroll to my chat with *@PitterPatterLetsGetAtHer* and begin typing.

@singlemomcatlady: Please tell me your day is going better than mine.

The ellipses immediately appear, telling me he's online.

@PitterPatterLetsGetAtHer: Well, that depends. Did your boss almost murder you and your coworkers today?

I pop a carrot stick in my mouth with wide eyes.

@singlemomcatlady: You win. What happened? Did you do something to earn it or is your boss just a jerk?

@PitterPatterLetsGetAtHer: He's not so much a jerk. Just demanding, which is probably a good thing. He's new and trying to make his mark. He and I don't see eye-to-eye on some things.

@singlemomcatlady: Ah. I see. I lucked out in that department. My boss is fantastic. It's my coworkers who aren't so much.

@PitterPatterLetsGetAtHer: When my coworkers are being asses, I usually just tell them so. But our workplace is casual like that. I'm guessing that's not an option for you?

I brush a curious ant from the wood picnic tabletop and dip another carrot in the hummus while I think about that for a second.

@singlemomcatlady: I don't love conflict.

@PitterPatterLetsGetAtHer: Sometimes I wish I didn't, but I kind of can't help speaking my mind most of the time.

@singlemomcatlady: You'll probably live longer not bottling things up.

@PitterPatterLetsGetAtHer: Tell that to my boss. And my therapist.

@singlemomcatlady: Therapy? That's very evolved of you.

And so is admitting it freely to a stranger. I'm kind of impressed.

@PitterPatterLetsGetAtHer: What can I say? I'm trying.

If he's being an open book, I suppose there's no harm in reciprocating.

@singlemomcatlady: My ex and I did therapy. It was really helpful.

@PitterPatterLetsGetAtHer: Not to be rude, but the word ex implies your therapist might not be so great at their job.

@singlemomcatlady: Haha. My ex and I are still good friends, and I think therapy made that possible.

@PitterPatterLetsGetAtHer: Talk about evolved. A healthy relationship with an ex sounds like the height of maturity.

@singlemomcatlady: Well, we share a child, so there's that. Also, neither of us cheated or anything.

I pause before deciding to hell with it and resuming typing.

@singlemomcatlady: He's actually gay. That was the nail in the coffin.

@PitterPatterLetsGetAtHer: The therapist or the ex? Just kidding. That'll do it almost every time.

That makes me laugh out loud, and I push my lunch aside so I can use both hands freely.

@singlemomcatlady: Right?

@PitterPatterLetsGetAtHer: I think it's cool, though, that you're able to co-parent peacefully and still like each other.

@singlemomcatlady: Yeah. But it's hard sometimes. You know, not having a partner anymore? We were together for fifteen years. Things started to get strained, and I had no idea what had changed. Then one day, I walked in the door from work and there he was at the kitchen table with a bouquet of flowers in his hands. I thought for a second that he was going to say we should clear the slate and start over, but as soon as I saw the look on his face, I knew it was over. Learning the reason why was almost a relief, you know?

@PitterPatterLetsGetAtHer: I can see that for sure. I mean, knowing that you didn't do anything wrong and there was nothing you could have done to save the relationship had to help.

@singlemomcatlady: Exactly. But he tortured himself for a long time, and I hated that.

@PitterPatterLetsGetAtHer: Sounds difficult all around. I can see why you're not ready to jump into another relationship.

@singlemomcatlady: I'm trying to get there, but I'm afraid of getting the rug pulled out from under me again, you know?

@PitterPatterLetsGetAtHer: Makes perfect sense to me. You'll get there someday, though.

As strange as it may sound, having validation from a stranger outside the situation makes me feel a little lighter.

@singlemomcatlady: Enough about me. How are things with your coworker crush? Did she survive the boss's murder spree?

@PitterPatterLetsGetAtHer: She doesn't work for him—she and I collaborate on more of a side project. I did make her laugh this morning, so that's good, right?

@singlemomcatlady: Definitely. Women love it when guys make them laugh. Sometimes, it can be the most attractive trait in a man, but don't tell anyone I clued you in. It's one of our secrets.

@PitterPatterLetsGetAtHer: Taking notes.
What else?

I grin down at the screen while I type. I know Ramona would say I should flirt instead of helping him woo another woman, but I don't care. I like talking to him.

@singlemomcatlady: Well, let's see. We like it when you remember things we tell you, no matter how small or inconsequential they may seem. Oh, and good manners still go a long way.

@PitterPatterLetsGetAtHer: Already ahead of you on the manners thing. My mom raised us the old-fashioned way.

@singlemomcatlady: That's sweet. Unless, of course, you mean the *really* old-fashioned way.

@PitterPatterLetsGetAtHer: Let's just say that anytime I got a tap to the back of the head, I more than deserved it.

@singlemomcatlady: A wild child, huh?

@PitterPatterLetsGetAtHer: Hey, I'm working on it. Remember the therapist? She said I'm not even close to the worst she's ever seen.

@singlemomcatlady: LOL. Thank god for mental healthcare.

@PitterPatterLetsGetAtHer: Not that I'm a deviant or anything. Don't want you to get the wrong idea. It's just time to work on myself, better myself so I can be at my best for the people in my life, you know?

I find myself nodding.

@singlemomcatlady: Yeah. That's really great.

@PitterPatterLetsGetAtHer: Oops. Gotta run.

@singlemomcatlady: Your boss hunt you down?

@PitterPatterLetsGetAtHer: Something like that. Talk later.

I set the phone down and pack up my things, suddenly ready to take on the rest of the day. I'm even able to successfully ignore both Jason and Maude until they leave to meet clients.

P.J. brings me my Kia keys an hour later, saying a mechanic dropped them off and my car is out back. I dread seeing the total on that bill. Thankfully, I won't need to pay it until Bobby buys a house.

My phone rings in the late afternoon, and I answer without checking the number. I curse myself when it turns out to be my dentist's office reminding me that I'm late on this month's installment for the crown I had to get a few months back. Those things are damn expensive for a little piece of porcelain, and my dental insurance through Farnsworth only covered a small portion of the bill.

I've been trying to pay it off, along with all my other bills, but things have been tight. Thus the reason my car never made it to the shop until Bobby interfered—something I can't think about right now. I take a mental inventory of my checking account and credit card balance and promise the woman on the line that I'll get the payment in this week.

Looks like the dishwasher repairs will be pushed off indefinitely.

I know my commission on Bobby's contract might be bigger than all my previous commissions combined, but I don't feel exactly right about it. It was Coco's contract, not mine. And, although I may not love Jason or Maude, I can admit I'd probably be unhappy with the situation too, had our roles been reversed.

I honestly don't know why he insisted on having me as his agent. Coco's reasons are clear–and delusional. Bobby's? Not so clear. I mean, he's obviously a flirt and enjoys making me blush. Maybe it's a narcissism thing?

No. I don't think narcissists fix your car or give you rides to work or open doors for you. Dammit! I can't think about this right now.

My phone rings again, and I start to think God is playing with me when I see it's Matty's school.

"Hello. Is this Ms. Sparks, Matthew's mother?"

"Yes. Is everything okay?" I check my watch and see that it's four-thirty. School ended an hour ago, and Matty should be home already.

"This is Mr. Finley, the vice principal."

Shit. I drop my forehead into my hand. "Hello, Mr. Finley."

"I'm afraid we had another incident today with Matthew, and he has been suspended for two days. It will be an in-school suspension starting tomorrow, and he will be unable to make up missed work for those days."

Dammit! Matty's grades aren't bad, but this won't help.

"I'm so sorry, Mr. Finley. I've been trying to talk with him and get him into counseling. What exactly happened today?"

"There was an argument with another student, and one of the teachers witnessed Matthew pushing the other child into a locker with a good deal of force."

Oh god. My head goes light. I have got to find out what is happening with my child!

"I am so sorry. I . . . I don't know what to say except that I am determined to figure out what is causing this aggression."

"Our guidance counselor did speak with both boys, but she said Matthew was tight-lipped about what preceded the incident. Perhaps you can get him to open up." He sighs before continuing, "Look, Ms. Sparks, Matthew is a bright kid, and records from his elementary school show no behavioral issues. It's important we get to the bottom of this so Matthew can return to his usual self. I'm a true believer that there are no bad kids, just bad behavior, and there's usually a reason behind it."

"Thank you. That's kind of you. I promise we'll get to the bottom of it. Believe me, I want Matthew to be happy and well-adjusted more than anybody."

"I believe you. I'll have the guidance department get in touch. I'm sure they can be of help."

"Okay. Thank you again. And I'll keep you updated."

"Sounds good."

Mr. Finley hangs up, and I sit for a few long minutes staring blankly at my phone. Then I get my ass in gear and pack up my things before driving home.

I find Matty in his bedroom, lying on his stomach on the bed, homework spread out in front of him like he's been innocently slaving away at it for hours. He's certainly no dummy.

Forcing myself to take a cleansing breath, I approach the bed and take a seat on the edge of the mattress. "Mr. Finley called. Tell me what happened."

Matty groans but he does turn to look at me, so it's progress, I suppose. "Raiden was talking crap, and I didn't want to listen to it." A lock of hair falls in his eyes, and I have to stop myself from reaching over to tuck it back.

"So you shoved him into a locker? Matty, that is not okay."

He stiffens and grits his teeth. "It's *Matthew*."

Right. "Matthew, that is not okay," I repeat.

"I know, all right?!" His head whips back around, and he shoves his homework off the bed, the books thudding loudly on the floor.

The hairs on the back of my neck stand on end, and I force a calm tone. "What did Raiden say to you?" So help me god, this Raiden kid might have more to worry about than my son if my current suspicions are valid.

Matty's response comes quickly. A little too quickly. "Nothing! It doesn't matter. I got suspended and it's over."

"Matthew," I begin, but he cuts me off.

"Besides, Mr. Rhodes said you've got to pay people back when they're rude. That's all I was doing!"

My chin shifts back. "Wait. What? Mr. Rhodes, as in *Bobby* Rhodes?"

"Yeah." Matty glances back at me again.

"Bobby Rhodes told you that you've got to pay people back when they're rude?"

He nods. "Yeah."

I draw in a slow breath through my nostrils, my hands twitching in my lap while I fight the urge to hunt the man down and strangle him. So much for nonviolence being the answer!

Fucking. Bobby.

He's not a narcissist. He's nothing but a *spoiled child*.

<h1 style="text-align:center">Chapter Eleven</h1>

Bobby

I'm still riding the high, having won at home last night against the Stingers, 4-2. I even scored one of the goals, which made Coach smile as the team celebrated. He probably strained a muscle doing it, but I counted it as a win. Maybe I can earn back his favor after all. Richie wasn't at my apartment after the game, which was a good sign that maybe he's foraging for his own food today instead of mooching off me.

And now, my favorite part of the day: I'm on my way to pick up Molly from her office to go look at a few houses before practice. This polo shirt can't be seen in a Kia, let's be honest. Burberry belongs in the Wolverine.

I earn myself a middle finger and an aggressive honk when I brake suddenly and turn onto the street before her realty office. Molly's on the corner, oversized bag over her shoulder, arms crossed over her chest, and her toe tapping out an irritated rhythm.

Before I can hop out and help her up into the truck, she

climbs up and slams the door shut. She looks beautiful in an emerald green blouse, straight-legged black trousers, and a pair of kitten heels that capture my attention more than they should when I need to be easing back into the flow of traffic.

"Good morning?" It comes out as a question because Molly is not even close to smiling. I swear I can almost see dark cartoon rain clouds hovering over her head. Or maybe it's an illusion from the steam coming out her ears.

"Good morning." Her tone is icier than the sheet I skate across every day. "Turn here."

I take the left she indicates with a flick of her hand. I keep darting glances at her, trying to determine whether she's in a bad mood in general, or if she's mad at me in particular. Thinking maybe being quiet right now might be better than telling her the blouse she's wearing makes her hazel eyes look like exquisite emeralds, I pull up to the first house we decided to tour since they were already having an open house. There's a flag outside the house that says, "*Come on in!*"

Leaving her bag behind, Molly hops out and climbs the walkway to the front door. I scramble after her. There's a man in a double-breasted suit waiting for us just inside the open door, his slicked back hair practically shouting that he's a realtor and drives an entry-level BMW. Molly shakes his hand, and I have to grind my molars together when he gives her a full body once over.

"I'm Molly Sparks and this is my client, Robert Rhodes." Molly gestures in my direction but doesn't bother to look at me.

Ah, back to Robert. Okay. She's mad at *me*, then. I shake the man's hand, giving him a death grip that hopefully says to stop eye fucking my realtor. If anyone's going to eye fuck her, it's me. And based on her temper today, no eye fucking of any kind is going to happen. Maybe some eye *gouging* if she ever stops clenching her fists until her knuckles turn white.

We enter the house and thankfully, the realtor lets us roam on our own after handing over a sheet with the house specs printed on heavy cardstock. Molly's giving me clipped, one-word descriptions of each room, and I don't even have a sexy pencil skirt to occupy my brain space. This isn't entertaining. If I have to adult, I want to be having fun doing it or what's the point?

When Molly turns to leave the spacious primary bathroom with heated tiles and a shower with four spray nozzles and space for a party of ten, I step in her way, pretending I didn't know she was going left. She stops on a dime, the pointy tips of her shoes almost stepping on my toes. Her startled gaze finally meets mine, and I feel like the sun is trying to peek out from behind the storm clouds.

"Sorry," I say calmly. But I don't move.

I watch the way the pink creeps into her cheeks, spreading down from her cheekbones to her neck. Her nostrils flare, and there should be nothing pretty about nostrils, yet hers are. Hazel eyes that change color based on what she's wearing and what she's feeling shift to a simmering gold. Her perfume is intoxicating, but I can't focus on that right now.

After much contemplation while following her from room to room, I've decided on the direct route. "Want to tell me why you're mad at me?"

In my family, we knew when someone was mad because it usually came in the form of a tackle to the ground and some-times a fist to the face. There wasn't much use in the silent treatment as none of us knew how to be silent. Disagreements were pounded out in a matter of minutes and then we got on with our day, problem solved. This perpetual storm cloud of irritation is completely foreign to me.

Molly scans my face and then tilts her nose in the air, voice crackling with righteous anger. "My son got suspended because of you, Robert."

She should have just punched me in the gut. That would have been less painful than hearing I had something to do with Matthew getting in trouble.

"What do you mean? What happened?"

Molly explains the situation, the anger only barely masking the pain in her tone as her loud voice bounces off all the damn marble in here. When she ends with Matthew echoing the comment I'd made offhand at his practice and then had promptly forgotten all about, I close my eyes and sag against the doorway.

"Shit," I mutter. Just when I think I might have left my screw-up self in the past, I go and fuck up something else.

"Yep. Shit is right." I feel Molly shift, like she's going to walk away from me.

My eyes fly open, and I grab hold of her arms. She glances down at my hands, and I lighten my grip immediately. "I made an offhand comment. I had no idea he'd take that as advice. I'll make this right, Molly. I promise."

Molly shakes her head, then pulls her arms away from me. "Please don't try. You've done enough."

We continue walking through the house and even tour a second home before I have to leave or I'll be late to practice, but we barely say two words to each other. By the time I drop her off at her office, I've discovered that having someone disappointed in you is far worse than having them angry. I'd take Coach's anger every day, all day, if it meant Molly would never be disappointed in me again.

I stay in the locker room long after the team has vacated

from practice. Everyone kept looking at me during practice and especially as we cleaned up afterward. I'm usually the comic relief of the group, but I just didn't have it in me to do the normal song and dance. As I skated my ass off in practice, I realized I have two modes of operating: cracking jokes to break the tension or cracking skulls if the tension gets to be too much. I should bring that up with Ashley later today when we have our virtual session. Maybe she can give me some insight as to how to navigate the murky gray area between those two modes.

When I hear kids flooding the rink for their league practice with Chloe, I head back out there, making a beeline for the thin kid with the dark head of hair that sports a hint of red. Thankfully, Molly is nowhere to be found. Matthew's shoulders are hunched forward, like he was just subjected to the same *I'm disappointed in you* treatment that I got this morning. I don't blame her. Us guys are mostly just a bunch of knuckleheads.

"Hey, Matthew!" I call out, trying to get to him before he steps out onto the ice.

He lifts his head and gives me the teen head bob that means hello. I sit down next to him on the bench as he begins to tie his skates. I don't have much time, so I don't bother asking about his day or talking about the fucking weather.

"Heard you got in some trouble."

His head whips up and his eyes shift left.

"I'm not here to come down on your ass about it," I assure him.

"I don't think you can say ass to kids." His mouth quirks to the side like he wants to laugh.

I shrug. "I never said I was good with kids. But here's the thing, man. You can't follow what I do."

"Why not? You're a professional hockey player." He says it with so much awe, I wince.

"I know. But that's because I can hit a hockey puck and slam someone up against the boards, not because I'm some moral paragon who should be imitated."

"Huh?"

I shake my head, wishing I was better at this. "Just . . . don't do what I do. I'm still learning how to do things without punching people, okay? I'm like a toddler learning to walk. I've got a ways to go."

"You like to punch people too?"

Shit. He's focusing on the wrong parts. Maybe this is exactly why Molly didn't want me talking to Matthew.

"It's not that I like to hit people, it's just that sometimes my fist flies before my mouth can say something."

Matthew nods vigorously. "I know! That's what happens to me! I mean, sometimes I just push people, but it's like I'm doing it before I even realize I'm doing it."

I put my hand on his shoulder. "Okay, so my counselor told me we have to get better at recognizing the signs of anger before it gets to that point."

"You see a counselor?" Matthew says it like I just admitted to getting regular enemas.

I puff up my chest. "Of course I do. I'm a grown-ass adult with an anger problem. It's my responsibility to get a hold of that before I hurt more people, don't you think?"

Matthew's nodding, furry brows drawn together in concentration. "You think I should see one?"

"I think it wouldn't hurt. What you're doing right now isn't exactly working, right?"

Matthew's nodding again. "So, how do you know you're mad?"

I review everything I went through with Ashley yesterday and he tries it, discovering that for him, he hears a whooshing noise in his ears and can feel his heartbeat pulsing all over his body.

"Okay, so when you notice those two things, I want you to take a deep breath and step back. Like, a physical step back. Just that little bit of time and awareness might help you realize what you're doing."

Matthew grins, transforming into a confident kid who'll have the ladies lining up around the block soon. "I'll try it. Thanks, Bobby."

We do the man-hug-back-slap thing, and he leaps away, gliding out onto the ice and joining the group of older kids warming up in a circle. I put my skates on and get out there too, helping Chloe as much as I can. I try to help at practice most days, but today, I do it with the mindset of being the kind of coach I didn't have growing up. One who lets the kids make mistakes without yelling at them. One who encourages and doesn't expect perfection.

When the parents come for pick up, I spot Molly easily. She's the quiet one, looking for her son with worried eyes. I skate over to Matthew before he leaves the ice.

"Remember what we talked about, huh?"

He nods at me and skates off. I help a younger kid who wipes out right at the entrance to the ice. His eyes fill with tears, but I tell him about when I fell in a game and broke my tailbone as a kid. He's laughing by the time his dad comes to collect him. I stand up and see Molly fussing over Matthew as he puts his skates in his bag.

"You're out of choices this time. You either have to talk to me or talk to your father, Matty," Molly is saying.

Matthew's expression turns to granite. He looks ready to blow, a feeling I recognize all too well. I step closer, not wanting harm to come to Molly, even if it's just hurt feelings. But I have nothing to worry about. Matthew closes his eyes, his chest inflating as he takes a deep breath. Then he takes a single step back from his mother and opens his eyes again, back in control.

"Mom, can you please try to use Matthew instead of Matty?"

Molly rubs her forehead. "Yes. I'm sorry, Matthew. I'm really trying."

Matthew sees me just past his mother and points at me with a proud grin. I wink back, an exchange Molly catches. She stares at me with a thousand questions in her eyes, but Matthew has picked up his bag and is walking out of the rink. Molly hurries after him, darting glances over her shoulder at me.

I can't help but give her a wink too. Only to see the blush track over her cheeks again.

Chapter Twelve

Molly

"He agreed to go!" I practically yell into the phone early the next morning.

"Dollface?" Blake's voice is little more than a croak. "What time is it?"

I glance at my dashboard clock and wince. "Um . . . six forty-five. Oops." In my excitement, I momentarily forgot my ex works nights now and probably just went to bed an hour ago. I, on the other hand, have been up since 2:36 a.m. I have no idea what it is about that time, but my brain has developed an internal alarm clock set for that time every night.

"No." I hear some rustling sounds, probably him getting out of bed. "It's fine. Who agreed to what now?"

"Matty!" My excitement is back as I pull up to a red light. "He agreed to go see a counselor."

"Ah, that's great. How did you convince him?"

"Well, I might have had a little help from somebody he looks up to." I still don't know what Bobby said to Matty, but whatever it was, he accomplished more in one conversation than I have in three months. It makes me feel a little guilty for giving him the cold shoulder yesterday, but I'll be sure to thank him when I see him. We're meeting up at a new listing before he has to go to practice this morning.

"Iron Man?" Blake guesses.

The light turns green, and I pull forward again. "Someone even bigger than Iron Man, if you can believe it. One of the Storm Chasers who helps out with his hockey league."

"Seriously? I didn't even know they were affiliated with that."

"I don't think it's official or anything, but a handful of the players hang out after their own practices sometimes. It's kind of a long story, but I'm actually helping this guy find a house too."

I might be imagining it, but Blake's tone sharpens a little. "Who is it?"

"Blake, when have you ever watched a hockey game?"

"That's beside the point. What's this guy's name?"

"Bobby Rhodes. Why do you want to know?"

"If he's having heart-to-hearts with my kid, I'd like to know the man's name, Molly."

Oh. I guess that makes sense. I slow down to allow someone to move into my lane and decide to shift topics for a second. "When are you back in town?"

"Early next week. I'll text you when I know more specifics, and I can make some plans with Matty. I miss the squirt. And you too."

"Aw. Sounds good. I'll let you know when I have more news on the counseling."

We hang up just as I'm pulling up to the modern Spanish-style home in Avila, an area outside downtown Tampa but close enough to be an easy commute. Bobby leans against his shiny silver truck in the driveway, sunglasses perched on his nose and muscular arms crossed over his chest. He's wearing a pair of linen shorts and a sixties-inspired polo, looking like he's posing for a fashion shoot. I can't help my smile, even as I'm shaking my head.

"Hi, Bobby," I greet as I open my Kia's door.

He pushes off the truck and comes my way, both dimples on display. "Oh, thank god. We're back to Bobby instead of Robert."

I laugh and let him take my bag for me. "I don't know what you said to Matthew yesterday, but whatever it was, thank you."

"Hey, I was only cleaning up the mess I made."

"No, I shouldn't have gotten so worked up about it. He's responsible for his own actions. I'm sure you didn't tell him to shove Raiden Voles into a locker. Although I still want to know what that kid said to Matty to make him so upset." I throw my hands up and start toward the house. "Sorry. I'll stop babbling."

"No!" Bobby intercepts me. "I want to hear." His brows draw together over his sunglasses. "And now *I* want to know what this Raiden kid said. He sounds like a first-class dirtbag. I mean, what kind of name is Raiden anyway? It sounds like an insecticide."

I smile again. "Slow your roll, Mister bigshot hockey man. The child is twelve. I've got it covered."

"Oh, right." He pulls the sunglasses from his face and has the good grace to look chagrined as we approach the front door. This gives me a better look at some bruising around his right eye that I noticed yesterday but didn't mention since I was annoyed with him.

"Nice shiner."

He runs a finger over the bruising. "It's nothing. All part of the job description. Got an elbow to the face from one of the Stingers the other night."

I do my thing with the key box and we let ourselves in. "I'm adding one more item to the list of reasons I like my job. No elbows to the face in realty."

Bobby laughs and lifts his eyes to scan the space. "Nice." His voice echoes off the walls of the empty house as we both admire the exposed wood beams and earthy neutrals of the decor.

I'm just about to go over the house's features when a loud siren sounds from outside with five short blasts. My startled gaze jumps first to the door and then to Bobby. His posture tenses, eyes narrowing as he cranes his neck to look out the windows.

"That sounds like a lightning siren, doesn't it?" He sets my bag on the floor, his eyes coming back to me.

"Maybe? I don't know. Isn't that usually one long air horn sound?" I shake my head to clear out the cobwebs. "Why do I have no idea what that siren means?" And why the hell am I panicking? It's probably nothing. Terrorists wouldn't come to Florida, would they? Oh god. They *totally* would.

Sensing my rising hysteria—which would be impossible to miss—Bobby comes close and takes both my hands in his large ones. They're steady and warm, unlike mine, which have begun trembling. "I'm sure everything is fine." His thumbs stroke back and forth over the backs of my hands, and it's almost hypnotic in the way it immediately calms me. "The skies are clear. Lemme just hop on my phone, and I'll find out what it is, okay?" Bobby is still on weather while I'm imagining nuclear war over here.

He waits for my nod before releasing my hands and pulling his phone from his shorts pocket. I worry my lip while conjuring a mental image of Matty's school. It's got a huge basement and concrete block construction, thank god. But still, the idea of my son crouched in fear in a dark basement has me breaking out in a cold sweat even as I remind myself his school is miles from here.

"Molly," Bobby says in a tone that tells me it's not the first time he's tried to get my attention.

My wide eyes flash to his face, looking for any sign of bad news, but his expression is indiscernible.

He raises a palm to me in a placating gesture. "It's nothing dire."

The breath whooshes from my lungs. "Then what is it?"

He opens his mouth to speak but closes it again before looking down at his phone. "It's . . ." He lifts the phone and points the screen my way. ". . . a snake."

"What?!" I'm clearly hallucinating. Or dreaming. Or maybe a tornado already ripped through the house and I'm dead. Because his words make zero sense.

Bobby's response is to shake the phone to get my attention. When I look down at it, the words are clear as day.

BURMESE PYTHON ESCAPE

Avila is on lockdown. Residents are instructed to stay inside and close all windows and doors until further notice. An illegally housed Burmese python has escaped a neighborhood home, and authorities are actively searching for the reptile. If sighted, DO NOT APPROACH. Call 9-1-1 immediately and retreat to safety.

When I turn my shocked expression back to Bobby, I see he's fighting a laugh, those matching dimples winking at me while he tries forcing his mirth down. At the look on my face, he loses the battle and bends at the waist as he guffaws. "You should see your face!"

"I can't believe you!" I bat at his arm. "This isn't funny. Do you know how long this could take? We could be here all day! And somebody's poor dog is probably being slowly digested by that thing this very moment."

Bobby's head snaps up, a look of panic replacing the amusement.

I prop my hands on my hips. "Not so funny when poor Fido enters the picture, huh?"

"Shit!" Bobby lifts his phone again. "I've got practice in just over an hour. Coach is going to have my ass if I'm late!" His thumbs fly over the phone as deep furrows form on his forehead.

"It's not like it's your fault," I argue, but he doesn't appear to hear me. I decide to investigate a little further on my phone to see if there are more details. My first search brings up a social media post from thirty minutes ago with a video captioned, "Florida Man Makes Public Appeal to Save Pet Python." Good lord.

An older man appears on-screen wearing a backward orange baseball cap and an unkempt beard, both hands steepled in front of him. "Please, if you see Betsy, don't hurt her. She's a sweet little thing and doesn't mean nobody no harm." He holds up a photo of himself with an enormous brown and tan snake draped around his neck. I fight a shudder. "She's never eaten anyone, I swear! I just want my Betsy back."

I quickly close the video to look for other information that does not include photos or bearded Florida men. Bobby sighs and drops his head back.

"Any luck?" I ask.

He straightens his head and runs a hand over his face. "Let's just hope they find him quickly."

"Her. Not him. Her name is Betsy."

"What?" His expression is both weary and confused, so I

give his bicep a pat, instructing myself not to notice his arm porn.

"Don't worry about it. Why don't we go ahead and tour the house since we're here?"

"Okay," Bobby responds, sounding no less weary or confused as I lead him through the entryway to the spacious living area beyond.

Two hours later, we've given in and made ourselves as comfortable as possible on the barstools at the kitchen island, the only pieces of furniture the owners appear to have left in the home.

The place is gorgeous, and even Bobby's distress over missing practice didn't dampen his appreciation for it. I have to say, seeing how seriously Bobby takes his job shows me a new side of him. That, coupled with the miracle he worked on Matty yesterday, has me thinking there might be more to this guy than muscles, dimples, and a flirty sense of humor.

Bobby's head is bent to his phone as he watches the Florida man video I finally directed him to.

"I'm going to text Coco to check in," I tell him.

I message her a quick update, and when I see Bobby's attention still trained on his screen, I scroll to the Catnip app on a whim, pulling up my chat with @PitterPatterLets-GetAtHer.

@Singlemomcatlady: So, just for research purposes, how inappropriate is it to be attracted to a client?

Bobby's phone pings while I'm waiting for a response. I look over to see him grinning at his phone. When he notices me, he says, "One of the guys from the team. They're a bunch of knuckleheads." He bends his head again to continue his chat.

My phone pings a few seconds later.

@PitterPatterLetsGetAtHer: Spill the tea.

I huff out a tiny laugh and look up to see Bobby glancing my way. I hold up my phone. "Coco." That sounds plausible, right? Wait. Why am I explaining myself? I shake my head and get back to my conversation.

@Singlemomcatlady: It's nothing. I just figured since you were in the middle of your own workplace attraction conundrum, you might have some insight.

I press send and notice Bobby's phone ping again. This time, my glance is more furtive. I can't have him suspecting I'm texting about him, can I? He's really sort of unfairly good-looking. He's also intently studying his phone.

The app pings me again.

@PitterPatterLetsGetAtHer: I guess it depends. Is this a long term client? If so, I'd say just enjoy the view but keep your distance.

@Singlemomcatlady: Very short-term.

Bobby is obviously still in a chat with his buddies because his phone continues to ping almost as quickly as mine.

@PitterPatterLetsGetAtHer: That's easy then. As soon as the contract is done, jump his bones. Why not?

Bobby chuckles, drawing my attention again, and I can feel my stupid skin heating at just the notion of "jumping" Bobby Rhodes's bones. I let out a quiet groan. I mean, can you imagine? This is ridiculous. Thank goodness he's oblivious to me and still focused on his phone.

@Singlemomcatlady: I'm not going to jump his bones! Besides, he's way out of my league.

I hit send as I scoff at the screen.

Ping!

@PitterPatterLetsGetAtHer: How so? I think you're probably selling yourself short, cat lady.

@Singlemomcatlady: How are things going with your workplace romance? Any luck?

Ping!

@PitterPatterLetsGetAtHer: I'm actually with her right now.

@Singlemomcatlady: Then what are you doing messaging me?! Go talk to her!

Ping!

@PitterPatterLetsGetAtHer: She's on her phone. Must be important too because she keeps mumbling to herself as she types.

@Singlemomcatlady: I think you should get her alone and tell her how you feel.

Ping!

@PitterPatterLetsGetAtHer: We are alone. She's showing me a house I think I might buy. But I don't want to make an offer because then I won't have an excuse to see her anymore. Is that crazy?

> @Singlemomcatlady: That's so weird! Oh, sorry! Not weird that you want to keep spending time with her. That's actually sweet. The weird part is I'm a realtor too! In fact, I'm showing a house right now.

Ping!

I grin and start typing another message saying that my client is the same one I was just . . .

My thumbs freeze as a buzzing sound rushes into my ears like a speeding freight train. Despite my strict instruction to stay still, my eyes fly directly to Bobby sitting two stools away at the gorgeous kitchen island. He looks like he belongs here. He also looks like he's really enjoying whatever conversation he's having on his phone.

Clearly sensing my gaze, he glances over quickly before returning his eyes to his phone. But his attention returns to me when he registers what I assume is my horror-stricken expression.

"What's wrong?"

When I don't respond—which, in my defense, is due to the crushing humiliation choking my windpipe—he rises from his stool and closes the distance between us. "Molly? What's wrong?"

The words come out in a stilted whisper. "P-pitter patter?"

His brows draw together as he studies me in the same manner one might examine a concussed patient. It takes two-point-three seconds before his brows change direction and spike almost to his hairline.

"Cat lady?!"

Chapter Thirteen

Bobby

This is amazing. I mean, maybe I should be upset that I've been talking to Molly this whole time on the dating app and didn't realize it. Maybe I should feel sheepish that I've been more honest with her online persona than with anyone in my real life lately. Maybe I should feel raw and exposed. But I don't feel any of that.

Because Molly thinks I'm hot. She said so in our chat.

I step closer, her bare knees above the sexy pencil skirt brushing my legs as she remains stunned, perched on her barstool.

"Molly?" My voice is soft, lower than normal. She just blinks at me, gorgeous eyes wide and frightened. And I can't have that.

My hands come up and sweep her auburn hair back, away from her face. Then I cup her jaw and bend down so we're eye to eye. "Hey. I have a crazy thought."

"C-crazier than what's running through my head right now?" she mutters, still gaping at me.

I grin, wishing like hell I knew what she was thinking. Molly's all buttoned up on the outside, a prim and proper realtor in her heels and skirts and proper manners. And yet I know she's trolling the dating sites in her downtime, looking to get laid. And since I'm a gentleman who wants to make every lady's dream come true, it's important that I offer my services. Like, right now.

"You think I'm hot?" I ask, followed quickly by my own confession. "I think you're ridiculously attractive."

I feel her swallow hard, but then she gives me the briefest of nods and it's all the confession I need.

"No take-backsies," I murmur. It's dumb, but the fear fades from her face, leaving her eyes filled with a heat I can feel from here.

As I move ever closer, her knees give way until I'm standing between them, one hand tilting her head to the side, the other tangled in her hair. She's wearing it down today, a nice change from her usual ponytail, since it allows me to bury my hands in it. Her eyes widen even more and then they flutter shut as I lean in.

I've kissed plenty of women in the past, but I've never taken such care to make sure it's good for them. I know more about Molly than most women I've kissed, and I want her to remember this moment. Remember me.

My lips briefly brush against hers. A test of sorts to make sure she's with me. Her hands fly up and for a split second, I think she might push me away. Instead, she takes a fistful of my polo shirt in each hand and yanks me closer. Our mouths crash together, hard this time, a mutual desperation making the kiss clumsy and so fucking hot I can't think straight. When my tongue flicks against her lip and she only hesitates a moment before opening for me with a whimper, I want to throw my fist in the air and gloat. I don't, because absolutely nothing is going to break this moment for me.

The whoop of a police siren right outside the house blares. *God-fucking-dammit.*

We pull apart, moment broken, both of us breathing hard and staring at each other. Where am I, and what the hell just happened here? I blink several times, trying to come back to the moment even as my dick strains to free himself like that Burmese python. He thinks it's playtime.

"The snake has been captured. Feel free to move about." A police officer on a bullhorn going through the neighborhood should be offering relief, but I curse the bad timing.

Molly's eyes go wide and fearful again. She lets go of my shirt and tries to close her legs. Considering I'm standing between them, pain radiates up my thighs as she squeezes.

"Argh!" I wedge myself from between her knees and rub the side of my left thigh. "Ease up on leg day, fluffernutter."

Her cheeks, red as the toenail polish she sports from those peep-toe heels, flame brighter. "Fluffernutter?" Then she licks the lips I just tasted, and I have to turn partially away or I'll tackle her to the ground and beg her to pretend we're still locked inside this house.

"Well, you're on the Catnip dating app."

Molly clears her throat and slides off the barstool, smoothing out her skirt. I guess we're just going to pretend that kiss didn't happen? "Oh, I don't care about cats. Allergic to them, actually. My boss signed me up for the app."

I turn back to her, realizing she's not getting my joke. "It's not an app for people who like cats," I say slowly.

Molly frowns. "What do you mean?"

"It's an app for cougars."

She jerks her head back, even more confused.

"Older women who like younger men," I clarify.

Understanding dawns slowly and incrementally. I know

when she puts all the pieces together because her chin drops to her chest and she wraps her arms around herself like she wishes she could disappear. I take a step toward her, my finger going under her chin. She lets me tilt her face back up, but she won't meet my gaze.

"If it makes you less embarrassed we can go back to pretending it's an app for cat lovers," I offer. "I'll call you fluffernutter and you can call me . . ." I rack my brain for an appropriate male cat name.

"Mister Whiskers?" Molly offers in a whisper.

We lock eyes and both of us smile. The tension ebbs, and while I'd love nothing more than to go back to kissing Molly, I know that the moment is gone. It's crystal clear to me I want more than a random make-out session with my realtor in a stranger's house. I want to take Molly out on a real date. And I can't do that if I push her too hard, too fast. She'll run scared, I just know it.

So I do what Bobby Rhodes has never done before and I take a step back. I assess. I don't go flying into the fray with a banshee cry and a flying fist of fury. I'm going to think twice. Maybe make a pros and cons spreadsheet like a goddamn adult.

Molly grabs her bag off the counter, and I take it from her. She locks up the house and we look both ways before venturing back to my car. I know they say they have the python, but it doesn't hurt to be careful. We climb into Wolverine, but I don't back out of the driveway.

"I like that house."

I can feel Molly looking at me, so I meet her gaze. "Want to make an offer on it?"

"Not really," I admit with a shake of my head.

She smiles, probably remembering how I told her on the app that I wanted an excuse to keep seeing my realtor. "How come I know so much more about you from our messages than all this time we've spent together in person?"

I hiss out a breath at the honest question. "I don't come from a family that talks about our feelings."

Molly lifts a shoulder. "Does anyone?"

She's probably right, but my family was next level. "I was just telling Ashley yesterday that I only have two modes: humor or fighting. It's probably not healthy, and she agreed with me."

"Ashley?" Molly's eyes are back to being guarded.

"My counselor," I rush to clarify. "Kaitlyn, my agent, has me seeing someone for anger management. I've gotten into a bit of trouble with my coach."

Molly's expression softens again. She reaches over to put her hand on my forearm. "Is he going to be angry you missed practice today? I can go with you and corroborate your story."

That knot that's had my shoulders feeling like they're being pulled like a bowstring loosens. I can't recall the last time I had someone in my corner. My brothers are the definition of "every man for himself." The world of hockey is cutthroat the higher up you go. Coach doesn't exactly like me. Hell, even my friend Chloe, treats me like the little brother she never wished she had. It feels . . . nice . . . to think Molly might have my back, for no other reason than she likes me. Genuinely likes me.

"You'd do that for me?"

Molly's full lips tilt up into a soft smile that hits me right in the middle of my chest. "I would. Will you keep talking to Matthew for me?"

I nod instantly. "You trust me?"

Molly's thumb shifts back and forth on my arm, distracting me. My dick decides he'd like a stroke too. I try to tell him Molly and I are having a moment, but he's not used to me ignoring him in favor of conversation.

"You know what? I do," she answers, sounding as shocked as I am to hear it.

Her trust feels like a gift she's given me. A very delicate gift that somehow weighs a lot due to its importance. I want to hold it carefully, making sure I don't damage it. I put my other hand on top of hers, squeezing her fingers.

"Go out with me, Molly. On a real date."

Her eyes flare with surprise, but she doesn't say no right away. She licks her lips again and I almost let a groan slip out. "I don't know. That might be against this realtor client relationship we have going."

"Then you're fired."

"Bobby!" She tries to pull her hand back, but I don't let her go.

I grin. "I'm kidding. But seriously, it's either go on a date with me or you'll be signing up for an endless amount of house showings, just so I can see you. Seems like even your boss would agree a date is a better use of your time."

Her eyes narrow. "Are you blackmailing me?"

"If that's what it takes, fluffernutter," I fire right back.

"That nickname is not going to work." I raise an eyebrow at her obvious attempt to deflect and she sighs. "Let me think about it?"

I pick her hand up and bring it to my mouth, kissing the soft skin of her knuckles. "Take all the time you need." Then I put her hand back in her lap. "As much as I'd like to drive you home, you brought your own car."

She jolts back, looking outside the passenger window to her beat up Kia parked next to mine. She chuckles and shakes her head. "You're distracting, Mister Whiskers."

I lunge for her, but she slides out of Wolverine with a squeal. Her laughter carries on the breeze as she heads for her car.

Chapter Fourteen

Molly

"It's not *that* funny," I insist for the second time.

Ramona puts a finger up telling me to hold on a sec while she continues losing her absolute shit. I sigh and turn my attention to the sidewalk café around us. A few customers dart furtive glances our way—I mean, it does sound like Ramona might be choking on something, not that I'm that lucky—but the rest ignore us while my friend laughs her ass off at me.

"Oh," she finally manages, "It absolutely *is* that funny, Molly. Or should I call you Mrs. Robinson?"

I knew I shouldn't have confessed everything to Ramona, but since I'm due to see Bobby again in an hour, I was at my wit's end.

"I've decided you're no longer my best friend," I respond as I lift my cardboard coffee cup to my lips. It's a treat to go out for coffee, but this conversation warrants it. My mind was pretty much blown by that kiss with Bobby, and now I don't know if I'm coming or going.

Ramona finally straightens in her seat and it only takes a few more sighs to tamp down her hilarity. "That's probably earned. When you said Coco signed you up for a dating app, I should have known it was Catnip–and that you'd assume it was a dating app for cat ladies."

"Thank you!" I nod. "You know I count on you for these things. I mean, if it weren't for you, I would still think the acronym IYKYK literally means 'Ick. Yuck.'"

"Oh." She stirs a sugar packet into her coffee. "And don't forget when you thought TBF was referring to my tuberculosis status. Why would I go around texting people about TB?"

"You're a nurse!" I attempt to defend myself. "Honestly, what is it with everyone feeling the need to shorten everything? Use your words, people!"

"No offense, but you sound old when you say things like that," she offers, straightening her glasses on her nose.

"I *am* old!" I remind her before dropping my voice low and leaning into the tiny café table. "Too old to date a twenty-eight-year-old beautiful hockey player, that's for sure!"

Ramona snatches up her own cup and meets me halfway. "Who happens to *like* the fact that you're old, you nasty cougar, you."

"Seriously, Ramona, what am I supposed to do with this?" I gesture at our surroundings as if Bobby is sitting at the next table over.

"I guess that depends. How was the kiss?"

My cheeks instantly flame at the memory. And is it my imagination, or do I smell Bobby's woodsy cologne mingling with the coffee aroma out here?

Ramona's eyebrows spike. "That good?"

"Better." I sigh. "Honestly, I don't think I've ever been on the receiving end of another person's complete and utter focus like that. I swear he was attuned to even my pulse during that kiss." My eyes go unfocused and my nipples tighten as I recall the sensation of being wrapped up in Bobby like that. "He was all in, and I mean it. *All. In.* We both forgot where we were." I fan myself at the memory.

"Damn." There's an almost reverent tone to Ramona's response, and when I snap myself out of my Bobby fog, I see her across from me, chin propped on her hand and a goofy smile on her lips.

I can't help my responding smile. "Yeah."

Ramona pulls in a long breath and squares her shoulders. "Well, you clearly have to go for it."

"Go for what?"

"Letting the hockey hottie put his focus on all your girl parts, that's what."

I frown at her. "You said, and I quote, 'a pro athlete like him would eat me up and spit me out—and not in the good way.'"

She shoos me off. "Yeah, I changed my mind. I think it will be in the absolute *best* way."

"Using Bobby Rhodes to scratch an itch or get my feet wet sounds like too much of a risk to me. I should start with some-one . . . simpler. Like maybe a mailman or a nice accountant."

Ramona points at me and scowls from behind her glasses. "Molly, an accountant isn't going to inspire the look I just saw on your face."

"How do you know?" I challenge, suddenly feeling protec-tive of my imaginary accountant boyfriend.

"Because I have an accountant. His name is Bryce, and I guarantee you he couldn't find your G-spot with advanced GPS technology and a sherpa at his side."

Perhaps she has a point.

"But what would make a hot young professional hockey player go for somebody more than ten years older than him? And with a kid, no less? It doesn't make sense."

"Hey, don't yuck someone else's yum. People like what they like. I happen to think the man has excellent taste." Ramona winks at me.

I can't help smiling at her while also shaking my head. "Yeah, well, just the thought of ending up in bed with the man makes me break out in a nervous sweat."

"We'll have to work on that."

I keep going over it in my head and coming to the same conclusion. In the Catnip chats, Bobby made it clear he was interested in this mystery colleague as more than a fling. Which means his attentions these past couple weeks haven't just been some natural flirting reflex like I previously assumed. Catnip Bobby talked about me like he wanted . . . a relationship.

And that scares the shit out of me.

As if reading my thoughts, Ramona says, "He asked for a date, not your hand in marriage. What can it hurt?"

I don't bother arguing anymore, not just because Ramona is impossible to sway but because I'm maybe kind of starting to like the idea.

The moment I spot Bobby by the bleachers at practice an hour later, I change my mind completely. He's wearing skates and form-fitting jeans, his dirty-blond hair a tousled mess and his head thrown back in laughter at something a tall, glamorous black-haired woman just said to him. He's turned fully into her where she leans against the bleacher rail and grins up at him. She has all his focus, and I suddenly feel like an idiot for thinking his focus on me at the house yesterday was something special. This is what he does—what he's good at. Making women feel like they're the center of his universe.

Ugh. What was I thinking?

I squeeze Matty's shoulder and paste on a smile. "Go get your skates on, okay?"

"K." He nods and runs off to join his new friend Eli where he waves at my son from down the bleachers.

Matty's attitude is much improved today, and I know who's responsible, even if I refuse to glance his way again. I don't have time to waste crushing on unattainable men with stupidly charming dimples! *My* focus should be on my child's emotional well-being and on earning enough money to put food on the table and clothes on our backs.

Matty deserves a mom who makes smart decisions and uses her time and resources wisely. The last thing I want is him growing up feeling insecure about his welfare like I did. Don't get me wrong, my parents have always loved me, but you can't eat love or sleep under its roof. And I refuse to ever let Matty question his own safety or well-being. It's Blake's and my job to provide those things and make that our top priority.

I suddenly feel ridiculous for slicking on a fresh coat of lipstick and curling my hair before bringing Matty here. I'll just leave and pick him up when practice is over. There's plenty of work I can get done on my company laptop using some fast-food joint's Wi-Fi nearby, I'm sure.

I swing back toward the entrance and run smack into a firm chest. "Oh! Sorry!" I say as strong hands grip my biceps to steady me. But when I look up, my surprise turns to delight. "Blake!"

My ex grins down at me. "I see you still don't watch where you're going."

All I can do is shrug. "Matty will be so happy you're here. They're doing a scrimmage today." I turn to wave our kid down, but Blake stops me.

"Just a second."

I shoot him a questioning gaze, but his eyes are scanning the practice facility. "Which one of these guys is Bobby Rhodes?"

I groan inwardly. I'm going to be forced to act like the mature adult I claim to be, aren't I? Little could make this situation any more humiliating than having to introduce my gay ex-husband to the guy I just kissed—the same one who is currently flirting with his next conquest right in front of me. Where is that python siren when I need it?

As if sensing the mortification rolling off me in sonic waves, Bobby turns away from the raven-haired beauty and starts in our direction. They've probably already arranged a rendezvous later tonight at some club where rich, beautiful people bang. A glance at his face reveals an expression I haven't seen before on him, and I can't quite read it.

Blake stiffens next to me, and then his arm wraps around my shoulders, his palm pulling me into him so I'm all but cradled into his side. What in the world?

"Molly!" Bobby greets me with a smile, but it's not the one that shows his dimples. This one is tight.

"Hi, Bobby," I reply as he draws near. For a second, I think he's going to lean in and kiss me, but instead, he stops short and sways back on his heels, his skates giving him at least an extra two inches in height.

Bobby's eyes rake my face before he shifts them to Blake and thrusts out a hand. "Bobby Rhodes."

Blake takes the offered hand and the two shake for what feels like an uncomfortably long time. "Blake Sparks," Blake says in a tone that begins to sound a little strangled by the end. What is going on here? They finally release each other. "So, how do you know my wife?"

My head whips up as I stare dumbly at Blake, but he won't meet my eyes. Before I can say anything, Bobby cuts in.

"I'm sorry. Don't you mean *ex*-wife?"

"Six of one," Blake inexplicably replies with a shrug. *Six of one? Really?* Since no one else is volunteering, I nominate myself as the adult in the room and turn to Bobby as I extricate myself from Blake's grip.

"Bobby, this is Blake, Matthew's father and my ex-husband. Blake, this is Bobby Rhodes, my client and one of the hockey instructors for the kids' league."

"Bobby," Blake begins again. "Do you mind if I have a word with my wife in private?"

"*Ex*-wife," I correct. Has he taken a blow to the head while on the road?

"Not at all," Bobby responds, reaching out to squeeze my bicep in a way-too-familiar gesture for current company. "We'll talk later, Sparkle." He winks at me, not giving Blake another glance before striding on his skates to the rink door.

Oh, for the love of god. Did these two men just metaphorically pee on me to stake their claim? Last I checked, one of them is gay, and the other was just securing a date with another woman right in front of me!

Before I can think of the appropriate words to express how idiotic Blake is being, he starts in on me with a whisper-hiss. "You didn't tell me you were *sleeping* with the guy!"

I draw in a sharp gasp and glance around to make sure nobody heard him. Thankfully, no one is paying any attention to us, so I erase all but one inch of distance between us and bite back, "I'm not sleeping with him. Oh my god! What are you doing here? Spying on me? I thought you were here to see your son play hockey!"

"I am," he retorts, each of us continuing in forceful whispers. "But I also wanted to make sure this guy mentoring Matty wasn't some deviant. It didn't occur to me that you're the one who'd need looking out for instead of Matty." His tone is accusing, and it has me grinding my molars together.

"I don't need 'looking out for,' Blake." I poke an index finger into his chest. "I can take care of myself. Besides, it's none of your business if I'm seeing someone."

"So you *are* sleeping with him."

That's it. I'm going to jail for murder. "No." It takes all I've got to force levity into my tone. We're in a public place, after all. "But that's beside the point. I could if I wanted to, and it would be none of your business."

Blake thrusts his fingers through his loose hair. "It's my business who's spending time with my wife and child."

"I'm not your wife anymore, Blake!" My voice rises to the point where we both glance around this time. I immediately spot Bobby watching us from the rink. Great. I sigh and turn back to Blake.

"You know what I mean," my ex says.

"No, I don't. We don't have that kind of relationship anymore. *I* decide what's best for me now. *I* take care of myself and count on myself. Nobody else does that anymore." Fuck. Why do I want to cry?

Blake looks wounded by my words. I'm usually so much more careful, but this day is kicking my ass. "You say that like I purposely abandoned you or something. You know that's not what happened."

"I know," I sigh and take his hand in mine. It's such a familiar hand, yet touching it brings not one tingle to my skin or kick to my heart rate. Again, my mind takes me back to that kiss with Bobby in the big Spanish-style kitchen where my entire body was alight. But I block it out. "I'm not blaming you. I'm just trying to explain that the stage of our relationship where you have a say in my personal decisions is over. When it comes to Matty, absolutely. But not me. Even if neither of us technically chose this path, this is where we are, and you've got to be okay with it."

"Fuck." Blake drops his head back with a heavy sigh. "I really screwed this up, didn't I?"

My lips twitch. "Yeah, you did a pretty spectacular job, I'd say. I mean, what was with that pissing contest with you and Bobby?"

He shakes his head and shrugs, looking down at me again. "Reflex?"

I raise a finger. "Not that it's any of your business, but Bobby flirts with everyone. I'm nothing special."

Blake's jaw tics, and I see him look over to the rink where I last saw Bobby. I refuse to follow his gaze, instead waiting for his attention to return to me. When it does, his tone is forceful. "Don't you ever say that, Dollface. You are the definition of special, and don't you forget it."

Tears spring to my eyes and I will them away, but not before Blake sees them. He musters a smile and switches to casual. "Anyway, I really did just come back early to see you and Matty—and to tell you some news, but that can wait."

"What news is that?" I'm as eager as he is to shove emotions aside.

"No, I already caused enough drama."

I bat at his chest. "You know I'll only worry if you don't tell me."

He grins at that. "It's really not a big deal. I was just going to tell you that I started seeing someone."

My eyes widen. "You did?"

"Yeah. I mean, it's early days but . . ." His eyes drop to his boots. "I don't know. It just felt weird not sharing it with my best friend."

"You know, you make it hard to stay mad at you," I scold, warmth infusing my chest. "I'm happy for you." And I am. This hasn't been easy for any of us.

"I know I'm going to sound like a complete hypocrite, but I want you to find somebody too." He cocks his head toward the rink. "Maybe not the guy who I'm pretty sure just broke my hand, but somebody."

"Ha! Well, like I said, there's no danger of that. He's just a world-class flirt, nothing more." Maybe if I keep repeating it, I'll convince myself.

Blake drops both hands onto my shoulders and gives them a squeeze. "You deserve the best, Dollface. Don't settle for less than someone who makes you the center of their universe."

I fight a wince at his use of the exact phrase I thought of minutes ago when watching Bobby flirt with the beautiful woman.

"Yes, sir. Now, go say hi to your son."

Blake gives me one last squeeze before jogging toward the bleachers and Matty. I watch Matty forget to act cool and instead jump into his dad's arms. Then I pull my phone from my bag and bring up my text chat with Bobby.

> Me: Thanks for asking, but I'm going to say no to the date.

Using every bit of restraint I can muster, I tuck my phone away and stride out the facility's doors without looking back.

<h1 style="text-align:center">Chapter Fifteen</h1>

Bobby

Well, that was as uncomfortable as that Gator jersey I had to wear one year for Halloween when I lost a bet with my brothers. Dad nearly disowned me, right after he ran me out of the house screaming about Bulldogs for life. What the fuck is Molly's ex-husband doing here engaging in a petty dick-measuring contest? I mean, I know I'd win the contest, but that's beside the point. I felt that guy's stare all through practice.

My wife? Shit, I didn't like hearing that guy call Molly his, nor did I care for his arm around her shoulders. Not that she's mine either, but considering they're divorced now, you'd think he could let up on the whole *my wife* thing. Whatever that was, it put me in a bad mood.

"Bye, Bobby!" Matthew gives me a wave from the exit door as I'm getting my skates off.

Blake wraps his arm around his son's bony shoulders and hustles him out of the arena with the other kids. Blake, however, doesn't bother with a goodbye, which is fine by me. It would have taken my entire adult ration of self-control to not flip the guy off.

I toss my skates in my bag and stand up again, stretching the kinks out. Coach went a bit psycho on me at practice today. Said I had some catching up to do since I missed yesterday's practice due to the python. Like it was my fault Florida Man struck again. Whatever.

My phone rings from the depths of my bag. By the time I find it, it's stopped ringing. Richie calls me right back though, always one to bother the shit out of me just for sport. Except there's also a text from Molly. I ignore the incoming call from my brother and read her message instead.

"Well, shit," I mutter. She turned down my date idea. Kind of. *I'm going to say no.* Which in my limited knowledge of proper English means saying no in the future, but maybe she doesn't want to say no right now? In other words, there's still hope. If the message had been *go fuck yourself, hell no to this date idea,* then I'd take that as a firm no. Her text is a firm maybe. I can work with maybe.

Practice was just as brutal today, though a bit shorter since we leave tomorrow morning for our road trip. I joined the old guys in the ice baths and I have to say, they might be onto something. I'm feeling spry as a spring chicken as I leave the rink.

My phone rings again. Goddamn Richie.

"Yo, Richie, why you blowing up my phone?" I answer,

slinging the bag over my shoulder and heading out of the facility.

"I've been trying to reach you. I'm a little low on gas. You think you could pick me up before we head to that charity thing?" he asks by way of greeting.

I close my eyes for a second. "Shit. I forgot about that." I check my watch. I barely have enough time to pick him up and get over to the center on time. Kaitlyn set everything up for me, including tipping off one of her favorite paparazzis. She'd never forgive me if I blew it off or showed up late.

"I'll be right there. Be ready to go. Clean shirt. No bull-shit, Richie."

"Since when do I–"

He doesn't even finish that ridiculous question before I hang up on him and sprint the rest of the way to Wolverine. Traffic is stupidly thick in the middle of the day thanks to the older set getting to their pickleball tournaments and doctor appointments.

Thankfully, Richie is dressed in a T-shirt that's not only clean but also doesn't have the name of a bar or a curse word on it. It's basically a fashion miracle. I probably shouldn't have asked Richie to come along to my charity work, but Ashley suggested it as a way for us to bond over something wholesome.

Richie and I pull into the parking lot my navigation system directed me to. A squatty building with an unfortunate orange paint job and above ground electrical wires streaming to it greets us. Two small windows should offer light into the place, but they're covered by security bars. The door has a handwritten sign that says *Bros 4 Bras*.

"Dude." Richie peers out the passenger window at the place. "That's some serious cable wire they got there."

I push open my door and slide out. "We're here to work, Rich. Just follow my lead."

Richie and I head inside where we have to blink repeatedly for our eyes to adjust. The overhead lighting in here is the stuff of nightmares for fitting rooms. The mega-watt halogen lights make my Gucci slides look sickly orange instead of Bulldog red.

"Can I help you?"

We look left to see an elderly woman with a bat in her hand, slapping it lightly against her palm in a menacing manner as she glares at us. We both put our hands up and Richie looks at me to take the lead. Kaitlyn's going to get an earful about this if I end up getting my ass kicked by an octogenarian.

"I'm Bobby and this is my brother, Richie. We're here to volunteer this afternoon?"

The woman's face clears and the bat gets tossed aside onto a pile of lingerie. Her facial wrinkles stack up as she smiles, making her look like our Grandma Betty Mae. The transformation is incredible.

"Bobby!" She leans in to hug me like she already knows me, a waft of minty muscle cream and denture glue hitting my nose. I pat her back and watch Richie look even more awkward than me when she gives him the same treatment. "Welcome, boys. I'm Betty, the manager of Bros 4 Bras. Sorry for the bat, but you'd be surprised how often we get robbed."

I look around the place, seeing bras on every surface. Six-foot tables and clear plastic bins are set up against all four walls and in neat rows filling the space in between. I had no idea this many bras could be in one place beside the bra factory. Television screens line the walls above our heads, maybe thirty of them in total. It's like a sports bar, but instead of whiskey and beer, it's bras and more bras.

"My husband Johnny, God rest his soul, started this place in 1972 when his sister did a stint on the streets." Betty puts her thin hand on my arm. "She was pretty well endowed, if you know what I mean. Had funbags the size of watermelons, that girl did."

Richie makes a choking noise he tries to disguise as a cough. I nod, giving everything I've got to keeping a straight face.

"Anyhoo, come to find out, it's hard to afford bras when you're homeless. Johnny rounded up his friends and started a nonprofit, asking all our female neighbors and friends for their old bras. From itty bitties to the bazookas, we collect them all. I've kept the place going and am proud to say we ship out over one hundred bras to every state in the nation every year." Betty pats my chest with her left hand and Richie's chest with her right. "That's where you two come in."

"I've got a bad back, but Bobby here can lift the heavy boxes," Richie offers. If Betty had her back turned I'd have flipped him off for trying to get out of working.

Betty's laugh is like tinkling wind chimes. "Oh no, sweet thing. I need you boys to sort the sizes. What good is a triple-D hammock to a woman who's got nothing but bee stings, you know? Proper sizing is imperative for good breast support."

Richie's face is turning the kind of purple that spells trouble for my image if he opens his mouth. I put my hand over Betty's, getting her attention. "You can count on us, Betty. We'll have hundreds sorted before our shift is over, don't you worry."

Betty smiles at me like I'm her favorite boy. The door to the place swings open and a guy with a camera pops his head in. "Bobby Rhodes?"

Shit, that must be the paparazzi Kaitlyn called. "Yep. Come on in. We're just about to start sorting the donations."

Betty gets us set up at a table in the back but gets pulled away when the phone starts ringing at the front. The camera guy stares around in all directions, probably wondering how his day led him to the land of brassieres.

Richie hands me a red lacy number. "I don't know, man. Is this a size three?"

I roll my eyes and take the bra from him, holding it up by the straps. "First of all, bras aren't sized that way. There's a band size that measures around the rib cage, and then there's the cup size." I hold it up and twist it this way and that while the paparazzi's camera clicks away. "I'd say this pretty thing is a thirty-two-C."

Richie checks the label. "Well, holy shi–oot. You're right. Thirty-two-C." He puts it in the correct bin and grabs another bra, this one a beige color with cups bigger than my head. "Guess this one."

I hold it up and assess. "Forty-two-F."

When I'm proven right again, Richie high-fives me. Even the paparazzi guy starts handing me bras to get my guess. Sometimes I have to put the bra on over my clothes and feel up the cups to get a good read on the size, but I'm ten for ten so far. Hot dog, I've finally found a charity I'm good at. We keep going like that until the paparazzi checks his watch and assures us he has enough pictures. He heads out and we keep sorting. Eventually Betty comes back with a bin full of remote controls.

"I forgot the best part! Johnny insisted on having as many televisions as possible for him and his friends. They'd spend hours in here sorting and watching sports. I've upgraded the televisions over the years and pay for cable."

"You're the best, Betty." Richie gives her a hug and takes the bin from her. I've got ten more bras sorted by the time he gets all the televisions on and tuned into different stations. He's gaping at the walls like he just stepped into Tampa's swankiest strip club. "I'm in heaven."

We shoot the shit over whatever's playing on the screens while we sort for the next hour. Ashley was right to suggest I bring Richie. Can't remember the last time we talked instead of insulting each other. My stomach starts to rumble and I put down the latest lime green bra to suggest we head out for dinner. We say goodbye to Betty and promise to return soon. I fire up Wolverine right as my phone rings.

"Kaitlyn!" I answer on Bluetooth speaker, feeling proud of myself. "You'll be pleased to know, we did good at the–"

"Why the hell are there pictures of you wearing a bra and copping a feel of your own boobs on social media right now, Bobby Rhodes?" Her angry voice floods the interior of my vehicle. Richie and I stare at each other in shock. Right before he doubles over laughing.

My skull hits the headrest as I stare at the ceiling. "Are you serious?"

Kaitlyn goes off for a good ten minutes about what a mess I've made of things before letting me go. I squeeze my eyes shut and try to count to ten while taking deep breaths. I recognize the signs of anger, but there's no stepping back from this one. All the things Ashley instructed me to do go out the goddamn window. Molly said no to a date. Coach is pissed at me for something out of my control. And now this. I tried to do something good, and it backfired.

Coach is right. I'm a screw up. Always have been, always will be.

I roll my head on the headrest. Richie is wiping tears from his eyes. "How does the Irish Rogue sound for dinner?"

Richie shrugs. "I can get us a discount."

I put the car in gear and head for the familiar bar. I just need some food in my gut and to wash it down with a stout beer. I'll try again tomorrow, but for today I just need some comfort food. We pull in and find a parking space easily. Richie greets his fellow bartender buddies inside the dark tavern. He gets us set up with a frosty glass of beer at the bartop while they fry up some disgusting food for us to eat. I take one long swig of the beer, all my worries melting away as the roasted malt hits my tastebuds.

"If beer's wrong, I don't want to be right." Richie smacks his lips after drinking half his pint.

I huff a laugh, taking another sip. I can feel myself slipping backward and yet I can't–won't–do a damn thing to stop it. I've tried most of the things Kaitlyn said to do and what has that gotten me? Nothing but frustration. Might as well enjoy the beer while I circle the drain of my career.

My phone vibrates in my back pocket. I put it on silent when we got to the bar, hoping to dodge any further phone calls from Kaitlyn, but when it buzzes again, I feel guilty for ignoring her. I pull the phone out and squint to see an unfamiliar number.

> Unknown: Hey Bobby. It's Matthew. You said I could contact you anytime. Is it wrong to bully a bully?

My spine freezes. I reply back as quickly as my thumbs let me.

> Me: Hey, Matthew. Depends. What's the bully doing?

> Unknown: It's mostly social media stuff. Just spreading altered pictures of someone and making fun of them. I wanted to spread a picture of the bully.

> Me: I think you'd be better served taking screenshots of what the bully's doing and talking to your mom. Or your principal about what's going on. Don't lower yourself to their level.

Unknown: I was afraid you were going to say that. Fine, I won't send the pic.

Me: Where are you?

Unknown: At the convenience store down the street from Mom's.

I look out the windows of the Irish Rogue. It's hard to tell with the neon beer signs, but it looks pretty dark out there.

Me: Does she know you're there?

Unknown: No . . . ? She thinks I'm studying.

Me: Stay right there. I'm headed over.

I reach into my wallet and throw a few twenties on the bar. Richie looks over at me with his eyebrows raised. I stand up and pocket my phone again.

"Gotta go. Can you Uber home?"

He nods, distracted when the bartender comes over with a plate of nachos and wings. I head out, suddenly not interested in beer or bars or bras.

Don't lower yourself to their level.

Time I took my own advice.

Chapter Sixteen

Molly

"Oh my god, babe! This would be the perfect spot for my reading room!" my client gushes as she paws her partner's beefy arm.

I glance around the tiny windowless room, barely making out the color of the walls in the dim light of the overhead fixture. "Um . . . absolutely!" I agree. "Very cozy."

Coco always says that when you're not working with an ideal listing, you need to help your clients imagine themselves in the space, offering as many possibilities for rooms as you can think of until you see the lightbulb switch on behind their eyes. Selling homes is as much about watching and listening as it is about talking, numbers, and neighborhoods.

"What kind of books do you read?" I ask Destiny, my tall, willowy client clinging to her partner Gabriel's arm. Getting to know your clients and taking an interest in their lives is another top priority, according to my boss.

"Oh, she doesn't read books. Says they're too boring,"

Gabriel answers, grinning down at Destiny and stroking her back. The two of them are handsy as hell. I swear I almost walked in on them screwing in the ensuite bathroom at a property last week.

Before I can ask the obvious question, Destiny clarifies, "I read tarot cards. Have you ever had a reading?"

The hairs on the back of my neck stand on end and I order them to calm their shit. "Oh. Um, no, I don't think I have." In fact, I know I haven't, and for good reason.

"Omigosh, you *have* to let me do a reading for you!"

"Yeah, you *have* to," Gabriel echoes with equal enthusiasm. "Destiny is *amazing*."

"Sounds . . . fascinating," I lie, trying to suppress the urge to excuse myself so I can scream into a throw pillow on the couch in the tiny den.

It's nothing against Destiny. She's lovely and has been a dream client so far. I've just had enough experience with shady scammers of the occult to last a lifetime. My mother is a huge fan.

But since I can't run screaming in the other direction, I paste on a smile and hope I'm convincing when I continue, "We should wait until we get you a house, though, right?"

Thankfully, it works.

"Totally," Gabriel answers for them both, and I hurriedly lead them down the hall to the primary bedroom, hoping like hell they're not going to declare it the perfect spot to summon the dead.

By the time we're finished touring the home, Destiny has approved its general aura, and the couple decides to grab some pizza and think about it. I take that as my cue to check my messages and emails.

The first thing I see when I pull out my phone is a text from Bobby. Crap.

Bobby: Please call me as soon as you get this.

I've been avoiding thinking about him since yesterday at the rink, and he's leaving for a road trip with the team tomorrow, so I'd been counting on having a little break from him to get my head back on straight. I'm still embarrassed I let myself get carried away and kiss him. The last thing I need is to hear his voice and let my lady parts start doing the thinking again.

Me: Hey. I'm at work.

Technically true.

Me: Is it about a property? Email me the listing and I can take a look.

I'm keeping this all business in case he's texting me about his offer of a date again. He wouldn't, would he? I suppose pro athletes don't often get turned down, though. Oh god, he doesn't think I'm playing hard to get, does he? See? This is what happens when I decide to dip my toe back into the dating pool! I start to obsess and overthink everything. He's obviously texting about a property.

Right?

Shit.

I drop the phone onto the passenger seat of my Kia—which has been purring like a sated kitten since its tune-up, by the way—assuming I'm in the clear when Bobby doesn't text back. Gripping the steering wheel with both hands, I tilt my head to look at my partial reflection in the rearview mirror.

"Get. A. Fucking. Grip, Sparks."

I jump in my seat when my phone rings as if I've just been zapped by a rogue wave of static shock. A glance at the screen shows Bobby's name—because of course it does.

Maybe I could have used that tarot reading after all to warn me of this.

Closing my eyes, I bring the phone to my ear and pretend I don't know who's calling.

"Hello? Molly Sparks speaking."

The gruff baritone of my name on Bobby's lips immediately flips my belly upside down. "Molly, it's Bobby."

A ridiculously forced lighthearted laugh spills from my lips. "Oh, Bobby. Hi." I sound completely deranged! "I didn't know it was you," I lie. Like he's going to believe I've suddenly switched to carrying around a mid-twentieth-century rotary phone wherever I go. I'm acting like a twelve-year-old girl with her first crush on the high school quarterback.

But instead of calling me out, he continues in a serious, very un-Bobby-like tone, "Don't freak out, okay?"

And just like that, every iota of embarrassment, attraction, and self-flagellation flees my mind, leaving nothing but thick, oppressive dread. "What happened?

My fingers tap impatiently on the steering wheel as I wait for the light to turn green fifteen minutes later. I can't believe I let Bobby talk me into not calling Matthew myself!

All I know at this point is that Matty is not at home where he's supposed to be, and that Bobby has eyes on him. Why my kid decided it was a better idea to call a hockey player instead of one of his parents to help him is beyond me. But I forced myself to push past the twin pangs of hurt and worry to give Matty what he deemed most helpful to him in the moment.

Bobby.

Who knew there were so many kids in need of therapy that the waitlist is two months long for an appointment? I found that out the day after Matty agreed to go to counseling. I called every place within thirty miles looking for anyone accepting new patients. The waitlist at one place was six months! How is that supposed to be helpful to a kid in crisis? I can only hope to do my best while we wait for Matty's turn, and right now it seems Bobby freaking Rhodes might be my best bet.

My tires squeal when I shoot forward as soon as the light turns green. I'm near home now, where I know the roads like the back of my hand, so I take the shortcut behind the half-deserted strip mall and pull into the parking lot of the little convenience store slash hot dog stand down the road from our house.

All the breath whooshes from my lungs when I spot Matty's familiar mop of brown and copper hair through a window. He's sitting at one of the tiny tables in the corner with his back to me, Bobby seated across from him and wearing a furrowed brow. Neither of them sees me as I unbuckle and head for the glass door of the shop, intent on getting to my kid.

I hurry inside and weave through the tightly nested aisles of Corn Nuts and ramen packets until I hear Bobby's voice and halt my steps just out of view.

"I'd bet my Gordie Howe bobblehead that this Raiden kid is being a jerk because he's insecure about himself."

Matty groans. "That's what adults always say. Bullies bully to prevent being targeted themselves."

It's pretty much word-for-word what I've told him before. Clearly, it hasn't proven to be a helpful bit of advice. I just *knew* there was something more to this Raiden thing!

"And you don't think that's true?" Bobby asks.

I venture forward another step and can just make out both

their profiles now through the space between two boxes of animal crackers. Neither one appears to notice me in my super-secret stake-out spot.

"I dunno. I just know he's a jerk."

"Hey, I'm not saying you need to be friends with the kid. Not everybody is meant to be friends and sit around singing 'Kumbaya' like in the movies."

"What the heck is 'Kumbaya?'" Matty asks, nose wrinkling.

"Uh, just some old people shi—stuff. Forget about it. What I'm saying is it's good that you're looking out for kids he's bullying, but don't let yourself become a bully in the process. Best to try to avoid him altogether."

I bring a hand up to stifle a tiny gasp. Pride warms my chest, and I'm not sure if it's from knowing that my kid is defending others or finding out Bobby Rhodes can dish out some really excellent advice.

"I still want to send that pic."

Huh?

"But you're not gonna sink to his level like that, are you?"

Matty sighs. "No. I'm gonna show my mom the stuff Raiden's been posting and let her talk to the school."

I stifle a growl and continue eavesdropping.

"Good call."

"Although . . ." Uh oh, I recognize that tone. "Seems a shame to have wasted my time making Raiden look ridiculous, though, right?"

"All right. Hand it over. But then we're deleting it, deal?"

"Deal." Matty quickly pulls his phone from his lap and scrolls for a few seconds before sliding it over the table to Bobby with a smug grin.

Bobby picks it up and squints at the screen. "Is that . . . Elmo?"

Matty chortles, chest puffed with pride. "Yeah. I took a

picture of Raiden eating a burger at lunch and edited it to make it look like he's kissing an Elmo doll instead."

Bobby's lip curls. "More like eating its face. Remind me to hire you next time I want to play a trick on my brothers."

"I like computers." Matty shrugs.

"It's good to be creative—not to mention have a good sense of humor." Bobby slides the phone back and folds his hands on the table. "But it's easy for a joke to get out of hand. Believe me, I know. I recently got into some big trouble for taking a joke too far. It could have cost me my job."

I didn't know that.

"Seriously?" Matty asks, just as clueless as me.

"Seriously. But I'm being more careful now. Less impulsive and more mature about things."

"Yeah. Me too." Matty straightens in his chair.

Bobby stifles a laugh. "Good to hear. Now, delete that photo." He waits for Matty to do as he's told before continuing, "Your mom is going to be here any minute and she's probably going to be all worried and want to love on you a bit before she lectures you about breaking rules. You've got to let her, all right? Moms worry. It's their job. They're also usually right about things, so make sure you listen, yeah?"

I bite back a smile. Bobby is *really* good at this stuff. I got a glimpse of it the other day, but this is next-level mentoring. He's made more progress in two chats than Blake or I have in the last three months!

"Okay. I will." Matty pauses and clears his throat. "Bobby, um, can you keep the part about what Raiden said to me the other day just between us?"

I huff out a frustrated breath through my nostrils. I am going to make sure this Raiden kid's bullying days are over if it's the last thing I do.

"You don't want your mom to worry," Bobby states instead of questions.

"Yeah."

Oh, god. I love my kid so much.

They're both silent for a long moment until Bobby replies, "I'll keep it between us if you promise to tell me or your parents the second Raiden says or does anything else, okay? *And* if you promise to keep your cool and do the exercises we talked about to control your temper. Got it?"

"Got it. Thanks for coming, Bobby. It's nice to have a dude that's not my dad to talk to, you know?"

My eyes suddenly fill with tears, but I shove them back, along with all my other regrets that serve no constructive purpose.

"A guy's got to have his boys, right?" Bobby extends his fist and Matty bumps it with his much smaller one.

They both push back their chairs, and I realize I'm about to get busted, so I hurry back through the aisles and sneak out the door before they turn the corner and see me. As soon as I'm outside, I turn back around and push through the doors again, entering the shabby fluorescent-illuminated shop to the confused expression of the cashier. I ignore him and wander toward the aisles.

"Mom!" Matty calls, and I pretend to be caught off guard.

"Matthew!" I rush his way and pull him into a hug. "Are you okay?" I sift my fingers through his hair and scan him from head to toe. He looks exactly the same as he did when he boarded the bus this morning, except there's an orange stain on his T-shirt. Since it matches the one on his lips, I use my remedial detective skills to conclude Bobby bought him a Fanta, his favorite.

"Yeah. I'm good. I also know I'm probably in trouble." He has the good grace to look sheepish.

"Why did you come down here?" It's one of the things my eavesdropping didn't answer.

"Ramona was fussing over me and asking me questions

and I was afraid I was going to lose my temper. So, I lied and said I was going to Tyler's. I just needed a minute to figure some things out, so I came down here." His eyes drop to his sneakered feet. "I know Bobby called you."

"Thank goodness he did. I would have been worried sick if I came home and there was no sign of you. Rules are there to keep you safe."

"I know. I'm sorry."

Bobby emerges from an aisle and steps closer. Now that I have more than an obstructed view, I can't help but take him in. He's clearly been running his fingers through his hair, leaving it a tousled and very sexy mess. Pair that with the light dusting of scruff on his chin and the form-fitting athletic shirt showcasing his pecs in glorious detail and I find myself a bit breathless.

"All right," I mutter to my son. "We'll talk more about this at home. Go hop in the car. I need to talk to Mr. Rhodes for a minute."

"He says we can call him Bobby."

"Mr. Rhodes is my dad," Bobby interjects. "If you met him, you'd understand."

I decide to leave that one for later and give Matty a gentle nudge. "Okay. Scoot." As soon as the doors close behind him, I turn back to Bobby and take a deep breath to steady myself. I barely even notice the stale hot dog scent filling the air. "I don't really know what to say. Thank you for . . . calling me." I don't want to let on that I eavesdropped, or I'd certainly thank him for a whole lot more than a phone call.

"No problem. He's a good kid. And he's got a decent head on his shoulders. I'll let him tell you what was going on today."

I nod, hoping to god he's right.

"So, uh, I'm headed out of town for the next five days so I'll be out of your hair." Bobby rubs a hand over the back of his neck. "I figured I should probably let some of your other clients get their fair share of time with you." His sheepish expression mirrors my son's so closely I want to laugh.

"Well, if I'm being honest, most of them aren't quite as fun as you."

"Oh yeah?" The dimples hit me with a one-two punch.

"Yeah." My responding smile is impossible to suppress. He's just so . . . tempting.

Bobby narrows his eyes and cocks his head to the side. "*Interesting.*" When he starts stroking his chin between a thumb and forefinger, I roll my eyes. I also start backing away while I'm still ahead.

"Thanks again. I'll talk to you soon, Bobby." I turn to the doors, throwing a wave over my shoulder.

"Is that a promise, Sparkle?"

Of course, I don't respond, but I can hear his laugh all the way to my car and my son.

Chapter Seventeen

Bobby

"What the fuck are you reading?" Alexi "Barzee" Barinov fires at me, kicking my feet where they're propped on my backpack.

My muffin almost rolls right out of my hand from the impact. I snatch it back, only losing a few crumbs to the floor. "Chill, bro. You almost made me drop my once-a-day sugary treat."

I snagged the last one from the tray of muffins when I joined the team for breakfast in a private banquet room at our hotel. I was late getting downstairs, mostly because I stayed up after our win last night, texting Molly until my phone hit me in the face and I had to admit defeat to the fatigue in the wee hours of the morning. Made me feel bad for Molly, who seemed to always be awake in those early morning hours. I make a mental note to ask the team trainer about that. Maybe there's something I can do to help her sleep better.

"Leave him alone. He's busy sexting some bunny again," Danny "Dan-O" Bright interjects as he walks by with his trash.

Somehow Coach talked him into being my babysitter for the trip and made him room with me like I'm some kind of juvenile that needs supervision. I thought he was asleep when I was texting Molly last night.

"Not some bunny," I snarl at his back.

"Ohhh, boy. Roadie's angry!" Pete "Forns" Fornier mocks me. He uses his uneaten banana as a gun, keeping it trained on me.

"Fuck off with that thing." I snap my book shut, convinced I'll never get back to it with these clowns around. And contrary to what everyone thinks of me, my anger management sessions with Ashley have been going well. I don't even have the urge to punch Forns in his ugly mug. "I'll have you know I'm messaging with a very respectable woman. Not a bunny." I glare at Dan-O as he comes back with napkins for all of us. He's such a dad.

"Is that right?" comes the flat voice of Coach Marsh.

We crane our necks and see him grab a plate off the table in front of the buffet before dishing up some of the eggs and bacon we nearly cleaned the hotel out of. With the help of Ashley, I've come to the conclusion that Coach Marsh isn't a bad coach, he just leads with tough love. And when you're new to the team and haven't taken the time to get to know us, that tough love just feels tough and not like anything close to love. Then again, this is his first time on this planet, so maybe he's still figuring stuff out too.

"Yes, that's right," I say proudly. "She's a businesswoman and a single mom. In fact, I've become somewhat of a mentor to her son."

Benny looks up from where he's been texting with Kaitlyn. He's having a hard time on his first road trip since Mei was born. Poor guy looks like he actually misses baby spit up and full diapers. It's a mystery to me, but he seems happy right now, shooting me a shit-eating grin.

"She finally gave you the time of day, huh?" He and Kaitlyn are well aware of my attraction to Molly. Mostly because Chloe has a big mouth and told them about me checking her out when she dropped Matthew off at practice.

Coach plops his plate down next to me. "I'd like to speak with Bobby privately."

The guys all look at each other in bewilderment before scraping their chairs back and heading out of the room. The silence is only broken by Coach shoveling scrambled eggs in his mouth. And that *does* make me want to punch someone in the face. I run through all the mental exercises Ashley's given me and then run through them again before Coach wipes his mouth with a napkin and addresses me.

"My wife seems to think you're the linchpin." He folds his hands over his slight paunch and assesses me.

"Uh . . ." I only met his wife once, the day after we were told Marsh would be our new coach. She was a small, dark-haired woman who was mostly unremarkable. I have no clue why she'd refer to me as a linchpin. I don't even really know what a linchpin is.

"She says that you're the key to getting this team gelling again."

I'm so confused. Is he mad at me? Little drops of spit aren't flying out of his mouth like I'm used to. He's just stating things and staring at me. It's highly unnerving. He's clearly waiting for an answer, and I have no idea what he wants from me.

"Uh, well. I would look toward Dan-O or Druggy for that. They've been with the team longer."

Coach is already shaking his head, and I brace for the inevitable yelling. "No, that's not what I'm looking for. You see, I came to Tampa, ready to lay down the law. Be the alpha. Get you boys in line." I'm nodding, yet I have no idea what the fuck he's talking about. "But it's not working. We're not gelling. We're not in a *flow* yet."

I pinch my arm and nearly jolt from the pain. Yep, not having a nightmare where I'm stuck in a conversation with Coach that makes absolutely no sense. When all else fails, I channel my inner Ashley and ask a question instead.

"How can I help you, Coach?"

It's apparently the right question because he smiles. Like, shows his teeth and his eyes crinkle up and everything. He claps me on the shoulder like my Dad used to do when us boys did something good instead of fucking things up.

"I'm impressed by your change in behavior so far, Bobby. I might not even have to saddle you with a roommate on our next road trip. How about we have dinner tonight and talk about it?"

I'm just barely able to hold back the grimace. Dinner with Coach is the last thing I want after an away game. First, no beer. Now, dinners with Coach? This growing up thing is utter bullshit.

"Can't wait, Coach," I finally squeeze the words through my throat.

He gives me a dismissive head nod and pulls out his cell phone. I take the opportunity to grab my backpack and get out of there. I have two hours before I need to be at the rink. Plenty of time to text Molly. I head for my room, only to see a tube sock hanging from the doorknob. I lift my gaze to the ceiling and groan. Isn't Dan-O too old to be whacking off to his wife on Facetime?

"Come on, Dan-O," I mutter, turning around and going back down the elevator to find a quiet place to curl up with my book and Molly. I end up in the courtyard of the hotel behind a green plant that's barely holding on in the Chicago chill air. I pull my jacket farther around me and crack my book open to page fifty-two of the *101 Questions to Ask Your Long-Distance Partner*. It's a little preemptive since we're not dating yet, but I saw it at the airport and figured it would be a good way to get to know Molly.

Me: Inquiring minds need to know: what's your love language, Sparkle?

Molly: Oh jeez, Ramona, my best friend, made me read that book after my divorce. Apparently, it's possible to score high in all five.

I wince, snuggling down into my jacket farther when the wind kicks up. Doesn't sound like she had a very good marriage. Clearly, she didn't, since they're divorced, but damn, did he not give her any forms of affection?

Me: Only extremely lovable people would score high in all five.

Molly: You're too kind. Or maybe a bit delusional . . .

Me: What's your ideal date?

Molly: April 25th

Me: ???

Molly: Oh my god! Have you not seen that romcom? You have to see it!!

Me: Invite me over to watch it with you when I get home Sunday night, and I'll make the popcorn.

Molly: I see what you did there.

Me: It's what I'm going to keep doing until you admit we'd have the best first date either one of us has ever had.

Molly: Think pretty highly of yourself, huh?

Me: No, I think highly of US.

Molly: Bobby . . .

Me: Molly . . .

Me: Do you think two people in a committed relationship should share their phone passwords?

Molly: What? Why are you asking me these questions? You asked a ton of questions last night too, now that I think about it.

Feeling like the jig is up, I pull out my phone and snap a selfie with my book purchase, a sheepish expression on my face. I send the picture to her and she answers right away.

Molly: That might be the cutest thing I've ever seen.

Me: Cute, as in, so cute I have to ask that man on a date??

Molly: Yes.

Me: I accept!

Me: Wait. Seriously, though. You're saying yes to a date? A real live, I'll plan it, pick you up, and pay for it date?

Molly: Well, yes, to all of that but the paying for it thing. We can split the cost.

Me: You'll have to fight me for the bill before I let that happen.

Molly: Bobby . . .

Me: Molly . . . Just let me bask in the warmth of your yes, okay?

Molly: Wish I was there to warm you up.

I squeeze my eyes shut and groan out loud. Fuck, why did this have to happen during an away streak? Molly is *flirting* with me. It's historic. Possibly a one-time thing. I don't want to give her enough time to rethink this date.

Me: What are you wearing? (And no, that's not a question from the book).

Molly: Well, I'm actually only wearing a towel. (And that's not me being flirtatious).

Me: Yes! See? Already feeling warmer. Wait, why are you in a towel? (And that's too bad. I like flirtatious Molly).

Molly: I went to a yoga class this morning that Coco recommended. And now I have a house to show one of my clients.

Me: So, it's true. I'm not your only client.

Molly: You're the only client I've agreed to go on a date with . . . (This is me flirting).

Me: All right I won't be mad. Especially won't be mad if you send me a selfie in your towel. (Just assume that every text I send you is me flirting with you).

I nearly melt the chair I'm sitting on when Molly sends me a selfie several minutes later. The lighting is low, and the high angle is perfect. I see her luscious boobs pressed into a white fluffy towel, the ends of her wet hair dangling into the shot. Her curvy legs below the towel end in fire engine red toenails that tempt me.

Me: Dammit, Molly. You're beautiful, and I can't wait to take you out on a date when I get back home.

Molly: You flirt very well, Mr. Rhodes. (PS-I intend to figure out your love language on our first date).

Benny yells across the courtyard that it's time to go. I slide the book in my backpack and hustle to the bus taking us to the rink for tonight's game.

I have three more nights to flirt with Molly. See, the key to a good date is knowing what matters to the girl. You don't show up with a box of chocolates if dairy makes her gassy. You don't take her to a wine and cheese pairing event if she's a recovering alcoholic. I'll get to know Molly as best I can long distance and then wow her on our first date. Like a proper fucking gentleman.

But first, I have to get through this dinner with Coach tonight.

Chapter Eighteen

Molly

"I did something," I confess the nanosecond Ramona opens her front door.

"Don't tease me." She beckons me in with impatient hands. She's still wearing her scrubs from work and has half of her dark braids arranged around the top of her head like a crown. When I start to speak, she shushes me. "Something tells me we need wine for this conversation. At least I hope so."

Once we're settled on the overstuffed couch in her living room, I'm finally permitted to share. "I agreed to go out on a date with the hockey player."

"Praise Jesus." Her eyes go to the ceiling. Ever since I filled Ramona in on everything from the kiss and the dating app snafu to Bobby showing up for Matty the other day, she's been firmly on Team Bobby.

Figuring I have nothing to lose, I decide to share every last detail. "And I sent him a half-naked selfie." I bite my lip and brace.

Ramona almost spills her Pinot Grigio on a throw pillow. "Shut the front door!" Good thing we opted for white.

I laugh and take a fortifying sip. "I honestly have no idea what's come over me, Ramona. We've been texting nonstop since he left town, and I'm starting to feel so . . . emboldened!" Who knew I could still flirt?

Bobby texting me that picture of him reading a relationship advice book was the straw that broke the camel's back and had me agreeing to a date. Although, I'll admit him opening up to me over the previous days' texts was probably enough. He's turning out to be so much more than I thought.

At this point, I can perfectly picture his poor mother surrounded by a gaggle of rowdy boys and pulling her hair out while his dad tried laying down the law. If Bobby's brothers are anything like him, their childhood home must have been filled with energy and humor.

He's just so thoughtful, not to mention funny and enthusiastic—and completely self-deprecating, which he must know makes me more comfortable letting my guard down. I even started telling him a bit about my childhood in return, something I don't usually talk about much.

We've texted about everything from his craziest hockey moments and his therapist to my path to Farnsworth Realty and my obsession with the nearly impossible to find key lime Twizzlers.

And then there's the genuine interest he appears to have in both me and Matty. Although, I'm hesitant to let Matty in on whatever this is between Bobby and me. He's finally started opening up a little, and I'd hate for him to get his hopes up about anything real happening with the man he clearly looks up to. Especially when this could crash and burn so easily.

"I'll tell you what's come over you," Ramona says, jarring me back to our conversation. "A man is finally worshipping the ground you walk on like every man should. You're a ten, Molly, just like I've always told you."

"To be fair, you didn't know me when I had bangs in high school."

"We all had bangs in high school. It's a right of passage." She sets her glass on the coffee table and focuses all her attention on me. "So, exactly how naked was this half-naked selfie?"

"All the important parts were covered."

Ramona nods and points at me. "Ah, leaving things up to the imagination. Clever move."

"I have no idea what I'm doing, but I finally just decided to throw caution to the wind and go on a date. How bad could I really be at dating, right? I mean, if Blake can date a man for the first time, I can date a *straight* man for the first time."

"Aha! I knew meeting Blake's new boyfriend would knock something loose."

She's right about that, of course. The other day, I dropped Matty off at Blake's apartment for the week. I'd called him after my talk with Matty about Raiden so he'd be up to date, and he mentioned he'd like to introduce Matty to his new boyfriend this week. When he asked my thoughts, I was at a loss since I didn't know how serious he and this guy were. But, in the end, I trust Blake, and I know he'll always put Matty first. That turned out to be the right move since Matty texted me this afternoon in good spirits and said he's having a great time.

What I didn't expect was to meet the boyfriend myself when I dropped Matty off. Blake pulled me aside and apologized for blindsiding me. Apparently, he and Luke, the boyfriend, got their signals crossed and Luke wasn't meant to be there when we arrived. It was probably better that way, anyway, though. Matty wasn't fazed at all, and I didn't have time to obsess or worry over the first meeting. Luke turned out to be really gracious and sweet.

But seeing the way he and Blake interacted left me full of all sorts of feelings. Their unconscious gestures of affection—a hand on the small of the back or a warm private smile—just further highlighted how very off my relationship with Blake had been. How forced it was by the end. Blake and Luke are clearly deeply in like, if not love, and I left the apartment with a sense of emptiness I haven't felt in a while.

I sigh and run my finger over the base of my wineglass. "I just . . . didn't expect it to make me feel so lonely."

Ramona tilts her head and sinks back into a cushion. "I think that makes perfect sense, babe. I mean, if Amir started dating someone, it would depress the hell out of me."

I choke out a laugh. "Ramona! You're still married to him and madly in love. It's hardly the same."

"Madly in love, my ass. I told you he ate my Chinese leftovers!"

"You're still mad at me about that?" Amir appears around the corner dressed in shorts and a form-fitting T-shirt. What is it with all these men and their pectorals on display?

Ramona purses her lips. "It was *shrimp dumplings*, Amir. It's gonna take more than six hours for me to get over it."

I take a sip of wine and smile up at my neighbor. "Hey, Amir, what is your love language?"

He dips his chin and looks at me like I just asked him to be my sperm donor. "My what language?"

"Never mind."

"Mine is food, obviously." Ramona glares at her husband. "Shrimp dumplings, in particular."

"I don't think that's one of the options," I inform my friend.

"Well, it should be."

Amir puts in a set of earbuds. Smart move. "I'm going for my run. Good luck, Molly."

Once he's out of earshot, I ask, "How long are you going to make him suffer?"

"Probably just a couple more hours." Ramona leans forward and snatches up her wine glass again. "Okay, so, back to your date with the young stud. Are we going for hot fling or potential relationship?"

I throw a palm out to her. "I have no idea. I can't think about that yet." But I drop my hand to the couch and ask, "It's crazy to consider actually dating a guy so much younger, isn't it?"

Even if he's starting to check all the boxes.

"I don't know. They say women and men reach their sexual peaks years apart, so it might be perfect. But you're probably right. Don't think about it too hard and just enjoy yourself."

"Every time I think about actually dating, my sweat glands go into overdrive. I haven't been naked in front of any man but Blake for *seventeen years*. You've seen Bobby. His body is like a marble statue. Mine is like . . . a child's Play-Doh version."

My words have Ramona rocketing forward in her seat, spine straight as board. "I know what you need! Do you trust me?"

Her maniacal expression has me draining my wine glass. "No. Not even a little."

"Why is he looking at me like that?" I mutter surreptitiously out of the side of my mouth.

Ramona and I watch the tall man with zero visible pores and immaculate head-to-toe black clothing in the mirror. He's eyeing me like a science project gone wrong.

"I think he's evaluating your bone structure to determine the right haircut," Ramona whispers.

My eyes go wide. "I think there's been a mistake!" I spin my chair to face Ramona where she stands beside me. "You said *makeover*, not haircut!"

She throws her hands up. "A haircut is part of a makeover. Have you never seen Oprah?"

"Ramona, my date is *tonight*! I don't have time for makeup *and* a haircut, even if I wanted one. I haven't even picked out my outfit yet!"

"I've got that covered, I told you."

The man, who introduced himself as Lars a few brief minutes ago, runs an index finger over my ponytail and interrupts, "The hairpiece is tragic."

I meet his eyes in the mirror. "It's worse without it, I assure you. Can we just skip to the makeup?"

He purses his lips and studies my face again. "Am I permitted to address the unibrow or is that off limits too?"

I gasp and bring a hand up to cover my forehead. "I don't have a unibrow!"

Ramona drops a hand onto my shoulder and bends down. "Molls, you may have gotten a little lazy with the tweezers. Let the man work."

I drop my hand to my lap and scowl. "It's probably my eyesight. It keeps getting worse every year." I shoot my gaze to Lars again. "Fine, do what you must." I throw up a finger. "But no haircut."

Twenty minutes later, I've completely given up and

decided to let Lars and Ramona have their way with me. It's much easier this way, and besides, Bobby is texting me.

> Bobby: Our flight is getting in a little early. You mind if I come at six-thirty instead of seven?

> Me: It's been a while since I've been on a date, but even I know a guy can't show up early.

> Bobby: Then I'll try to amuse myself until seven. You sell any houses since this morning?

> Me: No, but I finally got my commission check from my toughest sale yet. Cocktails on me tonight!

> Bobby: Congrats! But I'll be paying for the cocktails.

> Me: We'll see.

> Bobby: What are you up to right now?

Since there's no way I'm telling him I'm getting a makeover, I fudge a little.

> Me: Hanging out with my friend Ramona. You know, girl stuff.

> Bobby: Ah. In other words, I should mind my own business?

> Me: Ha! Maybe.

Bobby: Okay, I'll let you go. I've got some guy stuff to do anyway. Can't wait to see you tonight.

I grin down at my phone just as Lars spins my chair back around. When I look up into the mirror, I hardly recognize myself. My hair has been styled into soft waves that disguise my thinning areas, and my makeup is a couple notches above what I'd normally do while still managing to look natural and effortless. Lars's deft hand has made my eyes look huge, and I somehow have the cheekbones of a Hollywood starlet.

"Now that's what I'm talking about!" Ramona declares. I meet her eyes in the mirror and laugh. My laugh turns into a coughing fit, however, when she continues with, "Time for your waxing appointment. That kitty's not gonna strip itself!"

Chapter Nineteen

Bobby

"You need to calm down," I tell myself in the rearview mirror of Wolverine. Myself doesn't listen.

Wolverine does though. Soft music flows through the speakers. I'm parked half a block down from Molly's place, twenty minutes early for our date, knee jumping in nervous anticipation. I scrub a hand down my face and turn away from the mirror in disgust. Since when does Bobby Rhodes get nervous about a girl?

Maybe since the girl is way too good for him.

That stupid voice in my head won't shut up. It was squawking as I bought the biggest bouquet of flowers the shop had. It whispered in my ear as I went to three different stores before I found key lime Twizzlers. It was practically screaming as I checked my favorite Gucci wallet for condoms before heading out the door. Not that I intend to sleep with Molly tonight. *But a guy can't be too prepared*, has always been my motto. Actually, I've never had a motto. Mottos would mean I put time and thought into it, and let's be honest, I usually just fly by the seat of my very stylish pants.

I rest my head back and close my eyes, taking long, measured deep breaths. My session with Ashley early this morning involved visualization, a technique used for things that chronically make me angry. Turns out it's pretty useful for nervousness too. The bats in my stomach are finally calming down. Maybe Coach should have Ashley do a session with the whole team. Now that he and I are pals, maybe he'll take my suggestion.

I laugh out loud as I visualize that dinner with him. Talk about awkward. He ordered oysters first thing, and I thought maybe he was trying to hit on me. What guy orders oysters at dinner with another guy?

Coach actually just loves oysters, which is one of the many things I found out about him. He tried to be my friend, which was a move I wasn't expecting. I obliged, and by the end of dinner, I found myself actually liking the guy. He's still a dick on the ice, but taking the time to get to know me on a friendly level somehow makes his tough love palatable.

I suggested he do the same with each guy on the team. Which is why I'm laughing, thinking of all my teammates having to endure dinner with Coach. Serves those fuckers right. They gave me so much shit about my book and texting Molly, they deserve to slurp oysters with Coach over candlelight.

I check my watch again and put the car in drive when I see it's ten to seven. Close enough. We can just get to our reservation at the Rusty Pelican early. I already tipped the maître d' enough to warrant getting a table a little early when I went in and begged for a last minute reservation straight off the airplane.

My heart starts beating fast and hard as I see a single light on in her house. I turn off the car and tug on the cuffs of my shirt, which is lime green to match the Twizzlers. I grab the bouquet of flowers with the package of candy tucked inside and head for the front door. I could swear the curtains on the house next door move, but then Molly's big white door is opening and my entire being is focused on her.

"Damn . . ." I mutter under my breath, completely taken aback by the vision in front of me.

She's clutching the door like it's holding her up, but when I see the mile-high stilettos on her feet, it makes sense. She's in a new pencil skirt, this one lacy and a deep burgundy that matches her lipstick. The black silk blouse has a flouncy bow at her breast, making her look like a present I want to unwrap and devour. Her gorgeous eyes are wide and unsure as she looks at me from under thick lashes. Her hair is down and curled, looking thick enough to get both of my fists lost in the strands. She looks fucking amazing. But also different.

I try to shake off the fog and act like the gentleman I lectured myself about being. "You look . . ."

"Ridiculous?" she offers, forehead wrinkling.

I step inside her house, my loafers toe to toe with her heels as I hold the bouquet out to the side so I can look deep into her eyes. Shit. I'm already fucking this up if she's belittling herself because I can't seem to form words.

"No. You look stunning. Unbelievably good. So good I could forget dinner entirely and just eat you. So fucking hot I don't know if I want to take you out and share you with other people. You look so beautiful I want only my eyes on you, or I might be insanely jealous of everyone else."

Her eyes widen and I keep going, refusing to be another man in her life that makes her feel less than. My free hand skims over her hip and slides around her waist, pulling her into me. "I've been waiting for days to lay eyes on you and now I know why. You're like oxygen, necessary and life-giving."

Her lips purse and tremble as she blinks up at me. "Wow."

I nod, arm tightening around her waist. "Yeah," I whisper back, leaning down to pluck a kiss from her lips while inhaling her familiar scent. She opens for me immediately, her hands sliding up my arms and over my shoulders. I step farther into her and she steps back. I follow, my tongue delving inside to taste her, desperate for more from this woman. Feeling like we're on display and not wanting that, I flail my leg and whack the door. The thing slams shut and the noise makes Molly jump in my arms. She gasps and then grins at me while we both breathe hard.

"I'll say it again. Wow."

I think I might make it a personal challenge to get more wows out of her before the night is up. I release her just the tiniest bit and offer her the flowers. She looks down at them with surprise, like she didn't see them when I knocked on her door. I really fucking like that she only had eyes for me too.

"Oh my god, you found the Twizzlers?" She looks up at me, mouth popped open. "You remembered?"

I frown and pluck the candy from the bouquet. "Of course I remembered. My girl says she likes key lime Twizzlers, you bet I'm going to find them for her."

Heat sweeps across Molly's face. "Your girl, huh?"

I put the flowers down on a small dining table a few feet away from us. Her place is small but charming, exactly as I would have envisioned Molly's space. Back in front of her, I rip open the candy. "Lucky for you, we're a little early for our reservation. Plenty of time for me to feed you a Twizzler." I slide one out of the package and tease the end against her lips. "Open, baby."

Molly tips her head back and opens her mouth, eyes twinkling in the lamplight coming from beside the couch behind us. I slide the candy in and watch her tongue circle it. Everything below my belt tightens painfully.

"Can't tell you how much I like you trusting me," I say

roughly, incredibly turned on watching her take my candy in her mouth. And yes, I wish that was a euphemism for something else.

Molly closes her mouth on the candy and bites down, snapping off the piece that's in her mouth. "Now you try it."

I hand her the candy. "Feed me." She grins, sucking on her candy while she does a helicopter move I've seen moms do to their toddlers. I burst out laughing and that's when she pops it in my mouth.

"Suck on it and tell me if you like it," she says with a voice so sultry, I'm not sure how I'm going to be able to make it through dinner in public without being indecently turned on. I bite off a piece and wince as the sugary tart taste bursts in my mouth.

"I like it, but I like tasting you better," I answer.

Molly shifts closer, her hand trailing up my torso, making every muscle twitch in her wake. Her finger slides into my open collar and touches the skin at my neck. Why does her innocent touch feel better than all the puck bunnies who ever existed combined?

"Molly?"

"Huh?" Her eyes look like she's drugged, half-mast and thoroughly distracted as she traces back and forth over my exposed skin.

"If you don't stop touching me right now, we're not going to make it to dinner." My voice is barely above a rumble at this point. Pretty sure I'll have to think about oysters and dinner with Coach if I'm ever going to get this erection to go down enough to be in public.

Molly's eyes widen as she finally focuses. Then, with a wicked arch to her brow, she reaches up with her other hand and unbuttons my shirt so she has more skin to caress. My body is humming with excitement, not at all concerned with skipping dinner. That's a green-fucking-light if I've ever seen one.

"I warned you." I give her one last chance to say no, but the little vixen tweaks my nipple instead. Not to the point of pain, but hard enough all the blood rushes through my ears as it heads south.

I slide my hand to cup the nape of her neck and slam my lips down on hers. I'm not careful or sweet or tentative as I take her mouth. She tastes like key lime and MILF. This woman has driven me crazy, and I need her out of these proper clothes right fucking now.

My hand fumbles with the zipper at the back of her skirt, then slides up her silky-smooth back to find some way out of this blouse. Her skirt falls to the floor, but my watch is now caught in her blouse. I break away from her mouth and take in the black lacy panties she's wearing. Combine that with the sexy stilettos and the tiny little puffs of air coming from her lipstick-stained lips, and I'm fucking done for.

"Can you get this blouse off before I rip it?" I manage to ask between clenched teeth.

Molly huffs out a laugh, but reaches below her armpit to some secret zipper that only women know about. Down it goes, and suddenly my watch is free as I get the blouse over her head and thrown to the ground. Her breasts are absolutely insane in a matching black lace bra that pushes them up and together. I drop my forehead to hers and squeeze my eyes shut so I don't embarrass myself like a teen boy.

"Fuck, Molly," I groan.

"Fuck good or fuck bad?" she whispers back.

My eyes fly open. I grab her hand and press it against my fully erect cock. "You tell me, baby."

Her eyes go wide but she doesn't pull away. I let go of her hand, and still she stays there, stroking light fingers up and down my dick over my pants. A shiver racks my body.

"Damn that feels good."

"I want you to feel good," she whispers back sweetly.

I run my fingers through her hair and kiss her again before breaking away. "Anything you do will make me feel good. Believe me. I just gotta last long enough to make sure *you* feel good."

Molly's teeth find her lower lip. Then she says something and I swear I'm trying to listen but her fingers keep stroking me and it's nearly impossible.

"It doesn't always happen."

Belatedly, my brain kicks into gear. I pull back and stare down at this beautiful woman, sure I misinterpreted. "What doesn't always happen?"

She shrugs like I asked if she wanted chocolate ice cream or vanilla. But this topic is like heading to the finals and losing to Toronto and asking if I'm upset about the loss. It's a big fucking deal.

"Orgasm through sex."

Now I'm angry. Not in the lose-my-shit-and-make-a-mess-of-things kind of way. More like, I will prove this woman wrong if it's the last thing I do on this green earth. I let go of her, only to dip down and pick her up, princess style. She lets out a surprised whoop and winds her arms around my shoulders. I stalk over to the couch and sit her down, shoving her knees apart with my shoulders and making room for myself as I crouch down.

"Lift," I bark, hooking my fingers in her panties and tugging. She complies and I peel them off her body, tucking them into my pants pocket. She's wet, glistening in the lamplight. The skin around her pubic bone is bright pink, waxed clean. Molly shifts her hips, like she's nervous.

I wrench my gaze away from the prettiest pussy I've ever seen and stare her down until she looks at me. "Did you wax this for me, baby?"

She licks her lips and nods, face taking on the same shade of pink. I grin, insanely touched that she put in so much effort for our date, also assuming we'd end up right here. "I love it. But for future reference, you don't have to go to those lengths for me. I don't like you in pain for some beauty standard you think you have to hit. Now put those heels on my shoulders so I can finally taste you."

Molly sucks in air, but does as she's told, resting first one and then the other calf on my shoulders.

"That's it. Now relax and let me prove you wrong."

Molly huffs, but it quickly turns to a moan as I kiss my way up one inner thigh and then the next. Her skin is so soft. So fucking perfect. I'm shaking by the time I let myself lick her center, one long drag, bottom to top, that tells me just how wet she is for me. Molly gasps above me and I smile against her flesh. It's going to be so much fun proving her wrong. Over and over again.

Molly

I'm having an out-of-body experience right here on my own couch—the same one where I watch *The Office* with my kid and eat Pringles out of the can while promising myself I'll start my diet next week.

And the only stitch of clothing I'm wearing is the black lace push-up bra Ramona insisted I buy. Best friends are absolute geniuses! She also made me promise to allow myself to let go tonight and live dangerously, and I'm so glad she did.

It's thrilling being a wanton vixen for once in my life, taking chances and doing whatever strikes me. I pinched Bobby's nipple and threw myself at him, for goodness' sake! And he clearly liked it! Maybe this is the start of Molly 2.0 and I'm finally entering my sex goddess era.

I moan into the quiet of the room, my back arching off the couch and causing me to slide farther down. Bobby murmurs something against my clit before flicking it with his tongue. I react by digging my heels into his shoulder blades so hard I'm afraid I might impale him with my stilettos.

Does every straight adult man know how to do this expertly, or did I just luck out with Bobby? Because I can say with certainty that my two high school and college boyfriends were complete amateurs. And Blake? He generally avoided the task, which was fine with me. The last thing you want is for your sexual partner to engage in an activity that doesn't turn them on.

But I can tell from the sounds Bobby is making over my clit that going down on me is his version of a kid in a candy store. Who knew? I can't wait to return the favor.

He licks and nuzzles my center again before his tongue delves inside me, and a shiver of ecstasy consumes my entire body. I'm hot and cold, relaxed and restless, excited and scared shitless—all at the same time.

"Fuck, you taste good," Bobby rumbles when he comes up for air, never giving me a moment of reprieve as his fingers take over where his tongue left off. They twist and swirl, working me into a frenzy that has only one place to go.

His lips and clean-shaved chin glisten in the lamplight, and I'm too turned on to be embarrassed or freaked out to know it's my own arousal on his skin. I open my mouth to say something, but the only thing to come out is another moan when he hooks his finger inside me and hits the bullseye like a master archer. Damn, he's good at this—and I refuse to ponder the reason. Nope.

When his tongue rejoins his talented fingers, it's only seconds until my cry of release bounces off the living room walls. It's so loud I wonder afterward if Ramona and Amir heard it and thought a cat was dying outside. My body trembles and spasms with aftershocks as I revel in the feeling of an orgasm that wasn't self-induced for once. Bobby groans in satisfaction and licks my center with a thoroughness that reminds me of the way I clean up the last remnants of brownie batter from the mixing bowl.

My fingers begin screaming in protest, and it's only now I realize that I've had a death grip on the edges of the couch cushion under me this whole time. I release it and try catching my breath as I shake my cramped hands out.

"Hmm." Bobby's head pops up from between my legs and he shoots me a smug grin as he watches my flapping hands. "That's a new one. Must have been quite the orgasm if you're fingers are on fire."

I scowl at him, still breathing hard from said orgasm. "My hands are cramped." My eyes shift from his face to my thighs where they cradle his head and then to my belly where the silver of my stretch marks catches the light from the lamp. I was so caught up in the moment, I forgot to be self-conscious of all my body's flaws. I reflexively snatch up a throw pillow and drop it on my belly.

"What the—" Bobby gets cut off when a tassel tries to blind him.

"Oh! Sorry!" I unhitch my legs from his shoulders and scramble to a seated position, the throw pillow acting as armor.

Bobby rubs at his eye, dropping back to rest his butt on his heels. Then he puts his pro athlete reflexes to work by swiping the pillow from my lap and hurling it across the room in one fluid motion.

I gasp.

Bobby grins.

I cross one leg over the other and cover my belly with my arms.

Bobby eyes my barely covered breasts, eyebrows raised in challenge.

"Bobby." I frown at him.

"Baby," he coos at me. "Cover all you want. It just means I get to unwrap you again."

"Bobby," I say again, this time popping off my death-trap stilettos and stopping him with a bare foot to his chest when he creeps closer. I just need a second to get my head together.

But my date clearly has other plans. He removes my foot, cradling it gently in one hand while he wipes his mouth and chin with a swipe of his shirt sleeve—all the while closing the distance between us until my knees are pressed into his gut.

"Baby," he whispers this time, right before he leans into me and kisses me long and deep.

I've always thought a lover calling me baby would be a mood killer, but coming from Bobby, it's an absolute turn on. I lose focus on whatever I'm supposed to be thinking about. Something about not moving too fast? Or reminding myself this is only about fun? Whatever it is, it will have to wait for later.

I free my arms and hands from where they're crushed between us, one going to the back of Bobby's neck and the other reaching out to the side to switch the lamp off. There, that's better. The kiss continues, and I revel in it until I hear another click and open my eyes to see that Bobby has just switched the lamp on again.

Not so fast, wise guy. I break the kiss to let my lips travel to his jaw and then his ear. He hisses when my tongue finds a spot that has him shivering. I lick it again and click the light off.

Bobby jerks back and reaches over to switch it on again. "On," he insists.

I bat his hand away and switch it off. "Off." When he reaches for it again, I grab his hand with both of mine and bring it to my mouth where I slide his index finger between my lips and swirl my tongue around it before giving it a firm suck.

"*Fuuuck meee*," he groans distractedly. "Off it is."

Before I can even momentarily revel in my victory, Bobby rises to his feet and finishes unbuttoning his shirt one-handed. With the light off, I can barely make out the firmly muscled chest and abs I've felt through his clothes. I continue teasing his finger until I have to let him go to allow the shirt to drop to the floor. Then, with alarming speed, Bobby shucks his slacks and underwear in one motion, releasing what I'm sure is a rock-hard cock. But I can't really see it, dammit!

Not letting my squinting eyes stray from the man before me, I reach out for the lamp once more and click the switch. "On."

I hear him chuckle, but my eyes are riveted to the thick, long, impossibly hard cock that bobs between us. My mouth begins to water. I've never in my life had my mouth water at the sight or thought of a man's cock. Yet here I am.

He says something, but I'm too busy admiring his penis to register what it is until he repeats himself. "Molly." My eyes dart up to meet his, and I find two warm brown pools gazing down at me with molten desire.

It's a look I don't remember ever having seen before from any man. Like if he can't have me right now, he might actually perish.

And I feel the exact same way.

So, I uncross my legs and stand, allowing my arms to fall to my sides before I reach behind my back and unhook my bra. The flimsy scrap of lace falls to the floor and there I am. There *we* are. Fully naked. Fully revealed.

Bobby swallows hard before speaking in a tight voice. "God, you're beautiful."

"So are you," I whisper. My heart is a bass drum in my chest, booming faster and louder each second as we stand and look at each other.

Bobby finally reaches out and pulls me to him, letting his hands rove my curves as his mouth takes mine again. My hands are happy to do their own exploring. He's smooth and firm everywhere. Even his ass is perfectly tight, which probably shouldn't surprise me. He is a professional athlete, after all. It's his job to be fit. But I can't believe this is my life right now!

Our embrace becomes a fever-pitched contest to see who can cover more ground than the other with our roaming hands and lips until I find myself pinned down under Bobby on my living room carpet. I hear the vague crinkling of what I deduce is a condom wrapper. Shit! I hadn't even thought about that. Shows how out of practice I am.

Bobby rises to his knees and wastes no time rolling the condom on his length and then settling his weight over me again. His elbows fall to either side of me, supporting his weight as his eyes roam my face and his thumbs brush my cheeks. The fever has ebbed for a minute as we stare wordlessly at one another.

I realize he's waiting for me—giving me a chance to back out if I want to. But I am fully on board with this, so I let my fingertips skate down the ridges of his broad shoulders and back until I slide one down to reach between us and take him in my hand. When my knees fall open, he slowly lowers himself to drop a gentle, almost reverent, kiss on my lips as he notches himself at my entrance and nudges into me with care.

"Bobby," I sigh his name as he retreats and presses forward again until he's half seated.

"Fucking hell, Molly. You're so tight," he practically wheezes, and something about it makes me laugh. This, in turn, makes him groan loudly and shut me up with a hard kiss to my lips. When he pulls out this time, he holds nothing back, thrusting forward to fill me completely. My head falls back on a silent cry as I wrap my legs around him, ready to take everything he has to give.

I'm more full than I've ever been, but I need him to move. I need friction and pressure along with this delicious fullness.

But I don't need to tell him that because, in the next moment, Bobby pulls halfway out before thrusting all the way in again, beginning to establish a rhythm that works me up into a panting mess.

The strokes that began carefully increase gradually in power and abandon, our sighs and groans filling the air around us. My eyes fall shut as I focus on everything he's doing to my body. He's in complete control of it, working me up to what I fear might be an orgasm big enough to kill me. But what a way to go.

He smells like clean sweat, sandalwood, and pepper, and I breathe him in as if he's life-giving oxygen while our bodies, slick with perspiration, slide against one another's. My eyes flutter open to see his intense gaze locked on mine as he powers in and out of me. It's the hottest thing I've ever experienced in my life, and I don't want it ever to end. Of course, I change my mind when a familiar fluttering sends my pelvis pulsing and Bobby fuses his mouth to mine in a searing kiss as I begin to come apart.

Chapter Twenty-One

Bobby

Molly is everything I love about older women. Younger women almost scare me with their enthusiasm and eagerness to show their bodies. I prefer an older woman who leaves things to my imagination, because believe me, my imagination is better than anything you can show me in a short skirt and see-through shirt. Take for example, Molly's pencil skirts. Those things have had me twisted inside for weeks. And then I get to peel one off her like she's some kind of present under the Christmas tree? I'm officially feeling like that mind blown emoji.

"I need to take care of this condom but I don't think I can feel my toes," I huff, out of breath, sure I'm squashing her into the floor, but helpless to do anything about it.

"I think I have rug burn on my back," Molly replies and then starts giggling, her body shaking.

Which makes her muscles clench around me, and I'm suddenly interested in another round right this very second.

But not on the floor. Jesus, I didn't even take her out on our date, and I just gave her rug burn fucking her on the floor. I'll be damn lucky if she's not pissed at me. I pull out of her warm body and make quick work of things before coming back to her with a fresh condom in hand. Gingerly, I pick her up off the floor, cradling her in my arms.

"What are you doing?" Molly's suddenly wide awake, slapping at my bare chest. "Put me down. I can walk!"

"Nuh uh." I sweep her out of the living room, only to face a hallway I've never seen before. "Point the way."

She sighs, probably realizing I have no intention of putting her down. "Over there. Last door."

I grin at her tone, liking that about her too. That motherly tone does something to me that might make me sick in the head if I examine it too long. I probably won't be mentioning to Ashley that I get off on being scolded. Not really an anger management issue, unless you count a vigorous fucking as an inappropriate reaction.

My foot nudges the door open and her bedroom appears, looking just like her. Neat bed spread, decor simple but feminine, and her perfume infused through everything. Now's probably not the time to tell her I stole her perfume. I put her down, pull back the covers, and help her get under them before sliding in behind her and spooning her backside. She yelps when I tighten my arm around her and tuck her head under my chin. My dick presses up against her luscious ass, already halfway to where I need him to be for round two.

"Shh. Just let me hold you for a second. I'll be ready to go again in minutes. I promise."

She begins to shake again. "Ah, youth."

My hand roams, finding her breasts and getting a handful. I didn't get a chance to pay them much attention before and I'd like to correct that error as soon as possible. Her nipples stiffen under my fingers. Molly lets out a soft moan and reaches behind her to grip my dick. Her shocked, "Oh!" makes me grin.

"Told you." She scoffs and goes to roll onto her back, but I hold her in place. "Let me touch you for a bit. With all those flickering lights, I didn't get to feel this incredible body of yours."

"It was a bit like a strobe light," she admits on a sigh as I roll her nipple between my fingers. I lean down and kiss the back of her shoulder. I can feel her tensing everywhere I touch her, and that just won't do.

I roll her over onto her stomach, hands massaging her shoulders and back. Long sweeps up her spine, followed by deep rubs with my thumbs into her low back. When I feel her finally relaxing, I go a little lower, paying special attention to those curves that have teased me in her skirts.

"Bobby," she starts. Probably to say something ridiculous about her body that I won't agree with.

"Shh," I say. My hands grip her hips and tug upward. "Lift up, baby."

She does after a single second of hesitation. I feel between her legs, smiling smugly in the dim light of the moon when I feel how wet she is for me. I roll the condom on, making sure I keep one finger on her swollen clit. My other hand leaves her hip to notch myself at her entrance. I slide in, a little easier this time but no less impactful. Molly arches her back like a cat.

"Fuck, Molly," I moan, eyes squeezing shut to try to tamp the urge to unleash on her.

"Don't hold back. Please, Bobby," she whimpers.

"Ah fuck." I release the hold I had on myself and thrust hard and fast into her, watching the way her ass jiggles with each movement.

The slap of my flesh hitting hers is loud and glorious, and makes me want to slam into her harder. Her moans have turned to cries and for a split second I worry I'm being too hard. Molly takes that second to push her hips back onto my dick like she needs more, right fucking now. So I give it to her, over and over again until her body flattens into the bed with a loud, boneless cry and she's pulsing around my cock. I grip her hips and take what I need to get there, spilling into her and collapsing on top of her yet again.

After a few hours of pillow talk that makes my cheeks hurt from smiling so much, we eventually fall asleep, but something wakes me up several times in the night. Each time, I use the opportunity to fuck her again since she seems to be awake too. Around four in the morning, she begs me to make it stop after she comes long and hard, nearly bent in half and her toes hitting the headboard.

She's not in the bed when I wake up the next morning, which is disappointing. I had plans for her to ride my face so I could look up at her spectacular boobs.

I slip on a pair of pajama pants I found in her second drawer. They're a bit tight and have dancing chickens on them, but I'm pretty sure my underwear is out in the living room so this will have to do.

I find Molly in the kitchen, a silky blue robe tied around her waist and her back to me as the coffee pot burbles on the counter. There's a knock at the door that ruins my surprise of sneaking up behind her. Molly nearly jumps out of her robe at the knock and then sees me, jumping again. Her gaze instantly falls to the ridiculous outline of my dick in these chicken pants. I shrug. But she has bigger troubles because her front door is opening, and a woman's voice is calling.

"Knock, knock, anyone home?"

Molly rushes past me, but I snag her arm and pull her back, sneaking a quick kiss on her lips. "Good morning, baby."

Her entire face goes up in flames. "M-morning."

I release her and she hustles to intercept a dark-skinned

woman with twinkling eyes under a head wrap. But the woman sees me before Molly can make herself a human screen, her mouth dropping open as she gives me a full-body once over. Maybe I should cover up, but then again, Molly invited me over. It's this woman who's interrupting our morning together.

"Well, I guess that's my answer about how last night's date went, huh?" The woman's face lights up and I instantly like her. "I'm Ramona, Molly's BBF."

I walk over and stick out my hand to shake hers. "Did you mean BFF?"

Ramona flashes a brilliant white smile. "Nope. I'm her best bitch forever. BFF is kind of basic, don't you think?"

I take my hand back and wrap my arm around Molly's waist, tugging her into my side. She lands with a soft grunt and wrings her hands in front of her waist. "Best bitch has a better ring to it," I agree. "Did you want to join us for some coffee?"

Ramona instantly agrees. I look down to see Molly giving her a deadly glare. "It's okay for Ramona to join us, right, fluffernutter?"

Molly's elbow jabs me in the gut the same time Ramona barks out a belly laugh. "Oh my god, I love it. Please tell me she has a nickname for you too."

"Actually, I need to get to work, so you better take that coffee to go, Ramona." Molly finally finds her voice. Ramona and I just share a look and head for the coffee pot.

"She likes to call me Mister Whiskers," I share as Ramona pours a cup and hands it to me black.

Molly interrupts. "No, I don't. That was a joke."

I shrug and take a sip. Ramona dumps several spoonfuls of sugar into her cup. "I call her baby and Sparkle too, but she hasn't called me anything cutesy. Although, when she calls me Robert, that also does it for me."

Ramona is looking back and forth between us like seeing us together has made her entire week. "Oh, I bet. Molly can do a really good teacher voice."

"Yes!" I snap my fingers. "I've heard it and it's . . ." I waggle my eyebrows.

Ramona points to the tight pants I'm wearing. "Oh, we're all too aware of how much you like it, believe me. Not that I'm complaining."

Molly drops her flaming face into her hand. "Don't you have a practice to get to, *Robert*?"

I put my mug down and stand right in front of her, cupping her face to make her look at me. "See, there you go again, using that tone, baby." Her hands drop to my chest and the problem with the pants gets worse. I place a kiss on her lips, making her eyes go wide. "I do have practice to get to, but can I get a re-do on our date? Since we never made it out of the house?"

Ramona gasps behind me, but my focus is on Molly. Her skin feels like the face of the sun in my hands. I release her to wrap my arms around her waist and draw her into me one last time. "Please. I'll be a perfect gentleman. Except if you wear a pencil skirt. Then I don't think I can be held accountable for my actions."

Molly huffs, but nods. "I'd like a date with you."

I'm grinning ear to ear. I kiss her again, lingering a little longer this time. I just can't help myself around this woman. "Okay, I'll call you when I get out of practice."

And then I let her go so I can grab my clothes off the floor where we left them last night, ignore the fact I can feel two sets of eyes on my ass in these pants, grab my keys, and head out to my truck. I don't even care if the neighbors see me in Molly's pajama pants. I'm too happy to be worried about the fashion police. An hour later, when I finally get to practice after showering and changing at my place, I still can't wipe the grin off my face.

"What is wrong with your face?" Druggy asks in his heavy accent, warming up before sliding onto the ice.

"Nothing, dude. This is called a smile. You should try it sometime." I copy his moves.

"I save all my smiles for Chloe and Ayana."

I roll my eyes. "Yeah, we know." Those two are the only humans on the planet that can make Druggy seem like a normal, happy guy.

"Uh oh, Bobby finally got a date with the MILF?" Cappy sing-songs as he skates by at a snail's pace in his warm up pads.

I feel irritation at anyone else calling her a MILF, but oddly, there's no pounding heart or sheet of red that coats my vision. "It was only a matter of time, boys. Watch and learn from the master."

"More like master-*bater*," Dan-O snickers as he takes the ice.

"Says the guy spanking the monkey in our hotel room with your wifey on the phone," I holler at his back. The guys just cheer him on. There's no shame among hockey players.

"At least I have a wife, Roadie!"

The boys all hoot and holler, a few even shouting "burn!" like we're in fifth grade. I step out onto the ice and grin like an idiot, happy for the day, happy to be with these assholes, and happy I have another date to plan with my woman.

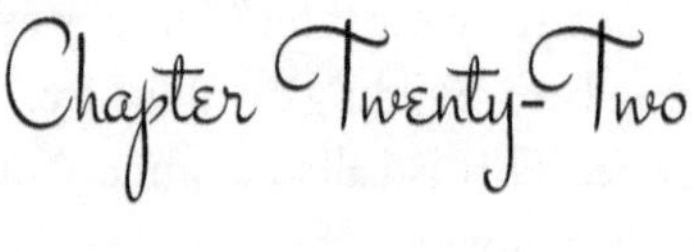

Chapter Twenty-Two

Molly

"Did we leave room for dessert?" the waiter asks with a lift of his manicured eyebrows.

"Actually, we've got that covered already," Bobby answers before I can even contemplate forcing another bite of food into my full belly.

It's been four days since Bobby modeled my pajama pants for Ramona in my kitchen, and they've been the best four days of my entire year. Bobby is so attentive, full of energy, and easy to be with he makes me feel like I'm in my twenties again. And he's performed a miracle on my sexual confidence.

The waiter nods and retreats as I shoot my date a quizzical look. He's dressed in a knit polo shirt with charcoal slacks that fit him like a glove and his hair tamed with some type of styling product. He looks good enough to eat—if I weren't already so full, I mean.

"I picked up a key lime pie earlier. It's back at my place."

"Ah, very sneaky."

"I have no idea what you're talking about." He feigns innocence, both dimples popping when he can't hold the expression. I wonder what the other patrons would think if I climbed over the table right now and straddled him right there in his chair.

"I should probably tell you now that I get Matty back tomorrow, which means no more sleepovers, Mr. Rhodes." I dab my lips with the white cloth napkin and drop it on my empty plate.

"*Mr.* Rhodes? How formal. But you forget I've seen you naked, Sparkle."

The waiter returns to drop our check, but Bobby hands him his credit card before the leather folder even hits the table. As soon as we stepped into the restaurant two hours ago, I made up my mind not to fight Bobby for the check. The menu doesn't have prices listed, which told me it was *way* above my budget. I'll pay when I choose the restaurant. I hope Bobby likes ramen.

I wait until we're alone again to respond, "How can I forget? Every time I move a muscle, I'm reminded of our activities."

Bobby frowns. "You didn't tell me that. Did I hurt you?"

I laugh. "No. I'm just way out of practice, that's all."

"Well, I'm more than happy to get you back into the habit."

"How very noble of you."

Bobby signs the check and then stands to escort me through the dining room. I catch more than a few pairs of eyes trained our way, reminding me I'm out with a local celebrity and have opened myself to public scrutiny. Damn.

I can't help the heat rising to my face when a woman whispers to another at her table and they both laugh. They don't even try to pretend they're not talking about us! What happened to female solidarity?!

When we step out onto the sidewalk, the night is unseasonably cool, and the breeze feels fantastic on my heated skin. Bobby drapes an arm around my shoulder and pulls me closer as we walk to the valet stand.

"You cold?"

I shake my head and muster a smile, not wanting to let him in on my discomfort. I went into this with my eyes wide open. I knew he was a public figure just like I knew I was twelve years older—and look it. Why do I even care what other people think?

When we get to his building, he parks his truck in the underground garage and opens my door like a gentleman before we take the elevator to the thirtieth floor.

"Soon, you'll have a house and won't have to wait for elevators or make five trips to get your groceries upstairs anymore," I say as we head down a carpeted hall.

"Would it be tacky of me to admit I get my groceries delivered most of the time?" he asks with a sheepish look that only makes me smile.

"Not at all."

Bobby pulls out a set of keys and unlocks a door at the end of the hall before holding it open for me. I step through, craning my neck to tell him I'd do delivery too in his shoes when a stranger's voice has me jumping in my heels instead.

"I promise I'm not jerking off this time, Boberto!"

"Motherf—" Bobby cuts himself off, quickly shutting the door behind us and sidestepping me to place himself between me and whoever just spoke.

"Richie! I swear to god I'm taking back your key."

Richie? His brother! Crap! I'm not ready to meet his family!

Bobby turns to face me, apology written all over his face. "I'm so sorry, Molly. I had no idea he was here." He raises his voice on the next comment. "*He was supposed to be at work!*"

"Wait, who's here?" Richie asks, voice getting louder as he approaches the entryway.

Well, there's nothing I can do about it now, so I may as well woman up and make the best of it. Plastering on a smile, I step around Bobby and raise my hand in a friendly wave at the guy standing there. He bears some resemblance to Bobby, but his hair is a mess and he's taller. And his fashion sense is decidedly different if the "Who farted?" T-shirt and cut-off sweatpants are anything to go by.

Richie looks me up and down as a grin overtakes his lips. "Well, this is a surprise."

Of all the things he could have said, I suppose that's one of the better options.

"Hi, I'm Molly," I say. "You must be Bobby's brother."

He approaches, but when he takes my hand and turns it to kiss the back, Bobby shoves him away—hard.

"Don't touch her, asshole," Bobby snarls, but it only makes Richie laugh. Bobby looks down at me, nose wrinkled. "He doesn't wash his hands."

"He lies," Richie tells me. "Can I get you a drink, Molly?"

Bobby curses under his breath again. "Dude, this is *my* apartment. *Get out.*"

Richie scoffs and addresses me again. "What's a classy lady like you doing with this rude, lying reprobate?"

I decide not to go with my reflexive answer of *orgasms* and settle on, "He's been a perfect gentleman so far."

Richie cocks his head. "Color me surprised. My brother must be on his best behavior with a real lady instead of his usual puck bunnies."

"That's it!" Bobby lunges for his brother and puts him in a head lock.

Richie laughs and tries fighting Bobby's hold while elbowing him firmly in the gut. I flatten my back against the wall to keep from getting taken out by any stray limbs. Both men grunt and swear as they battle each other until Bobby gets Richie's arms twisted behind him and frog-marches him to the door.

Bobby lifts his chin to me. "Mind getting the door, baby?"

"Baby?" Richie's eyebrows spike as they stagger my way. "Wait till I tell the boys!"

I can only shake my head as I hold the door open and step out of the way.

"Nice to meet you, Molly!" Richie yells as the door slams behind him.

Bobby secures the deadbolt, chest heaving from exertion, and then turns to face me again. "I am so sorry about that. I had no idea he would be here, and I am officially disowning him starting this moment. In fact, first thing tomorrow, I'm going down to the county courthouse to change my name legally."

I blink up at him, still recovering from the whole scene. He looks so earnest and apologetic that I can't help but pat his chest and offer him a grin. "It's fine. Family is never easy, in my experience."

"That's putting it mildly."

"You know, you might find this crazy, but I'm actually a little jealous of you and Richie."

"Jealous? Why would you ever wish for a two-hundred-pound leech with poor hygiene and an overinflated ego?"

"Well, when you put it that way . . ." I laugh. "No, I just mean it might have been nice to have a sibling, that's all."

"Well, you can have all four of mine if you want." Bobby pulls me in and drops a kiss on top of my head before leading us both into the apartment's living space.

It's not at all what I expected for a professional athlete with Bobby's very specific taste. It feels too . . . generic for him, from the beige walls and carpet to the vertical blinds covering the windows.

As if reading my mind, Bobby props his free hand on his hip and says, "You can see why I'm looking for a house." We both glance around the space. "I only got this place because it's close to the practice facility. I'm so used to being traded every season that I never put any thought into my living arrangements before. It was never worth it."

"And now?" I ask. I didn't know he'd been traded around so much. It must be tough not getting to decide where you live or work.

"Kaitlyn got me a six-year contract with the Storm Chasers last year, so I can finally breathe."

"Kaitlyn's your agent, right?" I'm not quite sure how all this works.

"Yeah. She and my teammate Benny are the ones who just had a baby." He gets a goofy look on his face that makes my ovaries perk up. *Settle down, bitches!* "You might have met her, actually. She was the dark haired woman I was talking to at Matthew's practice when I met your ex. She's around the facility a lot."

A lightbulb turns on. "Oh! *That's* who that was."

Bobby cocks his head. "Wait. Did you think . . . I was hitting on her?"

Heat crawls up my neck. "No!" I deny too quickly, knowing I've been caught. So I go on offense instead. "Hey, your own brother said you usually go for 'puck bunnies.'" I use air quotes.

Bobby gasps. "I'm going to tell Kaitlyn you just called her a puck bunny!"

"No, I didn't mean that!"

"Kinda sounded like you did."

"I just meant she's young—and beautiful, and stylish, and . . . sexy."

"Now you think she's sexy too? I'm sure she'd like to hear that as well."

"No! That's not . . . I'm going to shut up now."

Bobby chuckles and turns, drawing me into his chest and wrapping his arms around me. "I'm just giving you shit."

"Well, don't be surprised if I just kick you in the shin." I sound like a third grader.

Bobby's warm chest shakes against my cheek where my head is cradled. He's so solid and comfortable. It feels good to be able to lean on him and let myself exhale for a minute.

"Hey." His voice is quieter now and I can feel his breath ruffle the hair on top of my head. "About what Richie said, he doesn't know anything about my love life or who I do or don't date."

"It's really none of my busin—"

Bobby cuts me off. "Yes, it is. And I'm telling you right now that you're the only woman I want to date."

As good as that feels, I have to bring up the elephant in the room. "I'm forty, Bobby. And I have a kid."

"So? You just said you thought Kaitlyn was my type, and guess what? She's forty and has a kid too."

"Wow! She's got great skin," is my only response.

"She probably moisturizes with the tears of endangered baby seals."

I choke out a laugh. "What?"

"She's a hard-ass, to put it mildly. I'm actually a little frightened by her. Scratch that. A lot frightened."

"Bobby?"

"Yeah?"

"You should definitely continue seeing your therapist."

His chest shakes again, and I smile against the soft fabric of his shirt. Yeah, I could definitely get used to this.

Chapter Twenty-Three

Bobby

I'm nervous. Not because my dumbass brother was here. Not because our dates haven't gotten better every single day this week—they most definitely have. I'm nervous because I want more, and I brought Molly back here to try to get her to agree to being official. I feel like I'm sixteen again, trying to ask a girl to be my girlfriend.

"Okay, so hear me out."

Molly groans and pulls her head off my chest. She tips her head back with a pout and her red painted lips look so kissable I want to forget about everything I was about to say and just take her straight to my bed. And because I have the attention span of a gnat and the libido of a bull, I do. I dip my head, nibble on her mouth, and sweep her up into my arms to stalk into my bedroom. The lights are off and not even the half-moon shining through the windows can illuminate enough for my preferences. I refuse to not see her beautiful body while I strip her naked. Why deny myself that pleasure?

Laying her on the bed, I pause to light two candles I had in my room mostly for hurricane season in case the building lost power. After several sleepovers at her place, she's finally stopped fighting me on the lights, but I also figure candlelight might be a nice compromise to make her more comfortable.

"Hey. Is that my perfume?"

My head whips up to see the incriminating bottle still on my nightstand. Shit. I really should have returned that to her.

"Umm. Yeah. You left it in Wolverine that first day." I try to brush it off and distract her by prying the heels off her feet and tossing them over my shoulder.

Molly pins me with a pointed look, one eyebrow hitched higher than the other. "Have you been sniffing my perfume, Robert?"

"Oh fuck," I whine. "You can't call me Robert and not expect me to tell you all my secrets. Yes, I sniffed your perfume and even whacked off to it one time. Just once, I swear. I want you, Molly. *Have* wanted you. Happy now?"

"Yes, actually," she answers softly. She positions herself up on her elbows and nods toward me with a silent request. I quickly divest myself of the polo and slacks. When I'm down to the latest funderpants that I bought with her in mind–floating black stilettos on a bright pink background–she tosses her head back and laughs, exposing the long column of her throat. Fuck, she's sexy as hell without even trying.

"See? It's fun to watch, isn't it?" I tease her, wanting to see that blush on her face. After shoving the funderpants down my legs, I grab the base of my already hard cock and get my wish.

"When the naked specimen is that nice, yes."

I crawl over her body and she flattens to the mattress below me. My dick bops her on the chin. It's hilarious to watch her try to decide whether she should look me in the eye like a proper good girl or watch my dick like she wants to.

"See that evidence, Molly?" I point at the erection that's lengthening even more under her scrutiny, like it's trying to reach her mouth. "Believe me when I say the naked specimen I get to watch is even nicer."

She drags her wide-eyed gaze back to my face. "Can I try something?"

"Baby, you can do anything you want." And I mean it. Watching Molly's sexual confidence grow in just the last week has been fascinating to witness. I really don't think she was ever sexually satisfied in her previous relationships. Which means I have plans to fulfill every fantasy she never knew she had.

She lifts up and strips her blouse over her head, quickly unlocking the front clasp of her bra and peeling that off too. Her gorgeous boobs tumble out, more than a handful each. She cups her own breasts together and looks up at me. "Fuck my tits, please."

If I'd been any younger, I would have come on the spot. The visual of Molly's breasts served up on a platter for me, her request to fuck her, even the use of that language from her proper mouth. Damn. This is why I like older women: confidence that grows by leaps and bounds.

I grit my teeth hard to hold myself back. "Give it a little lube, baby."

Molly lifts her head and takes my cock in her mouth, her tongue swirling around the tip before taking me deeper. I groan and try to recall some of my stats just to keep my brain busy. When my cock is nice and wet and I just might explode, I pull out of her mouth and slide between the softest pillows known to man. Molly watches intently, licking her lips.

"I'm . . ." I grunt, that familiar tingle starting in my lower spine way sooner than I want it to. "Not gonna last."

Molly nods and lifts her head again, this time to lave the crown of my dick with her tongue every time I thrust through her breasts. The feeling is insane, soft and enveloping on the shaft, wet and warm on the tip.

With another thrust, I grip the headboard like I just might break it in two, spilling into her mouth as she opens wide and swallows me down. The orgasm keeps coming, the visual below me too compelling. Holy fuck, I'm going to store this away in my spank bank for future viewing when Molly's not here to give me the real thing.

I fall onto the bed beside her, lungs heaving. When I'm able to pry a single eye open, I realize I didn't even get her fully naked. "Give me a second. I promise I won't leave you hanging."

Molly snuggles into my side, her bare foot rubbing up and down my calf. "It's fine. We can just sleep."

I frown at my ceiling. Does she not know me at all? I roll on top of her with a growl, pinning her wrists to the mattress above her head.

"Sleep? Oh, you wanted to sleep tonight? Our last night together before you're back home with Matthew and you think I'm going to let you sleep? Baby, I'm just getting started." I laugh like I'm a bit demented and fuck, maybe I am. I'm obsessed with this woman. Which reminds me.

Rolling right off her after threatening her with sleep deprivation, I grab the flat box off the dresser and return to bed. "I have something for you first. Then I'll debauch you. Wait, is debauch a verb?"

Molly huffs out an amused laugh and sits up, her arm immediately coming up to cover her breasts. I bat her arm away and she bats me right back. I win the tussle though, because she doesn't cover her breasts this time, just points to the box in her lap. "What is this?"

"It's a present for you. Open it."

She gives me a look I ignore. I nudge the box closer, and

she sighs, opening it. She pulls out familiar gold and black material, holding it up. "A Storm Chasers jersey?"

I take it from her and turn it around so she can see the back side, which has my last name emblazoned across it. "Not just any jersey. *My* jersey. It's for you to wear. I also have one for Matthew, along with tickets for tomorrow night's game." My heart beats erratically. It's a fifty-fifty chance she turns me down and I probably should have warmed her up with an orgasm or two. "I know we haven't discussed it, but I'd like to go public that we're dating. And to do that, we need to tell Matthew first."

Molly's arms drop the jersey to her lap. Her cheeks are flushed, and her hair is mussed. Those unique eyes are staring me down, trying to find answers to the thousand questions swirling in her brain.

"I can literally hear your thoughts spiraling," I whisper. She nudges me with her foot.

"Being a good mom is the most important thing to me," she starts. I know this, of course. You only have to talk to her for a few minutes to know that Matthew is her world, as he should be. It's one of the things I like about her most. Only second to the pencil skirts. "He's already acting erratically at school. I don't want to endanger his stability."

I nod. "I completely agree. But he's also old enough he won't appreciate us lying to him about our relationship." I take her hands in mine, hoping she'll see I'm not joking like I usually am. "I want to date you, Molly. I want to take you out on the town, to my games, to events where the other hockey players bring their wives and girlfriends. I want to have simple dinners at home with you and Matthew. I want to continue to help him at hockey practice. Let me be in this for the long haul."

Molly's eyes dart back and forth between mine, considering. I hold my breath.

"Long haul?" she finally asks, nose wrinkling.

"Wrong phrase." I grab the jersey and the box and toss them both to the floor. "I'm into you, Molly Sparks. I want you to be my girlfriend. I want to put my jersey on you, so all those other fuckers know you're mine."

Molly wraps her arms around my neck and we fall back on the bed. "There are no other fuckers."

"Good!"

I seal our lips together and spend the rest of the night worshipping her body. Around three in the morning, when I wake up and see she's staring at the ceiling, I shift until my head is between her legs. I lap at her, moaning as her taste blooms on my tongue. I get her right on the edge of yet another orgasm, but I don't give it to her until she agrees to officially be mine.

"Blackmail," she pants, arm flung over her eyes as she catches her breath.

I grin into the darkness and pull her into me, spooning her from behind. "Smart negotiation," I correct her.

I run my fingers through her hair and freeze when some of it pulls away with my hand. I pop up onto my elbow and stare at a clump of hair I must have pulled from her scalp. It's hard to see in the dark, but it doesn't look like a small amount either. Surprise and horror have me gasping.

"Oh my god! I'm so sorry!"

Molly's eyes fling open. She snatches the clump of hair out of my hands lightning fast and tosses it to the ground. "It's a hair piece!"

"A what piece?" I peer over the side of the bed, but Molly pulls me back.

"A thing women use to make their hair fuller looking. Don't worry about it."

I stare down at her, then shake my head slowly. "I'm not sure I'll ever understand women."

Molly grabs my arm and wraps it around her, forcing me back into our spooning position. "I'm not sure I understand myself sometimes," she sighs, then yawns.

Laying there in the dark, I let that sit with me for a bit. I'm not even sure if Molly's still awake, but sometime later, I whisper into her hair. Or at least what I think is her hair, who the hell knows anymore? "You don't need to do that shit for me. I love you just the way you are."

I have exactly thirty minutes to be part of this conversation with Matthew. Molly and I planned to tell him after my practice and before the game. We both agreed to keep it casual and not make it a huge deal. We're dating, not getting married.

Afterward, I have to get back to the arena and get ready for the game. Molly and Matthew will drive there on their own and find their seats. I bought the tickets right next to Kaitlyn's normal seats. She told me she'd stay as long as she could to keep them company until Mei got sick of the loud noises. For the rest of the season, I'll be sure to get them passes for the WAGs suite.

Running up the walkway, I don't bother knocking. "Hey! Anybody home?" I call out as I stick my head inside Molly's house. Stepping inside and glancing around, I studiously ignore the spot on the floor where we made love that first time. *Stay focused, dickhead.*

"Hey, Bobby," Matthew calls back, appearing down the hallway and coming closer with a happy smile on his face. "Mom says we have tickets to the game tonight?"

We do a fist bump, handshake thing, and then I hand him

the box with the other jersey. "Yeah, dude. Got great tickets and a jersey for you."

Molly rushes down the hall, looking cute as a button in ripped jeans, Ugg boots, and my jersey on. I have to bite my lip to keep from leaning over and kissing her when she sidles up to Matthew to watch him open the gift.

"I get a jersey too?" he asks, ripping the box open and holding up the shirt. "Thanks, man!" He goes to dart back down the hallway to put it on, but Molly tugs him back.

"Hold up a second, Matthew. We wanted to talk to you real quick."

Matthew's eyes open wide, all that hockey game excitement gone. "I didn't get in trouble today, I swear, Mom."

Molly laughs, but I can tell she's nervous. She refuses to look at me or step too close. "Actually, that's not what this is about. Bobby and I wanted you to hear it first." She pauses, swallows hard, then clears her throat.

Silence.

Oookay. She's not good at this. I step closer to them both, slide my arm around Molly's waist, and pull her into my side. She's stiff as a board, so I take over. "What your mom is trying to say is that we're dating."

Matthew looks between us and then gives me a man-to-man head nod of approval. "Okay. It's kind of sus, but then again, having my mom date a hockey player isn't all bad." Matthew leans in closer to me, his face a mask of seriousness. "Be nice to her though, or I'll have to kick your ass."

"Matthew!" Molly snaps, appalled.

Matthew steps back and grins. "What, Mom? Just tellin' it like it is. It's a guy thing. Right, Bobby?"

I nod, but pull my arm from Molly's waist to step aside with Matthew. "Can you grab us some water, Molly?"

She huffs, but then decides to leave the room and give the two of us time to chat. I don't take her trust around her son lightly. I round on Matthew, making sure I'm looking him straight in the eye.

"Hey, I'd never do anything to hurt your mom or you. If there's ever a problem, a misunderstanding, or I step on your toes, I want you to know you can come to me. We'll talk it out and make it right, okay?"

Matthew nods. "Okay." We shake hands and then he tosses the jersey over his shoulder and backs down the hallway. "Wait 'til I tell my friends. They're gonna shit themselves."

"Watch your language, Matthew Sparks!" Molly comes back in the room with two water bottles.

"Sorry, Mom!" His door slams shut, and Molly and I stare at each other.

"That went . . . well?" I say tentatively.

Molly nods, her teeth worrying her bottom lip. I reach up and pull her lip away, then dip my head to kiss her.

"It went great. Quit worrying." I pull her into my arms and sway us side to side. When I feel her body start to relax in my arms, I whisper, "You look fucking hot in my jersey, baby. Can't wait to fuck you while you wear it."

"Bobby!" She slaps my chest, and I laugh, feeling like everything in my life is finally working out.

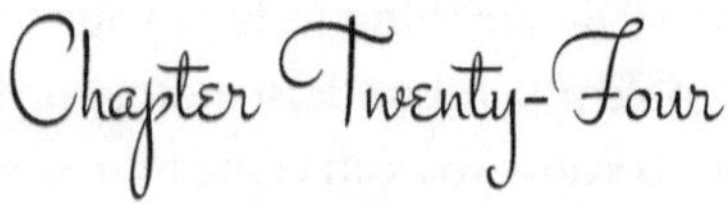

Chapter Twenty-Four

Molly

"Whoa! We're so close to the ice!" Matty exclaims as I shuffle sideways into our row and pull him with me. He's so distracted by all the music, lights, and people that he almost tripped down the stairs just now.

"Thank god for the glass between us and the pucks. I don't know about you, but I don't feel like sustaining a head injury tonight."

"There's Bobby!" Matty points to the rink where a stream of players in gold and black take the ice. My heartrate jumps at the sight of my kind-of boyfriend all geared up and speeding across the rink. This is more exciting than I thought it would be.

"I'm gonna go down and bang on the glass to see if I can get his attention." Matty lunges for the stairs again, and I just barely catch the sleeve of his jersey.

"Hold up, Speed Racer. He's working. Let him focus on the game. We'll have plenty of time to see him after."

Matty reluctantly takes his seat, and I do the same.

"Besides, who's going to eat this candy if you abandon me?" I pull a box of Milk Duds from my purse and Matty's face lights up.

"I can take care of that for you," my kid assures me, snatching the box from my hand and tearing it open like a bear raiding a camper's cooler.

I've never been to a professional hockey game before. It's almost giving me sensory overload and the game hasn't even started yet. My gaze tracks Bobby in his #62 jersey as he whacks a puck toward the goal and sneaks it past the goalie before he circles around to grab another puck. Why is my heart beating so fast?

"Did I tell you Coach Chloe scheduled our first official game?" Matty asks over a mouthful of caramel and chocolate. "She said she's gonna let me be a winger."

I smile at Matty, pretending to know what that means. "That's great!"

"I guess I'd better make sure I don't get grounded between now and then so I don't let down Coach and the team." He shoves another two candies in his mouth and turns his attention back to the players warming up on the ice.

I tap his temple with my finger. "Good thinking." I've been tiptoeing around the subject lately since I haven't had any more calls from the school and Matty's mood appears less troubled. But I suppose now is as good a time as any, since he brought it up.

"You know, I got a call from the counseling place I told you about. They said they can finally fit us in right after Thanksgiving."

He doesn't look away from the players as he shrugs. "Okay, but I should probably tell you a couple more details since you're going to find out anyway." My mom senses go on alert, but I stay quiet. If my tween is volunteering private information, I'm not about to do anything to deter him.

He finally turns to look at me. Damn, in these seats, he's the same height as me. How did that happen? "So, it's pretty much just been this Raiden guy making trouble, like I told you. The kid he's been bullying the most is gay like Dad, so I've been sticking up for him and, you know, it's making Raiden give me a hard time too. That's what most of the shoving and name calling has been about."

I knew some of this already, but not that Raiden was seeking out gay kids or that Matty himself was a target. I've suspected it, but he never said for certain until now. When Matty showed me the screenshots he'd taken, I sent them to the school, but I haven't heard anything since. Now that I know Matty is a target, though, I'll be calling again for sure.

"So, he's bullying you?" I ask just to make sure.

"I can handle it, Mom." Matty shrugs before turning his attention back to the ice. "Bobby!!" He waves his hand wildly and shouts to his new hero.

I'm too distracted to even look to see if Bobby has noticed us. I'm not sure whether to laugh or cry or hug the snot out of my kid. But before I can decide, Bobby's agent, Kaitlyn, appears beside me, her dark hair pulled up into a topknot and a carseat balanced in one arm.

"Hi! You must be Molly and Matthew." She smiles warmly at us. "I'm Kaitlyn."

"Oh, let me help," I say, unfolding the empty seat next to me so she can set down the carseat. As soon as she does, we shake hands. "It's so nice to meet you."

"The pleasure is all mine," she says as she takes the seat next to the baby carrier. "Believe me, I have been starved for adult interaction since this little lady showed up." She lifts the blanket covering the carseat to reveal the most precious baby with wispy black hair and a rosebud mouth.

"She's *gorgeous*," I gush. And no wonder. Kaitlyn is drop dead beautiful, and I'm pretty sure I did a double take the first time I laid eyes on her fiancé, Banks Bennet. The man is *fine*. The two were destined to have runway-model babies.

"We definitely lucked out. Mei sleeps through anything. If only she'd do it at night instead of during the day." Kaitlyn pulls a pair of baby pink headphones from her bag and carefully secures them over her sleeping daughter's ears. "Just in case." She grins as more fans trickle in and take their seats.

"Boy Scouts have got nothing on moms. We're always prepared for any eventuality."

"I'm trying," Kaitlyn sighs. "But I've got to confess, I feel like I have no idea what I'm doing most of the time. We're both first-time parents."

"Aw, you're doing great, I'm sure." I gesture to Matty whose got his nose buried in the program now that the players have left the ice. "I can't tell you how many rookie mistakes we made with Matthew, and he somehow turned out okay." More than okay considering his current situation. "It's a constant learning experience. Just when you think you can predict your kid's behavior, they change it up on you and you've got to figure it out all over again."

"Oh my god, yes! I swear a good back rub would calm Mei down like a charm for the first few weeks, but now? She ratchets up to DEFCON one if I so much as lay a hand on her back when she's upset. Why can't they just speak from birth, so we know what we're doing wrong?"

I laugh. "Hang in there. It'll get easier once she starts sleeping through the night." Lack of sleep is enough to drive the sanest person batty—I should know. Although, on the nights I spend with Bobby, my insomnia has gotten remarkably better. I'm assuming it's sexual exhaustion.

Kaitlyn drops her head back and closes her eyes. "I can't wait to get rid of these bags under my eyes." She straightens and begins to remove her jacket. "And poor Banks. He kept insisting on getting up with me to feed Mei in the middle of the night. I finally had to put my foot down when he fell asleep in his truck in the parking lot and missed practice. He's got three years left on his contract, and we're not risking the wrath of Coach Marsh. My man is staying on the first line until the day he hangs those skates up."

I bite back another laugh. "I think my low point was pouring orange juice into my coffee instead of milk and then being too tired to pour myself a fresh cup. Ten out of ten do not recommend."

"Oh, I don't mess around when it comes to my coffee," Kaitlyn responds with a tone usually reserved for the most serious of offenses. Coffee means business. Noted.

The lights suddenly drop in the arena, and all eyes go to the ice. "Here they come!" Matty announces as spotlights begin dancing on the ice and cheers go up from the crowd. Both teams enter the rink to the tune of an old Aerosmith song and file to their respective benches. The excitement of the crowd is palpable, and I'm literally on the edge of my seat already.

When Banks's name is announced for the starting line-up, Kaitlyn lets out a deafening whistle and I clap extra loudly. Mei sleeps through it all like a champ.

From what Bobby has told me, he plays on the second line of four, and they'll all switch out every few minutes throughout the game.

When Banks skates up to the circle in the middle and the puck drops, the crowd goes crazy. I dig in my purse for my glasses I hardly ever wear, but it's almost impossible to follow the puck without them. It zooms from stick to stick in what looks like a choreographed dance between players.

Matty and Kaitlyn both cheer and boo in sync when various things happen. My knowledge of hockey is pretty limited, so I stay mostly quiet, waiting for someone to score a goal that I can cheer or boo.

A few minutes in, one of the opposing players from Detroit takes his stick and blatantly jams it into Storm Chaser number 23's stomach, causing the guy to double over and fall to the ice. The crowd gasps and boos as play continues, and I turn to Matty.

"They're allowed to just do that?"

He shrugs, so I turn to Kaitlyn whose eyes never stray from the ice as she answers, "Dan-O will be fine. Refs missed it, but Visick will pay for it. You'll see." She gestures to the bad guy.

"That sounds ominous."

The player she referred to as Dan-O gets to his feet, still holding his stomach, and skates to the bench, a teammate replacing him as he throws his leg over the barrier. Play continues for another couple minutes when all the players switch out with teammates from the bench and a familiar jersey catches my eye.

Number 62. Rhodes. My pulse immediately races.

"There's your guy," Kaitlyn says.

Instinctively, I open my mouth to protest, but then I snap it shut again. Because Bobby *is* my guy. My lips spread in a smile I'm sure is goofy as hell and I train my eyes on my man again.

By the middle of the second period, the Storm Chasers are up two to zero with Dan-O, who I learned is team captain Danny Bright, having scored one and Banks having scored the second—something that had Kaitlyn out of her seat and bellowing like one of those beer-bellied fans you see on TV. I'm starting to pick up on the game a little better and manage not to wince when the puck goes racing a hundred miles an hour toward our goalie Drugov's face.

But I'm still completely unprepared for what happens next.

Bobby comes off the bench and switches out with Banks, but the rest of our players stay on the ice. Kaitlyn lets out what I can only describe as a cackle, but my attention stays on Bobby as he skates directly for one of the Detroit players and abruptly slams him into the side of the rink. In a flash, both Bobby and this opposing player have their helmets and gloves off and are in a literal fist fight–right there on the ice!

The crowd goes batshit crazy, half the crowd chanting "Fight! Fight! Fight!" and the other half booing. When I catch sight of the Detroit player's jersey, I realize it's that Visick guy who jabbed Dan-O with his stick earlier.

"Is that . . . blood?!" I ask no one in particular, my voice high-pitched.

"Yeah!" Matty yells with obvious relish. Good god, has he developed bloodlust or something?

"I think so," Kaitlyn responds, casual as can be.

The referees allow the fight to continue for almost a minute, for some reason, before they intervene and pull the two players apart. Bobby turns back toward the bench, his hands raised in victory. The players on the bench let out a chorus of "Roadie! Roadie!" as Bobby and the other guy each go to their respective penalty boxes and the game starts up again like nothing happened.

Kaitlyn is still clapping and does a double take when she glances my way and notices my look of horror. For some crazy reason, it makes her laugh and grab my arm.

"First game, huh?"

I nod dumbly.

"Didn't Bobby tell you he's the enforcer?"

"Um, I think he mentioned it, but I just thought it was another nickname like all the guys have."

I look over to Matty again to see him keenly focused on

the game. Am I the only one who thought that was nuts? I mean, sure, I saw Bobby roughhousing with Richie last night, but that's what brothers do, right? And nobody got punched in the face. But Bobby literally picked a fight with this other player out there in front of all these people–while doing his job! I'm really not sure how I feel about that kind of violence —especially when my kid is starting to see Bobby as a role model. Dammit!

Clearly not sensing my inner freak out, Kaitlyn snickers into her chest before getting her shit together and spelling it out for me. "Okay, so every team has an enforcer and usually a pest. The enforcer's job is to protect the star players by keeping the other team in line. It's actually really important. When Visick threw that stab, he knew he was out of the ref's sightline and he'd get away with it. Not only is Dan-O the team captain, he's probably the second best player on the team." She brings a hand to her chest. "After my baby daddy, of course."

"Of course," I echo robotically, trying to process this information about Bobby and his role.

"If we let something like a stab at Dan-O slide, then Detroit will start ramping things up, possibly seriously injuring one of our key players. So it's Bobby's job to get physical and put Visick back in his place. It's an unwritten code of sorts." She points to the bench. "You see number 44? That's Fornier. He's the pest. His job is to get under the other team's skin and throw them off their game. Taunt them so they make stupid mistakes—something he's really good at because that boy can be annoying as hell."

"And this is all . . . allowed?"

"Well, fighting gets you a five-minute major." She shrugs. "And if you take it too far, there can be other consequences. But Bobby never takes it too far." I guess that's something.

"A five-minute major?"

"Five minutes in the sin bin—the penalty box." She

gestures to the scoreboard where a penalty clock is counting down toward two minutes as the teams keep battling for the puck and racing around the rink. "Fun fact: that's where that band Five for Fighting got its name."

"Oh." I'm still wrestling with everything she's said.

Something tells me I've got an uncomfortable conversation ahead of me. Who knew a simple game could put me into an existential crisis?

"Hey, Mom," Matty says, leaning into me and smiling. "Bobby stood up to a bully just like I did."

Well, damn.

Chapter Twenty-Five

Bobby

My phone buzzes in my back pocket as I pull up to Molly's house. We're due at another house I want to see in thirty minutes. This one isn't quite as lavish as the others I was looking at, but the pictures made it look gorgeous inside and it's tucked away in a gated community that feels incredibly safe. I even saw a few basketball hoops in driveways and bikes left in the front yards when I looked it up on Google Earth.

I pull out my phone to see it's Ashley again. Shit. I missed another session this morning. That makes three in just two weeks. Molly exits her house, looking like a million bucks in my favorite deep burgundy pencil skirt and silky black blouse. She's literally trying to kill me with those stiletto heels. I thumb back a quick message, saying I'll call Ashley later today. I'm out the door and kissing Molly before she makes it even halfway to my vehicle.

"Good afternoon, Mr. Rhodes," she purrs.

My hands steal down her hips to her ass, wanting to take

her right here on the driveway but knowing I can't. Pretty sure there are laws about public indecency, and I have about ten indecent things I want to do to Molly. Something about seeing her in the stands at my game last week, wearing my jersey and cheering for my team, sealed the deal for me. I just had to look left to see Matthew going crazy when the Storm Chasers scored, then see him hug his mother in his excitement . . . it all made something click in my head.

"Good afternoon, Ms. Sparks," I murmur back, stealing another kiss before forcing myself to release her. I hold my hand out and she walks to my truck, letting me help her up into it and buckle her seatbelt. I may cop a feel of her breast in the process, but she doesn't slap my hand away so I'm not going to apologize.

In the car on the way to the walk through, we chat about all the things that have happened with Matthew here all week. He went back to his dad's last night. I would have come over right away since I miss holding her each night we're apart, but we got back late from a quick away game in North Carolina.

I pull up to a gate and have to give my name to the guard out front of the neighborhood, which Molly assures me decreases crime on average by 25 percent. I mostly just watch her face as we pull up in front of the house. We start the tour and Molly's head is on a swivel, an excitement in her tone I didn't hear in the other houses.

"Bobby?" Molly turns around in the chef's kitchen and puts her hand on my chest. "Are you even looking at the double ovens?"

"Yeah, they're great." I know because her face lit up when she saw them.

Molly's eyes narrow. "You didn't even look at them," she challenges.

I shrug and slide my arm around her waist. "I don't need

to look at them to know they're great. If you like them, that's enough for me."

Her head tilts. "Bobby, this is *your* home. *You* have to like it."

I lean down and pluck a kiss from her red stained lips. "I'll like anything. What I need to know is if *you* like it so I can get you over here every chance I get." I pull back and scan her face. "Do you like it?"

Molly's face softens into a smile I know all too well. Her face does that every time I do something she likes and she's about to let me do whatever I want. Fuck, I love that expression.

"Yes, I actually love this house. It's beautiful, but not so over the top to be ostentatious, you know? And it's safe. Not far from your job."

I cut her off, not needing any more reasons other than she loves it. "Let's make an offer."

Her face lights up even more. "Really? This is the one?"

She means the house, but I mean so much more when I reply, "This is most definitely the one."

Molly squeals, kisses me, then spins out of my arms to snatch up her laptop bag. We head back to my truck for privacy from any homeowner cameras, but don't leave the curb while she writes up the offer. I suggest full price and she scoffs, telling me that's why I hired her: to save me from making a mistake that will cost me money. I don't think she has any idea how many zeros Kaitlyn negotiated in my contract. If she did, she wouldn't be squabbling over twenty-thousand dollars.

But that's one of the things I love about her. Yes, love. She's down to earth and not sporting stars in her eyes because of my profession. I can trust her, and in the harsh world I grew up in, trust is everything.

My phone buzzes again and I take it out, ripping my gaze

away from Molly's feet in those heels. I was envisioning them on my shoulders, a repeat of our first date. This time it's Ashley calling me, instead of texting. I answer, wincing when she immediately gives me shit for missing our morning session. Molly gasps and I realize Ashley's talking so loudly Molly can hear her every word.

"You missed your session, Robert?" Molly asks me in that sexy scolding mom voice.

I cover up the phone. "Yeah. A couple, actually." Molly's mouth forms an accusatory O. "But I've been doing so well!"

Ashley chirps in my ear. "Is that Molly? Put me on speaker so I can ask her exactly how well—or not—you've been doing." The two haven't officially met, but I've talked freely with each of them about the other.

I hang my head but comply, hitting the button on my dash to put Ashley through the Bluetooth speakers. "Ashley, this is Molly. Molly, this is Ashley," I grumble.

"Hi Ashley. I apologize for Bobby wasting your time this morning. I hate it when I have clients who do that to me."

Well, shit. That makes me feel even worse. I can't believe Molly's had clients do a no-show on her. I make a mental note to ask her for exact names later.

Ashley chuckles. "Nice to meet you, Molly. It's fine. I work from home so I can just do laundry or something when a client ditches our scheduled meeting. But, I'm committed to my clients getting better and if they miss, we can't work on their issues. Bobby is doing so great, but it's not like you can reprogram an entire childhood in a few weeks, you know?"

Molly moans. "I totally understand that. Therapy is life-long, actually. I spent months in therapy after my ex-husband and I divorced, and that was amicable!"

The ladies keep chatting back and forth. I finally grab the door handle, thinking I'll give the two of them some space to chat without me, but Molly snags my arm, her nails digging in just enough for me to know she means business.

"Do you have time right now to work with Bobby? I can step outside to give you privacy," Molly offers.

"I sure do!" Ashley responds.

Molly reaches for the door handle, but I pull her back. "Stay. Please?"

Molly searches my face and then finally dips her head in agreement.

"We left off talking about childhood issues, Bobby. Do you feel comfortable talking about your mother?"

I rest my head back and wonder how the hell I got here. Then I feel Molly take my hand, lacing her fingers through mine, and I know exactly why I'm here. I want to do everything in my power to be a good man. A man she trusts her son with. A man she can open her heart to. Maybe it started out with saving my job, but I'm in this to win Molly.

Lifting my head, I look her in the eyes. "I don't have any secrets from Molly, so let's chat."

"Ahh, that's so sweet," Ashley gushes over the speakers. Molly squeezes my fingers, and I shoot her a wink. "So last time you said your mother was your favorite parent. Can you explain that comment?"

I blow out a breath and think about growing up the youngest of five boys. The way my father ruled our house with a raised voice and physical reminders that he was more powerful than us. He was never what I would consider abusive, but he wasn't warm and cuddly either.

"My dad is the kind who thinks crying is for pussies, pardon my language. He'd yell at us all the time and wasn't afraid to wrestle us boys into submission when we gave him problems. Mom, on the other hand, is sweet. To this day I can't fathom how she ended up with my dad, but they make it work."

"She sounds like a safe haven. Is that how you see her?" Ashley asks.

I roll that around my brain. "Yeah, I would say so. She would always come to my room after Dad yelled at me or my brothers beat the snot out of me. She'd sit on the side of my bed and stroke my hair, talking softly about anything and everything until I was ready to talk about the argument. She made living in that house tolerable."

Molly sniffs, and I'm horrified to see a sheen of tears in her eyes. She waves my concern away and blinks rapidly. Ashley makes some affirmative noises before speaking.

"I wonder how much that maternal influence has to do with your relationship with Molly. You're a mom, right, Molly?"

"I am. My son is twelve and he can be described as a handful with a heart of gold."

"I love that. Sounds familiar," Ashley says. "Bobby, did you know she was a mom when you first met Molly?"

I nod, then realize she can't see me. "Yes, I met her at the rink when she would drop off Matthew for practice. She's a good mom. One of the best. I love that about her."

Molly's sniffles are back. "Thanks, Bobby."

"I think you like her softness. I think her kindness reminds you of the only love and comfort you received as a boy. Would you say that's correct?"

I tilt my head, thinking about all the various reasons I like Molly. Her being a mom is just one of them. "Sure. But I don't just like her for that. I actually love her for a lot of things."

Molly inhales sharply and I realize I've just confessed my love for Molly on a phone call with my therapist. Fuckity fuck. I tug on our conjoined hands and face her fully to salvage this. "Molly. I love you. I know it's early, but I'm not one to fake how I feel." Molly's eyes have widened and her mouth's doing that O thing again. It's cute as hell, but I can practically feel the breeze from her brain spinning out of control. "I don't need you to say anything back. I just wanted you to know."

"Oh, my gosh! That's the most adorable thing I've ever heard!" Ashley coos loudly from the speakers. She's giving me the feedback I wish Molly would.

Molly's face flames with embarrassment, and if I could, I'd put myself in a headlock for choosing such horrible timing.

"Gosh! This is such great progress," Ashley powers ahead, oblivious to the awkwardness inside this car. "Bobby, how's your relationship with Matthew? Do you treat him the way your father treated you?"

I scoff, severely offended by that idea. "Absolutely not. We talk things through, and I try to be there for him any way I can. He's safe with me."

Ashley must hear my tone. "I bet he is," she assures me before abruptly switching topics. "Do you want more kids, Bobby?"

"Of course," I answer the same time Molly blurts out, "It's too early for that."

I haven't actually put much thought into it, but I always envision myself with kids around me. A chance to do things differently than how I was raised. I always envision them way in the future when I have things more figured out, though. It takes me a second to realize what Molly said.

I feel her stiffen. When I glance at her, she's looking down at her lap, teeth worrying her lip. "Molly?"

She lifts her head, eyes full of tears again. I lift her hand to my mouth and kiss her soft skin. I hate to see her cry.

"What's wrong, baby?" I forget all about Ashley being on the phone. All that matters is finding out what I said to make Molly cry.

"Bobby," her voice breaks and she pauses to clear her throat. "I'm forty. I don't know if I can have more kids."

My brain scrambles. What does she mean? "But there was that singer in Italy that gave birth at fifty-six. Or Janet Jackson! She was fifty. Oh! Kaitlyn! She just turned forty and had Mei!" I could give even more examples if she gave me time to Google it.

"That's a beautiful thing. For *them*," Molly answers, squeezing my hand so hard I can't feel my fingers. "But that doesn't mean I can. I'm already experiencing perimenopausal symptoms."

"Peri-what?"

"Um, excuse me?" Ashley's voice startles both of us. "I don't mean to interrupt but I'll be late for my next client if we don't wrap this up. I think maybe we better continue this conversation next session?"

"Sounds good," I say absently and hang up the phone. I nearly crawl over the console to get my hands on Molly's face, cupping her jaw and making her look me in the eye.

"This isn't a make it or break it issue for me. Please don't cry."

"And I wouldn't mind having more kids, but time's not on my side, Bobby. If you want more kids, I'm not sure you should be with me."

My heart starts pounding and not in a good way like when I'm about to beat someone's ass for messing with my captain. "Hey. Don't say that. Let's table that topic for now. One thing at a time. Right now I want to take the lady I love to lunch so we can submit an offer on a house. As my mom would say, let's not borrow trouble."

Molly's smile is watery, but it's there. "Okay."

I kiss her softly, savoring the scent of her filling my car. Instead of arguing about hypothetical kids in the distant future, I need to make Molly see how good we are together. That it's not too early to talk about a future together. About how she can trust me with every aspect of her life. How much fun we have together. After parking by the restaurant, I make sure to tuck her into my side as we walk together.

"Maybe over lunch we can discuss the naked plans I have for you in each of those rooms we just looked at."

"Bobby!"

"What? Can't blame a man for having dreams and aspirations, baby."

Chapter Twenty-Six

Molly

"What are your thoughts on Freud?" I ask from the doorway of Coco's office. She's sitting at her desk jotting something down with a gold pen.

"I could never date a man so obsessed with everyone's childhoods," she replies without looking up.

I step closer and cross my arms. "He's been dead for a hundred years, Coco."

She finally looks up, bringing the pen to the side of her mouth. "I've always found the German language to be dreadfully guttural, haven't you?"

This was clearly a mistake, so I laugh and turn to go. "I'd like to retract my question. I need to meet a client anyway."

"Oh, goodness, you're serious, aren't you? Take a seat," she commands. And, since I'm the one who invited this conversation, I do as I'm told and sink into the leather wingback chair across from her.

Coco pats her perfectly coiffed hair. "I'm sure Freud

would have a field day with me and all my preferences and idiosyncrasies, but I could not care less what some old dead man thinks about me." She points her pen at me. "And you shouldn't either."

"I know. I'm just . . . conflicted."

"This is about Bobby Rhodes, I gather?"

It's been a week since Bobby dropped the love bomb on me in his car—with his therapist! And I've spent way too much of the week examining my feelings and getting nowhere. When I'm with him, it's so easy, so natural. I don't overthink when we're together.

It's when I'm up in the middle of the night—that 2:36 a.m. witching hour—that my mind races with doubts. I've never been a leap-before-you-look person. I grew up with two parents who made it their life missions to fly by the seat of their second-hand pants, and I know the devastation that can come from that.

Spending Thanksgiving with Matty, Blake, and Luke didn't help clear my confusion, either. Bobby was disappointed not to spend the holiday with Matty and me, but his team had away games before and after, so he was on the road. When Matty asked if I'd come with him to Blake's for dinner, I couldn't exactly refuse.

Watching Blake and Luke so happy together made me miss Bobby like crazy. But it also made my head spin with doubt. Blake and Luke make sense together. They're close in age and economic status, and they have numerous interests in common. Luke even plays guitar like Blake.

Bobby and I, on the other hand? We have nothing in common, and he's too rich and young. It would never work long term, no matter what my heart tries to tell me. Having developing L-word feelings for someone or being sexually compatible are not firm grounds to base an entire future on. Are they?

"He told me he loves me, Coco. What am I supposed to do with that?"

Her lips tip up. "Revel in it? Make him your sex slave? Say it back? Your pick."

"It's not that easy, and you know it."

"It's only as difficult as you make it, darling."

"I don't have the luxury of making mistakes. That's like advising someone to go on a lavish vacation when they have no money in the bank and tons of bills to pay."

"Love is free. And so is sex. All the best things are . . . except precious stones, of course. And cosmetic surgery."

"Oh god, I'm so confused. I have no idea what I'm doing here. It was supposed to be a fun adventure, and now there are all these *feelings* involved. And not just Bobby's or mine. Matthew's too."

"Darling, you deserve to have a man fall head over heels in love with you. And so does Matthew." She abandons the pen and folds her hands together on the desktop. "How do you feel about Bobby? What does your gut tell you when you're not overthinking it?"

"I'm too busy overthinking it to figure that out!" I slouch in the chair in defeat. "I have such a good time with him, and he's so kind and generous and funny. But I have to put Matty first, and what if Bobby just *thinks* he loves me and figures out a month from now that it was only the novelty of it all? That a more age-appropriate woman suddenly looks more appealing?"

I huff out a frustrated breath. "And he wants to have babies, Coco. *Babies.*" I circle a finger over my belly. "My baby-making factory is having a going-out-of-business clearance event right now, and having a baby isn't something you can just jump into because the window is closing."

"Those all sound like what-ifs," my boss replies.

"Speaking of what-ifs, what if he really does have an

Oedipus complex and I find out I'm a dead ringer for his mom?! You know, part of the Oedipus complex is seeing other men as rivals and acting aggressively toward them. Did you know Bobby's job with the Storm Chasers is picking fights with opposing players? Real fights, Coco! With punches and . . . and . . . fisticuffs!" My breathing is almost ragged now.

"Fisticuffs?! Oh my!" She clutches her pearls, and not in a metaphorical sense. She's literally wearing a diamond and pearl necklace. But her tone drips with sarcasm.

"Coco." I frown at her.

"I'm sorry. I couldn't help myself. You sounded like my Grandmother June, and she's been dead for thirty years." She makes a shooing motion in the air before continuing. "Do you know what makes you a good realtor, Molly?"

"Learning from you?" I guess.

"Your work ethic. Your attention to detail. And your natural problem-solving abilities."

My chest warms at her compliment. "Well, thank you."

She forges ahead without acknowledging my thanks. "But do you know what would make you a *great* realtor?" Oh. Okay. "Opening up your imagination to embrace *all* the possibilities." She spreads her hands in the air like she's revealing a marquee. "Reaching for what you want and not even entertaining the option of failure."

"You have a point, I suppose. But blind hope hasn't ever really appealed to me." Practicality and good planning are far more reliable.

"Not blind or simply wishing on a star. Trusting yourself and believing you can make things happen." Coco abandons the imaginary marquee and focuses on me again. "Did you know the first property I sold was an empty, rundown, two-bedroom manufactured home that had been on the market for eighteen months? My boss gave it to me to watch it blow up in my face—an odious weasel of a man named Tony Lamont whom I recommend avoiding at all costs—but did I let it deter me?"

She answers her own question. "No. I did not. I spent a week scrubbing floors and windows and another cleaning up the lawn, planting flowers, and painting the entire inside. A third week scouring thrift shops and friends' and relatives' homes for mirrors, lighting, and furniture to create a vision of what the house could be.

"It wasn't a dilapidated, unkempt hovel anymore. It was a charming starter home for a young couple. I loved that house. I *put love* into that house. And because I did, the people I scrounged up to view it loved it too. I got two offers within a week. I made a thousand dollars and earned three new contracts."

"So, you're saying if I throw caution to the wind and go all in with Bobby, two other women are going to fall in love with him three weeks from now?"

She completely ignores my snarky comment. "Look, I know you have to put Matthew first, but I'll bet he'd tell you to take a leap and trust your heart."

I sigh and glance at my watch. "Now I actually do have to meet a client." I stand and send Coco a warm smile. "Thank you for the advice. I'll keep you posted."

As I leave her office, she, of course, has to have the last word. "And I'll start shopping for my maid of honor dress. Can we go with emerald green? It's my best color."

This is the second time my client is viewing this town-home north of Tampa, so I'm hoping it's a sign that she's close to making a decision. That's one reason I haven't hurried her along as she inspects every closet for the third time.

I surreptitiously glance at my watch to see it's past four. I want to reach for my phone to make sure Matty got off the bus and is home safe, but it can wait. The worst thing I can do right now is interrupt this client's "process."

"What did you say the HOA fees are?"

"$300 per month," I reply without having to look at the listing. I've got the thing memorized at this point. "It will be a godsend not having to do lawn work, I promise you." I smile.

She nods. "I'm just going to look at the primary bedroom closet one more time."

I gesture for her to go ahead.

By the time I drop her off back at the office in Coco's BMW, it's past five. I pull out my phone to see I have five missed calls, four from Matty and one from Bobby. Crap! I immediately pull up the phone tracking app and am baffled to see Matty's location is his school, not our house.

"Hey, Mom," he answers on the second ring. "I think you forgot today was the Spanish Club event after school."

I suck in a breath and drop my head to the steering wheel. "I was supposed to pick you up at four-thirty! I completely forgot you weren't taking the bus home today! I'm so sorry. I'm on my way right now." I can't believe I forgot my kid! I scramble from the driver's seat and lock the car before racing toward the office to drop the keys off.

"No hurry. Bobby's here and we're hanging out."

"Bobby, as in Bobby Rhodes?" I send an apologetic nod to Maude as I slip past her. She frowns.

Matty laughs. "Uh, how many other Bobbies do we know?"

"Good point." I drop the keys and reverse direction.

"I called him when I couldn't get you, and he came over,

even though school won't let me leave with him. You gotta add him to the list, Mom."

"Right." I hop in my Kia and turn the key in the ignition. "Um, okay. It's going to take me another twenty minutes to get there."

"Like I said, no hurry." He diverts the phone from his mouth but I'm still almost rendered deaf when he yells, "Hey, Bobby! Tell them about the Detroit game!" He hurriedly mutters, "Bye, Mom," before hanging up.

I connect my phone to the Kia's Bluetooth and pull from the parking lot as I place a call to Bobby.

"Hey, baby," he answers, and I swear I can hear his sexy smile in his voice.

"I fucked up." No use mincing words.

He barks out a laugh. "Not at all. We're having a good time, me and the boys." The chatter of adolescent males bleeds through the phone's mic.

"Thank you so much for trying to pick him up. Blake must have been away from his phone like I was."

"Um, actually, Matthew's second call was *me* after he couldn't reach you."

"It was? He should have called his dad instead of bothering you. I'm sorry." I wave to a guy in a red Mazda who lets me merge in front of him.

"Don't be. I dig that he feels comfortable enough with me to reach out. Seriously."

My breath catches at the sincerity in his tone. "Wow. I don't . . . know what to say. Actually, that's a lie. You're too good to be true, Bobby Rhodes."

"Flesh and blood, baby. Right here. Always."

My heart rate skyrockets for some reason and my vision starts to blur as tears form. I have turned into such a crybaby recently. Damn perimenopause. I swipe them away because I'm currently driving a car through Tampa rush hour traffic and can't afford to crash just because I'm all up in my feelings about a guy.

"I need to concentrate on driving before you make me cry."

"Take your time. I'm having a little impromptu press conference with half the seventh grade. Drive safe."

"I will."

I do a little Lamaze breathing the rest of the way there to calm my shit, and by the time I pull into the school parking lot, I've returned to a semi-normal state. I laugh out loud when I see Bobby on the school steps surrounded by a dozen kids and half of their parents.

"Good god," I mutter to myself as I park and get out. When I make my way over to the steps, Matty spots me before Bobby does and breaks through the circle to come over. Looks like my kid is anxious to get home. He's probably starving.

But he surprises me by grabbing my arm and pulling me into the circle to Bobby's side. "This is my mom. She's Bobby's girlfriend," he announces to everyone, his man-boy chest puffing.

Oh god. What fresh hell is this?

I feel my skin turn to fire as Bobby reaches out to throw an arm around my shoulder and pull me into his side. "Hey, baby."

All eyes are on us while Bobby's gaze skims over my face as if inspecting every detail for signs of what I might be feeling. I'll never understand people who crave being the center of attention. "Hey," I manage as I will my skin to cool.

"Bobby, what is Roman LaFontaine like?" one of the dads asks.

"Roman?" Bobby's eyes stay on me as he starts to answer, and I realize he wants me to signal I'm okay. This man is so attuned to me, it's hard to believe sometimes. Only when I nod does he turn to the man. "He's a little too full of himself, to be honest." Everyone laughs. "Nah, I'm just kidding. He's a legend, and he was a great mentor for the season we played together."

We stand there while Bobby patiently answers questions and shakes hands with everyone. He even signs some kids' backpacks before the crowd starts to disperse and our crew of three heads back to my car.

"That was so cool," Matty gushes. "The kids whose parents were on time are gonna be so mad they missed it."

Bobby and I both laugh and Matty shrugs, a huge smile spread across his cute face as he climbs in the Kia and closes the door with a quick, "Later, Bobby."

I rest my back against the car and look up at my guy as he closes the distance between us and settles his hands on my hips. Why have I been questioning this? Bobby is the perfect boyfriend. *My* perfect boyfriend. He's wearing a half smile and a look in his eyes I recognize well by now. It's a look of pure affection. It tells me there's nobody else in the world he'd rather be standing across from right now.

So I pull my big girl pants up and trust my heart. "Bobby Rhodes, I love you."

Chapter Twenty-Seven

Bobby

Good times don't last, boy. You gotta work hard for what you want, then work even harder to keep it.

Those are the wise and depressing words of my father. The glass is neither half full nor half empty in Dale Rhodes's world, it needs constant refilling. But I've never believed in the shit that man would spew, which is probably why I got my ass handed to me over and over again while growing up.

To be fair, I got an incredible work ethic from him that sealed the deal on my hockey career, but it also left some wounds even Mom hadn't been able to heal. Right now, there's a voice in my head, sounding suspiciously like my father, telling me that things are too good with me and Molly. That the other shoe is about to drop.

As for me, I refuse to believe that. Life is good. Molly, Matthew, and I have started a rhythm of sorts that suits us all. My career is on an upswing. Coach is off my ass, for the most part. My first house is going to close in just under two weeks.

The Christmas countdown has begun, and I've never looked forward to the holiday like this. Matthew's first few hockey games have gone well, and with the exception of a few battles of will with Molly and Blake, he hasn't gotten into any other fights at school.

And Molly. Damn, things are good with Molly. Once she said she loved me, she slid right into being the world's best girlfriend. She doesn't even try to cover herself when I strip her naked these days. Plus, she's been going to all my home games, sitting in the WAG section and sending me flirty waves that I swear make me skate faster.

"Molly!" I holler, letting myself into her house with the key she gave me. Matthew's going home with his dad after school today to start his week with him. That means I have plans to get Molly naked and keep her that way until I have to leave for practice.

"Back here!" she calls back.

I follow the direction of her voice, gripping the doorway of her bedroom when I see her in a short, silky emerald green nightie with lace cutouts that give enticing glimpses of her milky smooth skin. She's laid out on the bed, her knee cocked up and one hand behind her head. Her auburn hair is spread out on the pillow. But it's her confident smile that takes my breath away.

"Have I been a good boy?" I can barely breathe.

Molly lets out a hearty laugh, then controls herself, giving me a throaty answer in the mom voice I love so much. "Such a good boy. Why don't you come over here and let me show you how good?"

My phone rings in my back pocket, but I can't take my eyes off Molly. I take it out and throw it on the nightstand without looking at it. Molly lifts her arms in the air, and I take a flying leap to land on the bed, careful not to squash her. She squeals as I pounce on her, quick to get my lips on every available inch of skin.

"Mmm, baby. You smell so good," I murmur, taking my time to kiss every inch of her.

My phone rings again and Molly's head turns toward it. "Ignore it," I tell her, then push her knee to the side to see matching panties under this lingerie. "Yes," I whisper, celebrating with myself. If I didn't mind taking my hands off Molly, I'd high five myself for what I'm about to enjoy.

The phone rings a third time and with an irritated moan, I lean over her to snatch it up and silence it. Except I see that it's my dad calling me. I must pause or grimace or something because Molly pushes up on her elbows.

"You need to take that?"

Dad never calls me. Except when we lose a game. Then he calls and tells me all the ways in which we fucked up and deserved the loss. "Um, maybe. It's my dad."

Molly pushes the phone toward me. "Take it!"

Fuck. I grab her hands and bring them to my lips, kissing her fingers before hitting accept and putting the phone to my ear. "Dad?"

"Bobby! 'Bout time you answered. Your mom's in the hospital."

I'm frozen, absorbing his words as if through a tunnel stuffed with cotton balls. I feel Molly shift, pressing her ear to mine to hear what he's saying. He keeps talking, but I can't make out the words. Fear, the kind that grabs your gut in a vice and won't let you take a full breath, is running the show. I've felt this way a time or two out on the ice, but I was always able to breathe my way through it. Not this time. Not with Mom.

Molly nudges me. She mouths the word "okay" and I say it back.

Dad finally penetrates the fog, probably because his voice

breaks in the middle of his sentence. "Just get here quick, okay, son?"

I say okay again and hang up, still holding the phone in the air. Molly is up on her knees, her hands cupping my face.

"Bobby? Honey, can you hear me?"

"Wha . . .?"

Molly slams her lips to mine, her tongue delving into mouth and stealing what breath I have left. She leans her warm sweet body into mine. My hands find her hips and suddenly the heat of her seeps into me. My shoulders drop and my hands slide around to her ass, cupping her.

She pulls away just enough to stare into my eyes. "You with me?"

"I'm with you, baby."

"Okay." Her thumbs stroke my cheeks, so sweet and comforting I want to curl up into her. "We need to get you to Georgia, honey."

She tries to pull her hands away from my face, but I hold them there. "Come with me." It's not a question. I need her there with me. I need her by my side in my hometown more than ever. I'll beg if I have to.

Molly's eyes go wide and then she nods. "Okay. I just need to call Coco and pack a bag."

"You'll come?" When she nods again, I kiss her, hard. "Thank you."

I travel a lot for my job, but I've never taken a better plane ride than this one. We were able to snag last minute seats in the very back row of the airplane by the bathrooms. The baby in front of me must be related to Mei because she's been screaming almost the whole flight. Molly's held my hand the whole time, her thumb stroking back and forth like a metronome of comfort.

Molly remembered to call Richie, who said he was working a shift and couldn't leave until tomorrow. I didn't want to wait that long, so we took off for the airport immediately. Molly informed me that Dad said something about a heart attack on the phone. That must have been the part I didn't hear. When I went to Google heart attack survival rates in women, Molly confiscated my phone. Instead, she's been coaxing out every single memory I have of my mom.

I'm mid-story about that time Artie punched George, who fell into Richie, who backhanded me accidentally. Being the littlest, I went flying and broke Mom's vase. The one her mother had given to her years ago. It was a family heirloom and I'd broken it. Will, the oldest, came out of the bathroom and looked at the mess, shaking his head, saying we were going to be in so much trouble. Never mind the fact that he was supposed to have been watching us. Mom came home, took one look at our tear-stained cheeks and bowed heads while we stood over the shards of glass, and made us all go outside. She cleaned up the mess then came outside in her swimsuit. The sprinklers flipped on, and she laughed like a crazy woman as she ran through. Then we all started running through them and we had what became one of my favorite days of summer ever.

"She sounds like a strong woman and a beautiful soul. I can't wait to meet her," Molly says, still holding my hand as we file out of the airplane.

I get our bags and a rental car before making the drive out to my little hometown on the northern outskirts of Atlanta. I don't bother going to the house. I go straight to the hospital, pull into the valet spot, toss the keys over, and hustle us both inside the bright hospital. It smells like antiseptic and sadness, even in the lobby.

"Sue Rhodes please?" I ask the lady at the information desk. She looks up her name on the computer and directs us to the second floor, room two-twenty-four.

The elevator ride is slow and tortuous. The doors finally slide open, and I race forward. Molly pulls me back, a worried expression on her pretty face.

"Hey. I'm just going to wait outside while you find out what's going on. When you're ready, just stick your head out and I'll come in. Or I can just wait to meet everyone later."

I'm already shaking my head. "No. You should come in."

"Your mom's been through a medical event. Let her see her sons before you go and introduce a stranger. Please, Bobby."

I don't like it, but she has a point. "Okay. It'll just take me a second." I kiss her quickly and we walk toward the right room. She takes a position in the hall against the wall and shoots me an encouraging wink.

When I step inside the room, the lights are low and machines are beeping. There's a curtain around the bed, but I see shoes underneath. Shoes that probably belong to my older brothers. I push the curtain aside and see Mom for the first time. She looks pale and sickly, smaller than I remember her from the last time I visited. There's oxygen going to her nose and she's hooked up to an IV and has those electrode things on her chest. Her eyes are closed. My heart squeezes so hard seeing her like that I think I might be having a sympathy heart attack.

"You came." Dad steps next to me and claps me on the shoulder.

"Of course I came," I mumble back. I only have eyes for Mom. It hits me with startling clarity that she was the only truly good thing about my childhood. Through my sessions with Ashley and time spent with Molly as she parents Matthew, I've come to realize that my childhood wasn't normal. "How's she doing?"

"She had a heart attack, dumbass. How do you think she's doing?" Will answers, stepping closer with that stupid smirk on his face that used to make me daydream about punching him in the nose.

I hold up my hand, shaking my head. "Just tell me how she is. We can do the name calling later."

"Ohh," Artie hoots. "You've gone soft now that you're a famous hockey guy? No name calling allowed in the league?" He and George snicker like school children.

I ignore them all and head over to the bed, kneeling down to put a hand to Mom's cheek. Her eyes flutter open, unfocused for a moment. Then she sees me and she breaks out into that familiar lopsided smile.

"Hey, my sweet boy. You're here."

"Hi, Mom. I heard you needed some attention so you faked a heart attack."

She grins more, a look of pure affection in her eyes. "Heard it was the best way to get my Bobby fix. You know I can't go too long without seeing you."

"Don't wear yourself out," Dad grouses, stepping over to the other side of the bed. He gives me a hard look I try to ignore.

"I brought someone with me to meet you," I say to Mom.

"Oh? Is it a woman?" She seems to perk up. Mom's been giving me grief about settling down since I turned sixteen. Said I was her only hope for grandbabies.

"It is. Her name's Molly and she's a mom too." I lean in closer so only she can hear. "She's the one, Mom."

Tears fill her eyes.

"Dad!" Artie hisses. "Bobby's making Mom cry!"

Will immediately bats me away from the bedside with a

hard shove. "You brought a woman to the hospital? What's wrong with you? Can't you just be there for Mom without a parade of puck bunnies?"

"Boys!" Mom wheezes. Dad bends over her, trying to comfort her when what she really needs is for him to keep these jackasses in line.

"Don't touch me." I bump Will's chest with mine, both of us puffed up and ready to fight. He used to be bigger than me, but I outwork all my brothers combined in the gym these days.

"Or what? You'll call your baby mama in here and she'll give me a spanking?" His smirk is out in full force. "I might like it and have to steal your girl."

I don't notice any of the warning signs. I just pull back my fist and let it fly.

Molly

The unmistakable sound of flesh and bone colliding has me rounding the corner into the hospital room before I can form even one coherent thought. A metaphorical wall of testosterone brings me to a halt when I see five iterations of Bobby Rhodes, one clearly older than the rest. Everyone in the room is shouting, their fists tightly bunched as Bobby scuffles with one of his brothers.

My eyes flash to his mom in the hospital bed looking frail and tiny in comparison to the giant men surrounding her. I lunge toward Bobby, intent on separating him from who I assume is Will, not pausing to think about the wisdom of using my smaller frame to intercept two grown, battling men. But I'm pulled back at the last second by a pair of strong arms and turn to see Bobby's father, his brow furrowed and jaw tight.

"Hold on there, young lady. You don't want to get caught up in that." He sets me aside and barks at one of the bystanding brothers, "Artie, pull those two knuckleheads apart! Dammit all! Can't you boys see you're upsetting your mother and embarrassing yourselves? What is wrong with you?!"

Bobby grunts and throws another punch as Will drives his head into Bobby's gut, grabbing him around the middle and bashing him into a wall. By the time they're separated and held apart by their brothers, Bobby has a cut over his eyebrow and Will's nose is bleeding. They're glaring hard at one another and breathing even harder. I'll admit I'm just as breathless as they are. What in the world is going on with this family?

"Apologize to your mother right now," Bobby's dad commands.

Will shakes off Artie's grip and stalks from the room, purposely bumping Bobby's shoulder on his way out. Bobby snarls at him, and when he turns to watch him go, he finally spots me. His expression goes from wild aggression to what I can only describe as devastation in the blink of an eye.

"Fuck," he mutters, bending at the waist and propping his hands on his knees.

I can feel everyone's eyes on me, but I can't stop looking at Bobby's bent frame and heaving chest.

"I apologize for my sons," Mr. Rhodes says, his voice gruff with annoyance. "Clearly none of them are fit for respectable society, especially that one." He gestures to Bobby. "I hope you're not too invested is all I can say."

"Don't lump Artie and me in with those dipshits," the one who must be George complains. "At least the two of us know how to treat a woman." To prove his point, he sidles up next to the bed by their mother.

As if pulled up by an invisible puppet string, Bobby straightens and robotically shuffles to the door of the hospital room, only pausing to mutter a quiet, "I love you, Mom. I'm sorry," before passing through and disappearing around the corner.

His mom's eyes shine with tears, and part of me wants to go hug her, but I don't know her. I don't know any of these people. But there is one person I know, and he's in a whole lot of pain right now. So I excuse myself and run after Bobby.

The man is quick, I can give him that. He's already outside the hospital entrance and striding down the walkway by the time I catch up to him.

"Bobby!"

I know he hears me, but he doesn't slow down. Good thing I wore my flat boots today.

"Robert Rhodes, stop running away. Talk to me."

He still doesn't slow down, but at least he acknowledges me this time. "They're right, Molly. I'm no good for you. I'm an impulsive asshole and I'll never be good enough for you." His voice is tight and low, and it sets my heart racing faster than the sprinting I'm doing to keep up with him.

"That's a bunch of BS, and you know it!" I'm finally able to grab the fabric of his shirtsleeve and pull him to a stop—not from my superhuman strength but because I'm not letting go and he doesn't want me dragging on the sidewalk behind him getting road burn. See, he always looks out for me, despite what his current mindset is telling him.

"It's not, Molly. I've been kidding myself that I'm becoming a better man. I'll always be a hot-headed Rhodes boy, scrapping and lashing out, trying to claw out a space for myself. You deserve better than that. Matthew deserves better than that."

I let go of his shirt and prop my hands on my hips. "Don't you think I at least deserve some input on what Matty and I do or don't deserve? You're upset, and understandably so. I mean, damn, I thought *my* family dynamic was rough."

He drops his head back on a frustrated growl as a light

breeze ruffles his hair. "You're making excuses for me. I literally got into a fistfight in front of my mother while she's fighting for her life."

"Okay, fair. I'm not about to say I liked seeing you and your brother bloodying one another. And, yes, your timing could have been better." I step right up into his space and grab both his hands. He straightens his head to look down at me, strain lining his mouth and eyes. The setting sun casts him in a golden light that highlights his perfect bone structure. "But I could feel the tension in that room strung tight as a bowstring from out in the hall. Hell, I'm pretty sure people out in this parking lot felt it, it was that intense. Emotions are bound to run high at a time like this, but it was more than that. You've talked about it before, but I didn't really get it until today. It's toxic, and that's not on you."

"I should be able to handle my own shit, Molly. I'm a grown man." He pulls his hands from mine and covers his face. "Fuck! My mom."

I pull a bottle of water from my bag and hand it to him. He takes it and wordlessly opens it to draw in a long swallow. I want to get a better look at that cut on his eyebrow, but he needs more reassurance first.

"Your mom knows your family dynamic better than anyone, I'm sure. And I'm sure it's scary as hell to see her in that hospital bed, but she's going to pull through and be fine. I know she will. They didn't even have her in the ICU, so that's a great sign. And then the two of you can carve out some time together—maybe away from the rest of your brothers, yeah?"

Bobby pulls the bottle from his lips and shakes his head, but I notice some of the tension has drained, so I must be getting through to him to some degree. "I shouldn't have brought you here."

I grip the fabric of his shirt with both hands. "I'm glad you did. I want to be here for you like you're always there for me.

And to be honest, I kind of want to punch your brother in the face for running his mouth like he did. Your family makes an art out of shit stirring, don't they?"

This elicits the smallest of lip quirks. "It's an Olympic sport and they're all gold medalists."

I smile up at him, infusing all the warmth I can in my words. "Stick with me and I'll bring the peace."

Bobby brings his hand up to cup my jaw, his thumb caressing it as he stares into my eyes. "That's exactly what you do, Molly." His voice catches. "You settle my soul and give me that calm I didn't even know I needed so badly."

"I love you, Bobby, and we're going to work through this. Together." The sting of building emotion hits my nose.

"I have no idea what I did to deserve you, baby," he whispers as he leans down to rest his forehead against mine.

"Right back 'atcha, Mister bigshot hockey man." I slide one hand up to wrap around the side of his neck. "How about we patch up that eyebrow and get something to eat. Then maybe you can call the nurse's station and get a full update on your mom?"

"I do get a little cranky when I'm hungry." This time, his smile is closer to the Bobby I'm used to.

I pat his chest. "I know." Then I take my man to dinner.

"You've told me a few things about growing up, but I get the sense you don't like to talk about it, so I haven't really brought it up," Bobby says an hour later as we both lay our napkins over our empty plates at a diner near his family home. Drama and grief sure do work up an appetite. "Now that you've had the full Rhodes family experience, I kind of feel like it's my turn. If you feel up to it, I'd like to hear what growing up in the Hooker household was like."

I pause with my drink straw halfway to my mouth. "You just like saying my maiden name."

"I don't *not* like saying it."

I bark out a laugh. "Believe me, I was happy to get rid of it when I married Blake." After sipping my drink, I set it back on the Formica tabletop and pause for a moment. "I don't know, I guess our family's story isn't that uncommon. Money was tight, utilities weren't a given, depending on the month. I had to grow up fast."

Bobby leans in and rests both forearms on the table. I get momentarily distracted by the arm porn he so casually lays out there. "Being an only child in that situation must have been rough. I mean, my brothers are assholes, but it doesn't mean we never had fun. And Richie has always been fairly tolerable."

"Yeah. It was lonely." I spent way too much time alone as a kid. "It wasn't fun growing up feeling so insecure about everything, so I don't know that I would have wished that on another child."

I shake my head, allowing the memories to surface. "For a while, I was too young to understand that not everyone's mom spent rent money on telephone psychics and nobody else's dad relied solely on get-rich-quick scams to keep the family fed. There was no true adult in charge, and I didn't know until I was older how that really messed with my head." I lean forward, infusing my words with all the conviction in me. "It's why I'm so adamant about giving Matthew a strong foundation and letting him be a kid. I don't want him worrying about adult stuff yet."

Bobby winces. "And then I go and fuck things up by acting immature and probably making you relive some childhood trauma."

"No, Bobby. You didn't." I reach over the plates and grasp one of his hands. "My parents never took any responsibility for anything that went wrong in our lives. They'd chalk it up to bad luck and blindly promise next time would be better. They never owned their own shit. One of my very first conversations with you was about how you were in therapy to improve yourself and show up for the people in your life. You own every ounce of your shit and you're not afraid to work hard for what you want."

One of his dimples pops. "Were you a cheerleader in high school? Because you are damn good at building up a guy's confidence."

I give his hand one more squeeze and lean back in my side of the booth. "Nope. I was working from the time I was fifteen, so I didn't have time for normal high school stuff. But I could still do a mean herkie. And I could work a deep fryer like nobody's business."

His eyes widen. "Stop turning me on, Sparkle." Then he sobers and sighs. "I really hate that you had to go through all of that."

I shrug because life is going to life, no matter what we do. I'm just glad I have him in mine. "Everybody's got family baggage. Ours just might be a matching set, Mr. Rhodes."

Chapter Twenty-Nine

Bobby

With Molly by my side—and my brothers still at the hospital —we head to my parents' house. I show her my room, the pictures on the staircase wall that showcase my terrible haircuts over the years, my hockey trophies, and then the shade tree in the backyard where all five of us boys carved our initials.

Seeing my childhood home through Molly's eyes reminds me that there's been a lot of good that's come out of this house too. The Rhodes boys are far from perfect, but there's love underneath all the immaturity. Maybe with a little more therapy, I can tap into the love and not just the immaturity.

I call the hospital again and they inform me that Mom's staying overnight for more tests to be sure she's stable, and that visiting hours have ended. I figure Dad and my brothers will be home soon, so I take Molly to the nicest hotel in town. It's still not much, but I get us a room on the top floor and breathe a sigh of relief knowing we don't have to stay at the house with my brothers.

Molly sinks onto the fluffy comforter and swings her legs up to lay down. Today's been an emotional rollercoaster, but there's nothing I want more in this moment than to show this incredible woman how much I love her. Hearing her fight for me, for us, was everything I needed to get my doubts to shut the fuck up.

I slip into the bathroom and lay a mat down on the floor, then kneel to run the hot water. Soon, the bathtub is nearly full, so I dump in the entire travel bottle of bubble bath the hotel provided and turn off the water. The scent of lavender and something woodsy fills the bathroom. Standing back up, I head into the bedroom and see Molly thumbing out a text.

"Everything okay?"

She puts her phone down and smiles up at me. "Yeah. Just checking in with Matty. He had his second therapy appointment today."

"How did it go?"

"He said the counselor is easy to talk to, so that's a good start, right?" She shrugs and I nod in reassurance. "Anyway, he told me he's studying right now and I am going to trust that isn't a lie."

I reach down and slip her boots off her feet, tossing them behind me. "You being a good mom is incredibly sexy, Molly."

Her grin turns to a smirk. "You should see me yelling at him when he's about to miss the bus."

"You being a realtor and prancing around in your heels and pencil skirts is incredibly sexy." I unzip her jeans and peel them off her legs.

"What else?" Her breathing has picked up and I'm sure she expects a few of those orgasms I always deliver. But first, I want her to relax.

I reach behind her and pull her up into a seated position so I can unbutton the blouse behind her neck and peel it over her head. Her bra is a lacy black material, matching her panties and designed to drive a man insane. Fuck. Maybe we could skip the bath? I mentally give myself a smack across the face. *Focus, Rhodes.*

"I think you coming between me and my brother today was incredibly brave and most definitely sexy as hell." I reach around and unclasp her bra, letting it fall from her shoulders. I can't help but cup her breasts in my hands, feeling their weight and watching her nipples pucker under my gaze. But I force myself to release her, pulling her to the side of the bed so I can strip her panties down her legs.

She lets out a yelp as I swing her up into my arms and carry her across the carpeted bedroom. "What are you doing?"

"Bubble bath for you, Ms. Sparks. You've worked hard controlling this idiot." I shoot her a lopsided grin. Molly kisses me and we stop right there in the bathroom for a long moment with her in my arms and our lips locked. Reluctantly, I pull back and set her on her feet in the tub. She sighs and sinks down under the bubbles.

"I don't think anyone's ever drawn me a bath. Not since I was a toddler." Molly leans her head back against the porcelain and closes her eyes, lost in bliss.

My heart aches, knowing she's been fending for herself for far too long. I make a promise to myself: I'm going to spoil the hell out of her. I'm going to turn all that energy I spent being an idiot and funnel it into making her life easier. Seems like drawing my woman a bubble bath is a better use of my time than punching my brother in the face. Way easier on my knuckles too.

I slip out of the bathroom and get ready for bed. Coach has texted me, so I update him on my mom. He isn't pressuring me to get back, but I know we have a game the day after tomorrow. I just need to go see Mom again in the morning to know she's on the mend and to formally apologize for being stupid. I also want to introduce her to Molly. She's going to love her, I just know it.

A good half hour later I hear water splashing so I go into the bathroom to dry off every inch of Molly's skin before she can get her own towel. She giggles when I get to her belly and gets that hazy-eyed look when I give her breasts plenty of attention. When she's fully dry and has tried to stifle a yawn for the third time, I get her back in my arms and deposit her under the covers.

I climb in behind her and pull her in close, tucking her head between my chest and arm. My hand glides across her hip and stays there. Despite how badly I want to slide between her legs and hear her chant my name as she comes undone, I force my hand to rest. She'd let me, I know, but more than sexual release so good it makes my eyes roll back in my head, I want her happy and content.

"I love you," I whisper into her hair. It hits me that I almost lost her today. Lost this. Lost us. My eyes slide shut as I will away the emotion. I refuse to let that happen again. Molly's mine. Forever, if she'll have me.

She reaches up to the arm that's cushioning her head and intertwines her fingers with mine. "I love you too."

We fall asleep that way, only waking once around two in the morning. Molly's eyes are open, staring up at the ceiling.

"Can't sleep?" My voice is barely an audible scratch.

She shakes her head. "That stupid 2:36am. It's my nemesis."

I grunt and slide beneath the covers, rolling over her leg until my face is above her pretty pussy. Sadly, I can't see her and I contemplate turning on the light, but my whole focus is on making her sleep. Dark it is.

My left hand snakes up her torso to cup her breast. "Bobby," she breathes, already squirming under me.

I spread her open with my right hand and dive in, leaving

not one inch of her unexplored with my tongue. Since it's the middle of the night, I get serious, zeroing in on her clit and pumping two fingers inside her tight heat. Molly says my name again, but it's muffled, like she's buried her face in the pillow. I grin against her flesh and flick my tongue with reckless abandon until she goes stiff beneath me with a loud bark of my name. Her limbs start to quake and then she relaxes every single muscle. I kiss her still, lapping up her taste and wondering if she'd let me do this every night around 2:36.

Eventually, I climb out from under the sheets and pull her into my arms again. It only takes a few seconds for Molly's breathing to even out as she goes back to sleep. It takes me a little bit longer to make my dick realize it's not happening for him right now and then I'm out like a light too.

The next morning, we head back to the hospital as soon as visiting hours start. My brothers are night owls, so I have a feeling we'll get Mom all to ourselves. Molly starts acting nervous when we get to the hallway that leads to Mom's room.

I spin her into the wall and press her into a kiss too hot for a hospital full of sick people. "She'll love you just like I do."

Molly bites her lip, looking up at me. "I hope not *just* like you do." Her cheeks flare with color and I know she's thinking of what I did under those sheets to put her back to sleep.

"I like it when you talk dirty, baby," I whisper against her mouth, intent on saving that poor lip from her teeth.

A throat clearing behind me has us parting. I spin around to see a nurse in scrubs leaving Mom's room. She's biting back a smile. "Here for Sue? She's sitting up and ready for visitors."

"Thank you." I take Molly's hand and we enter the room. I poke my head behind the curtain to see Mom sitting up with a tray of food in front of her. Molly, being the genius I've fallen in love with, convinced me to stop and pick up Mom's favorite pastries in town, informing me that hospital food sucks.

"Good morning, Mom," I say quietly, not wanting to scare her.

Mom looks up, a ready smile on her thin face. "Oh! Bobby!" She holds up her arms and we hug.

Then I turn to Molly. "I want you to meet my girlfriend, Molly. Molly, this is my Mom, Sue Rhodes."

Molly comes to the bedside and holds out her hand. Mom lifts her arms again, to which Molly smiles and gives her a hug. It's a surreal moment to see my mother and my girlfriend hugging. I never envisioned this day happening.

"It's so good to meet you, dear. Bobby has told me all about you. Sorry about how I look." Mom swipes a hand through her hair. "They're all fussing over a little heart murmur."

"I think you look amazing. All the boys care about is you feeling better. In fact, we brought you some contraband to help you get out of here sooner." Molly holds up the pastry bag so Mom can see it.

Mom gasps. "Oh, you're now my favorite, Molly. Did you get the cinnamon rolls?"

"Of course we did. Got two of them, actually." I wink at Mom, just happy to see some color back in her face. "Did the doctors confirm it's a heart murmur?"

Mom lifts her nose in the air, a sure sign she's about to lie. "Well, it was a heart murmur for sure."

"Mom." I fold my arms across my chest. I can feel Molly looking between us.

Mom sighs. "Fine. It was a heart murmur right before the heart attack."

I take the pastry bag from Molly. "Maybe we should throw these away. I'll talk with the team nutritionist and see if she has some suggestions for you."

"Robert Rhodes, you'll hand me that cinnamon roll if you know what's good for you!" Mom turns to Molly when I don't instantly hand over the goods. "Did I ever tell you about the time I caught him jacking off to an American Dolls catalog?"

"Mom!" To say I'm horrified is an understatement. Molly sputters a laugh that has heat climbing up the back of my neck. "You said we'd never speak about that."

Mom rounds on me, plenty of energy in her now. "That was before you stole my cinnamon rolls out from under me!"

I shake my head, finally seeing my resilient mother back in action. I'm filled with such relief I hand over the pastry bag. "You're lucky I love you."

Mom holds my hand instead of ripping into the bag like I expected. "Yes, I am. I'm the most blessed mother on the planet to have you, Bobby. Santa granted my wish early by sending you out here to see me."

Tears sting my eyes. Mom and I share a moment. I could have been ten, sitting there in the warmth of my mother's love and feeling a level of comfort I haven't felt in a long time.

"You're going to be okay," I whisper.

"Of course I am. Never doubt that." And then she lets me go, reaching into the bag, and jamming a huge bite of dripping cinnamon roll into her mouth.

When she searches the bag for a napkin, she comes up empty but, of course, Molly pulls an entire stack from her purse.

We leave the hospital a half hour later, mostly so I don't run into Dad and my brothers. I'm convinced Mom is in good spirits and I even got to chat with her doctor when she came around to check on Mom. The team's nutritionist has already texted me back with several resources for what Mom needs to do to rehab from the heart attack. I have plans to place a few calls later today and get Mom into regular physical therapy visits and to schedule healthy meals to be delivered. I promise to come back and visit as soon as I have a stretch of off days, but she knows that doesn't happen often in season.

We load up the car with our luggage from the hotel and still have two hours to kill before we head back to the airport. I look at Molly over the hood of the rental car.

"Do you mind if we stop somewhere special?"

"Anywhere."

I take one wrong turn because they tore down the Dairy Queen and put in a Cook Out that throws me off. We eventually make it to the local ice rink where I practiced for hours each day growing up. I sign shirts, skates, and random pieces of paper for the kids just finishing practice. Here, I'm not a screw up, just a local boy who made it big. Frank, the owner who's been here since I was in middle school, has lost more hair and grown his belly a bit more.

"You two have time to skate?"

I look at Molly. "Want to take a spin?"

"Oh, I don't know. I'm not very good on skates."

Sliding my arm around her waist, I tuck her into me. "You've got a professional skater right here, baby."

Molly doesn't look so sure, but she gives me a nod. I help her with her skates and hold her hand as we step out onto the ice. She wobbles, but I stay by her side the whole time. This isn't about me. This is about introducing Molly to my life, my past, my future. I want her to know every part of me, even the not-so-nice parts.

When I feel like she's had enough, I take in her pink cheeks, bright smile, hair gone curly at her temples as strands escape the ponytail, and I don't think I've ever seen a more beautiful woman. I let her glide right into my body and put my hands on her hips to absorb the impact.

"Oof!" Molly laughs. "I don't think I know how to brake yet."

I shake my head, thinking I don't know how to put the

brakes on how I feel about her either. I'm head over skates in love with this woman. Somehow, I need to do everything in my power to be who she needs in her life so she'll keep me. Because from where I'm standing, I'm getting way more out of this than she is.

"I don't either," I mutter, making her frown with confusion. And then I kiss her, hot enough to melt the ice.

Chapter Thirty

Molly

I punch my pillow for the third time and throw off my covers. It's too hot in here. Or maybe I just miss lying next to Bobby. Either way, it's been an hour and a half, and I'm clearly not falling back asleep, so I get out of bed and pad to the kitchen with my phone. The screen reads 4:02.

I lay my bill folder and checkbook on the kitchen table and switch on the coffee maker, turning on only enough light so I can read. May as well use my insomnia to be productive. With the commission from my biggest sale this year in the bank now, I can finally afford the dishwasher repair and even add something extra to my retirement account and Matty's college fund.

We're set to close on Bobby's new house next week, but I refuse to count my chickens on that one before they hatch. Because that commission is going to be huge. Sure, Coco gets her cut, but my measly 3% is still going to be three times this latest one. Just one more thing I owe Bobby for.

Maude and Jason shared plenty of smug looks when they found out Bobby chose a house in a lower price bracket than they expected, but I ignored them the best I could. The house is perfect for Bobby, and that's all I care about.

I sift through the bills and see one for Blake's gym membership, so I do what I always do. Take a photo and text it to him. I swear I'll still be getting mail for him at this house in ten years.

When my phone vibrates on the table, I glance at it to see Blake calling me.

"Hey, what are you doing up?" I ask as soon as I accept the call.

"I was just about to ask you the same thing." His voice is scratchy.

"Oh, haven't I told you about the wonderful new midlife gift Mother Nature has bestowed on me? Insomnia. Every freaking morning at 2:36am for some reason."

"Damn, that sucks. You used to sleep like a rock."

"Those were the days. But seriously, why are you awake? You never go to sleep until at least two."

"We got a dog."

"You got a dog? You, who travels half the year?" I smile into the phone.

"Okay, *Luke* got a dog. A puppy. And the damn thing has to go outside to pee every hour, I swear. I'm standing outside in my pajama pants right now."

The visual makes me snicker quietly. We used to have a rabbit way back when, but Blake always swore dogs were too much trouble and expense. I guess it goes to show how your mind can change on a lot of things when love is part of the equation.

"I'm surprised Matty didn't say anything. He's been home for three days."

"We just got Posey on Monday."

Now I'm outright laughing. "Posey?"

"Don't start." I hear him pull the phone from his mouth. "Go potty. Go on," he coaxes the dog.

I mimic zipping my lips even though he can't see me.

"So, I hear from Matthew you're still dating that hockey player?"

"Yeah."

"Hm."

"What does 'hm' mean?"

"Nothing. I just . . . I don't know. I didn't really realize it was going to be a thing."

"A thing?"

"Yeah, you know. A relationship." When I don't respond, he takes that as permission to continue. "I didn't mean anything by it. I just thought . . . because he's so much . . . younger . . ." he trails off.

"How old is Luke?"

"Forty-three. Why?"

"Well, since we're making a thing out of the age of my significant other, I figured I should know Luke's too."

"Okay, okay. I'm sorry. You've got to acknowledge the age gap is a little worrying, though, right? When I was that age, I felt like I was still a kid in a lot of ways."

"We were pregnant with Matty at his age. Hardly kids."

"Don't you remember how clueless we were?"

"Every first-time parent is clueless, Blake."

"I'm sorry. I shouldn't have brought it up. I just don't want you—or Matty—getting attached and then ending up hurt. That's all. I love you guys and don't like seeing either one of you in pain. Matty talks about Bobby *all* the time. Maybe taking things a little slower would be better where he's concerned? Just in case?"

Shit.

"Blake, I know this is coming from a place of love, and I'll really give the Matty thing some thought. But Bobby and I are doing great—just like you and Luke and Posey, I'm assuming."

"Luke is gonna kick my ass when he hears about this conversation."

"Take your dog inside and go back to bed, Blake. We'll talk later."

I hang up and stand from my chair, phone gripped tightly in my hand as I start to pace the laminate wood flooring. It's still pitch black outside, and the wind whips the end of a tree branch against a nearby window, causing a shrieking sound. I need to trim that thing before I start having nightmares about vampires or Freddy Krueger.

Blake's words play back in my mind. *Matty talks about Bobby all the time.* I'm sure it's not easy as Matty's dad to hear him going on about another adult male figure. Maybe that's where it came from? Or is he right? Am I setting Matty up for heartbreak by diving into this relationship with a twenty-eight-year-old man and just assuming things will work out? If I let myself stop and be my usual practical self, I can admit the odds are not in my favor.

Guys get hotter and more virile in their thirties and even forties, as unfair as that is. When Bobby is thirty-eight, I'll be fifty. He'll be Captain America and I'll be Driving Miss Daisy.

Nope. I can't think about this or the next thing you know, I'll be spooning Ben and Jerry's into my face while tearfully examining every wrinkle and gray hair in the mega-magnification makeup mirror I pretend I don't own.

I consider texting Ramona to see if she's awake and able to talk me off this ledge. But I'm not up to date on her current schedule since I've been around less than usual. Shit. Am I being a bad friend *and* a bad mother?

No. Ramona is thrilled for me. In fact, she said just the other day that she's living vicariously through me since, as she put it, I'm in my "honeymoon phase" with Bobby and haven't reached her and Amir's era of scheduling sex dates on their calendars so they don't forget to bang.

Blake and I never did that. We just stopped having sex altogether—understandably, in hindsight. I guess I've never actually been in a normal sexual relationship as an adult. Bobby and I have a sex life so active it's downright exhausting at times, but Ramona has a point. It can't always be this way. And then what happens when the attraction goes from rampant lust to more of a slow burn? Bobby does not strike me as a slow-burn kind of guy.

I lift my phone and scroll to my text thread with Bobby, rereading the last message he sent last night.

Bobby: I'll see you at Matthew's game tomorrow. Call me when you get up. I like hearing your voice to start my day.

The tightness in my shoulders melts and I smile down at the phone. What am I doing getting all worked up about some random comments? Maybe I need to have my head examined. Or maybe I just need a good night's sleep.

"Honestly, I consider it a win that nobody cried," Coach Chloe says as we stand rinkside while the kids all head to the locker rooms. "Hey, I've been meaning to tell you what a great kid Matthew is. He's been so much fun to coach."

"Thank you. I'm so glad."

"Nikolai says we should try him at goalie, but I said I'd mention it to you before I let him talk to Matthew. I figured you might have visions of teeth scattering to the ice like

Chiclets." She cocks her head. "Do they even make those anymore?"

"I don't think so, but I'm sure none of these kids would have heard of them anyway."

Chloe shrugs. "And . . . now I want gum."

I smile. "Let me think about the goalie thing. I'm saving up for braces, but not for fake teeth just yet."

Bobby skates up and comes to a stop, throwing snow at the boards before propping his hands on the door to the ice. "What are you two talking about? Forns's new tattoo? I told him not to get my name inked over his heart, but he said he had to live his truth."

"What is wrong with you?" I laugh and shake his arm. He catches my hand and brings it to his lips with a sexy smirk. What a ham.

"I'm assuming lead poisoning as a child," Chloe responds. "If only we'd known not to drink out of the garden hose as kids."

Bobby releases my hand and turns to Chloe. "Uh, first of all, I am in excellent health—nay, *perfect* health. And second, how did you not know not to drink out of the garden hose as a kid? There were warning labels all over the place?"

Chloe and I look at each other. "No there weren't," we say in unison.

"I'm pretty sure I drank more water from the hose than the tap as a kid," I say with a grin.

Banks Bennet approaches from behind us. "Yo, Roadie. Kaitlyn is looking for you."

"Hey, Benny," Bobby greets his teammate with a chin lift. "Did you drink out of the garden hose when you were a kid?"

Banks considers the question for maybe a nanosecond. "Of course. Everybody did. Except these two kids down the street whose parents were scientists." He rubs his chin between a thumb and forefinger and smiles his movie-star smile. "Probably should have given that a little thought."

Bobby frowns, propping his hands on his hips and scanning the entire rink as if looking for an assist. He opens his mouth to respond and then shuts it again before finally exhaling and settling on a quiet, "Never mind."

Chloe rolls her eyes. "It took him this long to realize we're all elder Millennials and he's a Gen Z-er," she says with a laugh.

Banks joins her, but I can only blink as her comment registers in my brain.

Bobby throws his hands up. "I'm a Millennial too! Well, depending on what chart you look at." he protests.

But my head is starting to spin because I just realized my child and my boyfriend are from the same generation. What madness is this?

"I'm surprised you haven't brushed up more on Gen X since that's your preferred dating pool, Rhodes," Banks jokes.

I notice Chloe kick his shin.

"Ow!" Banks bends over to rub his leg.

"You looking for a fight, Benny?" Bobby postures with his arms out, but his tone is joking. "I was gonna save it for the Titans but I'm ready if you wanna go."

My mind continues to whirl as I take in the action around me in what feels like a blurred alternate reality. Bobby is *known* for dating older women? I mean, I know that dating app was for younger men and older women, but I didn't realize he has an actual *reputation* for it. I just assumed he didn't like to concern himself with age. Not that he's had a parade of geriatric women just like me.

Am I . . . a joke to people?

Kaitlyn sweeps into the circle, a fussing Mei in her arms. "Bobby, I need a word about a new charity for you since your breast obsession ruined the last one," she says over the baby's intensifying whimpering.

"Hand her over." Bobby thrusts his arms over the closed rink door toward Kaitlyn. "Let Uncle Bobby have a crack at it."

Kaitlyn hands Mei over, blanket and all. "Oh, thank god."

I blink a few more times and refocus, pasting a good-natured smile on my lips even though I feel like crying. Or screaming.

Bobby skates backward from the door, cradling the baby in his arms and making faces at her. As soon as his skates start moving, she stops fussing.

"Aha!" Kaitlyn says. "Skating calms her down this week! Hot Shot, we're moving into the practice facility." She pats Banks on the chest.

We all turn to watch Bobby continue skating and talking to Mei. Something cracks in my chest when his head pops up and his mouth spreads in a huge smile, both dimples on display. "She smiled at me! For real this time! Not just farts."

"Aww," Chloe gushes. "Okay, my turn!"

"What do you say we slip away and take a nap?" Kaitlyn asks Banks. "They've got it under control here."

Bobby glides closer, never taking his eyes off baby Mei's face. A baby just smiled at him for the first time. I've had a million and one baby smiles, and I cherish each one. I've had a marriage. I've changed jobs a dozen times. Started a new career. Had a mortgage for fifteen years—reached that halfway point on the thirty-year loan. I've raised a human. I'm *raising* a human. So that he'll have confidence and security and freedom to start his life. Matty's got his whole life ahead of him.

And so does Bobby.

Unless this geriatric ball and chain gets in his way.

Chapter Thirty-One

Bobby

"Hey, Bobby!" Coach waves me over as all of us file out of the locker room after practice.

Cappy gives me a wide eyed look of terror that does nothing to calm the butterflies that kick up whenever Coach singles me out. I haven't been the recipient of his wrath recently, but you just never know.

"Yes, Coach?" I force my hands to relax by my sides. My instinct is to always bunch them into fists, a habit Ashley clued me into the other day. She told me that I need to retrain my body to not always be ready for a fight. Apparently being in fight-or-flight mode all the time isn't healthy.

Coach claps me on the shoulder. "You've been stepping up lately. I've definitely noticed."

"Thank you, sir. I've been trying my hardest to be the kind of teammate the Storm Chasers need." *Please don't trade me, please don't trade me.* I've actually started to build a life here. That crazy list of Kaitlyn's has turned my life around.

Coach dips his head once. "I'm not going to lie to you. I had some offers to trade you, but if you keep going in this direction, I can toss those offers in the trash." He claps me on the shoulder again. "Good work, son." Then he marches down the hallway, leaving me sagging against the wall once he's out of sight.

I lean my head back and squeeze my eyes shut, doing that deep breathing shit Ashley always tells me to do. Thank fuck he's not going to trade me. I imagine I'm not entirely out of the woods yet, but it has to be a good sign my head's not actively on the chopping block. Good thing Molly never found out how close I was to being traded, or she never would have let me put an offer on the house.

When my heart rate comes back down, I head out to my truck, moving on to the next thing in my life that needs to be addressed. Molly. After a final walk-through yesterday, she handed me the keys to my new house. She didn't have time to celebrate with me since she had one more night with Matthew before he went to his dad's, so I didn't bother staying there, either. The house would seem huge and lonely without her with me.

Which is why I have big plans for tonight. Richie actually helped me pack up my things in boxes last week, in exchange for free rein in my refrigerator and pantry. I'm headed back to my apartment now to load up Wolverine with the boxes and then start my night of seduction plan at the new house. Okay, it's not all that elaborate, but I've got a shit ton of candles and blankets to set up in front of the fireplace. Food and champagne is being delivered a bit later, and Richie has strict instructions not to swing by.

As I go through the motions, my brain is spinning. I can't quite put my finger on what's bothering me, but there's definitely something going on with Molly. We still see each other every single day I'm not on the road, and we text back and forth constantly, but there's been some weird vibe between us. I even caught her studying me at the rink the other day, not in a   I-can't-wait-to-get-that-man-home-and-rip-his-clothes-off kind of way. More like she was studying me . . . and finding something lacking.

And I don't fucking like lacking.

If there's something in her head telling her that I'm not right for her, I want to know what it is so I can set the record straight. I'm most definitely right for her. Or at least she's right for me. She's the one I want. Forever. So if I need to change something to be what she wants, she just has to say the word. More counseling, less fighting, more dates, less sex . . . whatever it is.

Though I do hope it's not less sex.

I barely have time to find the box of towels that Richie packed with the few picture frames I own. Why he put those together, I'll never know. But I get a shower and take the time to put on my sexiest funderpants: the speedo pair with the picture of a bright red bow on the crotch. It's not my normal boxers, but I hope they'll get a smile out of Molly.

I top the funderpants with a pair of khaki slacks, a deep blue polo that she's told me in the past she loves, and a spritz of cologne. The food and champagne has been delivered, and fresh red roses sit in two different vases, one on the picnic blankets and the other in my new bedroom. I light every single candle and then wonder if we might have a problem with the smoke alarms when I eventually blow them all out. Too late now, I guess. The doorbell rings and I spin toward it with a huge grin.

The door swings open on well-oiled hinges to show Molly in a sexy pencil skirt and blouse. The heels tell me she came straight from work. I pull her inside, take the heavy purse off her shoulder, and pull her into a kiss.

"Hey, baby," I murmur against her lips. "I've missed you."

Her hands slide up my chest. "You saw me yesterday."

I sneak another kiss, my hands already busy feeling up her backside. I can't help myself when she wears these damn skirts. "Yeah, but I had to sleep alone," I pout.

Molly doesn't laugh like she normally would. In fact, she pulls back a bit, like she needs space. Warning bells go off in my head. Feeling a rush of panic, I grab her hand and pull her into the house, walking toward the living room where I have the picnic all set up.

"I have a surprise for you," I say, turning back around to her when we get to the living room. I catch a look of sadness on her face before her eyes go wide with surprise, taking in the surroundings. Candles flicker from every surface. Red rose petals are scattered over the blankets. Our food is set out under fancy silver domes.

"Oh Bobby," she whispers, hand going to her mouth. Her eyes go shiny and something in my gut tells me they aren't good tears.

I tug on her hand, telling myself to calm down and just talk to her. "Hey. Is everything okay?"

Molly swallows hard, staring up at me with eyes gone more brown than green today. She doesn't seem to have an answer, so I plunge ahead, desperate to make everything okay.

"I want to celebrate this house with you. I want you to be comfortable here with me. You and Matthew both. I envision a lot of happy days and nights with you two here. We can start by getting a huge Christmas tree this weekend. If there's something bothering you, just tell me. We can work it out."

Molly swallows again. I stroke my thumb over the back of her hand. "I, uh, just feel bad." She smiles, but drops her gaze to stare at the button on my polo shirt. "I can't stay. Something came up with Matty and I have to go."

If this were a gameshow, someone would be hammering the buzzer right now, indicating a blatant lie from one of the contestants. Molly slips her hand out of mine and hooks her thumb over her shoulder.

"I've got to go. Thank you for . . ." She looks around the room behind me, mouth dipping down at the corners. "Everything. I'm sorry." Then she spins on her heel and walks back to the front door.

After a second of disbelief where I'm frozen to the spot, I follow after her. I barely catch her at the front door, my hand holding her forearm. "Hey. Call me later. I need to know everything's okay with Matthew."

She doesn't turn back or look at me. Just dips her head in agreement and leaves. I watch her go, my insides an absolute mess.

What the fuck just happened?

And why is she lying to me? Blatantly closing me out. Pulling away when I thought everything was so good.

"Fuck!" I slam the door, hands going to my hips. I'm breathing hard and that rush of wind in my ears is enticing me to punch something.

Ashley's advice runs through my head, and I try to take a deep breath. I take a physical step back. I count to ten. I make my fingers open wide instead of closing into fists. I pace the foyer, up and down, up and down.

I still want to fucking hit something. A huff of laughter explodes out of me. Where's Richie when I need him? I lift my gaze to the ceiling and growl like an animal.

I don't understand what's happening. Plain and simple. I think about calling up Ashley, but we don't have an appointment today. I could call one of my teammates, but those fuckheads don't know dick about women. The only ones who do are married and I don't want to hear about marital bliss when I can't get my girlfriend to even talk to me. Plus, they'd give me shit for months if I talked about my feelings.

Then I think of one person who knows Molly better than

anyone. Someone I don't really want to talk to, but will, just for the sake of figuring out what's going on here. I pull my phone out of my back pocket, scroll to the contact I added for emergencies, and hit call before I can talk myself out of it.

He answers right away, the noise level in the background quite high. "Bobby? Everything okay?"

"Hey, Blake. Molly and Matthew are fine." I blow out a breath. "But I was hoping you'd chat with me anyway."

There's a long moment of silence. It's no secret that Molly's ex-husband and I aren't besties. I can't help feeling jealous that Molly gave so many years of her life to a guy who didn't give her what she needed in return. Then again, those years together might give him the insight into Molly that I need right now.

"Please, Blake," I add, not too proud to beg.

He sighs. "This is weird."

"Yeah, I know. Believe me, I didn't want to call you, but I'm desperate."

I hear a door close, and it gets a lot quieter on his end of the line. "Okay, shoot. What's going on?"

I rub the back of my neck, back to pacing my foyer. My footsteps echo off the naked walls. "I'm in love with Molly and she says she loves me too. I thought things were going good, but she's been acting distant and won't tell me why. Is there something I'm doing that makes her unsure of our future? Has she said anything to you?"

Blake's deep chuckle makes me irritable as fuck. "You gotta understand that Molly's the most practical human on the planet. She doesn't fly by the seat of her emotional pants. It's got to make sense in her head or she won't budge."

I'm nodding. "I know. She told me about her parents."

"Yeah, they're real pieces of work. She and I fought all the time about finances. There's a reason I didn't get to be with my band full time when we were married. Molly would have freaked if I didn't have a regular nine-to-five. Being financially stable is very important to her. So is being able to trust someone completely. I fucked that up too."

"Hope you don't mind, but she told me what happened there. Congrats to you and Luke, by the way."

Blake chuckles again. "Thanks. I have to admit, I wasn't too high on you and Molly together. Seems like an age gap that large might be more than just a number. I can't speak for Molly, but to me, it seems she needs to know that she's it for you. If you're just passing time with her, you should let her go."

Well, that right there just pissed me off some more. "I'm not passing time with Molly! She's everything to me. I have plans to ask her to marry me as soon as she looks like she won't run away when I drop down to one knee."

There's silence again. So much so that I pull the phone from my ear and make sure the call didn't drop.

"Well, hell, I didn't know you felt that way about her."

"How could I not? She's fucking amazing! The best mother. The sweetest partner. A badass realtor. Fuck, she's way too good for me, but I'm selfish enough to want her anyway."

Noise in the background swells again. "Shit, I gotta go, Bobby, but for what it's worth, I'm rooting for you two. Tell her how you feel. Make her believe you mean forever. She deserves that."

"Thanks, man."

And without another word, he hangs up. I stare at my phone and pace some more. I thought I'd been telling her how I felt. Sure, I haven't said anything about proposing yet. Didn't want to say anything until I had the ring made. Blake brought up a good point though. She needs financial stability and to know I want more with her than just sex and date nights every other week.

An idea pops into my head and I quit pacing. "Fucking genius!" My voice bounces off the walls. I pull up our text string. This isn't the way I wanted to do this, but Molly walking out tonight has forced my hand.

> Me: Hey, Sparkle. I know you have a thing with Matthew tonight, but I wanted to ask you a question. Would you and Matthew move in with me? I bought this house knowing you loved it too, envisioning us here together. What do you say? Will you think about it?

It doesn't take long for the bubble to pop up that tells me she's writing back. I start pacing yet again. This will be perfect. Without a house payment to make every month, she'll be better off financially. We can be together all the time. Matthew willl have a stable home here. And we'll be one step closer to getting married.

> Molly: Oh, Bobby. That's a really sweet offer, but I don't think that's in Matthew's best interest. In fact, I was going to suggest we take a step back. Really think about what we're doing together long term.

A step back? I can't believe my fucking eyes. *A fucking step back?*

"Fuck!"

Clearly, I shouldn't text her back in this state. Instead of responding, I pull up Ashley's number and hit call with a shaking finger. I'm going to need a marathon session not to take my frustration out on my new drywall.

Chapter Thirty-Two

Molly

"Why won't you stop calling?!" I yell at my phone where it sits innocently on the passenger seat of my car. I really thought I silenced it after ignoring my parents' sixth call since yesterday morning. There's a reason we don't keep in touch, and if I needed a reminder, I sure got it yesterday.

I pull to a stop at a red light and reach over to possibly chuck the damn thing out the window when I see a different name on the caller ID than I anticipated. I quickly click accept and bring it to my ear.

"Hi, Andrew," I greet Matty's counselor, forcing my tone to go from pissed off to pleasant.

"Hello, Molly. Just checking in real quick to let you know I'm filing Matthew's monthly report, and I'm really pleased with the progress we've made in such a short time," Andrew says in a friendly manner.

Thank you, God, I mouth silently to the ceiling of my car as I continue waiting for the light to turn. "That's great to hear. Any big concerns?" We've been making strides, and Matty is talking to me a little more. He still loses his temper now and then and withdraws sometimes, but there haven't been any more fights at school. Knock on wood.

"Well, it's always good to be vigilant when bullying is involved, and Matthew is still working through a few issues on that. But it takes time."

"I understand. Well, thanks for the update, Andrew. I appreciate it."

"No problem. I'll email you a copy of the report and see you both next week."

"Great." We hang up and I exhale loudly, dropping my head back to the headrest. Well, at least one thing is going right.

The light changes and I accelerate through the intersection while continuing to draw in calming breaths. Anger isn't one of my go-to emotions, but my parents have a special way of teasing it out of me, so I've been a bit of a hot mess the last twenty-four hours. At least anger feels more productive than continuing to mope around about Bobby.

Maybe the call with my mom was just the thing I needed, though, to reassure me that I'm making the right choice by pumping the brakes with Bobby. The minute I heard my mother's voice yesterday morning, I knew exactly why she was calling, even though she started out with the usual pleasantries.

It was the same old song and dance, though. She and my dad had thought something was a sure thing and, as usual, it fell apart, leaving them broke. Again.

"If you could just spare a few thousand, it would make all the difference, sweetie," my mother coaxed. Just hearing her voice made my skin feel too tight and brought back all the memories I try never to think about. Like how she stole all the birthday and Christmas money I'd been collecting over the years from my grandparents and spent it on call-in psychics and scratch-offs. Or how my dad scammed my friends' parents and then my friends weren't allowed to come over anymore. Or how the only way we had decent food to eat and heat in the winter was because I worked my ass off at after school jobs.

My parents have always lived in an alternate universe where you can just wish things into being by sheer will or hope. They have no use for practicality, as is evidenced once again by their latest catastrophe. I learned from experience that the majority of times, things don't work out like you want, and the sooner you smarten up and accept that, the easier your life will be.

"You know I would never ask if it wasn't an emergency," my mother continued as I focused all my energy on not freaking out my son by screaming bloody murder into the open refrigerator.

"Mom, I'm sorry, but I can't help," was the response I repeated at least four times throughout her lengthy explanation. Sure, I've got the money coming from Bobby's commission, but that's Matty's and my money, and I'm not the same young, naive teenager who thought it was her job to be responsible for grown adults who make terrible choices and refuse to learn from their mistakes.

The call ended when I lied and told her I had to leave for work. To her credit, she only sighed and said she loved me. I told her I loved her too because I do, despite how hard I've tried not to. It turned out to be a bad decision, however, because it apparently made my dad feel like he had permission to call an hour later. I chose not to answer that time—nor the four following times.

I have spent my entire adult life determined not to make any of the same mistakes my parents made. I got my associate's degree while working two jobs, I always pride myself on being a model employee wherever I work, I'm frugal and thoughtful in how I spend my money, and I don't deal in fantasies and pipe dreams. Ever.

Until very recently, that is.

Sigh.

I turn into the arena parking area as the sun drops toward the horizon, and I find a spot on the outskirts of the wives and girlfriends parking. Good thing I'm wearing sneakers tonight. I am not, however, wearing Bobby's jersey. It just didn't feel right.

It's been radio silence since I texted Bobby last night about stepping back. I know doing that by text was the coward's way out, but the man asked my kid and me to move in with him via text, so it was more of a reflex than anything. Part of the reason I'm going to tonight's game is to speak to him in person afterward.

His impulsiveness always has him putting the cart before the horse, even if it's not in his best interest. He may think he wants us to move in right now, but that could change. And did he assume it wouldn't be a big deal for me to uproot our entire lives to play house with him? Talk about impractical! I mean, sure, if our relationship was further along and we knew for certain we had a future together, it might make sense, but we've only been officially dating for a month! Even if it feels like it's been a whole lot longer. I've dated jackets for longer than that before cutting the tags off.

The guard scans my ID and I head to the stands to climb to the upper deck where the wives and girlfriends suite is. But then I pause. What am I doing? If we're taking a break, why am I going to watch with all the wives and girlfriends? I'm standing at the landing, considering my options when I see Kaitlyn waving to me from down by the Storm Chasers' bench. She never watches in the suite, preferring instead to be closer to the action. And the violence.

Crap. Now that she knows I see her, I have to go down there.

"Hey, Molly!" We hug in greeting.

"Where's Mei tonight?" I gesture to her empty hands.

"Banks's family is in town. His mom took possession of Mei the second she walked in the door and hasn't given her up since."

I laugh. "Sounds heavenly." Blake's parents used to do that sometimes, and it was always a welcome reprieve.

"You headed up to the WAGs' suite?"

I hesitate, and before I can come up with an answer, I hear my name being called. We both look to the ice where Bobby is standing by the bench looking our way. "Meet me down there!" he yells, gesturing to the right.

Shit! I didn't want to distract him before the game, but it looks like it's too late. I muster a smile for Kaitlyn and head over to meet Bobby by a set of doors being guarded by a security guy.

"Aren't you supposed to be warming up?" I ask as soon as Bobby emerges. He's dressed in all his gear and holding his helmet in one hand. With the skates on, he towers over me.

"I was afraid you weren't going to come." He's wearing a nervous smile, and it's so hard not to go on my tiptoes and kiss him. But I really need time to think and reassess, and he deserves to hear it in person. Even if being around him makes me want to change my mind and ditch rationality in favor of rainbows and unicorns and orgasms.

"I wanted to see you." I have to raise my voice to be heard over the announcer and the swell of cheers from the crowd. "We can talk after the game."

His eyes drop to my sweater and his jaw tics. Clearly, he's noticed I'm not wearing his jersey. "No, I want to talk now."

"Bobby." I glance around nervously as the lights dim in

the arena. He needs to get his butt out of here and rejoin his team.

"Molly, I'm sorry if I made you feel pressured by asking you to move in. I just love spending time with you and Matthew, and I wanted you to know how sure I am about us."

"Bobby, I . . . how can you be so sure? You haven't even thought of all you might be missing out on by hitching yourself to an instant family, much less an older partner. When I think about my twenties, I feel like I was a different person back then. You're supposed to be able to grow and change as you go through your thirties, and you should absolutely do that."

"And I'm sure I will. With you."

I shake my head. "It doesn't work like that. *I* don't work like that. We've only been dating for a month, Bobby. This is just all too fast, and I need to take a step back to do what's best for my family."

He clenches his teeth, then releases. "By step back, you mean you're breaking up with me?"

I swallow hard, my pulse thumping in my neck. "If that's what you want to call it," I croak.

His chin drops to his chest as the announcer's voice booms through the speakers and he begins introducing the Gold Rush's first line. I can barely hear Bobby, yet I make out his words. "I can't believe this. I love you, Molly." The look in his eyes says he's not lying one bit, and my heart tears apart.

I go on my tiptoes to make sure he can hear me. "And I love you. But love doesn't automatically fix everything. Believe me." I've got a whole suitcase full of examples from my life.

"Why not?"

I almost want to smile at the question because it's so . . . Bobby. "The fact that you're asking that question tells me I'm making the right decision. Let's take the holidays apart and then we can talk in the new year."

His nostrils flare. "So, your mind is going to change in the new year?"

I owe it to him to be truthful. "I don't know."

"I think *I* do." A series of flashes go off, and we both turn to see a photographer snapping our picture. "Shit!" Bobby bites out, turning so his back is to the guy.

"Bobby, I think you need to go." I gesture behind him. "Your team is taking the ice." I don't want him getting into trouble with the coach on top of this awful conversation.

He gives me a hard look, one that shows all his conflicted feelings. And I want to pull him in and kiss him. Make it all better. But that won't work. Instead, I let him go and wander the stands until I find an inconspicuous spot from which to watch the game.

It's evident from the second Bobby's skates hit the ice in the first period that he's on edge. He's hogging the puck and misses every time he shoots for the goal. The coach is going hoarse yelling at him and then lecturing him when he hits the bench. In the second period, he gets two penalties and spends more time in the penalty box than on the ice. By the third period, I can't stand it any longer. I leave when Bobby trips his own teammate, Pete Fornier, and the Gold Rush steal the puck to score. The tension in the arena is palpable, and I can't help feeling like it's all my fault.

"What are you doing here? You're supposed to be off for the next week." Coco stands with her arms crossed beside my office chair the next morning.

"I'm just grabbing a few things, I promise, boss." I rifle

through my top drawer for a flash drive I need in case clients reach out over the holiday. Just as my fingers close around it, my cell phone vibrates on top of the desk. "Don't answer it!" I yell.

Coco pulls her head back and stares at me like I just spontaneously morphed into a dragon right before her eyes and might barbecue her. "Are you okay, darling?"

I shake my head. "Sorry. Just a bit jumpy." I muster a forced smile as I grab my phone to shove it back in my bag. But that's when I see it's Matty's school calling, not Bobby or my parents again. Shit! To think that we almost made it to Christmas break without more drama.

"Hello, this is Molly Sparks," I answer, immediately pulling my lip between my teeth to gnaw on it.

"Ms. Sparks, this is Vice Principal Finley."

"Is there a problem with Matthew?" I get straight to the point.

He pauses, making me wonder exactly how bad it is that the man can't speak. Finally, he says, "In a manner of speaking. Are you available to come to school?"

Crap, crap, crap!

"Of course." I check my watch. "I can be there in twenty minutes."

"I'll see you when you get here. Just come straight to the office."

I hang up and hike my bag up onto my shoulder. "Damn!" I turn to Coco. "Sorry, Coco, I have to run. It's Matty's school."

"Oh dear," she responds. "Good luck." When I thank her and book it to the back door, she calls out behind me, "Text me later so I know everything is okay!"

I make it to the school in record time, pulling into a parking spot just as the buses are lining up to take kids home from the half-day before break. This is so not how I wanted to start the holidays. It's bad enough that I have to break it to Matty that Bobby won't be around for Christmas. Now I might have to ground him too. Merry freaking Christmas.

When I go through security and then step up to the front desk and give my name, the woman behind the desk gasps. At first, I think maybe someone famous just walked in behind me, but I quickly realize her attention is focused only on me.

"Oh my god!" she exclaims, her salt and pepper curls bouncing around her face. "You're Molly Sparks."

"Um . . . yes." I did just introduce myself, so I'm entirely unclear why this news is so noteworthy.

"I was just reading about you and that hot young hockey player of yours! Lemme grab it." She digs around in her purse while the blood drains from my face.

"Oh! No need!" I try. "I'm just here to see Vice Principal Finley."

But she's entirely undeterred, practically squealing as she unearths the device and swipes her finger over the screen before turning it my way. And right there in vivid color is a shot of Bobby and me from last night's game, deep in conversation and oblivious to prying eyes.

She turns the screen back to examine it herself with an almost hungry expression. "What I wouldn't give for a fling with some young stud like Roadie." She lifts her eyes to me. "We might have a few more miles on us, but even us older women have needs, am I right?"

It takes everything I have not to turn around and flee. But I must be on God's rotation today because the vice principal chooses that moment to stick his head out of his office. "Molly?"

"Yes!" I practically shout and then stride toward him in case he was thinking of coming out for some small talk with me and the young-hockey-stud enthusiast.

"Enjoy yourself for the rest of us!" the woman calls behind me as I step into his office. Dear god.

"Hey, Mom."

My head whips around. Matty leans against the far wall of the office. But instead of a worried or guilty expression, my son is wearing a devilish grin.

Uh oh.

Bobby

Coach leans in, the fury behind his eyes enough to have me wincing. "I ought to call back every single team that had an interest in you. One more game even close to the absolute shit show of last night and your ass is done with the Storm Chasers. You got me?"

I nod, anger like I've never felt before coursing through me, along with an ache in the right side of my ribs. Sammie, a smartass young player on the Gold Rush, started rough housing me every time I took a shot and missed. By the third period, I saw that Molly was missing from the stands and I tripped my own fucking teammate, and Sammie stole the puck to sink it into our net. Coach was so pissed he couldn't even look at me last night. Our assistant coach had to be the one to tell me to show up this morning at seven to have a meeting.

But what really has me pissed is that I didn't resort to fighting like I so badly wanted to. And I'm still in deep shit.

All that work, and I'm in the same fucking hot seat with my career on the line.

"Answer me when I talk to you," Coach barks, making me wince yet again.

"Yes, sir. I'm sorry, sir. It won't happen again."

Coach sneers. "Where have I heard that before?" He shakes his head and moves back around his desk to sit down. He folds his hands over his belly and leans back. "Frankly, Bobby, I feel sorry for you."

Well, I don't like that one fucking bit. My spine straightens, my whole body ready to defend itself. But Coach is on a roll.

"You have so much potential. You're phenomenal out on the ice. And then you go and fuck it all up. Letting your emotions run wild." He keeps shaking his head and it's pissing me off. Then again, everything is pissing me off since Molly ruined everything between us. "I don't know who hurt you, but you need to figure that shit out. For you, for this team, for everyone around you. Fix your shit and grow up, son. Now get out of here. I'm sick of looking at your face."

I grit my teeth and offer a nod of acknowledgment, pushing up from the chair and hightailing it out of his office before I do any further damage to my career. My phone pings as I leave the practice arena. We have five whole days off in a row for Christmas. I planned to spend every single minute with Molly and Matthew, but it looks like my schedule is wide open again.

Ashley: Call in five minutes.

I give her message a thumbs up as I make my way back to my vehicle, trying to breathe out the anger that's strangling me. I called Ashley last night and requested daily sessions for a few weeks. She obliged, but only if I also started seeing a certified psychologist alongside our anger management sessions. Probably should've been seeing a shrink all along. I'm more fucked up than any of us realized. I'm parked outside the practice rink sitting in Wolverine when Ashley calls right on time.

"Did you schedule with Dr. Barnhardt?"

"Yep. I'll see him this afternoon." I rest my head back and close my eyes. I'm going through the motions again, doing all the things Coach and Kaitlyn want me to do, but it seems pointless. It won't get Molly back. It won't make her see that we're perfect together. She's made up her mind that I couldn't possibly love her for the long term. And after my kindergarten-level play out on the ice, I might actually agree that I shouldn't be distracted dating someone.

"What are your holiday plans?" Ashley asks out of the blue. She normally gets right down to business, so this idle chit chat isn't what I expect. Or want. I just want to fix whatever's broken inside me. Maybe then I can turn my attention to getting over Molly.

"Um, not sure."

"Why don't you and Richie fly home and spend the holidays with your family?"

My eyes fling open. "The whole point of these sessions is so I quit getting in fights, Ashley."

She sighs, probably not appreciating my sarcastic tone. "I know. The best way to do that is to go to the source. Your behaviors were learned in your home growing up. You need to go there and talk to the adults who should have given you and your brothers better coping mechanisms. You need to confront those memories and have those conversations. It's easy to blow up and walk away. It's not easy to confront the things that make you angry and choose to work it out. Your team. Molly. They want you long term, Bobby. You can't blow up and walk away like you do with your family."

"No, that's what Molly does. Just walks away," I grouse,

feeling sorry for myself. I'm not sure what's worse. Feeling angry or feeling devastatingly sad.

Ashley's voice is so damn patient. "I'm sure Molly has her own past and her own reasons for what she did. But we're talking about you, Bobby. You can't make her do what you want. You can only work on yourself. So are you going to mope around the whole week you have off or will you take that time off to work on yourself?"

I scrub my hand over my face, knowing what my answer should be and yet not wanting to say it out loud where I'll have to actually follow through with it. "Ugh!"

A giggle comes through my speakers.

"I'm glad my agony is entertainment for you," I snap.

The giggle just gets louder. "Oh, Bobby. I'm sorry. I shouldn't be laughing, it's just you are the cutest grump I've ever heard! You're usually so funny and right now I'm picturing you wearing grumpy pants with your arms folded over your chest and a big ol' frown."

My lips twitch, the closest I've gotten to a smile in twenty-four hours. "Grumpy pants? Really, Ashley?"

That only sends her into another peal of laughter. I roll my eyes and check the time. If I leave now, I can work on Richie, convince him to fly home with me, pack, and then book our flights for tonight.

"Maybe when you're done laughing, you can give me something useful to work on," I say loudly, firing up the car to head home. Ashley composes herself and is thrilled to hear I'm going to talk to Richie.

"Tomorrow at ten?" Ashley confirms our call for tomorrow. "Hopefully you'll be calling me from Georgia!"

"I can't believe you're voluntarily going home." Richie toes off his tennis shoes the second he clicks his seatbelt on. I grimace at his airplane etiquette but decide I can't focus on that right now. I have bigger issues to deal with. "I mean, I know you were just there, but it took Mom having a heart attack."

"Well, it's not exactly a warm and fuzzy place for me," I tell him, glad I spent the extra money for first class so there isn't anyone sitting next to us.

He gives me an exaggerated pout with his baby voice. "Ah, did Mommy's favorite not have a fun childhood?"

I turn toward him, refusing to take the bait. "Actually, no. I didn't, Richie. I had a traumatic childhood, probably similar to yours, except you had someone younger than you to bully. I had no one."

Richie frowns, crossing his arms over his chest. "What do you mean, *bully*?"

"Well, you four blamed everything that went wrong on me. You made me fetch you water and snacks and shit or you'd threaten to beat my face in. Will gave me my first shiner. You all gave me shit for how much hockey I played. Said I was wasting Mom and Dad's money on all the equipment. You're the only brother who showed up to congratulate me when I was drafted. What part of that sounds warm and fuzzy and loving?"

Richie's head starts to bob up and down. "Hmm, you're right. That sounds kind of awful. Though to be fair, the older ones beat my ass too. You're not the only one who had to fetch them snacks or face an ass whooping."

Richie points to the faint scar above his eyebrow that has been there for as long as I can remember. "This is from Will when I stole one of his T-shirts from his room and wore it on a date with Allie. Remember her? She let me kiss her, tongue and everything. Then I got home and Will saw me in his shirt. Dumbass punched me right in the face and ended up getting blood on it, ruining it."

I put my hand on Richie's arm. "Dude, that's messed up. How come I don't remember that?"

Richie shrugs. "I guess we were all just doing our best to survive. Grow up. Move out."

I sit back in my cushy seat and mull all that over. I think of Molly and Matthew and how much they enjoy spending time together. That's how families should be. My abused heart squeezes out a trickle of sympathy for Richie. For all of us boys.

"I don't want to just survive our family, Rich. We're all grown now. We should move past all that childish shit and support each other."

He looks over at me and I brace myself for him to grab me in a headlock or burst out laughing at my ridiculous idea. Instead, he rolls his lips in like he's choked up. He nods then sticks out his hand. We shake on it, and he pulls me into a backslapping hug before letting go. He turns to stare out the window, clearing his throat. And fuck if that doesn't get me all up in my feels too. About my brothers, my career, my Molly.

The flight is uneventful and thankfully, Richie puts his shoes back on before we land. Richie drives the rental car while I text our brothers on the brother group chat that goes silent except when someone wants to give one of us shit.

> Me: Family meeting at Mom and Dad's house at eight tonight. Be there.

Will: Who the fuck made you king of this family?

Artie: Pretty sure just because you make a shit ton of money doesn't mean you get to boss us around, Bobby-boy.

George: Wait. Are you back in town again?

Me: Just meet me at the house. Please? I have something I want to talk to everyone about.

Will: Really? Mom has more important things to worry about than your love life problems. Just because you and that woman are all over the news today doesn't mean you can swoop in here and demand we all meet up, fuckhead.

Me: Wait, what? What news??

Artie: Like you don't know you were the main topic for a full ten-minute segment on ESPN this morning.

"Fuck, fuck, fuck." I blow off the rest of their bullshit comments to pull up a few websites, all of which have pictures of me and Molly from before last night's game.

She looks so pretty in jeans, boots, and a sweater. My jaw clenches about her deciding not to wear my jersey. One shot shows her looking up at me, her beautiful hazel eyes searching for something from me that she clearly didn't get or didn't see because the next shot shows her walking away. The speculation on who she is didn't last long. They've found out her name, her occupation, and have a running list of theories on what she means to me. Not a single one has the truth.

I'm so in love with this woman, not even her breaking up with me will make that love stop.

"We're here," Richie says calmly.

I put my phone away. I can only handle one thing at a time. Molly would hate having pictures of her on the internet, just like she'd loathe all the speculation about us, but it was inevitable dating a professional hockey player. If she wasn't already done with me last night, I'm sure this latest invasion of her privacy isn't going to help things.

"Ready to try something different?"

Richie barely gets out a yes before Will's yanking the passenger side door open, nearly ripping it off its hinges.

"This better be good, jackass."

I stand up, facing the brother who's always been the worst of the bunch. The leader of the bullies. Instead of puffing up my chest or taunting him back, I force myself to relax. Will works hard as a general contractor here in the town we grew up in. It can't be easy to watch his little brother making seven figures. Couldn't have been easy to help raise all us boys. Ashley's right. Will's got his own past and his own reasons for being the way he is. I just need to see if we can see eye to eye as grownups.

"You couldn't have had it easy being the big brother to all of us and dealing with Dad directly. I just wanted to tell you I love you, Will."

His face remains stony for several long beats. Richie comes up to my side and claps him on the shoulder. "I love you too. Love both of you." Then he throws his arms around us both and pulls us into a group hug. Not a precursor to a tackle. Just an honest-to-god hug.

Will lets out a belly laugh that gets us all laughing. He pats us on the back before pulling away. He looks confused, but also softer. Like maybe he isn't planning our murder in his head. "You two are weird as fuck. Why don't we do this inside, so the neighbors don't think we're drunk off our asses?"

We traipse inside where we have the first honest conversation we've ever had as a family. Mom cries happy tears, Dad apologizes for being too tough on us sometimes, and no one gets tackled to the ground. It's not a fucking kumbaya song around a fire with linked arms, but it's progress.

Molly

"What made me think this was a good idea again?" I whisper
to Ramona from my spot next to her on their cushy loveseat.

We both watch as Luke models the new scarf Ramona
gave him while Blake looks on like he's hatching plans to use
the scarf to tie Luke to his headboard and have his dirty way
with him later tonight.

She throws an arm around my shoulder and whispers
back, "You're in the running for goddamn mom of the year for
giving Matty both his parents on Christmas." When Blake
leans in to kiss Luke, she springs to her feet and announces,
"Time for Christmas morning Bloody Marys!"

"I'll help!" I jump at the chance to escape for a breather. I
mean, sure, I'm happy for Blake and Luke, but I'm also fresh
off a three-day Hallmark holiday movie marathon where I
spent the better part of each film yelling at the characters that
love is a lie and they're better off alone. Yeah, I've had better
weeks.

I can't stop thinking about how I allowed things to get so out of hand that Bobby and I actually had a conversation about having babies together! Babies! What was I thinking, traipsing off into la la land like that and not thinking rationally? Ripping it off like a Band-Aid was the right move, even if it had me emptying every tissue box in the house.

"Who's Bloody Mary?" Matty asks.

"An excuse for your Aunt Ramona to drink her breakfast," Amir replies as we duck into the kitchen.

"Thanks again for being so awesome and letting us crash your Christmas," I say as I dig through her fridge for the tomato juice. Matty and I had planned to spend the day with Bobby before everything fell apart, and I wanted to give him something better than a morning hanging out alone with his mom.

It was Luke's idea to combine parties and spend the day together once Matty spilled to Blake that Bobby and I are on pause—a thoughtful gesture that makes me feel even worse for being a love Grinch today. I haven't had the heart to tell Matty that Bobby and I are likely over for good.

"Please, girl. Any excuse to avoid Amir's mother for a few hours." She slams the freezer door after grabbing the vodka. "Did I tell you she suggested I might want to buy the next size up in dresses the last time I saw her?"

"Yikes."

Ramona waves a hand and sets the vodka on the counter. "Matthew's having a good time; that's all that matters."

"He asked me earlier if I could take him to give Bobby his present."

"Damn. What did you say?" Ramona asks with a wince.

"I panicked and told him where I was hiding the Christmas candy. Thank god he's so easily distracted."

"What did Matthew get him anyway?"

"A hockey bobblehead. Some player named Roman

LaFontaine? He said it was a joke between them." I frown down at the jug of tomato juice and then feel Ramona's hand on my shoulder.

"You'll get through this, Molly."

I muster a half smile and put my hand over hers. "Then why do I feel so awful?" When I woke up this morning, I had a few beautiful seconds where I forgot Bobby wasn't in the bed next to me. Those tiny seconds felt like the best Christmas in history. Until reality crashed the party.

"Because you made a grown-ass adult decision, and you're facing the fallout like a grown-ass adult woman."

I sigh and return to the fridge for the celery. "I'm never dating again."

"Hm."

I poke my head over the top of the open fridge door to look at my friend. "What does *hm* mean?"

But Ramona only shakes her head. "Nothing. Hand me that celery."

I straighten instead. "Ramona Nasiri, don't you lie to me."

"Fine," she huffs and pushes her glasses up on her nose. "I was just thinking about the next guy you'll likely date."

"I just said I was never dating again."

"Don't pretend you're not a realist. You'll get back out there, and you'll bag yourself a homely fifty-something investment banker with an impressive golf handicap, a membership at the yacht club, and an affinity for Cuban cigars. Either that or a librarian."

I scowl at her and hand her the damn celery. "Shows how much you know. Golf is boring, I get seasick, and the smell of cigars makes me want to puke."

"You'll adapt. Or go for the librarian."

We're both silent for several beats. "Matty would hate those guys."

"Well." Ramona shrugs, infusing the single word with a

whole lot of ambiguity while at the same time making me feel like she just won an argument. How does she do that? "Speaking of Matty. You never told me what happened the other day at school with the latest fight."

"Oh my god." I shake my head at the memory. "That child."

"This sounds like it's gonna be good. Was it more shoving, or did he actually punch someone this time?" she asks as she empties half the juice into a glass pitcher with candy canes on it.

"Neither. It turns out that Raiden kid hasn't let up on his bullying at all, and Matty got together with a couple of his other victims and hatched a plan." I cross my arms and lean against the closed refrigerator while Ramona mixes the drinks. "Apparently, Raiden has a habit of stealing choice items from other kids' lunches, so they brought bottles of soda that day and made a big deal about it so he'd notice. Sure enough, Raiden came over and swiped Matty's soda from his hand and started to drink it. But the boys had punched holes in the bottles, so when he upended it, it all spilled on his pants."

Ramona slaps her hand over her mouth, her shoulders shaking with laughter.

"And because they're twelve, all it took was one kid to yell, 'Raiden just peed himself!' before the entire cafeteria was laughing."

"Ha! You have a burgeoning genius on your hands, Molls."

"I don't know about that, but I do have to give him points for creativity." I shrug. "I mean, the school's hands were tied since Raiden is pretty sneaky about his bullying, so I guess I can't be mad that the kids took things into their own hands—especially since it was nonviolent."

In fact, the vice principal appeared to agree, although he didn't say as much. He just told me he'd continue keeping an eye on Raiden and let me know what Raiden's parents had to say about the incident after the break. I'm just hoping getting a taste of his own medicine is enough to settle Raiden down.

"Mom! I'm getting ready to open Dad's present, so you gotta get in here!" Matty shouts from the living room.

"You got this covered?" I ask, and Ramona shoos me out of the kitchen to go hang with my patchwork family. The look on Matty's face when he opens the guitar Blake bought him is almost enough to make me forget about what could have been a very different Christmas.

Chapter Thirty-Five

Bobby

"Merry Christmas, Bobby," Mom whispers to me from the couch where she sits with a cup of steaming decaf coffee clutched to her chest. The Christmas tree before her is lit up in all kinds of colors and mismatched ornaments we either bought or made over the years.

Considering I didn't see her there, I nearly jump out of my socks on the way to the kitchen. "Hey, Mom. Merry Christmas. What are you doing up so early?"

Mom shrugs and pats the cushion next to her. "I couldn't sleep. I just kept thinking how lucky I am to be here another year after my little scare." I change course and sit next to her. She puts her head on my shoulder. "And having you here again so soon is just an added bonus."

"Thanks, Mom."

I'm glad someone around here is happy. I've spent hours talking with my brothers the last three days, talking with Ashley and my new psychologist through all my emotions, and even spent some quality time with Dad fixing the Christmas lights out front that went on the fritz. There was zero shouting or back-of-the-head slapping. A goddamn Christmas miracle.

I just fucking miss Molly. And Matthew. And the life I thought we could have together.

"I wish your heart wasn't hurting, my boy," Mom whispers.

I kiss the top of her head. "It's okay. I'll move on somehow. Plenty of fish in the sea, right?"

Mom lifts her head and frowns at me. "Don't do that. Don't pretend like you don't feel heartache. That's the kind of crap your brothers do. You've always been different from them, Bobby. You feel things deeply."

She puts her coffee cup down on the side table before grabbing my hands and holding them in hers. "I always doted on you more than the others. I know it put you in their crosshairs, but you needed more attention. You've got a beautiful, tender heart, Son. Don't be afraid to follow it. If Molly is who you want, you need to go after her."

My chest squeezes when I think about chasing Molly. I want to go after her, more than anything. But she's a grown woman who's made her decision. Defeat tastes bitter.

"I want to respect her wishes, Mom."

Mom shakes her head. "From everything you've told me, Molly hasn't made any kind of decision, except to be scared of you and what you have to offer. Or maybe you haven't been clear about wanting forever with her. You do want forever, right?"

"Of course I do! I asked her to move in with me. She asked to take a break." I pull my hands from hers and stand, needing to move my body or I might go insane. "I'm going to start making the pancakes. When are the boys coming over?"

Mom studies me for a long moment, but lets the topic of

conversation go. "They'll be here early for pancakes and bacon. They actually get up for free food." She laughs, like it isn't super annoying to have grown men coming over and raiding your kitchen at all hours. My mom is a goddamn saint.

She and I move around each other in the kitchen like we used to when I was younger. There's a calming rhythm to being back home, surrounded by people who love you, even when you're a giant pain in the ass. Dad gets up and sits at the kitchen dinette table with the newspaper and his coffee, occasionally chiming in with a comment. I take in the moment, filing it away as a good memory to pull out and relive when I think everything is crap in my life.

"Bobby the baconator!" Artie's loud shout breaks the quiet morning. He and Will shove through the front door without knocking, dropping some gifts under the tree that look like a kindergartener wrapped them. "I smell breakfast!"

Richie stumbles out of his old bedroom, clad in only boxer shorts. His hair sticks out in every direction. "Why is everyone shouting?" he shouts.

Will and Artie tag team him with a bruising hug. Dad yells at them to quit roughhousing in the kitchen. They take the crazy into the living room, the volume only increasing when George arrives and professes he can't stand to hear them bickering until he's had some caffeine.

"Let's eat, jackasses!" I call out when Mom and I have everything ready.

It's like a goddamn stampede as the boys file in to load up their plates. I give them the stink eye, and Will remembers our conversations over the last few days.

"Hey, Mom. You go first. Everything looks delicious."

Mom beams, patting Will on the cheek. He sticks his tongue out at me as Mom passes. I roll my eyes, but I'm pleased they remember some manners. We all get food and have a seat in the living room like we've done for as long as I can remember. At first, there's just the sound of us gorging on food, but pretty soon someone starts rifling through the gifts and handing them out. We tear into them in utter chaos. We aren't a house that slowly unwraps each gift and thanks the giver.

Except when Mom opens my gift. She gasps and everyone settles down to see what's got her in a tizzy. She has one hand pressed to her mouth and tears welling up in her eyes.

"Oh, Bobby," she sobs.

Dad gives me a head nod like I've done something right. My brothers are all trying to get a look at what she holds on her lap.

"I found an exact replica of the vase we broke. The one your mother passed down to you. There were only fifty made in the whole world and only about ten left that are known. One of the owners was willing to sell." I shrug like it isn't a big deal when it took me months to track down an owner willing to sell. And it took an extraordinary amount of money to convince them to part with the vase.

"Damn, Bobby. You showing us up again?" Will snaps.

"Yeah. I thought our rule was fifty bucks or less for gifts," Artie chimes in.

George, always the quiet one, just glares at me.

Richie tilts his head, watching Mom gaze at the vase lovingly. "I think it's kind of nice. Like, really nice."

"Thanks, Rich. Guys, it's not a competition. I'm the one who ultimately broke the vase. Sure, you all played a part, but I'm taking responsibility. Mom should have her vase back."

I'm taking responsibility for more than just the vase, a deeper meaning to my words that my brothers seem to under-stand. Will gives me a sullen head nod. He's not happy, but he's willing to move beyond what he considers a slight. And since he's the oldest brother, the rest follow suit. Artie goes back to ripping open his gifts, George gets up for more coffee, and Richie tries on the new beanie he received while giving us all a few flexes of his nonexistent muscles. Jeez, the guy should really try manscaping.

"Put a fucking shirt on, Dick!" Artie yells.

Mom leans over and snuggles up to Dad. I put on the reindeer slippers I was given—complete with antlers made of rubber that look absolutely ridiculous. Rich gives me a knockoff Burberry scarf that feels like burlap, but I'll wear it just to make him happy. It'll go good with my red Gucci slides.

When all the gifts are open and the living room floor is a mess of wrapping paper and boxes, Will stands up. I stand up with him, the two of us approaching Mom and Dad like we planned.

"Mom. Dad. The boys and I have decided we need new family pictures. As our gift to you this Christmas, we've hired a photographer to come over tomorrow morning." Will hands Mom an empty picture frame. It took the five of us two hours to agree on the frame at the department store yesterday. We won't mention that fact.

"We'll get the pictures printed out and you can put it on the fireplace mantle," I add.

Mom and Dad love the gift. Will gives me another appreciative head nod. Technically, the pictures were my idea, but I wanted us boys to do something together for once. We spend the rest of the day cleaning up, eating more food until we have to take a midafternoon nap from all the calories, and no fighting to burn it off.

Mom finds me at the dinette table as I'm staring at my phone after dinner. My thumbs itch to reach out to Molly with a simple text wishing her a merry Christmas. Mom lays a hand on my phone and grabs my attention.

"I'm proud of you. You're miserable and yet you didn't pick a fight with your brothers." She shakes her head, smiling proudly. "I've changed my mind about things. You've grown up so much, Bobby. If Molly can't see that, maybe she isn't the one for you."

I mull over her words long after she leaves the kitchen with a fresh cup of coffee. I have changed. Not for Coach. Not for my agent. Not even for Molly. I've changed because I wanted something better from my life. I wanted to break the generational dysfunction. Pride fills my chest, taking up a tiny bit of the space currently harboring heartbreak. This has been both my best and worst Christmas.

Because, yeah, I've changed. But what good is all this hard work if I still don't have Molly?

Molly

"You made it!" Chloe pulls me into a hug and bustles me through the front door.

It's two days after Christmas, and I've been unable to talk my way out of attending this gathering of hockey women at Chloe and Niko's house, no matter how hard I tried.

"Well, when you said you'd kidnap me if I didn't show up, I figured I'd save you the trouble."

Chloe chuckles and links her arm in mine. She's wearing a festive red sweater that shows off her decolletage and some spike-heeled leather boots I want to steal. "Hey, everyone! Molly's here!"

We turn the corner into a gorgeous open living space where I expect to see a dozen or more hockey wives and girlfriends gathered. But, to my surprise, only Kaitlyn, Sara, and a woman I don't recognize sit relaxed on the oversized couches.

I turn a confused gaze to Chloe. "Am I early?" I know I'm not since I spent the last twenty minutes in my car talking myself out of driving right back home. The last thing I want is to spend an afternoon pretending I'm not miserable and keeping up some pretense that Bobby and I are just fine. Hell, I have no idea if he's told anyone we broke up or not, so I don't know how to act at all. "I thought all the WAGs were coming." After all, that's what the invitation said.

"Change of plans," Kaitlyn says before gesturing to the stranger. "Molly, this is Olivia LaFontaine. Her husband, Roman, used to play for the Storm Chasers, and the two of them can't seem to decide whether they live in North Carolina or Tampa, they're here so often."

"I don't know about that," Olivia responds with a grin. She's around my age and has the prettiest honey brown hair. "He spends enough time with the hockey boys at Blue Ridge U, I might have to buy a second house there."

"Roman runs the hockey program at BRU," Chloe explains. "But right now, he's throwing axes with our guys. There was too much testosterone in the place, so we kicked them out."

I nod and paste on a pleasant smile, having no idea what's going on here. "Nice to meet you, Olivia. My son just bought a bobblehead of your husband, I think."

Sara laughs. "Our kids have them too. They worship Roman. Danny got jealous and ordered a dozen of his own Dan-O bobbleheads to scatter around the house."

Chloe gestures to an empty loveseat. "Take a seat, Molly. What can I get you to drink?" she asks.

"Oh. Water is fine." I gingerly perch on the edge of the loveseat.

"They're all drinking wine. It makes them laugh a lot," comes a girlish voice from the far side of the room. Niko's daughter, Ayana, skips toward the women, her blond hair pulled back into two braids.

"Pump and dump, baby," says Kaitlyn, raising her wine glass up in the air.

"Hi, Ayana," I greet the little girl. She's on the younger hockey rec team that practices with Matty's group. "Did you have a good Christmas?"

"Uh huh." She nods. "You're Matthew's mom, right? He's kind of nice—for a boy, that is."

Everyone stifles their laughter at that.

"Well, I'm glad to hear it."

Ayana turns to Chloe. "Don't worry. I'm not crashing your lady time. I just came to get Paul. We're playing beauty shop in my room."

Before I have a chance to muster too much sympathy for this Paul child, a German Shepherd trots through the room toward Ayana. She throws her arms around him. "Come on, Paul! Let's see what color eyeshadow goes best with your fur." The two scamper down the hall, leaving us all smiling after them.

"She's adorable," Olivia gushes. "I always knew Niko had a soft spot, and it's clear where he got it."

"Life can be pretty sweet, that's for sure," Chloe responds before turning her gaze to me. "But it can also suck sometimes."

Oh, crap. Is this what I think it is?

When all four women aim identical concerned gazes my way, it's confirmed. I just walked into a fucking intervention.

"I know I'm a total stranger, Molly," Olivia begins. "But believe me when I say I'm very familiar with the complications of life with a hockey player."

Oh god.

"Oh, no. Really, I'm fine." I try to wave her off, but Kaitlyn leans forward on the couch and cuts me off.

"We all know what happened, Molly, and we're here to help. You and Bobby broke up right before the Gold Rush game, and he's been flailing ever since. Not that you're to blame!" she hurries to add. "We just figured you're probably hurting too and might need a friendly ear from women who've been in your shoes."

Shit. "That's really kind of you." I scan the women's faces. "But I'll be okay. I'm sorry if I messed things up for the team."

All the women protest at once with such vehemence that I almost want to smile. Almost. "Listen, we all know Bobby can be . . . a lot sometimes," Chloe adds.

"But you two seemed so happy together," Sara chimes in.

Kaitlyn jumps on board with, "We just want to know if there's any way we can help."

I quell the rising panic in my chest and respond, "If you're asking if there's anything you can do to get us back together . . ."

"No! That's not what we're doing at all," Olivia exclaims.

"Uh, yeah it is," Chloe objects.

Olivia throws her arms out. "I'm sure Molly thought through her decision before she called things off, and we need to support her."

"We *are* supporting her," Kaitlyn interjects. "Can't you see how miserable she is? We want her all swoony and smiley like she was when she was with Bobby."

"You didn't see it, Olivia. They're adorable together," Sara informs my only ally.

"Excuse me!" I raise my hand. Everyone shuts their mouths and turns my way again. "Olivia is right. I did think things through. I'm *still* thinking things through."

"Sorry, Molly. I guess we got carried away." Chloe's expression is a bit chagrined. "You're both just such awesome people, we loved the idea of you two."

"I did too—when I let myself lose sight of real life there for a while," I admit.

"What do you mean?" Kaitlyn asks.

I shake my head with a sad smile. "It never should have been anything more than a fling, but I was stupid and let emotions get in the mix. Pretty soon, Bobby was buying a house and asking my kid and me to move in with him. After a month!" I look around the room, expecting at least some degree of allegiance. I don't get it.

"I fell in love with Roman in less than a week," Olivia shrugs.

"I'm pretty sure I was in love with Niko after our first kiss," Chloe adds.

Sara furrows her brow. "It took a few months for Danny and me, but he was twenty-two and trying way too hard to play it cool. I went out on a date with another guy and *bam*! Danny was at my door the next morning with roses and a ring." She shakes her head.

"I don't think Bobby could ever play it cool. He wears his heart on his sleeve." My voice catches on the last couple words and all the women spring from their seats and gather close.

"Oh, honey," Sara says. "You love him, don't you?"

I tilt my head back so the tears can't fall while I try gathering myself together. Only when I'm sure they've receded do I lower my chin again. "It doesn't matter. Better to cut things off now before it got more complicated. I have to put Matthew first."

"That's her son," Kaitlyn informs Olivia.

"Oh. Did your son and Bobby not get along?" Olivia asks.

My responding laugh is almost maniacal. "Matty worships the ground Bobby walks on." Since I know I'm not getting out of here without spilling my guts, I turn to Chloe and say, "I changed my mind. I'll take the wine."

Twenty minutes later, I've downed an entire glass of Pinot Grigio and spilled my guts about my parents and my vow to raise Matthew in a home life that's stable and secure. They listen intently as I share all the other factors that went into my decision: the lingering scars from my failed marriage, Bobby's unexplained predilection for dating older women, our age gap and my fear that he'll have regrets, our opposite personalities —Bobby's impulsivity versus my pragmatism and cautiousness. All of it.

"I hated Banks for the first ten years I knew him," Kaitlyn is the first to speak when I've quieted. "Well, technically, I liked him for a couple hours when I met him, but then I hated him for ten years." When I cock my head at her, wrinkling my nose in confusion, she laughs. "What I'm saying is I got in my own way because I thought we were too different. Turns out, our differences complement one another." She shrugs.

"Roman is younger than me. And I had no idea what to do with the idea of dating a celebrity," Olivia says. "Turns out it's pretty easy to shut off all the noise when it's just the two of us."

"Niko's younger than me too!" Chloe says.

"Banks too!" Kaitlyn laughs.

Chloe squeezes my arm. "Niko is a grumpy sourpuss half the time, but he needs my positive energy. It's okay to have differences. And we all tune out what other people are saying. Who cares what some strangers think about your private business?"

She reaches for the wine bottle and refills my glass. "I'm not trying to talk you into anything, so just take this for what it's worth. Bobby has a big personality, no doubt. But that means he loves just as big. The guy can't help it. He gives a hundred percent to whatever he commits himself to."

"As his agent, I can tell you I've never seen a client so ecstatic to find a team that was as ready to commit to him as he was to commit to them. What can I say? The guy knows what he's got and doesn't take it for granted." Kaitlyn shrugs and takes a sip of her wine.

"You guys aren't doing a very good job of helping me get over the guy, you know," I respond with a hint of a smile.

They all laugh and toast each other while my mind reels.

"Hey." Kaitlyn squeezes my hand. "You know yourself better than we do, of course. If your heart is telling you you're better off without Bobby, that's okay. Just don't let your *head* do all the decision making, okay? Been there. Done that. Got a bucketful of regrets for wasting so much time."

I squeeze her hand in return, but when I draw in a breath to tell these women how great they are, I'm cut off by a barking German Shepherd streaking through the house with a little girl at his heels brandishing a can of body glitter and a pink hair bow. "Paul! We're not done yet!"

I can only shake my head and drink another sip of wine.

Chapter Thirty-Seven

Bobby

I made sure my location is off on all my social media apps. The boys would never let me live it down if they knew I was at Coach's house. Voluntarily. I ring the doorbell, and it takes years for someone to swing open the huge wrought iron door. Coach stands there in an elf costume with a confused look on his face. And he doesn't look like a cute elf from the North Pole, but more like Buddy the Elf from the movie Elf. It takes everything I've got not to give him a full-length perusal to take in the green tights and pointy shoes. There's not enough eye bleach in the world for that.

A snicker bursts out of my mouth before I can swallow it back, and Coach's face turns to thunder. Which is the opposite of why I'm here two days after Christmas. I force my face into neutral and hold out the platter I'm carrying. I stopped by the finest seafood restaurant in Tampa just to pick up this bad boy.

"Merry Christmas, Coach!" I really want to add in a hearty

ho, ho, ho, but I don't think he'd appreciate it. "I brought you and the Missus your favorite oysters!"

He looks at it like it might be poison. I shake the platter, and he finally takes it with a disgruntled harumph. A much cuter elf comes up to his side and gasps at my offering.

"Bobby Rhodes! Thank you so much!" Coach's wife leans in to give me a hug, which I return. She has a curious accent that I can't place.

"You're welcome. I just wanted to say sorry for being a jackass at our last game and I know how much Coach loves oysters, so . . ." I scratch the back of my neck, feeling like I walked into some weird role-playing game they've got going on.

"Come in, come in!" His wife grabs my arm and drags me inside the house. "We have at least fifteen minutes before we have to leave for our party. Isn't Andre the cutest elf you've ever seen?"

I force a smile to match hers as we both glance at Coach. He stands there with the oyster platter, looking like he hates his life. My smile turns into a chuckle. He sticks his finger in my face, but his wife bats it away.

"Oh, he's such a grouch. I don't know how you boys put up with him."

I really want to suggest he go to the costume party as the grinch, but I've reached the level of maturity that lets me think things through before I say them out loud. "Well, we're pretty hard to put up with too. Which is why I'm here with my sincerest apologies."

Coach huffs, setting the tray down on a coffee table fit for a king. He gestures to the couch behind me, and I sit. He and his wife sit across from me. Thankfully, Coach puts a throw pillow across his lap so I don't have to worry about my eyes accidentally seeing anything in those tights.

"I appreciate the peace offering. I know I can come down

on you pretty hard, Bobby, but I see your potential. You could be our starter for the next ten years if you get your act together."

His confidence in me makes the weight on my shoulders lift a little. "Thank you, sir. I promise I'm doing everything to get my personal life in order. I just spent the holidays healing some of the things that get under my skin." I wince. "Now if I can just fix the woman situation . . ."

"Ohh, honey," his wife interjects. "I can help, if you'd like. Women are complicated creatures. When Andre and I were dating, we broke up for a little while. He would never answer his hotel room phone when I'd call while he was on the road with his team. I began to believe he was keeping time with women in every city his team played in." She laughs while Coach rolls his eyes. "Come to find out, he was learning Italian with his headphones on to surprise me. Never heard that phone ringing! After he convinced me to give him another chance, he proposed in front of my family back in Italy. And he did it in my native language!"

I look over at Coach to see the tips of his ears bright red. "That's really romantic, Coach. You got game."

He huffs, but his wife just keeps on going. "So, tell us what's going on. I bet we can help."

And so I do. Over a plate of shared oysters, I tell them about Molly, Matthew, my family, therapy, and what I see for my future. By the time I leave, they're late for their party, I feel like Coach and I came to an understanding that cements my position on the team, and I'm horny as shit from those fucking oysters.

Kaitlyn texts me on my way home from Coach's house.

Kaitlyn: Where the hell are you? The boys are all going to this axe throwing place off the 19 for some team bonding. Please go and make sure Banks doesn't cut off a hand. He can't change a diaper with only one hand, Bobby.

Me: I'm on it. Although I'm pretty sure you can do lots of things with just one hand. Diapers included.

Kaitlyn: When you've changed a blowout diaper, you'll know you need at least five hands to contain it.

I don't want to know what a blowout diaper is, so I just give her message a thumbs up and head toward the axe throwing place that just opened in Clearwater.

The boys are already there, taking up three bays and causing a ruckus. I join them, getting hugs and back slaps and questions about my Christmas. Druggy gives me shit about my new snow boots that are entirely unnecessary in Florida, even in the winter, but are super stylish. Banks shoves a beer bottle in my hand. Cappy says I stink like the inside of a fish barrel. Honestly, I missed these fuckers. They're everything I ever wanted in a team. We're a family already, and now that I know I'm staying here for a few years, I can settle into being a part of it.

Turns out that throwing axes at a target is hard work. Most of mine bounce off the wall and fall to the floor instead of sinking the blade into the bullseye. By our fifth round, I take a break and crack open a fresh beer while sitting on one of the couches they provide in the back of each bay. Benny throws his arm around me.

"How come you aren't at Molly's tonight?"

I give him the stink eye. He knows damn well why I'm not

with Molly. He and Kaitlyn gossip like a pack of middle school girls. "She dumped my ass, remember?"

The boys all suddenly lean in like they've been waiting for this subject to come up. Cappy is the first to lob out a question.

"We heard, but why? We thought things were going good?"

"Yeah, I thought you were going to ask her to move in with you," Money pipes in.

"If you looked at another woman and hurt her, we will all kick your ass next practice," Druggy growls.

I hold up my hands. "Easy, killer. I haven't looked at any woman except my mama. Molly ended things because she doesn't believe that I want her long term, even though I asked her and Matthew to move in with me. I've been doing a full court press for our entire relationship while she stomps on the brakes. Why would she think I'd suddenly not want her? I just . . . I don't get it." I stop talking and swig some beer instead.

"Dude, that sucks," Cappy laments with me.

Druggy just frowns at me, but that's nothing new. "Wait. She already has a house, yes?"

"Yeah. Why?" Half the time I don't even know what Druggy is saying.

He spouts something off in Russian, then translates. "It is nice being a guest, but it is nicer at home."

We all stare at him, trying to make sense of his Russian-isms. I don't even try. I pat his knee. "Well, thanks for that, Druggy. I feel so much better."

Benny holds up his hand. "Wait, wait, wait. It scares me a little, but I think I understand Druggy." He turns to me. "You invited Molly to move in with you, but what kind of security does that actually give her? She's not on the title. There's no ring on her finger. You asked her to give up the home she's made for her and Matthew to be a guest in your house. I would have turned your ass down too."

I gape at him, horror pushing out all the heartbreak I've been feeling over the holiday. Is that what Molly thought? That I'd asked her to give up all her security and familiarity to play house with me?

"That's not what I meant!"

"Doesn't matter what you meant, that's what she heard," Dan-O shakes his head. "You're a good guy, Roadie. One of the best on this team. We give you a lot of shit because we love you. *We* know you meant well, but maybe you didn't address what she actually needs, you know?"

I listened to her fucking ex-husband, the guy who didn't give her what she needed their entire marriage. For shit's sake, I'm an idiot. I jump to my feet, slamming my beer down on the side table. "I fucked this up."

"Most definitely," Druggy drawls.

I dig in my pocket for my keys, glad I only had two beers over several hours and I'm good to drive home. "I gotta go."

I barely get my goodbyes said before I'm racing out of the axe throwing place and back to Wolverine. Once inside, I pull up Coco's number from the agency's website. Say what you want about the woman, but she has more class in her pinky finger than I do in my entire designer closet.

And she knows Molly inside and out.

Molly

"Hey, Dollface."

I jump in my chair with a surprised yelp, spilling coffee down the front of my fleece robe. "Holy crap, Blake. You scared me."

"Hey, Mom," Matty pops out from behind his dad, handing me a wad of paper towels.

"What are you guys doing here?" I take them from him and start blotting the front of my robe. Matty is supposed to be staying with Blake until school starts back up again next week. "I might have to confiscate everyone's keys to avoid third-degree burns."

"Sorry about that," Blake says, resting a hand on Matty's head. "The spawn forgot his headphones."

Matty steps toward the hall but stops at the last second and turns to me, giving me a quick hug before rocketing off again.

I watch him go and turn to Blake. "A hug? What did you do to him?"

"Let's just say we had a long heart-to-heart last night, and he's working on some feelings."

My chest tightens. "Is everything okay?" I gesture for my ex to sit down while I grab another mug from the cabinet and fill it with hot coffee.

"Yeah." He pauses, extending his long legs under the table. "I think it will be, that is."

I hand him the fresh mug and slide back into my chair across from him. "That sounds cryptic. What happened?"

But instead of answering, Blake studies me for a minute and runs a hand through his hair before asking, "You and Bobby still taking a break?"

"Can we not talk about that? I'd rather talk about our son." It's been damn near impossible to keep the man out of my head as it is. My insomnia has gotten even worse because of all the intrusive thoughts. I finally decided at four-thirty this morning that I might need to get a cat after all. Allergies be damned, I need someone to keep me company in bed.

Blake lets out a long exhale and ignores my wishes entirely. "You know, I think I judged Bobby without getting to know him. I saw his age and his social status and made assumptions about him. About you and him. About his influence on Matty. A lot of things."

I give up on salvaging my robe and drop the paper towels to the table. "Blake, I'm happy you're on a journey of self-discovery and all, but what does this have to do with Matty?"

He doesn't appear to hear me. "You know, you spend a lot more time and energy making sure everyone else is okay than making sure *you're* okay."

I shrug because that pretty much describes every mom I know.

"Even with our divorce, you were more concerned about me and Matty, and I let that happen. I was selfish." He spins his coffee mug on the table in front of him, eyes trained on the movement.

"Blake, you didn't wake up one day and decide to be gay," I remind him.

"No, but I made it all about me—and Matty, to some extent. I didn't focus enough on how it must have felt for *you*. I knew it hurt you, but looking back, I think I was more worried about you being mad at me than you being genuinely okay." He meets my eyes again. "I'm really sorry, Molly."

I reach out to lay my hand over one of his. "It's been hard on everyone. And it was a huge struggle for you, so don't downplay it."

"Right back atcha, Dollface." He flips our hands over so he's holding mine now. "Don't downplay how it all affected you either, especially considering the number your parents did on you. You spend your life waiting for the other shoe to drop, and I was supposed to keep that from happening. Then I basically smacked you in the face with the damn shoe!"

Since he did not, in fact, hit me in the face with any shoe, metaphorical or otherwise, I move to protest. But he holds his free hand up. "I know I didn't *choose* to be gay, and I didn't take the whole thing lightly, but deep down I knew, even when I asked you to marry me, I think. And that's on me."

"Blake, I don't regret our years together. You're my best friend. And you gave me Matty."

"I don't regret it either, but I do regret that I hurt you and made it even harder for you to trust yourself and other people."

I shrug again because . . . that's life. "I'm just wired to be wary, I guess."

"Yeah. About that . . ." He gently disentangles our hands and brings his mug to his lips for a sip.

"What?"

He speaks over the rim of his mug. "Ramona might have mentioned on Christmas that Bobby asked you and Matty to move in with him, and you freaked."

I gasp. "She had no business telling you that."

"Well, I'm glad she did because . . . I'm pretty sure it's my fault."

I pull my head back and eye him. "How could that possibly be your fault? I just said I'm wired to be wary, and that started well before our marriage crashed and burned."

"Bobby called me," Blake confesses.

"Wait. When? *Why?*" What would possess my boyfriend to call my ex-husband?

"A few days before Christmas, he called asking for my advice because he felt you slipping away. I told him you needed to feel secure in his feelings for you so you wouldn't wonder if he was all in or not."

My jaw drops. "So you told him to ask me to move in with him?!"

"No! I swear I didn't know he was going to do that. I thought maybe he needed to spell out his feelings or something. Maybe go public with your relationship? I don't know." Blake shakes his head.

"Look, Blake, I was already putting distance between us before he asked me that. There were a lot of reasons."

He rolls his eyes. "So, you don't love him?" When I don't respond, he jabs a finger in my direction. "You *do* love him. Well, holy shit."

I glance behind me toward the hall to make sure Matty isn't listening. "This doesn't change anything, Blake," I whisper-hiss.

He doesn't bother to whisper his response. "As far as I can tell, the guy is out of his fucking mind over you. So, what's the problem?"

I cough out a laugh and chug the remains of my coffee.

"Come on, Blake. We live in the real world. Bobby is basically a movie star. Our kinds don't end up together." I slam the mug to the table to punctuate my point.

Blake is unimpressed. "Why not? Two years ago, I was married to a beautiful woman, and today I own a dog with a man who posed for last year's first responders calendar."

I cock my head. "I could have guessed that about Luke. Those biceps."

"Stop trying to distract me when I'm making an important point."

"And what point is that?" I ask as I stand to take my mug to the sink. I hesitate at the last second and grab Blake's from his hand as well.

"Hey! I was drinking that."

If he's going to lecture me in my own kitchen, I'm taking his coffee.

Unfortunately, he continues with whatever point he's trying to make. "I could have stayed married to you and pretended for the rest of my life."

"And we both would have been miserable," I reply over the running water in the sink.

"It was the safe option. To stick with the status quo and not take the leap to be true to myself. I blew up our lives to live my truth."

This is ridiculous. I shut off the water and turn to my ex as I slump back into the counter. "And I'm glad you did. It all worked out for the best."

"I know. And I can't tell you how happy I am that I took the chance and didn't stay in the closet my whole damn life just because coming out would make life messy."

I know where he's going with this. "That's different. That was about being your true self."

"And it feels pretty fucking good to be unafraid to live the life I want. I highly recommend it."

"Yeah, Mom." We both turn to see Matty standing in the doorway. "Life is messy. Dad's gay. You love a hockey player. We can't just give up when things get scary. Everyone makes mistakes and then we forgive each other and move on."

"Come here, kid." I extend my arms and Matty moves in for a hug. When he finally pulls back, I grab both his forearms and take a good long look at his handsome face, those boyish features that will be too grown up far too soon. "I'd never give up on *you*, no matter what."

"I know. Dad said the same thing when I confessed something big to him last night." Matty and I both glance to Blake, and he nods to Matty. Our son drops his eyes to his feet and swallows hard.

"What's going on?" I ask.

"It's the Raiden thing." Matty meets my eyes again. "At first, I didn't want you guys to know anything about it, but my temper got in the way and that plan went out the window. I got in trouble for fighting, I'm sure you remember." I fight a grin when he studies my expression. "And then you seemed kind of proud of me when you found out I was only involved because I was sticking up for another kid." His eyes drop to his feet again. "A gay kid."

I glance at Blake in confusion. I know all of this already. Blake gestures for me to be patient and listen, so I do.

"But that's not the whole truth, and I've been struggling pretty hard with it until last night when I got mad at Dad's place and it all just . . . came out."

"What is it?" I squeeze his arms. "You know you can tell us anything, Matthew."

"I know. I was just . . . ashamed." He swallows thickly. "I mean, I *did* stand up for Grant. But then Raiden said, 'If you're sticking up for him, you must be gay too!' and I . . . I . . . denied it and yelled back, 'I'm not gay!' like it was something bad. And then every time he'd say it, I'd deny it over and over."

I look back and forth between my son and Blake. I have no idea what he's trying to confess here. Is he saying he's gay? I don't even know how far along in adolescence he is to be feeling anything in any direction. Is he worried I'd be . . . upset? "Matthew, I'm afraid I don't quite understand."

"He felt like he was betraying me every time he denied being gay."

I let out a sigh. "I see now."

"Like, I don't think I am?" Matty's face screws up. "I don't really know anything about it, if I'm being honest. I mean, I don't like dudes *or* girls in that way." I suppress a grin as he continues. "But if that's something a kid gets bullied over, I didn't want any part of it. And that's not fair to Dad."

"But you're not ashamed of your dad because *he's* gay, right?" I ask Matty just to make sure we're all on the same page.

"No," he responds. "It's just something that makes him who he is. Like being a kickass guitar player."

"Language," I remind him, though it's hard to be mad.

"Sorry." He sobers again. "But if Raiden had said I was a kickass guitar player—even though I'm not yet—I wouldn't have been quick to deny it like I was about the gay thing."

"You're right. Being gay or bi or straight is nothing to be ashamed about. It's something to be celebrated because it's part of who a person is. But you're twelve, kiddo. Don't be so hard on yourself. You're still figuring all this stuff out."

"And we have a plan, right?" Blake prompts.

Matty nods and musters a half grin. "Next time Raiden says I'm gay, I'm gonna look at him and laugh and say, 'Nobody cares besides you, so why do you keep talking about it?' Then, if he still tries to fight me, I'm gonna stay calm and take deep breaths like Bobby taught me. But hopefully he's done bullying us after our soda trick."

It pains me that after all the care I took to give my kid a worry-free childhood, he still ended up getting bullied anyway. I hate that I can't protect him from everything.

As if reading my mind, Blake says, "It's all going to be okay. You'll see."

"Yeah. I mean, if none of this had happened, Grant and I wouldn't be friends, and he's really cool to hang with. So, sometimes things happen for a reason, I guess." Matty shrugs and I muss his hair.

"It's good to have people to lean on. And I'm glad you finally told us about what's been going on. Feels better to let it all out, right?"

"Andrew, my counselor, says that I probably tend to take out my troubles on you guys because I know deep down you'll never abandon me. You'll always forgive me and want me no matter how hard I try to push you away."

"Andrew sounds like a smart guy," Blake says with a grin that's a carbon copy of Matty's.

"Yup. We'll never give up on you, kid," I agree.

"I won't give up on you either," Matty says. "And neither will Bobby, so you can't give up on him."

I open my mouth to protest, but Blake beats me to it. "I agree."

"Guys," I begin, not sure what I can say to make a dent.

"Mom, he loves you. It's soooo obvious. And I know you love him too. Why don't you want to be happy?"

I stare at my child, feeling dumbfounded. Does he really think I don't want to be happy? That I'm actively avoiding it? That's a horrible example to set.

"Matthew, I *am* happy," I start to reassure him, desperate to fix this.

"Not like you are when Bobby's around."

"It's . . . complicated." Even I am unimpressed with my reply.

"No, it's really not," Blake says, his grin turning annoyingly smug. "Who wants to spend the rest of their life wondering what if? Is that what you would have wanted for me?"

Dammit! I really hate it when other people have a point.

I grimace and watch my ex and my son through narrowed eyes. "I'm guessing you have a plan in mind?"

When their mouths spread in identical grins, I swallow hard and prepare my parachute. Looks like I'm about to jump.

Chapter Thirty-Nine

Bobby

I stare at the black box and the oversized diamond sparkling back at me, wondering if I'm making another huge mistake. Coco didn't seem to think so as she helped me pick this ring out. The boys didn't seem to think so when they each came up with a line I should use when I actually get down on one knee. The whole speech was a little cheesy, so I scrapped it, but I appreciate their effort. The point is, if and when I get a chance to talk to Molly again, I won't fuck it up this time. She'll know exactly how serious I am about her.

For the first time ever, I get that this isn't about me and my behavior ruining my own life. My behavior now affects Molly and Matthew. I have to get it exactly right. Practice starts in twenty minutes and if I don't get my ass in there, I'm going to be late. I click the box shut and nestle it in my gym bag, wondering when I'll get to actually pop the question. I don't care how long it takes, my heart belongs to Molly.

My phone dings and I pull it out, nearly bobbling it when

I see it's a new message from Molly on the Catnip app. I forgot I had the app still downloaded on my phone. Practice can fucking wait.

@Singlemomcatlady: Hey, PitterPatter-LetsGetAtHer. Still looking for a girlfriend?

I punch my fist in the air and let out a yelp that has Wolverine asking me if I need emergency roadside assistance. My thumbs are trembling as I quickly text back.

@PitterPatterLetsGetAtHer: Yes, but only if she'll let me call her fluffernutter.

@Singlemomcatlady: No self-respecting woman would go by that name.

@PitterPatterLetsGetAtHer: Sparkle then?

@Singlemomcatlady: That's much better. Doesn't even sound like a stripper name. Much.

@Singlemomcatlady: Any chance we can chat today?

@PitterPatterLetsGetAtHer: Absolutely. When works for you? Now?

@Singlemomcatlady: Don't you have practice?"

@PitterPatterLetsGetAtHer: I can cancel. Tell Coach I'm coming down with something.

@Singlemomcatlady: No, don't do that.
How about I meet you after practice at the
rink?

@PitterPatterLetsGetAtHer: Sounds good. I
can't wait to see you.

I hold my breath, hoping against hope she responds to that.

@Singlemomcatlady: Me too, Bobby. I've
missed you.

I let out the loudest holler, Wolverine once again insisting we call for assistance. I shout back that I don't need any damn assistance. I'm getting my girl back. Fucking *today*. I slide out of the vehicle and hurriedly type out a text to Coco, informing her of the progress.

Me: She's meeting me after practice!
Should I do it today?

Coco: Most definitely.

Me: It's not too soon?

Coco: If you love her and want to be with
her forever then it's just the right time.

Me: Definitely today then.

I'm literally running across the parking lot, my bag bouncing against my back as I book it to the locker room. Dan-O gives me a weird look as I crash through the locker room door and sprint for my stall. Druggy just shakes his head at my behavior, already fully padded up for practice. As long as

I'm not smashing faces, they don't care if I'm acting weird. Then I think of a tiny detail that's not tiny at all.

> Me: Can you somehow bring Matthew?

> Coco: Leave it to me. I can make a man do anything I ask. Go get your woman, stallion!

Practice is long and hard, but I barely register any of it. I could swear I'm gliding across cloud nine, not an actual sheet of ice. I have just enough time at our first water break to tell my teammates about Molly coming after practice. They swear to give us space and then file back out at the right moment. I know I can count on them to have my back and help this proposal to go smoothly.

I'm counting down the minutes until practice ends. Coach keeps us a little past quitting time, probably sensing I have stuff to do and purposely being an asshole. That's the last time I bring him oysters. I was really hoping to have time to shower before Molly got here, but he blows the whistle right as Molly has a seat on the metal stands.

My heart is pounding away, far faster than when I'm out on the ice in the middle of a tie-breaking game. She looks fucking amazing. Her hair is down, soft auburn curls around her shoulders. Her sweater is a deep emerald green, which I know will make her eyes more green than hazel. The tight jeans with a slight rip at the knees make my mouth water. I drink her in like a starving man. Noticeably missing is her huge purse. She gives a little wave as our gazes lock, looking happy to see me. The boys all leave the ice, but I barely notice them. All my attention is on this woman I want to make my wife.

I skate over, barely stopping in time. Ice sprays across the boards before I hop off and walk over to her. I probably stink and my hair is a sweaty mess as I take off my helmet, two problems I can't be bothered with right now. Molly hops up as I get near, her hands sliding into the front pockets of her jeans. Her cheeks are pink, and I hope it has more to do with me and not just the cold.

"Molly." I say her name like my entire soul has been longing to hear it.

"Bobby," she whispers back.

My whole body shivers hearing her say my name. Fuck, I love her so much. My gloves and helmet fall to the floor and even though I still have my skates on, I crush her to me, needing my arms around her more than I need air in my lungs.

She gasps, but I feel her arms come around my waist. She pulls back too soon for my needs, her head tilted way back to see me. I was right. Her eyes are sparkling green gems. "I wanted to say I'm sorry."

"No, I'm sorry," I say quickly. "I shouldn't have asked so much of you without explaining my full intentions."

Her hand comes up to my face, covering my mouth. "Shut up, Robert Rhodes."

My eyes widen, and even though I should be mad about being told to shut up, my dick goes semi-hard hearing her use my full name. Why is that so fucking hot? I hear noises behind her, but I can't look away from her sweet face to see what the commotion is. I don't really give a damn. I just need to make things right with my girl.

"I love you, Bobby, so much. I'm just scared. You asked me to move in with you and I pulled away and probably made you feel like it was your fault. It took me a bit to realize that I'm scared by how much I feel for you. If you decided you didn't love me anymore you'd absolutely crush my heart. So, I was a chicken."

"I woub neber thop wubbing ooh." Her hand only tightens on my mouth as I try to assure her of my feelings.

"Shh." Oh shit, she's using the mom voice. "I'm not done

yet." She tentatively takes her hand back from my mouth and rolls her shoulders back. "I was wrong to do that. I was wrong to not trust in your love, and I was wrong to walk away from you. It was all me, not you."

As far as I'm concerned, she can do no wrong and that's all behind us. I don't give a crap about that, I just want her back in my arms. I take a step forward to do just that, but she steps back and I freeze. She holds my gaze, looking as frightened as I feel right now.

Then she drops to one knee, her eyes filling with tears, looking up at me like she's pleading for something only I can give her. I'm so confused. I hear a tiny yelp and my gaze shifts to the swarm of people that have somehow formed behind her, all staring at us. Coach, every single one of my teammates, Kaitlyn, Chloe, Olivia, Roman, Ramona, Coco, Richie, and Matthew. Dan-O claps a hand to his mouth on another emotional sob. Druggy catches my eye and throws me the black box. I snag it out of the air, then stare down at Molly.

"I've never done this before, but I'm pretty sure *I'm* supposed to be on my knee, Molly."

"Not if I propose first," she snarks right back, pulling a simple gold band from her pocket and holding it up between us. "Bobby Rhodes, I love you. I love your fearless approach to life and the way you fiercely love me back. I love how much you love my son, and I want to see what a future looks like with you by our sides. I don't like being the center of attention, but I asked all of your teammates and their wives to be here today because you deserve to have your family around you, supporting you, cheering you on. And I want to be part of that family. Will you accept all my insecurities and marry me anyway?"

My heart, the one that sped up when I met Molly, slowed down when she let me hold her throughout the night, and then thumped helplessly when I thought we were done forever, squeezes hard in my chest. She stares up at me, tears in her eyes and so much hope in her expression that I want to pull her to her feet and crush her to me.

"Dude, say yes!" Matthew whisper-shouts. Ramona shushes him, but I don't ever want him to censor himself around me. I look over Molly's head and shoot him a wink.

"I can do you one better."

I drop to my knee, still taller than Molly, but way closer to looking her in the eye this way. Everyone behind her fades away, and it's just her and me and a whole lot of love between us. I pop open the black box and hold up the largest diamond the jeweler had, set on a thin band of tiny diamonds. Because my Molly deserves the best I can buy for her.

Plus, I want every asshole within a ten-mile radius to see this huge rock on her finger and know she's mine.

"Molly Sparks, I just have one question for you before I say yes."

Chapter Forty

Molly

I can't help my gasp at the sight of the most beautiful—and enormous—engagement ring I've ever seen. Bobby takes advantage of my momentary speechlessness to take my free hand in his and hit me with that devastating double-dimple smile that ties me up in knots every damn time.

"Will you make me the happiest man in the world and—"

"Yes!" I cut him off and hear laughing behind me. I know all eyes are on us, but for once, I don't care. I want to share my joy with everyone in the entire world, but especially everyone in mine and Bobby's.

But when I lunge toward Bobby, he stops me. "You didn't let me finish the question!"

I can't help myself. I giggle like a kid and smack a hand over my mouth as I rest my butt back on my heels.

"That's better. Sheesh." Bobby rolls his eyes and plays to the gathered crowd, who laugh even harder now. "What I was going to ask was will you make me the happiest man in the world and . . . let me pick next time we get takeout?"

Groans come from behind me. "I keep telling him he's not funny, but he won't believe me," Richie mutters, and my chest shakes with laughter. Maybe I shouldn't have been shocked, but nobody I called to join us here today was the least bit surprised that there would be a proposal on the table. If anything, they seemed frustrated it took us so long to figure our shit out. I guess when you're meant to be, sometimes you're the last to know.

I drop my hand from my smiling mouth to answer Bobby. "Absolutely. Anything else?"

He shifts on his knee, pretending to think on that for a few beats. "Will you wear pencil skirts and heels until you're eighty?"

I force myself not to laugh at his waggling eyebrows and bob my head back and forth. "Eighty might be pushing it, but I'll do my best. Anything else?"

This time, he hobbles closer on both knees until we're only a foot apart. "Just one more thing." He slides the diamond ring onto my finger and brings my hand to his lips. "Will you let me spend every day of the rest of my life showing you just how beautiful you are and how much I love and need you?"

My smile turns wobbly as emotion floods through me again. I can't believe I ever thought being apart from him was a good idea. This man is everything I've ever wanted and been afraid to hope for. And, dammit, I deserve to have my happily ever after.

"Only if you promise the same in return," I agree, my voice cracking as I hold out the gold band I bought.

It proves to be too much for Bobby because he pulls me to him, his lips crashing down on mine in a hard kiss filled with pent-up emotion. Everyone behind me cheers, so they don't hear Bobby when he says against my lips, "I prefer handsome to beautiful, but I can deal."

I barely get in a, "Shut up, Robert," before he pulls me in for a longer and, dare I say, indecent kiss that has Matty and Richie groaning and the rest of the crowd hooting and hollering.

"What are you doing?!" I shriek an hour later as Bobby literally sweeps me off my feet as we exit his new Raptor truck. He got rid of the Cybertruck in favor of something both of us felt more comfortable driving.

"Carrying my bride across the threshold." He pushes the door open and walks through.

"We're not married yet."

"Then consider it practice. I take practice very seriously, as I'm sure you know."

When he doesn't let me down and instead carries me through the foyer and up the wide staircase, I don't bother arguing. A girl could get used to this.

I received everyone's well wishes and gushing over the ring while Bobby showered in the locker room after our dual proposal. I still can't believe he had been thinking the same thing, proving once again that I should have trusted in the power of our feelings and not gotten so caught up in my head.

Bobby lowers me gently to his mattress when we get to his bedroom, and although I haven't had the chance to check the house out with his things in it, I don't bother with that now.

Not when my head's finally on straight and I have Bobby all to myself.

I lie on my back while Bobby arranges my limbs around him to make himself comfortable on top of me. He gazes down at me, both thumbs caressing circles at my temples. "What do you say if instead of you changing your last name to Rhodes, I change mine to Sparks? Bobby Sparks has a certain ring to it, don't you think?"

I bite back a smile. "Makes you sound like either a Nascar driver or a porn star." When Bobby starts looking a little too excited, I have to burst his bubble. "You know that's Blake's last name, right?"

"Oh, right. I forgot. Your maiden name is Hooker." His thumbs halt as he frowns. "Bobby Hooker doesn't hit the same, does it?"

"Uh, no. You should probably stick with Rhodes." I can't help my chuckle this time, but Bobby manages to zap my mirth with a hot kiss. When we finally come up for air, I have no memory of what we'd been talking about. Nor do I care.

"I missed you." Bobby's voice is hoarse, and I cup his cheeks with my hands.

"I missed you too. I'm so sorry."

"Shh," he silences me and comes back in for another kiss that takes my breath away. Then he strips us both of our clothing until we're down to just our underwear. I do a double take when I see he's wearing a pair of boxers made to look like a tuxedo shirt, complete with bow tie.

"Nice drawers."

He grins, both dimples popping again. "I figured they were on theme. I'm really getting into this whole groom thing."

"Then let's get rid of them and move on to the consummation part," I suggest with a wink.

Bobby doesn't argue, immediately shedding the tuxedo

boxers while I slide my panties to the floor. I take him in from his broad shoulders down to his narrow hips, strong thighs, and fully aroused cock. Clearly enjoying my appreciative gaze, he raises an eyebrow "See something you like?"

Instead of answering, I roll onto my hands and knees and crawl to get an up close and personal look at what we're dealing with here. Perfection.

Bobby groans my name as I wrap my hand around his length. When I stroke up and down a couple times and run the flat of my tongue across the head, his eyes squeeze shut. "I'm not sure this is going to end well for you if you keep that up."

I drop my butt to my heels and continue to slowly stroke as I grin up at him. His hips reflexively jerk forward into my touch, and I love that I can turn this powerful athlete into a quivering mess of desire so easily.

"I'm sure you can figure it out," I tease, giving him another firm squeeze.

He narrows his eyes at me. "You know, you act all innocent with those pretty blushes and that soft voice, but inside, you're one hundred percent vixen."

I start to laugh, but it turns into an "Oof!" as he springs forward and tackles me to the bed, pinning my arms above my head and nestling his rigid cock between my thighs.

"Nice try, fluffernutter." He smirks down at me. "But I'm going to be inside you when I come."

Heat immediately pools in my belly, and I have no desire to fight him on this. Bobby lowers his head and kisses me stupid, eventually rolling so he's on his back and I'm on top of him. His hands slide to my hips as he thrusts up against me. I drop my knees to the bed and lift up so I can position him at my entrance.

He reaches between us to guide his cock, and we gaze into one another's eyes as I lower myself to take him completely.

The fullness and stretch are so beautiful that I can't help but sigh.

"I love you so fucking much," Bobby says, voice strained.

My vision goes blurry with burgeoning tears, but I force them back. I don't want to miss a thing. "I love you too," I whisper, so thankful I got out of my own way and embraced my chance at happiness.

I roll my hips as I begin to find a rhythm, and Bobby groans beneath me. His hands roam my body, cupping my breasts and teasing my nipples as I rock against him. When I quicken my movements and begin to ride him for real, his eyes roll into the back of his head, and he starts moaning nonsense words. Despite his loss of mental faculties, his body is completely in tune with mine as he meets my movements with upward thrusts.

I pick up the pace as familiar flutters begin in my core. Reading me so well, Bobby snakes his hand between us, his thumb finding my clit and circling it expertly. The dual stimulation has me gasping, my nails digging into his shoulders.

"Bobby," I pant. "I'm close . . ."

"I'm with you," he grunts, his hips jerking more forcefully.

I cry out as my release crashes over me, my body shuddering. Bobby wraps his strong arms around me, continuing to piston up into me as I ride out my orgasm. With a final, deep thrust, he stills, pulsing inside me as he finds his own release.

We cling to each other, both panting like Labradors. Bobby drops soft kisses along my temple while his hands stroke my back and butt. I nuzzle into the crook of his neck, inhaling his scent and savoring his nearness.

When we've both recovered somewhat, Bobby rolls us so he's spooning me, his arms holding me tight and secure. It's only then that I get my first good look at his new bedroom.

"Um, Bobby?"

"Yeah," he murmurs into my hair.

"Is that . . . the Gucci logo all over your wallpaper?"

He lifts his head behind me, and I crane my neck to see his satisfied grin. "Yeah. Pretty tight, right?"

I bite my lip and reach a hand up to pat his cheek. "It's a good thing you're handsome."

Epilogue

Bobby

"This suit is the tits." I run my hand down the lapel of the killer velvet suit in Storm Chasers black. How could I pass it up when it goes so perfectly with my new gold Gucci loafers? "I'm going to be feeling myself all day."

Dan-O makes a retching noise. Druggy frowns and walks out of the guest room, grumbling something in Russian under his breath. Benny just throws his arm around my shoulders and takes a picture of us in the full-length mirror.

"It's the perfect material for Mei. She'd love to spit up on you."

I shrug him off me and straighten my tie. "I thought I'd be nervous on my wedding day, but I'm not."

Benny grins. "Just eager to marry her, right?"

An image of me and Molly curled up on the couch downstairs and Matthew buzzing through to get a drink out of the kitchen fridge runs through my brain. It's what our life has been like since our double proposal three months ago. Perfection. "Exactly."

"Bobby? Druggy said you needed me to do something?"

I turn from the mirror to see Matthew coming into the guest room in his own suit. Molly nearly killed me for spending so much on a growing boy, but I got him a matching velvet suit for the wedding. "There's my best man!"

I pull him into a hug and try to mess up his hair, but he pushes me off him with a teenager scowl. He'll take a lot of rough housing, but hates having that hair messed with now. Molly says it looks like a llama, and I have to agree. What's up with these youngsters these days?

"I got something for your mom. A little pre-wedding gift and I was hoping you'd deliver it for me."

I grab a flat black box off the dresser and pop it open, holding it out to Matthew for inspection. On the velvet inside lies a pair of sparkling diamond earrings and a necklace with my number 62 in diamonds. Molly's career has taken off the last few months with her newfound confidence. She even stood up to those jerks she works with who were pushing her around. I figure a few more diamonds might make them choke on their own jealousy a bit more.

Matthew whistles. "Holy shit. Mom's gonna love it!"

I don't correct his language. It's my wedding day, after all, and he's about to become my son. I snap the lid shut again and hand him a smaller box. "Got something for you too."

Matthew's gaze darts to my face. "You did?" He opens the box to see a luxury brand watch that's got everything from a compass to a flashlight to a step counter and sleep tracker. The back is engraved with today's date.

I put my hand on his shoulder. I could swear he's already starting to put on some bulk from the weight-lifting we've been doing together. "It's not every day I get to become someone's bonus dad. I'm not great at verbalizing feelings, but I want you to know that I can't wait to marry your mom for a whole lot of reasons, one of which is because it'll make you and me family."

Matthew's cheeks go pink, but he's smiling despite his embarrassment. "Thanks, Bobby. I was actually going to ask you something. I talked to Dad last night and he said he was okay with it. Can I call you Pops?" He rushes on, like he isn't getting me choked up already. "Or something similar? Daddy seems a little juvenile. Old man seems kinda rednecky."

"Matthew," I stop him. "Pops is perfect. I love it. And I love you."

His head dips, but not before I see his eyes fill with tears. I pull him in for another hug and this time I don't try to mess up his llama hair. "I love you too, Pops," he whispers into my chest.

"Jeez, who's cutting onions in here?" Benny hollers, swiping at his eyes and not bothering to pretend like he didn't just eavesdrop on our conversation. Cappy hands Mac a tissue before taking one for himself. Dan-O sheepishly puts down his phone. That idiot was recording everything.

I release Matthew and shove both boxes in his hands. "Can you give the gift to your mom before the ceremony starts?"

"You can count on me." Matthew gives me one last smile before darting out of the room.

Not even ten minutes later, the music starts downstairs. I rush out the door, down the stairs, and out into the backyard of my new house. The boys are on my heels, hurrying to find their women and take their seats, along with Ramona and her husband, Coco and her latest young boyfriend, and Blake and his boyfriend. Even Ashley is here, currently sitting next to Cappy who's flirting outrageously with her and getting nowhere.

Molly and I decided on a small ceremony with just our friends. Our families are both still a work in progress, so we decided to plan a reception for later this month with them. The ceremony is for our chosen family.

I take my place at the front of the chairs next to the minister. Matthew stands next to me, giving me a thumbs up, indicating he got the gift to Molly. The photographer flutters about, snapping pics and memorializing this moment. The music shifts and Molly comes out the back door of the house. Everyone stands up and my breath catches in my throat. She looks like a dream in a white lace dress that hugs her curves and then flares out along the ground at the last minute. It's like the pencil skirt of wedding dresses. Her hair is soft and curled, dancing around plump breasts that I already can't wait to get my hands and mouth on.

But it's her smile that makes tears flow down my cheeks unashamedly. She's not nervous. Just calm and happy and proud to be walking toward me. She glides down the five concrete steps and Matthew runs down the aisle to offer her his elbow. She gives him a kiss on the cheek and lets him escort her the rest of the way to me. That was a secret plan Matthew and I came up with weeks ago. She hands her flowers to Ramona in the front row as she walks by. Her tears match mine when Matthew squeezes her in a fierce hug and then stands next to me.

It feels like everything clicks into place when her hands slide into mine. The minister says some things and we respond, but I'm not really paying attention. I'm just swimming in Molly's presence, wondering how the hell I landed the sweetest, prettiest, hardest working woman in the whole world. I do hear the minister announce us husband and wife, the cue I can finally kiss this woman.

I take Molly in my arms and look down into those hazel eyes I know better than my own. "Today's just the start of an infinite amount of days where I show you how much I love you, my wife."

I dip my head to kiss her, but she shoves her finger over my lips. "Today's just the start of an infinite amount of days where you shock me with your fashion sense."

My mouth drops open. "You love this suit. Admit it."

She raises an eyebrow. "I love *you* . . ."

I clear my throat and reposition my hands on her body, attempting to wrap her up like a Burmese python and never let her go. "Do you mind saving this for later? I have to kiss my wife in front of all our friends."

She smiles, her finger leaving my lips and tracing across my dimples. "Yes, please."

I dip her over my arm and lay one on her that she'll remember for the rest of her life. Our friends cheer and Matthew groans something about adults being gross. All I care about is that Molly is mine and I take care of what's mine. I wasn't kidding about what I said to her. I intend to show her every day for the rest of our lives how much I love her and cherish her. I never thought something would occupy my thoughts more than hockey, but here we are. I'm obsessed with my wife.

After a disturbingly long time, I let her come up for air. Our guests have mostly wandered off to the tables in the back of the yard where Richie conned the Irish Rogue into catering our wedding. There's a beer keg on tap and all the fried foods one can eat. You'd be surprised how much greasy grub professional athletes can eat when they let loose.

Molly pulls a tissue out of the plunging neckline of her wedding dress and swipes it across my lips. "That's better. My lipstick clashed with your gold shoes."

I wag my eyebrows and hold her hand, lacing my fingers with hers. "There's some other places on me I'd like to find your lipstick, wife."

Her cheeks turn pink. "So no more Sparkle or fluffernutter? Now you're just going to call me wife all the time?"

Fuck, I love the way that sounds. "Damn right."

And then we celebrate with our friends all night.

Our chosen family that never gave up on either of us.

Bonus Epilogue

Roman

Winning the Cup the year I retired felt like it was the pinnacle of my life. Then I married Olivia and I realized that while the trophy and the fanfare were nice, waking up every morning next to her is even better. Way fuckin' better, especially when she lets me get her naked and show her how not-old I really am.

"What's that look on your face, ice bath king?" Olivia murmurs, snuggling into my side.

The crowd is cheering for their teams down on the ice like everything's on the line. And in some ways, it is. Years of practice and sacrifice and money and injuries have culminated in two teams making it all the way to competing to win the holy grail in the ice hockey world.

"Thinking about getting you naked," I reply with a wolfish grin.

Olivia jabs me in the ribs, hard. "Seriously. Why are you so uncharacteristically quiet?"

I look around us and see the wives, girlfriends, parents, siblings, and friends of the Storm Chasers in the suite with us. The team is giving it their all out there, sweat pouring down their faces despite the chill of the ice. It's game seven of the finals, and both the Storm Chasers and Pittsburgh have three wins. This game is for all the marbles.

The coaches, while looking spiffy in their suits, look like they're about to lose their ever-loving minds, gesturing wildly and tapping on their iPads to pull up stats and plays. The music is pumping through the speakers and fans are coordinating cheers. You can feel the manic energy in the air like a living, breathing thing.

Bobby hasn't gotten in any fights, having successfully handed off the responsibility of enforcer to Goose, one of the new guys. Druggy has stopped more pucks than I can count tonight. Banks looks like I remember him almost a decade ago, swift, cunning, and lethal. My feet itch to get out there on skates and join them, never mind being in my midforties.

I feel like a proud father, watching the young ones carry the torch all the way to the end.

It's tied 2-2 with only three minutes to go. Bobby starts mouthing off, and I'm too far away to hear exactly what he said, but I can imagine it's something off the wall and as hard hitting as a sucker punch. Some of the Pittsburgh players get in his face and Goose glides in there with a rough shove. The refs break them up but it's enough of a disturbance to make Pittsburgh a little too aggressive on the next play, purposely tripping Banks. We get the power play with a little over a minute to go, and everyone is on their feet.

The puck is flying, precision and perfectly practiced plays creating a dizzying back and forth that leads to Banks flying straight for the net. He pulls back and I swear to god, time hangs frozen in place. The crowd noise dims, and nothing matters but the flick of his wrist. Nobody knows more than me that certain moments in our lives can change absolutely everything. His steady wrist unleashes and it's so fast you can't even track the puck.

The buzzer sounds, the lights flash, and every black and gold jerseyed player holds their stick in the air triumphantly. The ladies are jumping for joy, Olivia's screaming my ear off, and I . . . well, I can't seem to see past the tears flooding my vision. These guys. These former teammates. These friends-turned-family. They mean the world to me and in twenty-eight seconds, that Cup could be theirs.

I don't make another noise, not even through the final buzzer where the fans go wild at another Storm Chasers win, or the suite that fills with confetti, not even when we're ushered down to the ice to watch the awards up close. I thought holding that silver cup in my own hands would mean everything to me, but watching the next generation hold it high in the air with ear-to-ear smiles on their faces with their wives and babies watching brings me even more joy.

A female broadcaster thrusts a microphone in my face. "Roman LaFontaine, how does it feel to see your team take home another Stanley Cup without you?"

I smile at the woman, knowing she couldn't possibly understand. "It feels exactly right. I know more than anyone how much these guys have sacrificed to be here, and I couldn't be more proud. Now go interview one of them and leave this old guy to blubber in the stands."

She laughs and swings the microphone to Banks as he glides off the ice. Kaitlyn kisses him, then hands him Mei. He holds her more carefully than the Cup, looking like the proud father I know he is. He expertly fields a question from the reporter amid the chaos.

Chloe and Ayana tag team Druggy as he comes over. He picks them both up and over the barrier, one under each arm and spins them around. Coach hands out champion hats to all the players, along with hugs. Dan-O takes a victory lap around the ice with the Cup held over his head before handing it off to another player and sweeping his wife and kids into his arms.

It's a surreal moment, one these guys will remember for the rest of their lives. Olivia wraps her arms around me and lays her head on my shoulder.

"You love them, don't you?"

"I love the sport, I love the guys, I love the victory, and even the defeat." I turn toward her, cupping her pretty face. "But never as much as I love you."

She beams and leans in to kiss me, but gets interrupted by Kaitlyn bellowing, "Oh my god! Look!"

We swing our gazes over, trying to figure out what got Kaitlyn all riled up. Bobby is doing his individual victory lap with the Stanley Cup held over his head. He locks eyes with Molly, who's standing on top of the first row of seats, a huge watery grin on her face. She lifts a poster above her head, matching Bobby's stance. We crane our necks and read the sign.

Congrats, Daddy! I'm pregnant!

Olivia shouts in my ear again and Bobby nearly drops the Cup. Thankfully, Cappy's nearby and snags it before it hits the ice. Bobby skates over faster than I've ever seen him skate, climbing over the boards to get to Molly.

"Are you serious, wife?" he shouts.

Molly nods, fully crying now, along with everyone else in our friend group. It's been a pleasure to witness Bobby's transformation into a man devoted to his wife and stepson. And now . . . a baby.

He whoops and spins her around, setting her down carefully, only to drop to his knees and start talking to her stomach.

Olivia lifts her gaze to mine, tears streaming down her face. "That's better than any Stanford Cup."

Laughter replaces the tears as I pull her into my arms. "*Stanley* Cup, honey. You'll get it one of these days."

Also by Marika Ray

Steamy RomComs - Blueball Band of Brothers:

Grumpy the Bear - Blueball Band of Brothers #1

S'more Than a Feeling - Blueball Band of Brothers #2

Home is Where You Park It - Blueball Band of Brothers #3

Set My Heart Bonfire - Blueball Band of Brothers #4

Pining For You - Blueball Band of Brothers #5

***

Wolfe Brothers:

A Package Deal - Wolfe Brothers #1

An Ex Affair - Wolfe Brothers #2

All Steamy RomComs Set in Hell:

Grumpy As Hell - Hellman Brothers #1

Bro Code Hell - Hellman Brothers #2

Friend Zone Hell - Hellman Brothers #3

Cougar From Hell - Hellman Brothers #4

Falling First Hell - Hellman Brothers #5

***

Ridin' Solo - Sisters From Hell #1

One Night Bride - Sisters From Hell #2

Smarty Pants - Sisters From Hell #3

Ex Best Thing - Sisters From Hell #4

***

Love Bank - Jobs From Hell #1

Uber Bossy - Jobs From Hell #2

Unfriend Me - Jobs From Hell #3

Side Hustle - Jobs From Hell #4

***

Backroom Boy - Standalone

Steamy_Small_Town_Christmas_RomCom:

Grumpy Little Christmas

Sugar Nookie

Steamy Small Town Summer RomCom:

Salt Love

Steamy Hockey RomCom:

Hot Flashes and Hockey Slashes - Hot Flash Hookups #1

Mood Swings and Hockey Flings - Hot Flash Hookups #2

Night Sweats and Hockey Nets - Hot Flash Hookups #3

Sleepless Nights and Hockey Fights - Hot Flash Hookups #4

Steamy RomComs:

The Missing Ingredient - Reality of Love #1

Mom-Com - Reality of Love #2

Desperately Seeking Househusbands - Reality of Love #3

***

Happy New You - Standalone

Steamy RomComs with Delancey Stewart:

The Spare and the Single Mom

Head Over Cleats

Falling For Mr. Safety

Sweet RomComs with Delancey Stewart:

Texting With the Enemy - Digital Dating #1

While You Were Texting - Digital Dating #2

Save the Last Text - Digital Dating #3

How to Lose a Girl in 10 Texts - Digital Dating #4

Sweet Romances:

The Marriage Sham - Standalone

***

The Widower's Girlfriend-Faking It #1

Home Run Fiancé - Faking It #2

Guarding the Princess - Faking It #3

***

Lines We Cross - Nickel Bay Brothers #1

Perfectly Imperfect Us - Nickel Bay Brothers #2

Steamy Beach Romance:

1) Sweet Dreams - Beach Squad #1

2) Love on the Defense - Beach Squad #2

3) Barefoot Chaos - Beach Squad #3

* Novella - Handcuffed Hussy

4) Beach Babe Billionaire- Beach Squad #4

5) Brighter Than the Boss - Beach Squad #5

* Novella - Christmas Eve Do-Over

Also by Sylvie Stewart

Ale's Fair in Love and War (*Love on Tap*, Book 1)

Smooth Hoperator (*Love on Tap*, Book 2)

Deja Brew All Over Again (*Love on Tap*, Book 3)

Stout of My League (*Love on Tap*, Book 4)

Asheville Collection (Standalone Stories from the *Love on Tap* World)

* * *

The Fix (*Carolina Connections*, Book 1)

The Spark (*Carolina Connections*, Book 2)

The Lucky One (*Carolina Connections*, Book 3)

The Game (*Carolina Connections*, Book 4)

The Way You Are (*Carolina Connections*, Book 5)

The Runaround (*Carolina Connections*, Book 6)

Carolina Connections Box Set 1

Carolina Connections Box Set 2

* * *

The Nerd Next Door (*Carolina Kisses*, Book 1)

New Jerk in Town (*Carolina Kisses*, Book 2)

The Last Good Liar (*Carolina Kisses*, Book 3)

* * *

Between a Rock and a Royal, *Kings of Carolina, #1*

Blue Bloods and Backroads, *Kings of Carolina, #2*

Stealing Kisses With a King, *Kings of Carolina, #3*

Kings of Carolina Box Set

* * *

Poppy & the Beast

Then Again

Full-On Clinger (FREE for a limited time)

About That

Nuts About You

Booby Trapped

Acknowledgments

Marika and Sylvie met years ago at a book signing, instantly hitting it off as they were both quite funny. Fast forward a few years and they were on the phone lamenting all the very real symptoms of peri menopause that were affecting their lives when they both had the grand idea that they wanted to write about it! The goal was to normalize conversation about the various side effects of the hormonal rollercoaster that is aging, while also reminding women of their inherent beauty no matter their age.

From Sylvie - A personal thanks to Allison, Carlie, and Annette for their support, and to my trusty neck fan for pulling me through my worst hot flashes.

From Marika - A big huge thank you to my husband, not only for his understanding, but also his patience when I yell at him for having the audacity to fall asleep so fast when I can't anymore. And his chewing. Dear god, the man's chewing!

Thank you to fellow romance authors for their enthusiasm and support of this book. You make a girl feel less crazy.

Last but not least...a huge thank you to Nancy Smay at Evident Ink for making this whole series shine with your editing and proofreading services!

About Marika Ray

Marika Ray is a USA Today bestselling author, writing small town RomCom to make your heart explode and bring a smile to your face. All her books come with a money-back guarantee that you'll laugh at least once with every book.

Marika spends her time behind a computer crafting stories, walking along the beach, and making healthy food for her kids and husband whether they like it or not. Prior to writing novels, Marika held various jobs in the finance industry, with private start-up companies, and then in health & fitness. Cats may have nine lives, but Marika believes everyone should have nine careers to keep things spicy.

If you'd like to know more about Marika or the other novels she's currently writing, please find her at www.marikaray.com.

If you want to take your stalking to the next level, here are other legal (ish) places you can find Marika:

Join her Newsletter - http://bit.ly/MarikaRayNews

Amazon - https://www.amazon.com/author/marikaray

Goodreads - https://www.goodreads.com/author/show/16856659.Marika_Ray

Bookbub - https://www.bookbub.com/authors/marika-ray

TikTok - https://vm.tiktok.com/ZMJvnQ2Cv

Instagram - https://www.instagram/authormarikaray

About Sylvie Stewart

USA Today bestselling author Sylvie Stewart loves dad jokes, dirty rom-coms, country music, and baby skunks—preferably all at the same time. Most of her steamy contemporary and romantic comedy novels take place across her favorite state of North Carolina, and her characters never run out of snarky banter or snacks. When her laptop closes, Sylvie is a sucker for hugs from her twin boys and a good laugh with her hot-nerd hubby. If you love smart Southern gals, hot blue-collar guys, and snort-laughing with characters who feel like your best friends, Sylvie's your gal. Stay up to date on all things Sylvie! https://sylviestewartauthor.com

Join her Newsletter - http://bit.ly/s-s-nl

Facebook Reader Group - https://www.facebook.com/groups/743238732533487

Facebook Page – https://facebook.com/SylvieStewartAuthor

Instagram – https://instagram.com/syvliestewartauthor

BookBub – https://bookbub.com/authors/sylvie-stewart

Twitter – https://twitter.com/sylvie_stewart_

TikTok – https://tiktok.com/@authorsylviestewart

Pinterest – https://pinterest.com/sylviestewartauthor

Goodreads – https://goodreads.com/author/show/15303783.Sylvie_Stewart

YouTube – https://youtube.com/@sylviestewartauthor